The Cure for Summer Boredom

Katherine Luck

The Cure for Summer Boredom

Prologue

Friday, June 14
Early o'clock

At sunrise on the last day of school, a naked, beer-maddened trucker ran amok on Main Street. I wasn't there myself, but a handful of reliable witnesses and a couple dozen of the unreliable variety reported that he jogged up and down the street just as bold as a yard dog let loose, his naughty bits swinging freely in the tender morning light.

Sheriff-Mayor Dolan was called out to collar the hooting and hollering hooligan. He rolled up in his spit-shined Cadillac, ill-tempered and clad in his robe and slippers since he planned on crawling directly back into bed once his duty was done.

As the first luminous rays of sunlight bejeweled the vast Fack Sex Furniture Distribution Warehouse on the edge of town, the sheriff-mayor proceeded to scamper after the trucker on foot. Drunk but wily, the trucker led our fair town's one and only lawman in an ungainly chase up and down our fair town's one and only thoroughfare.

It was said that Dr. Flo was the one who finally captured the screwball streaker. I heard she brought him to bay with nothing but a glass jar filled with cotton balls and a sterile latex glove.

Just another summer morning in Somwärin, Texas.

Chapter One
The Hootchie Doctor Hits Town

Friday, June 14
2:58 in the p.m.

How did all the trouble start?

Nine hours after the ruffian trucker made merry along the length and breadth of Main Street, I, too, went whooping and cavorting up the roadway. But I was fully clothed and motivated not by booze but by triumph. Against all odds, I had not been given detention on the last day of school.

There had been several close calls throughout the day. In health class, I nearly ran afoul of the Gentleman Gym Teacher. Fresh and crisp in his snowy Colonel Sanders suit and broad-brimmed plantation hat, he spent the entirety of the class lounging against the battle-scarred lectern, delivering A Little Talk about the menace of public drunkenness in general and men specifically.

Pricked by boredom, I piped up.

"Men like you, sir?"

The Gentleman Gym Teacher's well-brushed white hat paused in mid-fan of his gentile self. He offered the class a dark, yet courteous, scowl.

"Might I beg to inquire who said that?"

I ducked my head and kept my mouth clamped shut for the rest of the period.

At lunch, needled by ennui, I fashioned a food-based statuette I entitled "The Trucker in the Raw." Rashly, I exhibited it for the consideration of my classmates. When the Lady Principal swooped down upon us to see what all the tittering was about, I crammed the edible effigy into my mouth and gazed at her with innocent eyes and bulging cheeks until she swooped away.

By the final class of the day, I was determined to take no chances. I settled into my seat next to Annie-Belle Cutler, rolled my head back, and gazed up at the decorative tile mosaic on the ceiling.

As the math teacher enumerated the threats posed by tipsy truckers, I considered the yellow rose of Texas and Viking helmet, entwined in chummy camaraderie, fashioned from yellow and blue kitchen tiles donated by the Fack Sex Furniture Distribution Warehouse. Weaving between dusty beams of sunlight that spilled through the windows was a plump honeybee. It circled the mosaic as slowly as the second hand was circling the clock.

I was powerfully bored.

I watched as the bee drifted along the edge of the mosaic to hover just above the classroom timepiece.

"And now," said the math teacher. "I will tell you the most important calculation you must make, should you have the misfortune to encounter a trucker this summer—"

I cut her off with a shriek of victory. It was three o'clock!

My cry ricocheted off the ceiling tiles. The bee shot downward and flung itself stinger-first into Annie-Belle Cutler's exposed upper arm. She let out a cry of her own.

"Ruby Bejou," thundered the teacher. "That's deten—"

But judgement was not to rain down upon my head because, at that very instant, the bell rang.

I jumped to my feet, bashed open the classroom door, and fled into the bright sunlight.

School was out at last!

Outside, in the infernal June heat, I met up with my little sister, Pearl. Off we strolled to the Swedish Embassy & Beauty Parlor & Coffee Shop, Somwärin's preferred site for enacting the sins of envy, pride, and gluttony—all at the same time and technically outside of U.S. soil.

As always, the Swedish ambassador, proprietor and sole employee of the Swedish Embassy & Beauty Parlor & Coffee Shop, greeted our arrival with the silken words, "Välkommen till Konungariket Sverige: För Sverige i tiden."

We residents of Somwärin had agreed that this translated as, "Welcome to the Kingdom of Sweden: For Sweden with the times," which we further agreed made no sense. But the Swedish ambassador never failed to recite it in a formulaic voice whenever anyone set foot in this official government facility, so it was surely a crucial tool of Swedish bureaucracy.

Pearl and I chorused, "Hey!" which we had been taught was a genuine Swedish word. But our town's only native Swedish speaker didn't respond with a "Hey!" of his own. He contented himself with giving us a puzzled look before directing us to two ergonomic Fack Sex chairs set around an economical Fack Sex table.

"May I interest you girls in a coffee? Or a plate of lutefisk and a coffee?" he inquired. "I shall get your coffee."

We disappointed our township's only foreign dignitary by ordering a pair of sundaes and sodas.

"Fika, fika," the Swedish ambassador muttered disapprovingly as he set our chilly treats before us. "When you finish these, I shall bring your coffee."

I'd stuffed myself to bursting before I noticed that someone was missing.

"Where's Opal?" I mumbled through a mouthful of butterscotch.

"Where else?" Pearl said. She tossed a maraschino cherry into the air to catch in her mouth, but succeeded only in hitting herself on the forehead. She scraped it off the tabletop and tried again.

I dropped my spoon with a loud *plank*.

Could it be that today, just like every day after school, our big sister was holding court in the school parking lot with every male—from sixth graders to teachers—in attendance?

"But she promised to come!"

"Yeah, well," Pearl surreptitiously glanced at me, plucked the cherry from the floor where it had fallen, and tossed it skyward again. "She's gotta get hers while she can. She's gonna be too busy for masculine companionship this summer."

I stirred my liquefying ice cream and scowled. Our big sister had obtained herself a job this summer and planned to abandon Pearl and me to our own devices all the dull, sweltering days until September.

In Somwärin, there was little to nothing for the teenaged crowd to do during the interminable summer months. As elementary school kids, my sisters and I had glumly attended "Fun Time Swedish Language Learning Camp for Little Youngsters," put on by the Fack Sex Corporation. It had been a rotten trial, what with rising daily at dawn to sing the Swedish national anthem, writing gracious letters to the King of Sweden to thank him for being a beneficent figurehead, and the lack of any form of protein besides lutefisk.

"You must learn to love this good fisk!" our teachers would shout, displaying the Viking temper that simmered just beneath their pale skin, when we surly kids picked at our ammoniacal meals. The King of Sweden never wrote back, and our Swedish Language Learning consisted of memorizing such useful phrases as, "Ship three chairs to New Hampshire by Wednesday," and "Please forgive my late arrival, boss. I urge you to dock my salary." It was no fun time at all.

"So, what're we gonna do this summer?" Pearl asked, as she dropped the mangled cherry into her soda and scrubbed at the sticky red blotches on her cheeks.

"I dunno," I said.

"Well, we better come up with something, coz I don't guess either of us can stand another summer like last year."

Pearl was wise. Last summer, we three sisters had passed all our waking hours sprawled in various positions of lethargy in the living room of the Bejou family trailer as we watched the Sissy Spacek Movie Marathon on TV and took in vast quantities of grape soda and Almond Roca until we looked and felt like bloated corpses.

Too old to attend Fun Time Swedish Language Learning Camp for Little Youngsters, too young to put our scanty Swedish vocabularies to use in summer jobs at the Fack Sex Furniture Distribution Warehouse. Our prospects appeared grim.

"I have a bad feeling, Pearl," I said. "I have a feeling I'm gonna be so bored this summer. You got any ideas regarding what we can do to occupy ourselves?"

"No. I figured you might, being older and all," Pearl said.

"Maybe Opal will," I said.

I peered expectantly at the café door. Miraculously, at that very moment, it swung open.

A vicious blast of heat burst through the calm, cool air of the Swedish Embassy & Beauty Parlor & Coffee Shop. On the threshold stood, not Opal, but a sweaty, crazed-looking man.

Breathing hard, he gripped the doorknob for a moment, then staggered into our midst. His hair was wild and his face was red and he wore a thick suit jacket wrought in a subtle plaid pattern, like the one sported by the anchorman who introduced each movie of the Sissy Spacek Movie Marathon last summer.

"Oh wow!" whispered Pearl, her eyes bright. "Another drunken trucker! Maybe he'll take his clothes off for us."

The stranger stumbled to the counter, where the Swedish ambassador stood watching warily. The man hung his flushed head and drew in several deep breaths, his hands planted flat on the shining countertop.

"Välkommen till Konungariket Sverige," said the Swedish ambassador. "För Sverige—"

"Homagawd, so hat…hat…I hada walk…wicked hat…"

The Swedish ambassador cocked his head, puzzled.

"För Sverige i tiden," he said. "Would you like a coffee?"

"I hada walk so fah," the man continued, his voice rattling around the edges of an accent none of us could place. "Dacta Hershille…"

The Swedish ambassador flicked his eyes quizzically at Pearl and me, then leaned forward and scrutinized the man.

"Shall I bring you a coffee?" he enunciated.

"Hah?" the man said, lifting his sweat-soaked head and squinting at the Swedish ambassador. "No, no. Sorry, I'm just so…hat."

The Swedish ambassador's face brightened with comprehension.

"Ah! You are not from Texas. You are from faraway, yes?"

The man nodded, scrubbing the perspiration from his forehead with the Swedish ambassador's table-wiping rag, which lay folded neatly on the countertop.

"And what country do you hail from, please?"

"Bwastin."

"I ask your pardon?"

"Bwastin," he repeated. "Mass'chusetts."

The Swedish ambassador looked concerned. He reached beneath the counter and pulled out a thick stack of paperwork.

"Please announce your country of origin and purpose for visiting on these simple forms. You shall have a coffee while I inspect your passport. Have you any fruit to declare?"

"No, I just needa speak with Dacta Hershille."

The Swedish ambassador frowned.

"Who?" Pearl and I mouthed at each other.

The foreigner dug through the pockets of his Bwastin jacket and produced a letter bearing the Somwärin town seal of entwined yellow rose of Texas and Viking helmet, as seen previously upon the bee-ridden classroom ceiling.

"Dacta Florence Hershille?" the man read, proffering the letter.

"Dr. Flo!" Pearl exclaimed.

The Swedish ambassador and the outsider glanced at her. We girls hunched over our sundaes to conceal our eavesdropping.

"You wish to visit Dr. Flo?"

The man nodded vigorously.

"You are ill?"

"No, no, I just needa speak with her about my lodgings."

"Please, Mister—"

"Dacta."

"Please, Mr. Dacta—"

"Dacta Grant. Not Mista Dacta."

The Swedish ambassador pursed his lips.

"Please attend me here."

He turned on his heel and vanished into the kitchen.

The peculiar man sighed and swabbed his face with the rag

again. Pearl and I peeped at him over our spoons.

"Is he a trucker for real?" Pearl hissed.

"No, he can't be," I whispered, as I flicked my eyes over his person. "He hasn't got the characteristic baseball cap with a lewd saying, and he hasn't done the rebel yell even once to relieve his pent-up enthusiasm."

I realized the man was staring at my sister and me. I hunched down in my seat and pretended to eat.

The Swedish ambassador emerged from the kitchen bearing a steaming cup of coffee and a Swedish-English dictionary. He set the cup upon the counter and opened the dictionary with a flourish.

"Please indicate your nationality and country of origin for the immigration records of the Swedish-Texan corporate commonwealth of Somwärin," he read aloud.

The stranger slumped over the countertop, his shoulders hunched in defeat. But only for a moment. He inhaled deeply, lifted his chin, and raised his eyes to meet the pale blue ones of the Swedish ambassador.

"Please," he said. "Fathalovagawd, just tell me where I can find Dacta Hersh—Dacta Flo—whateva you call her. No one came to pick me up at the airport. I hada hitch a ride off a fammer driving an honest-to-Gawd turnip truck. He dumped me five miles outsida town and told me I hada walk the resta the way in this heat."

"That must've been Farmer Bill," Pearl whispered.

"Where is Dacta Flo?" the man articulated each syllable with the clipped precision of a tailor wielding a pair of pinking shears.

The Swedish ambassador hung his head in shame.

"I have failed," he said miserably. "Mr. Dacta, these two girls are native English speakers. They will assist you. I cannot."

Pearl and I looked at one another in surprise.

"Us?" I said.

"But we're still eating!" Pearl whined.

I kicked her under the table. Nothing this exciting had ever happened to either of us before.

"Please excuse me. I must file a report confessing my incompetence," said the Swedish ambassador.

He withdrew a clipboard from beneath the counter and trudged across the room to the beauty parlor section of the Swedish Embassy & Beauty Parlor & Coffee Shop. He slumped into one of the pink plastic hairdryer chairs, lowered the glass hood over his head, and covered his face with both hands, his entire frame radiating bleak Nordic sorrow. It was best to leave him alone when he fell into such moments of nihilistic introspection, so Pearl and I stood and motioned to the newcomer to follow us.

"This way," I half-shouted, to facilitate comprehension.

Out on Main Street in the downpour of torrid sunlight, the man began to sweat vigorously. He mopped at his forehead with the back of his hand, then opened his mouth to speak. Pearl and I perked up our ears, eager to learn his outlander dialect.

"Is it always this hat? It's only June—how can it be so hat?"

He paused and looked at me, then at my sister.

"I'm sorry about this. I can't imagine what your motha and fatha would say, you two helping some man you neva met before—"

"Oh, our daddy's a trucker, and he's off trucking around from one end of the country to the other and making trouble in every town he hits. He and Mama are long-divorced, so the likes of him wouldn't mind, I don't guess," Pearl burst out cheerfully, all in one breath. "And Mama's been known to say you've got to be neighborly to neighbors and neighbor-like types, so she wouldn't mind."

"As long as you aren't a trucker," I said.

"Are you?" demanded Pearl.

Every summer, for as long as I could remember, truckers had been showing up in Somwärin with their semis and their Class A commercial driver's licenses and their synchronized impulses to loiter destructively around town while the employees of the Fack Sex Furniture Distribution

Warehouse—including my own mama—loaded their trucks with easy-to-assemble Swedish furniture bound for stores throughout the great U.S. of A. and the lesser republic of Canada.

Somwärin was the sole North American distribution hub connecting the Fack Sex Corporation's clandestine manufacturing plant in Mexico (called "Southernmost Sweden" on the shipping receipts to Norwegianify the furniture's Hispanic origin) and the rest of the continent. Unfortunately, not a single Somwärinite in the company's employ had ever learned to read Swedish. Thus, the simple task of filling the waiting trucks dragged on and on during peak shipping season each June, during which time the warehouse workers— including my own mama—baffled their brains over invoices requesting mysterious objects such as fåtölj, skåpdörr, and nattduksbord.

With nothing to do during the warehouse workers' period of functional illiteracy, and with a handsome stipend from Fack Sex for each day they were idle, the truckers holed up in a gauntlet of seedy motels on the outskirts of town where they whored, drank, and mischieved the days away. When at last their trucks were fully loaded, the truckers always held a blowout of decadent debauchery and incomprehensible inebriation known along every highway and byway of the Northern and Southern Americas as the Trucker Jamboree. Then, sated and hungover, they drove off into the sunset, leaving us in peace. Until next summer.

Pearl and I crossed our arms over our chests and glared at the man. He blinked in confusion, then said, "Oh, the Teamstas Union! No, no, I'm not a Teamsta."

He laughed. We didn't see the humor, so we didn't join him.

"Then what are you? Nobody but truckers and Swedes from the home office in Stockholm ever come to Somwärin," said Pearl.

"And you, sir, are no Swede," said I.

The man held out his hand. I looked at it, wondering what

he wanted me to give him.

"My name is Richard Grant. *Dacta* Richard Grant, actually."

I narrowed my eyes at the sight of his ruddy palm, covered as it was with the sweat of his brow. I declined to shake it.

"I'm Ruby Bejou, and this-here's Pearl."

"I'm twelve and she's fourteen and Opal's seventeen and Mama says she's twenty-nine but she's really thirty-four and how old are you?" Pearl concluded with a squawk as I jabbed her in the ribs.

"Why're you here if you're a doctor? We already got ourselves a doctor in Somwärin," I said.

"Dr. Flo," Pearl supplied.

"Yes, I'm awara that. I'm with a federal program that sends dactas to medically underserved communities. A request for an ob-gyn was sent from this…town. So here I am. It sounded like a good idea when I signed up in med school," he sighed, swiping his hand like a windshield wiper across his dewy face.

"What's an opie gee whiner?" Pearl inquired.

The doctor smiled and replied, "Ob-gyn. It stands for obstetrics and gynecology."

"What's that?" I asked.

"Obstetrics is the care of mothas and babies before and afta birth. Gynecology is the diagnosis and treatment of disordas of the female reproductive tract."

Pearl and I glanced at each other, glanced at the doctor, glanced back at each other and burst out laughing.

"A hootchie doctor!" we squealed, holding our sides and gasping with giggles.

The hootchie doctor didn't look pleased.

Pearl and I snickered all the way to Dr. Flo's clinic, which was located three doors down from the Swedish Embassy & Beauty Parlor & Coffee Shop. To our collective dismay, it was buttoned up tight, the blinds firmly drawn and the front door locked.

"Wicked pissa," muttered the hootchie doctor.

"I bet Dr. Barney'll know what to do," I said.

"There's anotha dacta in this town?" the hootchie doctor

said.

"Dr. Barney's better than a doctor," Pearl said, steering him across the blazing pavement of Main Street. "He's an *animal* doctor!"

The hootchie doctor did not seem delighted by this news. Nonetheless, we ushered him through the welcoming door of the Vet 'n' Pet Shop, Pearl's favorite place in the whole wide world.

The physician grumbled in Bwastinese under his breath as Pearl darted between the dimly lit aisles of cages filled with furry fauna and creepy critters.

"Lookit, Ruby! Lookit the bunny! Lookit the salamander! Oh, I love you—what are you, a hedgehog? Lookit how cute he is, Ruby, look!"

Tipped off by the alarmed bleats of the animals my little sister was terrifying with adoration, Dr. Barney emerged from the back of the Vet 'n' Pet Shop, a mouse squirming in his hand.

"Well, hey there," he said, his eyes sliding from me to the stranger with mellow curiosity.

"Hey, Dr. Barney, this-here's a hootchie doctor, and—and he—"

I could not continue. I was overcome. I doubled over with laughter.

The hootchie doctor sidestepped me and gave Dr. Barney a smile.

"Hi, I'm Dacta Richard Grant from the—"

"Oh, the ob we asked for," Dr. Barney said, transferring the mouse to his breast pocket and reaching out to shake hands. "Howdy-do, Dick?"

Dr. Dick eyed Dr. Barney's mousy palm and unsubtly occupied both of his hands with the task of rustling his letter of introduction from his jacket pocket.

"I've been trying to track down Dacta Hershille."

"You mean Dr. Flo?"

"Is that really what she prefers to be called?"

"Well, I don't know if it's a matter of preference. We've just always called her that. Heck, my name's not Barney, it's Owen Maple. Don't ask me why they call me Dr. Barney, Dick."

"I—pardon me, but I'd ratha not be called 'Dick.'"

"Well, sure," Dr. Barney laughed. "But considering the line of work you're in, I think you'd better get used to it."

"Um. So where is Dacta…Flo?"

"County hospital," Dr. Barney said, as he slipped half a saltine cracker into his pocket, which began to undulate like an alien fixing to bust out of his chest. "Some kid got sick over at the school and she had to ride 'em in. She'll be back tomorrow. Maybe the day after, if the young'un takes a turn for the worse."

Dr. Dick looked alarmed.

"I see. The thing is, I undastood that she would tell me where I'm going to be living, where my office is, when my luggage is going to turn up."

"Oh, I don't know anything about housing or luggage, but I can show you your office right now, if you want. Dr. Flo put me in charge of getting it all set up for you."

Dr. Dick brightened considerably.

"Yes, I'd very much like to see it."

"Okay, just gimme a sec."

Dr. Barney turned and moseyed into the depths of the Vet 'n' Pet Shop. Dr. Dick and I followed him, leaving Pearl behind to coo over a profane parrot. Dr. Barney strode past the dog kennels and the operating room. He opened a nondescript gray door, flicked on a light, and withdrew the mouse from his pocket. He stuck it in a small wire cage bolted to the cheap wood paneling that covered the wall and began to wash his hands in a steel utility sink.

"Like it?" he inquired presently.

Dr. Dick smiled an uncertain smile.

"What?" he said.

"This space. I cleared it out as best I could. Used to be a storage closet. Feel free to take down the feline anatomy charts if you want; might give the ladies the wrong impression," Dr. Barney chuckled as he shook his hands dry.

Dr. Dick's eyes grew and grew and grew.

"You don't mean…"

"Dr. Flo said you'd only need a small space, since you deal in such a…restricted area of the ladylike body, as it were."

"This is a joke, right? Haze the new dacta, ha-ha, very funny, I get it. Where's my real office?"

Dr. Barney met Dr. Dick's desperate gaze with a mild smile.

"We can get you a shorter exam table eventually, once we have the funds. This-here's my old equine table, but we don't see too many horses 'round here nowadays, so I figured I could spare it. I may need to borrow it back at some point, though—just be forewarned."

"Oh my Gawd," said Dr. Dick. "The town physician can't possibly think I can practice medicine in the back room of a pet store—"

"Technically, this-here's a pet shop slash veterinary clinic, Dick."

"Is she insane?"

Dr. Barney shrugged and replied, "You'll have to take that up with Dr. Flo when she gets back."

"I…I…I…"

Dr. Dick's face had assumed an unhealthy, milky hue. I sensed he was overwhelmed. Dr. Barney gave me a little nod and I took him by the elbow to escort him away from the storage closet that was causing him such dismay. When Pearl saw the snow-white shade of Dr. Dick's visage, she abandoned her beloved beasts and trailed us out of the Vet 'n' Pet Shop without protest.

Back in the brilliant sunshine, my sister and I took a few steps back and observed Dr. Dick. Would he dash up and down Main Street in a rage, pausing only to lob a few stones through the windows of Dr. Flo's clinic? That's what I would have done.

Or perhaps he would entreat first the sun, then passersby, with a profanity-permeated plea for justice and a bottle of Southern Comfort to take his unfathomable affliction away. That's what Mama would have done.

In either case, Pearl and I would be eyewitnesses and much in demand when the gossiping began.

Dr. Dick stood very still for several minutes, squinting numbly into the sultry distance.

"I need a hotel," he said finally, frustration and a light sunburn putting some color back into his features.

Instantly, I set upon him in horror.

"Oh no! You can't go to one of the motels!" I said. "Only truckers stay there."

"Ruby…" Pearl said.

"Filthy hellholes, all of them. You so much as look at one of them motel beds and you'll catch a disease. A disease of your secret parts."

"Ruby…you're not thinking what I think you're thinking?" Pearl said.

"Come to our house. Mama will let you stay with us."

"Ruby, no!" Pearl said.

"She'd never forgive us if we let Somwärin's one and only hootchie doctor bunk down at a nasty ol' pay-by-the-day when we can demonstrate the Bejou family's sense of hospitality."

"You're gonna get us in so much trouble," Pearl said.

But I was the oldest and I had veto power, so we took him home.

And that's how all the trouble started.

Chapter Two
Perdee Dora's Superior Summer Shindig and Smörgåsbord

Friday, June 14
Three hours prior to sundown

Into the resplendent gloaming suffused with diaphanous clouds that soared heavenward from an unseen tire fire smoldering at the dump, my sister and I tugged our reluctant quarry. As we traversed the pitted and pocked dirt road leading out of town, Dr. Dick's expression grew more and more uncertain.

"Excuse me," he ventured again, for the fifth time. "Where exactly do you girls live?"

Dr. Dick's uneasy gaze swept the Texan desolation of merciless sky and lifeless earth.

"It's soon, soon, just past the lawn chair graveyard!" Pearl chirped. She took him firmly by the hand and began to tug him along in an ever-accelerating trot.

Before Dr. Dick could bolt, we reached it: the Somwärin Trailer Park and RV Pleasure Garden.

Our home.

Dr. Dick's face fell as he beheld the rusty ranks of tin can trailers slumping against embankments of oxidizing earth, the clotheslines of naughty panties stretching between the windows of the McMayberry brothers' school bus residence, and the dark enigma of the caravan that contained the Tooth Witch.

Pearl dropped Dr. Dick's hand and ran ahead to our trailer to announce the arrival of the town's crotch doctor to Mama and our big sister. I was left to parade the skittish gentleman at a slow clip through the trailer park, showing off the citified specimen to the locals who gawked at him from plastic lawn chairs with one foot in the lawn chair graveyard.

I was more than pleased with how the summer was starting. We Bejous would be purveyors of town gossip for months—and not its scandalous stars, for once.

I gave Dr. Dick a subtle side-eye and saw his Adam's apple going up and down and up and down. Clearly he was losing his nerve. The key was to chatter at him so he couldn't collect his thoughts.

"You're gonna love staying at our place," I began. "Me and Pearl will take good care of you and shelter you from the observation and photography of the overeager townspeople. Mama lets us stay up till eleven in the summer, which is fortunate coz the good shows don't come on until after the Sissy Spacek Movie Marathon ends every night. Last year, they showed back-to-back episodes of "The Dukes of Hazzard" every Thursday from nine o'clock until dawn. Opal particularly appreciated that programming choice, coz she thinks Boss Hogg is hot."

As we passed an aged El Camino poised precariously on cinderblocks, a low snarl sounded.

"What's that?" Dr. Dick said.

"Don't worry about it," I said. "Opal made herself a pair of Daisy Duke shorts once, and they looked like underwear, and Mama said she couldn't traipse around in public gadded up in such garb, but she did, and there were twelve car accidents on Main Street that Easter Sunday morning. What do you think of that?"

"Ah…um."

Another gravely growl vibrated from beneath the El Camino, which now lay in our immediate wake. I turned my head with feigned insouciance and spied a flash of tufty black fur slinking around the duct tape embellished back bumper. My eyes automatically roved the dirt for a weapon. Leaning against Quenton Keeton's homemade monster truck was a wooden flag pole with shreds of the ol' yellow-and-blue of mother Scandinavia wrapped around the top. Casually, I reached out and grabbed it.

"If you hate macaroni 'n' cheese, best say so now or that's

all Pearl will feed you. She considers it a luxurious treat," I said. "The lunch ladies at school say it's a Swedish food, coz they use them macaroni noodles to make Swedish meatballs. But Mama says the Fack Sex cafeteria cooks insist on noodles that're as flat as the fjords at midsummer for their Swedish meatballs, and macaroni 'n' cheese is un-Nordic."

At this particular moment, our neighbor's mad dog, Bitch-Girl, launched herself at us. As this was an everyday happenstance, I knew what to do. I mechanically battered at her flashy fangs with the flag pole as Dr. Dick coiled himself into a full-body cringe, his hands flapping about to protect his face.

"But the very best of the very, very bestest shows on TV is wrestling. They got a real professional wrestling league over in Big City, and one'a these days Mama is gonna take us to see it live and in person. She made us and Jesus a solemn vow to do it when Pearl almost died choking on a piece of Lundergarten's Lickable Licorice," I informed the cowering physician.

I got Bitch-Girl a good one on her tick-scabbed rump. She yelped; a sound like the ominous swinging of a screen door on rusty hinges in a slasher movie. Dr. Dick grabbed my free hand in alarm as she galumphed past us, spewing wrathful foam from her snout.

Safe and sound, I steered us between a pair of garden gnomes astride pink flamingo steeds. I halted. I swept my arm wide, pointing the flag pole with the aplomb of a carnival barker.

"Here we are," I announced.

Dr. Dick, whose eyes were hubcaps, came to a shuddering standstill in front of the Bejou family trailer. I hopped up the metal steps, only a few of which were broken, opened the dented front door, and beckoned to him. Dr. Dick hesitated, torn between the manifest terror presented by Bitch-Girl and the potential horror that might lurk within the nausea-green double-wide. He took a bracing gulp of hot afternoon air. Deep within the trailer park, Bitch-Girl bayed. In three strides, he was at my side.

"Enter of your own free will," I said. "Welcome to our home—välkommen!"

I tugged Dr. Dick across the threshold by the sleeve of his unseasonably sturdy suit jacket and steered him into the living room. I considered the TV, then its honor guard of tatty old couch and mud-brown armchair from the Fantastisk Fåtölj line, obtained at a discount by Mama when the Fack Sex Furniture Distribution Warehouse was clearing out excess stock six summers ago. I shoved Dr. Dick into the choicest seat, the fåtölj.

"Make yourself at home," I commanded.

Pearl dashed in from the kitchen with a cold can of soda. She thrust it into his hand.

"This-here's the rare strawberry-flavor soda, which Opal generally steals. But I hid it in a certain place and now you can have it!"

"It also reclines!"

I jerked the handle on the fåtölj and Dr. Dick went flopping backward, his feet pointing straight up at the imitation-gold kristallkrona hanging from the ceiling.

"There we go! Comfy? Good. Opal!"

"Hey, Dr. Dick, do you like macaroni 'n' cheese?"

"We can't have that tonight!"

"Why not? We have a guest."

"Because. Opal! C'mere!"

"You're not very neighborly, that's what Mama'll say. Guests like macaroni 'n' cheese, Ruby. Isn't that so, Dr. Dick?"

At this point, my big sister, Opal, emerged from the depths of the trailer in a state of great undress. She was clad, but only barely, in one of her shiny bra-and-panty combos. A button-down shirt, conspicuously unbuttoned, was thrown over her undergarments. This in and of itself was not what elicited the palpable silence from the fåtölj, however.

Opal had the biggest boobs in all of Somwärin.

Actually, Opal had the biggest boobs, full stop. No one from Somwärin to Southernmost Sweden had such massive melons. Even the implant-infused bazombas showcased in the nasty magazines that carpeted the motel grounds each summer were positively tiny in comparison.

Opal's boobs exceeded any size conceived by the human mind. Since the age of eleven, she'd been unable to find a bra that fit. Mama had been obliged to learn the arcane art of stitchery on a thrift store sewing machine and whip up a fresh batch of bras every few weeks to accommodate Opal's ever-expanding rack. And, to this day, they were still growing. I could fit one of my big sister's bra cups all the way over my head, roll it down over my face to settle in folds over my shoulders, and there was still plenty of room for Pearl and Mama to squeeze their heads in.

"Okay," she said, looming over Dr. Dick and sweeping her head from one end of the living room to the other. "Where is he? Where's the hoo-hoo hole doctor Pearl's so excited about?"

From Dr. Dick's horizontal position in the fåtölj, it surely appeared as if two great balloons of flesh were floating untethered just above his feet in defiance of the laws of gravity, and speaking English in defiance of the laws of God.

"Right here in the fåtölj," I said. "Dr. Dick, this-here's my big sister, Opal."

I turned Opal sideways so her view of Dr. Dick was no longer obscured by her gargantuan gazongas. She brightened and grinned at him over her shoulder.

"So, you're a—a sex doctor, huh?" Opal said. She pushed her dishwater-blond hair out of her eyes with a nimble hand and reached for him, her fingers twiddling eagerly.

"It's Oafy Gee Wine," I corrected.

"Well, you'll have yourself a mess of work once the truckers hit town," Opal said, her hand questing for Dr. Dick. "Fun-time girls with the clap, the gonorrhea, the crabs—"

She leaned down, the canyon of her cleavage nearly swallowing Dr. Dick's face whole.

"Syphilis, scabies, that one makes alla your hair fall out, even your eyebrows…"

She smiled and neatly pulled the strawberry soda out of his

hand.

"You ain't gonna drink that, are you?"

"Hey! Pearl saved that special!"

"Oh, he don't mind, do you, Dr. Dick?

"I'm gonna tell Mama! And it's your night to start dinner, and Pearl's in there trying to make us eat macaroni 'n' cheese—"

"Uff da, Ruby," Opal huffed, rolling her eyes.

She sailed out of the living room, her breasts coming to port in the kitchen a full ten seconds before the rest of her made anchorage. She raised her voice as she rustled through the cupboards.

"One time, when the truckers were in town, there was this girl who caught herself a strange and exotic affliction the likes of which no one had ever seen before. Her skin got plumb *sparkly*. Like she rolled around in glitter. Dr. Flo had to take her all the way to Houston to see a specialist."

"Fred Flintstone show's on right now, if you'd care to partake," I said.

I rummaged amongst the battered cushions of the fåtölj, which encased the supine Dr. Dick like a sarcophagus.

"Turns out it *was* glitter. Some jokester trucker superglued it all over her while she slept. Yep, you're gonna have a heap of work this summer. Dr. Flo isn't gonna be happy to have you here, though," Opal laughed from afar. "Not one little bit."

"Mama's coming!" Pearl called, as she swung through the living room.

"Hurry, Ruby!" Opal cried.

I flew into action with my sisters, setting the table, wiping the counter, and tidying up the islets of clutter that had somehow formed in the mere fifteen minutes we'd been home. Mama, spouseless, relied upon her daughters to serve as housewives to her breadwinner, a duty we girls collectively botched on a daily basis.

As we hurried along a slow-to-simmer pot of canned fiskbullar that Mama had nicked from work and searched for a subtle hiding place in which to conceal the dirty breakfast dishes, we completely forgot about Dr. Dick.

Suddenly, a shrill shriek rent the air.

"Who the hell are you?" came a familiar tobacco-ravaged voice at the front door.

Pearl and I rushed into the living room, and there was Mama: menthol cigarette clamped between her front teeth, banana-yellow high heels kicking like a kung fu champion, car keys stabbing the air above the reclining Dr. Dick.

"Now, Mama, don't be alarmed," I exclaimed, jumping between Dr. Dick and her lethal fake fingernails. "This-here's Dr. Dick. He's a legitimate man of medicine, new in town, and we didn't want him to stay at a motel—"

"Actually ma'am, the situation, uh, appeahs to be…" Dr. Dick wheezed, struggling to drag himself from the confining clutches of the fåtölj.

Seeking to diffuse the outrage in Mama's darting eyes, Pearl clutched her around her tiny waist. She tipped her head back to smile with sickening sweetness into Mama's heavily made-up face.

"He isn't a trucker and he's nice and clean and well-behaved. Can't we keep him, Mama? Pleeeeeease?"

"Opal! Did you drag this character home with you? I told you, I don't want none of your conquests crashing in my household."

"No, Mama, this one's those two's. And he's a specialist with regards to the wee-wee region," Opal announced from the kitchen doorway, dropping her voice into a secretive whisper.

"Pervert!"

"No, no, no! I'm the new dacta in town, but I'm afraid there's been a bit of a mix-up…"

"Well, hell's bells," said Mama, matter-of-factly.

She let out a sharp puff of air, sheathed the keys in her handbag, and kicked off her high heels. Thus disarmed, she stepped over to Dr. Dick and looked him up and down. She planted one hand on her hip and stretched the other hand out to him in an Opal-esque manner. With a practiced twist, she stubbed her cigarette out in the cut-glass askkopp poised on a little wooden soffbord by his head.

"I guess," she said. "We can feed and bed you for tonight. But this ain't no flophouse, understand? Even that one," she jerked a long, red fingernail at Opal, who was lounging in the doorway, her bosom casting a shadow as wide as a circus tent across the shag carpet. "That one there has to get gone when she turns eighteen. When the clock strikes midnight and ya turn into a pumpkin, that means it's time to roll along. Got me?"

Dr. Dick didn't look like he got her, but he nodded anyway. Mama nodded back, then padded into the kitchen. We girls trailed behind her.

"Didja get me my hairspray for Perdee Dora's shindig, Mama?"

"Pearl, I've been at work for twelve hours! You think I had time to fetch hairspray?"

"But Mama! My hair'll look so bad and Perdee Dora will make fun."

"Borrow some from your sisters."

"They don't share well!"

"Hey Mama, guess what happened out in the parking lot after school," said Opal.

"You promised me you'd get my hairspray before I left for school, Mama. You said, 'I promise I'll get it on the way home.' Ruby is my witness."

"Well, you were taking advantage of my morning disorientation, and I surely was lying."

"Annie-Belle Cutler fell slap down on the asphalt and started speaking in tongues," said Opal. "Glad it wasn't me. I'd hate to miss the smörgåsbord tonight because I was full of angels or Moses or what-have-you."

"So that's why you ditched me and Pearl after school?" I accused, more accusingly than I intended.

Opal rolled her eyes at me once again and hoisted the pot of steaming fiskbullar securely under the expansive awning of her bust.

"Don't be a baby, Ruby."

"Pearl, you best stop that moaning right this minute—I can hear you, sly and subtle-like. I'll get your hairspray this weekend."

"That's too late, Mama! Perdee Dora—"

"Perdee Dora, Perdee Dora! Never in alla my born days have I seen a worse tempered brat of a child. She'll be the ruin of the entire blamed town before she's done—mark my words."

"Yep, that was some high drama in the school parking lot. Y'all missed out."

"Well—well—me and Pearl found us a whole doctor, didn't we? Haven't ever seen you bring home one of those. You're the one who missed out, fannying around the parking lot, just like every single boring day. You didn't see how he babbled like an idiot and sweat bullets all over and—"

"Quiet!" said Mama.

She turned to Dr. Dick, who was hovering anxiously in the doorway, his eyes darting to each of our faces in turn. She flicked her frosted blond hair out of her face and indicated a chair with a hand hardened by years of lugging stout slaktblocks and broad bokhyllor around the Fack Sex Furniture Distribution Warehouse while perched on spindly spike heels.

"Please be seated," she said.

We watched avidly as Dr. Dick cleared his throat and hesitantly approached the köksbord around which we loomed. He withdrew the nearest köksstol and sat. We three girls sat on our köksstolar as well, swiped up our spoons, and lunged at the big pot of hot soup. The sound of a fist rapping once upon the battle-scarred köksbord-top—like the jewel-encrusted gavel that Judge Diamond Don Desmond from courtroom TV was always banging—stopped our utensils in mid-air.

"Hospitable manners!" Mama glared at us beneath double-layered false lashes. "Y'all ain't uncouth Greenlanders. Our guest first."

We girls retracted our spoons slightly and fixed hungry eyes upon Dr. Dick.

Dr. Dick glanced around the köksbord at each of us, placed a servett in his lap, and picked up his empty skål. He dipped his sked into the fiskbullar and dished a single sked-ful into his skål.

That was enough for us—he'd had his chance. We four dove into the pot and wrestled out our shares, squalling like alley cats. We fell wordlessly to slurping, jealously guarding our portions, and fighting over the dregs. None of us paid Dr. Dick any mind as he stared from us to his sad spoonful of soup and back again. In the Bejou household, you were swift of spoon and fleet of fork or you went hungry.

"So, you're some kinda doctor?" Mama demanded after four out of five of us had sated our appetites. She lit a fresh, minty cigarette and tipped the ash into her plate.

"Yes, I'm some kind of dacta. I'm an ob-gyn. Listen, I'm sorry for inconveniencing—"

"I've heard of that. My sister had one of them. You planning to set up shop here in Somwärin?"

"It would appeah so."

"Huh," Mama shot a grin at me. "Dr. Flo ain't gonna like that."

A swampy, sticky atmosphere descended upon the trailer after the dinner dishes had been cleared away. Mama retired to the great outdoors to cool her cheeks and smoke in the blue twilight, while we girls betook ourselves first to our bedroom to dress, then to the bathroom to primp for Perdee Dora's Superior Summer Shindig and Smörgåsbord. Dr. Dick wandered around, accidentally walked in on Opal hoisting on her most festive bra, and fled to the kitchen to hunker down at the köksbord and sweat.

Little did he know that greater terrors lay on the horizon. Refreshed by nicotine and the nocturnal breeze, Mama re-entered and spoke what she believed were comforting words.

"Ya best prepare yourself, Dr. Dick. My lady friends are gonna be here in ten minutes, and we intend to drink. Gotta have ourselves one last hurrah before our yearly curse descends."

"Curse?" we heard a bewildered male voice say. "Menstruation?"

In the midst of overhauling our natural appearances in the tiny bathroom, we girls covered our mouths and giggled hard and deep. Then we resumed our efforts to curl, crimp, plat, rat, glue, and staple our hair into concoctions of a scale and grandiosity befitting Perdee Dora's annual end of the year party.

Barely had we completed our renovations when Mama hollered at us from the living room.

"It's seven-thirty! Get going or it'll be over before you're there."

We rushed out of the bathroom, crammed our feet into our highest heels, and tumbled to the side door, where Mama stood tapping a small foot encased in one of her blood-red drinking party pumps and glowering out the window.

"Well, git! My lady friends are arriving as we speak."

Mama seemed to have forgotten the morning's nude harbinger of truckerly mischief, sending us unchaperoned into town on foot and after sundown as she was. I had high hopes that this fact alone would guarantee an exciting evening for us girls. We each kissed her cheek in turn and beat it for the wilds of the night.

"Y'all get yourselves home by midnight. No later, or I'll…well, my lady friends and I will think of some fitting punishment for the likes of you," she called.

"Okay, Mama," I called back.

"Bye, Dr. Dick!" Pearl yelled over her shoulder.

"I really do prefer 'Dacta Grant,'" he replied wanly from the kitchen.

As we stumbled down the metal steps in our sky-high footwear, Mama's lady friends—a blonde, a brunette, and another blonde—began pulling up in their various and sundry

Oldsmobiles. Hauling rawboned asses out of the drivers' seats, cigarettes jammed between their vice-like lips, they bore brown-bagged bottles and sneered at us in passing. We were only too glad to scurry away down the dim dirt road. Mama's drinking parties were no picnic.

The setting sun stained the sky a rosy-orange hue. The air was soft on our bare arms; a friendly sort of chill after the audacious heat of day. In the distance, a lone trucker trilled "Yeeeeeeee-haaaaaaw!"

"I don't know what to do this summer," I began in a complaining voice. "I'm afraid it's gonna be awful boring, just like last year."

"Hey, I know! Opal's working at the Burger Bower. Maybe you can get a job there?" Pearl said.

"No, they don't take on little kids. The manager says they're over-staffed as it is, but he squeezed me in coz I've got extra special qualifications."

"Ain't that a fact," I muttered, glancing at Opal's hooters before I could stop myself. Opal's hooters returned my gaze blandly, but Opal herself scowled at me.

"Knowing you, you'll either spend the whole dang summer flat on the couch in front of the TV, or you'll prowl the town making trouble. Hope you pick the couch, for your own good," Opal said.

I glowered at my big sister and thought of three nasty, cutting retorts. But I swallowed them down whole and said nothing in the interest of preserving the party mood.

After twenty blister-raising minutes, our teetering high heels brought us to the fanciest domicile in Somwärin. Perdee Dora Dolan's house was a wheel-less structure that Mama referred to as a "townhouse," though given Mama's unfamiliarity with the finer points of non-trailer architecture it was possible that the house was a split-level or a ranch-style or a geodesic dome for all we Bejous knew. It was painted a classy shade of blue with clean, white trim around the windows and door frames. There was an expanse of alligator-green grass both fore and aft. It had two stories, a wrap-around porch, and a cellar for the microscopic tornadoes that drifted lazily through Somwärin every couple years. The only time we were ever allowed inside Perdee Dora's house was for her Superior Summer Shindig and Smörgåsbord.

We girls paused a moment to admire the sheriff-mayor's patrol car parked out front. The glossy beast of a Cadillac loomed proudly in the faint starlight. Silver scrollwork etched its way along the sides and across the hood like the fancy piping on a singing cowboy's shirt. Every inch of the car, from stem to stern, was studded with red and blue lights that glimmered like snazzy sequins against the jet-black paint job. The convertible top was down, inviting the unwise to hop in and grip the steering wheel—an act that would surely be their last on this earth.

The word (put out there by the sheriff-mayor himself) was the car had once belonged to Elvis Presley.

"THE Elvis Presley," he always boomed, sticking his thumbs in his bullet-studded belt and rocking back on his heels. "But he didn't never drive it. Nawsir! Bought it for his identical twin brother, Jesse Garon Presley. Stillborn. Died the day Elvis and him was born. The minute he got famous, ol' Elvis bought his dead 'n' deceased twin a Caddie. Ain't that brotherly love for ya? You better believe it. And now it's ALL MINE!"

How it had come to be ALL HIS! was one of Somwärin's many mysteries.

Twangy country-western music resounded from behind unbroken windows as we approached. The shadows of dozens upon dozens of kids skimmed along behind the gauzy drapery. It was not a wild party—the somnambulistic Mrs. Dolan would never stand for that—but it was, bar none, the most popular event of the year for Somwärin's teenaged crowd.

Perdee Dora's Superior Summer Shindig and Smörgåsbord was held every summer on the last day of school. It was "superior" because, upon its inception following her graduation from kindergarten, she judged it (correctly, as it turned out) to be better than the town's other Summer Shindig and Smörgåsbord, which had been put on by the Somwärin school board for more than three decades. After Perdee Dora's glittering inaugural party, the Inferior Summer Shindig and Smörgåsbord quietly ceased operations and was heard of no more.

My sisters and I climbed the impeccably-swept front steps and let ourselves in via the polished brass doorknob. Immediately, Opal vanished into a swell of boys clad in their stiffest Levis and mightiest belt buckles. Pearl let out a squeal that was echoed by a gaggle of sixth grade girls, and off she galloped to hug and hop en masse as if they'd been parted for decades.

I was left all alone.

Ditched for the second time today by Opal, and now abandoned by Pearl, too.

Well, I could get on fine without them! I'd show Pearl who was unemployable and Opal who was incapable of entertaining herself. Since there was nothing I could do to secure a wage-earning position at this particular moment, I would bend my efforts toward beating back the encroaching swell of boredom I felt building on the horizon, like a bank of stygian thunderheads.

It shouldn't be too hard. I was at a splendid soiree, after all.

I squared my padded shoulders, tossed my immobile hair, and pointed myself at the buffet boards laden with the fete's titular smörgåsbord. Three massive tables—not a one from the Fack Sex Furniture Distribution Warehouse—stood draped with Mrs. Dolan's imitation Irish linen. They groaned under the weight of brand-name delicacies the Bejou household rarely saw.

Twenty kids from my grade loitered thereabouts, grazing and chit-chatting. At my approach, five cleared off. When I gave forth an engaging smile, ten more departed. When I said, "Looks like this party's gonna be *real fun*!" a further three scattered. I offered a wink to the two remainders, and when my eye opened, I was all by my lonesome.

Somewhat daunted, I piled a hoity-toity paper plate with

Cheez Whiz and Doritos and Oreos and Leksands Knäckebröd. As I gnawed upon the Knäckebröd with my front teeth, a lad from Opal's class approached. I offered him a conspiratorial grin.

"Do I ever have some great gossip! We got us a fella at our house who traffics in the private parts of women!"

The chap gave me a boyish look of dumb alarm. He dodged me, grabbed himself a fistful of Slim Jims, and beat a swift retreat well out of my reach.

Alone again, I scanned the crowded living room. Over by the genuine granite fireplace, Opal's chesties were having a conversation with two high school boys. They—boys and boobs—bounced with good-humored laughter. All four of them were having great fun.

Resentful but undeterred, I spun away from the unlucky smörgåsbord and pointed myself into the thick of the crowd. I would find a way to amuse myself if it killed me. My purposeful stride was cut short, however, when the music abruptly shut off and every light in the house went out.

From the thick blackness came uneasy giggles and awkward shuffling sounds. Ten seconds passed. Thirty. Suddenly all the lightbulbs in the living room blared brilliantly to full wattage. Everyone squinted and blinked and turned to the carved pocket doors that stood closed at the far end of the room. After a breathless pause, they slid open on silent rollers. There she was! Sparkling, resplendent, and utterly detestable.

Perdee Dora Dolan.

The one and only child of Sheriff-Mayor Dolan.

The rich aura of his power had been smearing itself all over her since she was born and now, at age thirteen, she was the juvenile dictatoress of Somwärin's Junior and Senior High School.

Our Glorious Leaderette had outdone herself this year. She'd been groomed at the Swedish Embassy & Beauty Parlor & Coffee Shop earlier in the day, likely just after Pearl and I imported Dr. Dick to our trailer home. Her clear blond hair was painstakingly curled into a foamy sea of ringlets amongst which swam a rhinestone tiara, three peacock feathers, and a little glowing orb that backlit her head with a halo that changed colors every few seconds. Her face was meticulously painted with makeup so exquisite that it hurt my eyes to look directly at it. Her slim yet tastefully developed body was shown off by a pink denim dress sprinkled with scintillating rose-colored sequins. I had seen that very dress in a Big City department store weeks ago. The price tag had exceeded Mama's monthly take-home pay by hundreds and hundreds of dollars.

"Hi, everybody!" Perdee Dora cooed. "I want to thank all y'all *ever so* for coming to my lil party!"

We all clapped, as was expected.

"I hope y'all are enjoying yourselves so far…"

She paused dramatically. She raised one little hand above her haute couture hairdo. She snapped her fingers, each topped by professionally-applied false nails embedded with maybe-real diamond chips.

At this none-too-subtle gesture, four grinning boys appeared behind her bearing a gargantuan cake that towered to a height of eight impressive layers, topped by sizzling Fourth of July sparklers that shot sparks to the ceiling.

We were expected to gasp and then cheer, which we obediently did. Perdee Dora preened, giggled, and flashed chemically whitened teeth at us. I made a sour face and rolled my eyes away from our hostette. I espied Pearl a few paces from Perdee Dora, listening attentively with a desperate-to-seem-genuine smile sewn to her lips. Opal was in the back of the room, sucking the jaw off a sophomore.

Perdee Dora unsheathed a shining silver blade, raised it on high, and amputated eight great chunks of cake for our delectation. Our respectful silence began to crack in places, coughs and murmurs daring to emerge from the mouths of the bravest of us. After a further two swipes of knife through cake, Perdee Dora grew weary of performing manual labor and relinquished the rapier to one of her cake-bearers. She turned to strut into the throng of well-wishers, where she expected to bask in groveling compliments.

But before she could, a great and dreadful twist of fate struck.

It happened, as these terrible turning points tend to, with a confusing rapidity that muddled later testimony. My view was partially obscured by the milling backs of my school chums, but it looked to me like the following five things happened in swift succession:

1. Perdee Dora, swiveling to show off her dress to her sympathizers, accidentally trod upon the toes of my sister, Pearl.
2. Pearl let out a yelp.
3. Perdee Dora, displeased by physical contact with a groundling, turned to sneer at Pearl.
4. "Sorry, Perdee Dora," said Pearl, grimacing in pain.
5. "Hmf," smirked Perdee Dora. "Nice hair. Didja let that no-good sister of yours fix it for you?"

This was a quintessential Perdee Dora insult. Her slyness was incomparable and as layered as the towering cake held by the quartet of boys behind her. I sliced the insult in my mind as swiftly as the gents were slicing the cake:

Her initial "hmf" adroitly dismissed Pearl's pain as inconsequential and yet, in acknowledging it, Perdee Dora called attention to the fact that she was shamelessly not apologizing for causing it.

"Nice hair" was spoken with just enough sarcasm to wound, but the vowels were infused with a cheery little lilt that made it possible for Perdee Dora to claim that the comment was sincere, should she wish to present herself as the aggrieved party after the fact.

Instead of impugning the shoe upon which she accidentally trod, Perdee Dora had chosen to insult Pearl's hair, which cunningly called attention to her own elaborate hairdo while simultaneously reminding everyone that she was rich enough to have it professionally styled, unlike Pearl.

By asking if Pearl had let one of her sisters fix her hair, Perdee Dora was accusing Pearl of being unable to craft her own coiffure, implying that she was grossly ignorant about feminine beauty techniques.

Her reference to Pearl's "no-good sister" could pertain to Opal or myself equally—a brilliant two-in-one insult.

There were probably several more layers to the insult, but I was not sharp enough to probe their depths.

"Hit her, Pearl!" I heard myself shout. "Hit her good and hard!"

Alas, alas! This was the very command I always issued when Bitch-Girl was bearing down upon my little sister. From pure habit, Pearl swung out her fist and slugged Perdee Dora in the shoulder.

Perdee Dora froze. Pearl froze. The entire party froze. I doubled-down.

"Hit her again!" I shouted.

With a roar, Perdee Dora threw herself upon Pearl. Shrieking, the two began tussling like a pair of frilly game cocks. Lacquered nails tangled in stiffly sprayed hair. High heels shot in and out like spurs. Rose-colored sequins flew through the air like feathers.

The crowd of kids in the living room maintained both its distance from the brawlers and its horror-struck silence. No one had *ever* dared to engage Perdee Dora in hand-to-hand combat.

The fight might have continued indefinitely. Both combatants were scrappy and resolute. But woe unto Pearl! From the outskirts of the crowd came the voice of doom.

"Civil disobedience!"

Sheriff-Mayor Dolan stormed into the living room, his crew cut bristling, his thick head turning this way and that to demonstrate his simultaneous awareness of, and control over, our potentially riotous crowd.

Every single one of us recoiled, then became perfect statues as the sheriff-mayor, puffing with rigorous wrath, threw himself into the fray. A couple of valiant boys bestirred themselves and dragged the battling duo asunder, leaving behind strands of hair that floated earthward like streamers in a ticker tape parade.

Locked in the sweaty grip of a strapping youngster, Perdee Dora screamed something at my little sister that sounded like, "Silly spaceship! White trash silly spaceship!" As I tried to work out the intricacies of this peculiar insult, Pearl made a renewed lunge. She was held fast by her adolescent detainer.

At this moment, Sheriff-Mayor Dolan finally came to an accurate assessment of the nature of the domestic disturbance in progress before him.

"Fighting! Fighting in my house! *My* house!" he thundered in a basso profundo that rattled the very light bulbs in their sockets. "My baby girl throws y'all a party, and you turn it into a brouhaha? Is that Pearl Bejou there?"

The sheriff-mayor took three steps on his tree trunk legs, planted his meaty fists on his intricately tooled leather belt, and menaced my sister from above.

"I got me a good mind to turn you over my knee, missy. Whoop you on behalf of your no-good mama for what you done to my poor lil girl."

Any one of us would have been reduced to a quivering tear-puddle under the red-eyed bulldog glare of Sheriff-Mayor Dolan. Pearl, however, simply blew a stay tuft of hair out of her eyes and stuck out her jaw.

"My poor little angel food cake, are you all right?" said the sheriff-mayor, turning his attention to the bedraggled and sobbing Perdee Dora. I tried to slip unseen through the crowd so that I might snatch Pearl and spirit her safely away, but our host wasn't done with her yet.

"Lawless behavior, that's what it is, plain and simple! Where the hell're them other Bejou girls?"

His bayonet eyes slashed the room and skewered me.

"Get yourselves outta here, pronto! Y'all is banned! Banned from my home. Go on—git!"

Every face in the room turned to me. The crowd parted in silence to allow me to slink over to my sister. I took her by the hand and we scuttled out, our high heels and Pearl's quick, angry breathing making a racket that echoed throughout the tastefully appointed living room.

I steered Pearl into the elegant foyer to wait for Opal. I leaned against the front door and let out a slow breath.

Shameless and tearless, Pearl combed her fingers through her wild hair with jerky rage. I had never seen my little sister like this before. She tended to cringe and cavil when taunted by Perdee Dora. She wasn't a hair-ripping party wrecker. Was it all my fault? Had I provoked her at just the right moment with my Pavlovian exhortation to strike? As we prepared to dishonorably discharge ourselves from the shindig, the Dolan doorbell chimed the first bars of "The Eyes of Texas are Upon You." I sprang away from the front door in alarm.

"Ah," came a hazy voice, then Mrs. Dolan wobbled into the foyer. She smiled vaguely at us, a suspicious beverage in one hand, a rope of pearls long enough to rig a ship coiled around the other.

"Hope y'all had a fine time now," she nodded at us, nodded again, nodded a third time, then turned and wavered to the front door. She opened it, the rust-free hinges making no sound at all.

From the front porch came a familiar voice.

"Good evening. I'm sorry to trouble you, but I needa speak to the mayah right now, if I may. It's very urgent."

Had Dr. Dick, our temporary lodger, abandoned the hospitality of the Bejou trailer after a mere three hours? I minced to the door, peeped around Mrs. Dolan's scrawny elbow, and spied the same Dr. Dick standing on the porch. He was looking much the worse for wear. What had Mama and her lady friends done to him?

"Well…" Mrs. Dolan eventually replied. "There's no mayor here. My husband is the *sheriff*-mayor."

A long, long silence was exchanged between Dr. Dick and Mrs. Dolan. Dr. Dick broke it first.

"May I…may I speak with him?"

"Oh no, he's quite busy. He's a very busy and significant man."

"Um…"

Dr. Dick reached into his sweat-stiffened jacket and

withdrew the much-handled letter of introduction bearing the Somwärin town seal. He proffered it. Mrs. Dolan accepted it. She let it flutter to the thick beige carpet like a Victorian lady's handkerchief without sparing it a glance.

She sighed. She rotated her glass languidly to make the ice cubes swirl in the turbid liquid. She twined her pearls between her ivory fingers. She pursed her lips in a faint half-smile and looked dreamily into Dr. Dick's eyes from beneath her heavy lids.

"I suppose…I suppose I ought to invite you in," Mrs. Dolan mused, in no way inviting him in.

"Can't believe it—can't damning well believe it!"

I sought to conceal myself behind the shimmering folds of Mrs. Dolan's white silk lounging kimono as the sheriff-mayor came blustering into the foyer. Pearl stood her ground and folded her arms across her chest.

"Little sugar dolly all mauled and mangled! Pearl Bejou, I ought to haul you straight into the jail for what you've done. Teach you to respect your hostess at a party."

Pearl's spine remained stiff, whilst I fell to my knees and cowered upon the carpet, my palms raised in supplication.

The sheriff-mayor turned to the open door and squinted out at the unfamiliar figure poised beneath the custard-yellow porchlight.

"And who's this here? Ain't we got enough goddamned people at this goddamned party?"

Perceiving the arrival of a figure of great authority, Dr. Dick perked up. He extended his hand and stepped across the threshold, straight into the awesome presence of Sheriff-Mayor Dolan.

"Hi, good evening, I'm the new dacta in town—"

"Whoa, whoa," the sheriff-mayor barked, holding up one hand to stop Dr. Dick, the other cupping his hip pistol. "I don't recall asking your own self to enter my house and home, and I sure as shootin' don't—"

"Ah—sorry, but your wife here invited me in, Mista Dolan, so…"

We three—Mrs. Dolan, Pearl, and myself—inhaled in acute distress and shrank back until our backs were flat against the hand-painted wallpaper.

You never interrupted the sheriff-mayor in mid-rant.

You never dismissively referred to the honorable Mrs. Gloria Dolan, née Buckwheat of the Big City Buckwheats, as "your wife here."

And you never, never, upon your life and all you held dear, *never* referred to the sheriff-mayor by the lowly appellation "Mister."

Sheriff-Mayor Dolan's beady eyes went wide. He took a slow step toward Dr. Dick, his shiny boots creaking ominously under his heavy tread. He leaned in and poked his sausage-sized index finger into Dr. Dick's chest.

"Listen here, bub. You best export your ass outta my town just as quick as you can, so's I don't have time to fetch either my deputies or one of my many, many, many shotguns. You hear me, son? You are under…*indictment!*"

Pearl, Mrs. Dolan, and I gasped.

It was suspected by the majority of the townsfolk that Sheriff-Mayor Dolan had never learned the exact legal meaning of the term "indictment." Under his regime, "indictment" meant that much-enlarged photocopies of your unflattering driver's license photo would be plastered all over the walls outside the courthouse, which was located within the Celestial Temple of Psychedelic Truth and City Administration. Bratty grade school boys would be permitted to deface your image with clumsily crayoned devil horns, nerd glasses, and word balloons containing falsified quotes attesting to your aberrant toileting habits. If you showed yourself in town before the sheriff-mayor decided you'd learned your lesson, you could be dragged straight to the jail, also located within the Celestial Temple of Psychedelic Truth and City Administration, by any half-sober yahoo who happened to spy you. Mama frequently found herself under indictment.

Poor, incautious Dr. Dick merely frowned at the sheriff-mayor.

"Well. Okay. The thing is, I just arrived in town and it seems my contact person isn't, uh, available. So I was hoping that, as mayah, you might have some infammation about my housing situation. You *are* the mayah, am I right?"

"I'm the sheriff-mayor, you got that?" Sheriff-Mayor Dolan bellowed, the wind from his mighty lungs fanning Dr. Dick's hair back. "Not just the sheriff, not just the mayor. Both! BOTH! Ooooohh, Gloria, I'm about to go off! Get out! Alla y'all! GET OUT!"

We got out. Pearl and I each latched onto one of Dr. Dick's arms and dragged him through the front door as fast as we could. Behind us, we could hear the sheriff-mayor raging and Mrs. Dolan calling drowsily, "Y'all come back anytime!"

We tugged Dr. Dick down the smoothly paved driveway, deaf to his protests. He had never tangled with an irate sheriff-mayor before. He didn't know how lucky he was to escape with no new holes in his body.

"You'd best not let the sheriff-mayor lay eyes on you for two months at least. You'd best hide out at our place until autumn," I whispered into his ear as I hauled him down the street.

"Now, wait just a minute—" he began.

Fortunately, Opal chose to stagger out of the shadows of the imported-from-Virginia shrubbery at this moment, her clothing in cleavage-baring disarray, her face besmirched by a lusty smirk. This stopped Dr. Dick in mid-phrase, as it would any man, even a cleric of the medicinal arts. Silence settled upon our little posse as we began the long hike home. As the road turned to dirt and fireflies replaced the street lights, Dr. Dick cleared his throat.

"I suppose you three are wondering why I went to Mista…Majah-Sheriff…the Dolan residence?"

I considered this. No, I had not wondered. Nor did I now. None of us replied, but that didn't stop Dr. Dick.

"Well, your motha's…uh…friends were ratha…innarested in my presence. They were ratha…aggressively innarested. I found it more comfortable to just relax alone in the kitchen, but as the evening progressed, they became ratha…rowdy."

Dr. Dick was being very chivalrous. Mama's drinking parties with her lady friends were sprees of burlesque bedlam. Four hardened, bitter broads staggering around the Bejou family living room with a bottle of Johnnie Walker in one hand and an oozing hunk of chocolate-banana-peanut-butter-lard pie in the other. TV blaring a trashy Bolivian telenovela as a panful of something slathered in butter, canola oil, Crisco, and yet more lard blazed into a perilous grease fire on the stove's backburner. Voices raised to the heavens to declaim the evils of the male sex as they shared tales of woe they'd personally suffered at the hands of kinsmen and lovers, complete with clumsy pantomimes and the occasional folk song.

"One of them began to discuss a very unfortunate case of sexual mistreatment she'd read about in the newspapah, and that set them all off—in a manna of speaking, I mean."

Dr. Dick was right to say "set them all off." I could only imagine the shrill cawing, the stomping of deadly spike heels, the lamp-knocking-over sweepings of bony arms that this story must have elicited. I shuddered to envision the crocodile tears, the whipping out of kitchen knives, the battle cries of, "Follow me, sisters! Gonna geld me a man tonight!"

Poor Dr. Dick.

"So then your motha became concerned about the three of you walking home at night without an adult, so she told—*asked* me to escort you back to the…the traila park, if that's what you call it. Although, I woulda presumed she'd worry more about a man she just met conducting her daughtas through a deserted stretch of…what is this, exactly? Fahmland? Oil country?"

"You wouldn't last a dead minute with me," Opal snickered.

"Beg pardon?" Dr. Dick said.

He turned to look at her, couldn't help being fascinated by her monstrous mammaries, then realized he was staring and looked away with an awkward cough.

"So…how was your patty?"

Pearl let out a shaky little sigh. All the steel drained from her clenched body. She gave a great sob, dove headfirst under Dr. Dick's tweedy jacket, and wrapped her arms around his waist. She began to weep piteously.

"Ah. Well. Okay," Dr. Dick said, patting Pearl's back hesitantly. His befuddled kindness only made her wail louder.

Remembering how my little sister threw down so bravely on Perdee Dora, a chuckle of delight escaped my lips—I couldn't help it.

Another chuckle came.

And another.

Then a great, gleeful guffaw.

"Oh, shut up," Opal said.

"You shut up!" I retorted.

"Now girls, please—"

"Håll käften!" Opal snapped.

"You håll käften!" I yelled.

"Girls! Please! I can't imagine what your motha and her…*lady friends*…will do if I bring you home quarreling."

For the sake of Dr. Dick's hide we ceased, but I gave Opal the evil eye the whole way home, and she in turn slung many glares back at me.

The Somwärin Trailer Park and RV Pleasure Garden loomed at the end of the road. The blue haze of bug zappers above every front door and the inferno-red glow from the laundry trailer welcomed us home. Pearl emerged from beneath Dr. Dick's jacket. She sniffled and rubbed the back of her hand over her wet face, smudging her makeup badly.

"Now, Pearl," I began.

"This is all your fault, Ruby!" she hissed. "You made me do it!"

"I didn't!" I said. But I knew it was true.

"You know it's true," said Opal. "You've trained Pearl to admire your reckless ways. Now she's gonna get it from Perdee Dora, Sheriff-Mayor Dolan, and Mama. You're the one who oughta be punished."

"Pearl has free will," I sputtered. "She could've resisted her instincts."

"You got free will yourself, and you can't never resist a single one of your instincts," Opal retorted. "You're a born troublemaker, just like Daddy, and there's no denying it the bigger you get."

"Well!" I growled. "The bigger your titties get, there's no denying you're gonna be a trucker toy out Motel Way!"

"You best take that back," Opal gasped.

"Girls!" Dr. Dick interjected. "Let's keep things civil, shall we? We're almost at your traila…house…traila."

I grabbed a large stick from the ground and brandished it.

Dr. Dick grabbed my wrist.

"Violence isn't the anssa!" he exclaimed.

I twisted out of his grip, raised the stick skyward, and swung it as hard as I could. Dr. Dick cried out in alarm.

Bitch-Girl, having thought herself cunning by lurking in wait beneath the porch of the laundry trailer, yipped and retreated in mid-spring. She hunkered down and gathered herself for another attack. I expertly bashed the stick about her muzzle without taking my eyes off Opal.

"I'll never take it back!" I said. "Never! You ain't nothing but a set of big boobs that gets invited to parties and parking lots and burger-flipping jobs. You're a terrible sister."

Bitch-Girl slinked away, snarling in defeat. We approached the Bejou family trailer.

"You…you…how could you say such a mean, mean thing?" Opal cried, her hand shaking as it turned the front doorknob.

"Because you're selfish and big-boobed and boring!" I bellowed, as I stepped across the threshold.

There came to my ears a queer, laden sort of silence. It was the silence of many people holding their breath. There in the living room sat Mama and her lady friends, their eyes nailing me down, their mouths agape to swallow me whole.

The air was redolent of menthol cigarettes, singed shag carpet, cherry schnapps, Charlie perfume, and caramelized Spam. On the Hi-Fi, Lee Dorsey was singing, "Workin' in the coal mine, goin' down, down, down…workin' in the coal mine—oops! About to slip down…" It was Mama's favorite liquor-me-up song and, she often said after her third shot, a word-perfect depiction of her daily life of toil and ever-souring fortune.

The room was lit by flickering tapers that dripped lush purple wax from the tall, gilt candelabra that Mama liked to trot out when drunk. Contrary to her inebriated belief, the golden candlelight was not kind to her complexion at such times, staining her face sepia like the mugshot of a lunatic from Edwardian-era Hell's Kitchen. Nor did it do her lady friends any favors, canted as they were at weird angles like moldy old scarecrows wrested from their cornfield crucifixes and tossed onto the sofa to ward me off from entering this place of womanly intemperance and disgruntlement. The linen-skinned ladies rustled themselves upright to simulate sobriety, crossed their gaunt arms sternly, and began to shake their heads at me in disgust.

Opal promptly burst into tears and ran past them into the depths of the trailer. Pearl followed suit. From afar, I heard the door to our shared bedroom slam.

Mama rose very slowly and very unsteadily from the fåtölj. She took three swaying steps toward me. She reached out two red talons, snatched up my earlobe, and bent down so she could whisper to me privately.

"WELL NOW!" she blared down my ear canal. "What's all that about? You think you're better than your sister? You think you can call names? Well, I gots a few I could call you, ain't that right, my lady sisters?"

Mama's lady friends nodded.

"Mmm-hmm!"

"You tell her!"

"Don't you go easy on her, Crystal-Lynn. That's how they getcha."

"I ain't raised you to disrespect your sister. You jealous of her popularness? Pop-yoo-lair-titty? If you grew yourself some titties, then you'd be popular too, so don't get all high and haughty. Lord, Lord, tell me how I coulda birthed such a troublesome child? Brother Jesus, why you wanna punish me so? There's nights I dream of nothin' but the sweet embrace of the crypt where there ain't no daughters bothering me with hairspray-wanting and name-calling and—hey, didja get to see the sheriff-mayor after all, Dr. Dick?"

"Oh, uh, well, yes…but…" Dr. Dick, dawdling diffidently in the doorway, looked for his part like he wouldn't mind a bit if Jesus were to swagger in from the kitchen, snap his fingers, and proclaim, "Yo! Time to go, bro."

"He weren't no help at all, was he? Ha! I told you!" Mama crowed, seizing a coffee mug smeared with three shades of pink lipstick while keeping hold of my earlobe. She slung her cleverly concealed adult beverage across the carpet in a wave, overcome with enthusiasm at her ability to accurately predict the failure of an enemy male.

"He ain't no good for nothing but growlin' and prowlin' while we women do all the heavy lifting for those damned Swedes!" she said.

"Need us a woman sheriff-mayor!" said the blonde.

"Ain't that a fact," said the brunette.

"Sheriff-mayor—what the hell good's one'a them, anyway?" said the other blonde.

Mama thought about this for ninety seconds.

"No good!" she declared.

"Uh-huh!" Mama's lady friends chorused, unfolding and re-folding their bony legs and flapping their colorful claws until the loose skin of their scrawny upper arms waggled.

Mama released my ear, tottered herself into a mostly upright posture, and leered at me and Dr. Dick in turn.

"Well, alright," she said. "Tomorrow, this one here'll escort you into town and hunt up Dr. Flo for ya. Then she's gonna buy a gallon of cleaner and scrub this-here trailer top to bottom, inside and out."

"That's right!"

"Crystal-Lynn sure knows how to handle the kids."

"Mmm-hmm!"

"But Mama! Opal was being so—"

"I raise my hand now!"

Mama raised her hand.

I fled, tears flowing.

I paused in the kitchen, found that I could still hear the insults being heaped upon my person, so I dashed out the side door.

I tripped down the back stairs and went sprawling in the dry dirt.

I commenced a loud fit of weeping. I beat the ground with my fists and cursed. I was never the good one, the sweet one, the big-boobed one. Always, always I was the troublemaker. It wasn't fair.

I lay on my stomach and watched the lights go out in our neighbors' trailers. I almost wished Bitch-Girl would take advantage of my sorry state and creep up to finish the fight. It was the only fight I had understood today.

Presently I heard the zealous commotion of Mama's lady friends as they staggered out the front door and stumbled to their vehicles.

"Just like ol' Don Bejou, that middle one."

"Worse the older she gets."

"Born troublemaker, same's her daddy."

I jammed my fingers into my ears until they roared away.

I cried until I grew bored. Then I scrubbed my eyes dry and dragged myself out of the dirt. Inside, the trailer was dark and quiet. I almost sat on Dr. Dick, who was slumped in the fåtölj, dozing fitfully. Mama and my sisters had gone to bed without a care that I might have been kidnapped by marauding truckers.

I went into the bathroom. The face in the mirror was as ugly as my mood: raw and red and dirty and slimy with tears. I began to sniffle again as I scrubbed the makeup and muck off my cheeks. It took half an hour to comb the hairspray out of my hair, leaving a flaky snowdrift in the sink.

I crept into the bedroom we three girls shared. All was still, except for my sisters' soft breathing. They didn't seem to truly be asleep, though. I climbed into the bottom bunk beneath Pearl's and squeezed myself into a ball. There was a hard, peach-pit cramp in my stomach. It took a long time, but slowly, painfully, I fell asleep.

Chapter Three
Dr. Dick vs. Dr. Flo

Saturday, June 15
The crack of dawn

How did I spend my summer vacation? On the very first day, I awoke to a bleak, empty home; a testy and interestingly-spelled note from Mama stuck to the bathroom mirror with a half-chewed wad of hangover-combatting spearmint gum ("Dozzen fools called in sick this a.m. so I gotta work the Saturday shift. You best by the gallen jug of cleaner cause your gonna clean ALL the trailor inside AND out!!?**!"); and the lingering sense that I was a horrible sister to both my older and younger siblings.

It was so quiet. I was so alone.

Sighing, I collected five dollars from the cookie jar. I gave the deserted kitchen a last, forlorn look, then I slipped on my sneakers and opened the side door.

I immediately tripped over our town's temporarily homeless and indigent gynecologist, who was sitting on the top step. I careened face-first into the gravel parking patch: a reasonable way to begin a miserable day.

"Oh Gawd, sorry, Ruby!" he exclaimed, springing to his feet. "You're not injured…are you?"

Was it my imagination, or was this last bit spoken a bit hopefully? Having no patients as yet, I supposed he had to shill his services at every opportunity; though, as far as I could tell, he was useless unless I'd damaged my vee-gee.

He held out a hand that had been inserted into God-only-knew how many female orifices over the years. I shuddered and allowed him to use it to restore me to verticality. As I brushed oily grit from my knees, I gave him a discreet once-over.

A single day spent in the bosom of Somwärin and a single night spent in the Bejou family fåtölj had done him no favors.

He looked as creased, crumpled, and cheap as an old dollar bill.

"I was starting to worry that you'd left without me," he said, rubbing his forehead, which was sweaty, reddened by exposure to our Texan sun, and filled with an unholy knowledge of the female body. "Last night, your motha indicated that Dacta Flo might not make time to meet with me unless I'm introduced by a local."

In addition to cleaning the trailer "inside AND out!!?**!" I had been charged with the care and handling of Dr. Dick on my first day of school-less freedom. On one hand, I ticked off the chores that my punishment for my sisterly misdeeds comprised:

1. Escort our guest into town
2. Acquaint him with Dr. Flo
3. See to it he secured quarters more hospitable than the fåtölj in which to sleep
4. Buy cleaner
5. Find some way to trick Opal and Pearl into cleaning the "trailor" for me

It didn't sound too difficult. I started walking and Dr. Dick followed.

"What's her story, anyway?" he inquired.

"Mama? She's divorced and available, but not at all desperate. She's a woman in the prime of her extended youth and weighs only six pounds more than she did before she got knocked up for the first time, lo these seventeen-and-a-half years ago. That's what she always tells us girls."

Dr. Dick stared at me bewilderedly, blinked thrice, and replied, "I meant Dacta Flo."

Was I really advertising my mama's charms after the unjust invectives and errands she'd plied me with last night? Perhaps I simply didn't want him to think that the head of the Bejou household was the intoxicated Virginia Slims chimney that Mama had transformed herself into under the corrupting influence of her lady friends. A sophisticated doctor from the Right Coast might not grasp the subtle waggishness of a 34-year-old mother of three letting loose to tipple a tad and defame the male sex in a spew of rural Texan patois, all of a Friday night.

"What do you wanna know about Dr. Flo?" I said.

"Well, I don't undastand why everyone keeps saying that she's not going to be pleased to have a specialist in town. As a family physician, her own practice won't be infringed upon. I would assume she'd be glad to have an expert to whom she can refer cases."

Specialist? Expert? Was Dr. Dick talking about himself? I espied a lofty look in his eyes as I guided us out of the trailer park and onto the dirt road to town.

"I don't know about alla that," I said. "Dr. Flo's never needed any other doctor to help her out. She can do everything and anything that falls under the umbrella of the medical sciences. Somwärin's very lucky to have such a dedicated lady doctor—that's what everyone says."

"*Lady* dacta?" Dr. Dick raised his sweat-bedewed eyebrows. "Is it significant to you people that she's a woman?"

I snorted.

"Of course! Women're better healers coz they're more compassionate, and naturally better at tending the sick, hurt, and emotionally unstable."

"Oh, is that so? And just where did you get this idea?"

"Mama, the Lady Principal, Dr. Flo," I shrugged. "Everyone."

"You know, Ruby, a dacta's sex has nothing to do with their ability to—"

"You said sex! Tee-hee!"

"Gendah, then. A dacta isn't a betta or worse practitiona of medicine because of their anatomy."

"I'm sorry, Dr. Dick, but that's plain bull. Don't worry: Dr. Flo will set you straight."

Dr. Dick pressed his lips together to contain some variety of defensive man-doctor retort. He remained mute as the dirt road evolved to gravel; then to asphalt booby-trapped with three-gallon potholes; and finally to lumpy, cracked concrete.

Though Somwärin was a highly abbreviated town, I had no

doubt Dr. Dick would find a way to lose himself in the three blocks from its outer edge to Dr. Flo's clinic at the heart of the municipality. I took him by his tweedy elbow and steered him a course straight and true past the Pubic Library, past the Swedish Embassy & Beauty Parlor & Coffee Shop, past the Celestial Temple of Psychedelic Truth and City Administration, past the forbidding Tree of Contemplation, to the antiseptic front door of Dr. Flo's clinic.

The structure was the newest and most Swedish in Somwärin besides the Fack Sex Furniture Distribution Warehouse. This was on account of it having been assembled from building materials left over from the construction of the Fack Sex Furniture Distribution Warehouse; said materials having been foisted upon the town in the form of a huge pile of debris abandoned in the middle of Main Street by the preternaturally cheery Nordic building crew imported from Stockholm for the task. The clinic was a perfect miniaturization of the Distribution Warehouse, minus the great golden sun of the Fack Sex logo that shone forth on high over all of Somwärin with promises of quality home furnishings at reasonable prices. Boxy and squat, with ultramarine roofing and siding, the clinic tended to blend, camouflaged soldier style, into the summer sky on a clear day. Left to his own devices, Dr. Dick would never have discovered it.

"Now, Dr. Dick," I said, lowering my voice as I reached for the clinic's gleaming, prophylactic doorknob. "It'd be best in more ways than I can explain if you let me do the talking. Dr. Flo really isn't gonna—"

"Be happy to meet me, yes, I've gathad that. Fine: you take the reins, Ruby."

"Keep your eyes downcast and bow your head to indicate your shame at disturbing the medical staff," I said as I turned the knob and gently pushed the door inward.

"What?" Dr. Dick blurted, too loud.

Every head in the clinic waiting room swiveled to the two of us.

"Shh!" I hissed as I stepped over the threshold. "You'll rile the receptionist and we'll be doomed."

Strict protocol ruled Dr. Flo's clinic. Patients were seated on tall kitchen stools in order of arrival along three walls of the waiting room. The fourth wall was dominated by the formidable reception desk: a birch laminate kitchen island with stainless steel facings and a polished granite countertop. Long-established procedure dictated that Dr. Dick and I should take the seats farthest from the desk and scoot ourselves closer, stool by stool, as Dr. Flo worked her way through the patients preceding us.

However, today I broke with customs immutably ingrained in every citizen of Somwärin. The score of sickly and injured townsfolk sensed the significant business I was about as I brazenly strode past them to approach the receptionist who guarded the door leading to Dr. Flo's exam room. The receptionist's face was cocked and loaded with suspicion, tempered by a trigger guard of curiosity. This was an unprecedented occurrence. Unprecedented occurrences were rare in Dr. Flo's clinic. The receptionist had seen it all—except the appearance of a besuited young man sporting an alarmingly sun-pinked face, accompanied by one of the Bejou girls on the first day of summer vacation.

Her eyes swept over Dr. Dick, narrowed slightly, then landed on me.

"Yes, Ruby, what is it?"

"Eh-hem," I announced loudly for all to hear. "This-here that I've got with me is Dr. Dick, a certified hootchie doctor from Out of Town."

Murmuring began on all sides. It abruptly ceased when Dr. Dick (madman!) strode around the kitchen island reception desk, cast his eyes without diffidence upon the receptionist, and thrust his hand presumptuously at her for shaking.

"I'm Dacta *Grant*, actually. I'd like to have a word with Dacta Hershille, if I may."

The receptionist's eyes met his and hardened into globes of granite and steel that perfectly matched the shade and texture of the front desk.

"Dr. Flo is with a patient right now. Take a seat and she will be with you in due course."

"As I'm a colleague, not a patient, I would prefer to wait in Dacta Hershille's office, if I may."

Dr. Dick was radiating defiance. Defiance was not tolerated in Dr. Flo's clinic. The receptionist raised her index finger threateningly. I yanked Dr. Dick away from the front desk and shoved him toward the pair of stools furthermost from the exam room door.

"Yes—yes, ma'am, yes!" I cawed in alarm. "Sit, for the love of your Bwastin God, sit!" I pleaded through a submissive, grit-toothed smile.

Dr. Dick eyed the motley folks ringing the room. Twenty pairs of eager eyes met his. Grudgingly, he sighed and eased himself up onto the tall kitchen stool next to mine.

A breathless hush filled the waiting room as all stared in wonder at the stranger in their midst.

Dr. Dick gave an uneasy half-cough.

Instantly a wave of whispers swept down the line of stools.

"Didn't cover his mouth!"

"Said he's a doctor, but he didn't cover his mouth."

"Maybe he's diseased!"

"You know who's diseased? Them truckers that come to the warehouse."

"Doesn't look like a trucker. Doesn't talk like one, neither."

"He don't talk like anyone I ever heard. He must be a foreigner."

"A foreigner from Out of Town."

"Maybe a foreigner from Afar."

"A Swede!"

"A Swede come in secret to inspect the warehouse."

"Bet they're fixing to fire some of us."

"Fire alla of us and replace us with Swedes that can read those damned shipping labels!"

There were many gasps, then a weighty silence overtook the multitude. Nudges and mouthed words were exchanged, then the patient perched on the stool next to mine turned her head and gave me a friendly, green-gilled grin.

"Hiya, Ruby! What brings you here this morning? Not sick or hurt, I hope?"

"Nope, not me, Miz Jackson. Mama just asked me to be neighborly and help out the new genital-fixer, you know how it is. How 'bout you? You don't look so good."

"Oh, well," she flapped her hand dismissively, then gagged. "It's the lingonberries again."

She glanced at potentially-Swedish Dr. Dick and lowered her voice.

"The meatballs in the cafeteria looked iffy last night, so a bunch of us on the late shift stuck to the pölsa and the lingonberries. They may taste sweet, but I tell you, that's no sign of wholesomeness, Ruby. This is the third time I've been poisoned this month."

She flicked her gaze again at Dr. Dick and reapplied her easy-going-employee smile.

"Anywho! Enough about me. How are you Bejous doing? How's your mama?"

I opened my mouth to put Miz Jackson out of her courteous misery and present her to Dr. Dick, so she could interrogate him on behalf of her fellow Fack Sex employees. However, before I could speak, Dr. Dick prodded my arm.

"Just how long will we have to wait, do you suppose?" he said, none-too-quietly.

"Well, Dr. Flo won't see us until she's treated everyone else. It looks like we're preceded by…"

I began to count heads.

"Next!" barked the receptionist.

A berry-poisoned young man in the chair closest to the receptionist's desk rose and shuffled through the aseptic exam door. Everyone in the waiting room grunted themselves up and scooted over one stool. Dr. Dick watched this, agog.

"Nineteen," I concluded.

"You can't be serious. Nineteen patients?"

I nodded.

Nudged by the elbows of her coworkers, Miz Jackson

swallowed her nausea and reached out a hand to Dr. Dick.

"Hello! Howdy there, I'm Evangeline Jackson. You must be that foreign fellow from Out of Town we've been hearing so much about."

"Dacta Flo is the only dacta in this clinic, correct?" demanded Dr. Dick, ignoring her proffered hand.

"Of course!" I laughed. "There's only one Dr. Flo."

"And she's planning to see all these people herself? Nineteen patients at fifteen, maybe twenty minutes each? That'll take her five or six hours at least!"

"That's quite some accent you got there! You aren't from around here, are you?" Miz Jackson persisted.

"We'll be here all day! Or she'll close up shop before she gets to us."

"Dr. Flo is a dedicated physician. She never ends her day until each and every person in her clinic has been helped 'n' healed. That includes us, even though nothing's wrong with me. Or you…I'm pretty sure."

"So, you're something other than a regular ol' American, am I right?" Miz Jackson said, leaning across my lap in a manner that was vexing, given her visible biliousness.

"This is insane. I'm not going to sit here all day, waiting for her to deign to talk with me! I'm her peer, not her patient."

"Now, Dr. Dick, there's a certain methodology one must follow if one seeks an audience with Dr. Flo," I began.

"No, no, no—nah-uh, no!" he said, his voice rising. "This so-called Dacta Flo didn't send anyone to pick me up at the airport. She didn't provide me with any kinda housing. She told the local veterinarian to set up my office in the broom closet of a pet shop. And now she expects me to wait here all day until she feels like squeezing me into her evah-so-busy schedule? No!"

Dr. Dick rose and shook his suit lapels straight.

"Dr. Dick, calm yourself!" I urged.

"Look, I'll be blunt," said Miz Jackson. "Are you, sir, a Swede?"

"Bwastin is his homeland, ma'am," I said. "Please, Dr.

Dick, sit back down!"

"Bwastin," Miz Jackson gasped. "That's sounds European, yes it does!"

"Y'all hear that? He says he's European."

"Swedes are European!"

"I heard the sheriff-mayor saying he placed some European hooligan under indictment for general criminality just last night."

"Must be him."

"Should we detain him?"

I grabbed Dr. Dick's wrist, but he tugged himself free. He stepped briskly toward the receptionist.

"Excuse me," he said in a loud voice.

"Good God in the morning," I moaned, sinking down low on my stool and covering my face with both hands.

"Pardon me, but this is quite important. I needa speak with Dacta Hershille at once," Dr. Dick proclaimed, bold as brass, to the receptionist.

"Dr. Flo is with a patient right now," said the receptionist in a nonsense-repelling tone. "Take a seat and the doctor will be with you in—"

"Look, how about I just wait for her in her office?" Dr. Dick said, striding across the no-man's-land of kitchen tile that led to a door marked "Private: Staff ONLY."

Shock rippled through the waiting room. Nobody, but nobody, defied the receptionist—even in the direst emergency, even if you were an ignorant foreigner from Bwastin. Her gaze went harder and flatter than I'd ever seen it. Wordlessly, she jabbed a large red button on her desk with a spiny finger.

The troublemaker button.

A shrill alarm sounded, making all of us clap our hands over our ears. No longer desiring to be associated with Dr. Dick, I wriggled my legs up high on my stool and vainly sought a magazine behind which I might hide.

The alarm fell silent as the exam room door slowly swung open.

Into the waiting room stepped Dr. Flo, barely five feet tall, plump as a peach, and sporting a grandmotherly bob of gray curls. She was clad in her customary white doctoring coat, which was so large it made her look like a mischievous tot playing dress-up. Her little hands were dwarfed within a pair of floppy latex gloves. Her blue eyes twinkled as they roved the room and landed on Dr. Dick, lending her a Mrs. Claus aspect.

The moment Dr. Dick beheld those plump pink cheeks and that cupid's bow mouth set in that wee, heart-shaped face of hers, his surly scowl cracked into an amused grin.

Unhappy Dr. Dick!

"Hi there, I'm Dacta Grant," he said, with fatal optimism. "You must be Dacta Hershille. Pleased to meet you finally."

He stuck out his hand for a shake, smiling broader than ever.

"I guess we just missed each otha when I arrived in town yestaday."

Dr. Flo eyed his outstretched hand with the disdain of a farmer sizing up a crow perched smugly on the scarecrow's arm.

"I'm sterile," she replied.

"Beg pardon?" Dr. Dick said, leaning down toward her.

Nineteen gasps were heard in the waiting room.

"Oh, lordy!" I moaned, squeezing my eyes shut.

Dr. Flo's spine stiffened, bristling her height up a centimeter or two.

"I am wearing sterile gloves. I won't shake your hand."

"Oh. Of course, yes, that's undastandable. Well! Shall we head on back to your office to discuss—"

"You," barked Dr. Flo. "Claim to be some sort of gynecologist. Is that right?"

Dr. Dick blinked, taken aback by her use of the qualifier "some sort."

"Yes, I'm an ob-gyn. The federal program that funded my medical school tuition received a petition from this town requesting an ob-gyn, so…um…they sent me," he emitted a nervous chuckle as punctuation.

"Are you aware that I filed an official opposition to that

petition? A petition which was submitted despite my repeated objections?"

Dr. Dick's uneasy smile slipped considerably.

"Could we perhaps discuss this in private?"

When Dr. Flo remained motionless, he awkwardly injected another chuckle into the silence that stretched taut between them.

"Well…it was suggested to me that…I mean to say, a few people indicated that you might not be exactly pleased. But…"

Dr. Flo folded her gloved hands behind her chubby back and began to pace the waiting room with a steady, deliberate tread. The patients seated along the walls tracked her progress like rubberneckers at a car wreck.

"This is a small town, Dr. Grant. A very small town. There is no need for more than one doctor. Somwärin's populace cannot sustain two: That's simple economics. We certainly cannot—and will not—support a full-time gonad technician."

"Now, wait just a minute," Dr. Dick snapped, fatally leaning down for a second time to aim a face now reddened by anger as well as sunburn at Dr. Flo's placid little visage. "I've been hearing that nonsense evah since I arrived. That—that cootchie dacta bullshit—"

"Hootchie doctor," I corrected. I went unheard, however, due to Dr. Dick's reckless use of a naughty word.

"Oooooh!" crooned the assembled patients.

Dr. Flo paused her pacing to paint Dr. Dick from head to toes with an icy glare.

"You will watch your mouth while you're in my clinic, young man. We have no use for the casual Yankee profanity of a Boston Brahman in our town. And we certainly have no use for a narrow-minded specialist who is useless in all medical circumstances not pertaining to the satisfaction of the male erection. Oh yes, that is a gynecologist's sole function—to aid and abet the sexual adventures of men."

"Of…of all the ludicrous, outmoded statements I've evah heard—"

Dr. Flo raised a diminutive finger, which she shook at Dr.

Dick.

"As a general practitioner, I diagnose and treat *all* ailments of the male and female body—including any reproductive complaints which might present themselves. You, on the other hand…" she lifted her rosy upper lip in a withering sneer.

Dr. Dick stared at her, his mouth ajar.

"Yesterday afternoon, a girl from our junior high school felt faint as she began to walk home—diagnosis!"

"What?"

"As she stopped to chat with friends, they noticed that she was breathing with difficulty, her face visibly growing flushed—diagnosis!"

"I fail to see the relevance of—"

"Exactly!" Dr. Flo shook her head with disgust. "That girl was Annie-Belle Cutler, a patient of mine since birth. You, a mere intercourse advocate, would not have recognized the critical symptoms in time. I, however, did."

"Hell, it sounds like—"

"Anaphylactic shock!" Dr. Flo proclaimed in triumph. "While you grasp in vain for a diagnosis like a first-year med student, I immediately assessed the symptomology. Young Annie-Belle had never before presented with an allergic reaction, but I have previously treated her mother and sister for just such a condition. I was able to ascertain that she had been stung by a common honeybee and required undelayed epinephrine and airway support, even though by the time I reached her she was unconscious and could give me no clues as to what ailed her!"

Every one of us in the clinic broke into applause, as was appropriate in the face of such medical bravado. Every one of us, that is, except Dr. Dick. He simply gaped in disbelief at Dr. Flo. She scooted across the waiting room to park her petite toes a mere inch from his. She tipped her little noggin back and peered up into his face sternly.

"When I first came to Somwärin some thirty years ago, I received no coddling or special favors. If anything, I was shunned in favor of the local faith healer simply because I was an outsider…and because I was a woman."

We all murmured disapprovingly at this, as was proper. Back in those benighted times, there had been no civilizing Norwegian employment hereabouts. Just a dusty, hangdog town called Boscoe County populated by draft dodgers dissolutely trying to find oil and growing Mary Jane.

"But the tide has turned! Now everyone comes to my clinic. Everyone! Except those lost souls who subscribed to the Fack Sex HMO and must trek into Big City every time they get sick."

Dr. Flo shook her gray head, then locked a pitiless gaze on Dr. Dick.

"I received no help when I established my practice, so neither will you. You'll have to sink or swim on your own merits in the back room of the Vet 'n' Pet Shop…Dr. *Dick*."

Her lips curled into a tiny, chilling smile.

"Oh, and yes, I do indeed have the key to your apartment, which is located above your office. Your luggage was dropped off there early this morning. But I wouldn't bother to unpack, if I were you."

Dr. Flo jerked a gloved thumb at the receptionist. She rose, goose-stepped over, and held out a shiny brass key to Dr. Dick.

We waited in breathless anticipation to see what he would do. The suspense was thrilling!

Dr. Dick raised his hand. He glared first at Dr. Flo, then at the receptionist, and then took the key. Without a word, he turned sharply and stalked out of the clinic.

Of course I followed him.

Out in the penetrating fury of the sun, Dr. Dick exploded.

"I can't—can't—cannot believe this! What—what—"

And then he said "pocket" in Swedish four times, which puzzled me.

"Fack, fack, fack, FACK!" he shouted.

He scraped a hand through his brown hair, spattering the sidewalk with sweat.

"She's sabotaging me! She'll turn every woman in town

against me. I won't have a single patient. Trouble pockets!" he added in Swedish, which puzzled me yet further. "No möda facken patients!"

"Ya wanna go for an ice cream at the Swedish Embassy & Beauty Parlor & Coffee Shop?" I said. "Always makes me feel better when I'm being persecuted."

"Then—then, she'll report me to the govament for not practicing medicine per my contract, and they'll—they'll…dear Gawd, what if they revoke my grant? What'll I do?"

"It's a head-scratcher, all right. Ya wanna soda instead of ice cream?"

"How will I pay my school loans? What'll I do for a living?"

"The Fack Sex Furniture Distribution Warehouse is always hiring."

"And she'll just smile and put it down to me being incompetent. Never mind that I'm being asked to perform gynecological and obstetric examinations in the back closet of a möda facken PET SHOP!"

Dr. Dick threw back his head and issued forth a brief, rather restrained scream at the sun.

He closed his eyes and lowered his head slowly, breathing hard.

For most folks in Somwärin, this was a remarkably mild reaction to so much abuse. Most folks would be high-stomping it up and down Main Street right about now, calling everyone forth to bear witness to the injustice done to their person. They'd fling the entire contents of their purse or pockets hither and yon. They'd drape every onlooker in a flamboyant tapestry of gutter-talk. And when the sheriff-mayor rolled up with the blues-and-reds going full bore, they'd strenuously resist arrest, beseeching friends and family to avenge them as they were hogtied and stuffed into the back of the flashy Cadillac patrol car.

That's what Mama did just last Sunday when we Bejous were kicked out of the Swedish Embassy & Beauty Parlor & Coffee Shop for disruptive bickering.

"Ya wanna check out your apartment, Dr. Dick?" I suggested.

Dr. Dick opened his eyes, then his fist. He stared down at the brass key, which had embedded itself into the flesh of his palm.

"What's the point?" he intoned dully.

I sighed.

"Well then, I'd best be getting along. Mama said I hadta secure you an introduction and habitation, and I guess I've done that."

Dr. Dick didn't reply.

"You sure you don't wanna stay with us a bit longer? At least until the sheriff-mayor lifts the indictment against you?"

I waited a full two-and-a-half minutes for an answer. When I received none, I sighed again and turned away.

"Well," I said. "See ya around, I guess, Dr. Dick."

I began to walk away, leaving him standing morose and motionless in the middle of Main Street. I kept expecting a cry of, "Ruby, wait!" But nothing came to my ears.

When I reached the end of Main Street, I turned to look back one last time. He was gone.

But somehow, I was sure I hadn't seen the last of Dr. Dick. Not by a *trouble pockets* long shot.

Chapter Four
The Somwärin Soothsayer:
A Not-Yet-Newspaper

Saturday, June 15
One hour before dinner

Much as I hated to admit it, Opal, Mama, and Mama's lady friends had a point: Whenever I got bored, I made trouble.

Just like Daddy.

Once upon a time, Somwärin had itself a daily newspaper, *The Somwärin Sentinel.*

"Can any of you kids tell me what a sentinel is?" I remember the enthusiastic editor asking my class of grubby kindergarteners when we took a field trip to the newspaper office, housed in the sturdy red brick building that has since become the Pubic Library.

"A sentinel is someone who watches," our town's only journalist said, rubbing his ink-stained hands together. "That's what a reporter does. They watch what's happening around them, then tell other people about it. What they tell them is called 'news.' News is printed in the newspaper, which is given to everyone in Somwärin. Isn't that amazing?"

It was not amazing, as I recall. What was amazing was the editor's inexorable descent into madness at the hands of Daddy. And it only took four short summers.

The summer after that memorable field trip, Daddy became bored during the tedious interval between his arrival in town and the stocking of his truck. So he decided to find an activity to occupy his creative mind and busy fingers. Recently divorced from Mama, with only a dumb, good-natured buddy with whom to while away the dull hours, Daddy took a long, hard look into the depths of both his imagination and the storage locker he kept on the outskirts of town. In the darkest corner of the latter, he found a box containing a gross of uncut keys attached to rectangular keychains made of clear plastic with a blank slip of paper inside, which he had failed to deliver to a hardware store six months ago. In an even darker corner of the former, he found the solution to his ennui.

Daddy lugged the box back to his motel room, set it down at the end of the bed, and strolled into town to ponder how he might carry out his plan.

As he ambled up Main Street in the early evening twilight, he came upon the editor of *The Somwärin Sentinel* hefting a sheaf of newspapers into the recycling bin in the alley behind the newspaper office.

"Howdy, friend," said Daddy. "Mind if I get me one of those?"

"It's old news," said the editor with a shrug, as he handed one of the newspapers to Daddy. "Why not?"

Fatal, fatal moment! How the editor would come to rue that thoughtless act!

Daddy took the out-of-date newspaper back to his motel room and sat down to read it. When he came to a throwaway bit of copy in the classified ads section, his eyes lit up with that sizzling light that Mama says often sparks in my eyes.

"Got a news tip for *The Somwärin Sentinel*? Call Enrique Hernandez at 325-555-3545," it read.

Daddy pounded on the motel wall and hollered at his buddy to come into his room—and bring a pair of complimentary motel pens with him. The two of them stayed up all night laboring over their task.

Bright and early the next day, the editor parked his car on Main Street in front of the newspaper office. The Swedish ambassador, whose place of employment was next door, hailed him.

"Mr. Editor," he said. "Here I have your lost keys. Surely you dropped them last night in your haste to cover the meeting of the town council."

The ambassador held out a set of keys attached to a rectangular keychain made of clear plastic with a slip of paper inside. Penned on the paper were the words, "Enrique

Hernandez, 325-555-3545."

The editor took the unfamiliar keys, frowned, and shoved them into his pocket. There were many sets of keys scattered throughout the newspaper office, unlocking such diverse doors as the front door, the back door leading to the recycling bin, the room that contained the printing press, the closet crammed with computer servers, and the lockers filled with photography equipment. The editor forgot about the keys in his pocket until noon, when he went out to get lunch at the Burger Bower.

"That'll be six-fifty," said the scrawny teen manning the cash register. "Here's your burger and fries. Oh, and..." he reached under the counter and scrabbled through the lost and found box. "Somebody turned these in last night. Here ya go."

The kid withdrew a set of keys attached to a keychain and handed them to the editor. The keychain was rectangular, made of clear plastic, with paper inside. The paper had the words "Enrique Hernandez, 325-555-3545" written neatly on it.

The editor took the keys and stared at them in bafflement. Twice in one day? Was he that careless?

A bit shaken, the editor ate his lunch and returned to the newspaper office. As soon as he sat down at his desk, the phone rang.

"*Somwärin Sentinel*," he answered. "How can I help you?"

"Hey, Ricky," said Dr. Barney. "Looks like today's your lucky day. I found your keys right out front of the Vet 'n' Pet Shop here. Bet you're relieved. Want me to swing by and drop 'em off?"

Then Dr. Flo's receptionist called. Then the sheriff-mayor. Then the Gentleman Gym Teacher. Then five employees of the Fack Sex Furniture Distribution Warehouse. All of them had the editor's lost keys.

It didn't stop that day. Nor the next. All summer long, citizens of Somwärin accosted the editor with sets of keys. The editor tried the first few in each and every lock in the newspaper office. None of them fit. He had never seen them before. The handwriting wasn't even his. What was going on, he wondered? What kind of terrible joke was this?

It didn't stop that summer, either. When Daddy at last departed in his truck, bound for stores throughout the contiguous United States, Canada, Alaska, and Mexico, he was armed to the teeth with several hundred sets of keys. Every single day thereafter, *The Somwärin Sentinel*'s telephone jangled off the hook.

"Hi there. I think I might have found some keys that belong to you."

"Is this Enrique Hernandez? Hey, I got your keys, man."

"Oui, êtes-vous Monsieur Ahn-reek Air-nan-day? J'ai des clés marquée avec votre nom."

"Hola? Señor Hernandez?"

"So I was ice fishing, and I hooked a set of keys, and—wait, are you all the way down in Texas? Wow, I'm in Nome! How the heck did your keys get up here? No, don't hang up! Is it sunny where you are? It's dark twenty-four hours a day here. I haven't seen the sun in months. No, don't hang—"

And so it went. The editor began to dread the ringing of the phone. Eventually he took it off the hook altogether, which severely hampered the newspaper's coverage of local news.

A year later, it was June once again, and Daddy was bored. He took a stroll into town one evening to see what sort of amusement might befall him. As it happened, he came upon the editor lugging a pile of the previous day's unsold newspapers to the recycling bin out back of *The Somwärin Sentinel*.

"Howdy, friend," said Daddy. "How about I take those off your hands?"

The editor's eyes narrowed. There was something oddly familiar about this man, this greeting, this situation.

"It's old news," said the editor slowly. He hesitated, then handed the stack of newspapers to Daddy. "Why not?"

Fool!

Daddy took the newspapers back to his motel room and pondered them, his chin in his hands. At that moment, his dumb, good-natured buddy bopped on in.

"Hey Don, lookit what I got!" he exclaimed, dragging a big box crammed with ghastly beige sweatsuits into the room. "Tampa sporting goods store refused to accept delivery, so that means they're all mine!"

Daddy pulled out a hooded sweatshirt and a pair of sweatpants and considered them. He looked at the stack of newspapers sitting mute with terrible potential on the edge of the bed. The sparks of a wicked notion kindled in his eyes.

When the editor arrived at work the next morning, nothing seemed to be amiss. He whistled while he worked, went out for lunch at the Burger Bower, and set his type without incident. Six o'clock rolled around. He yawned, stretched, and stood up. He grabbed a box of unsold papers to dump in the recycling bin before heading home. He opened the door leading to the alley and froze.

A creepy figure sat slumped against the recycling bin. Clad all in off-white, with a hood pulled tight around its face to obscure its features, the not-quite-right personage appeared to be asleep, drunk…or dead.

The editor set the newspapers down. He swallowed, flexed his ink-smeared hands uneasily, and cleared his throat.

"Hello?" he said. "Hey there. Are you alright?"

The individual did not respond.

"Should I get Dr. Flo? Are you sick?"

There was nary a sound nor a movement.

"Can you hear me?"

The editor ventured closer, took a deep breath, and gingerly shook the person's shoulder. He leapt back at the crunchy feeling of the flesh and the crinkly sound that emanated from the sweatshirt.

Frowning, he advanced on the sweatsuited figure. He touched it again. He poked it. He gave it a shove. It fell over, limp as a ragdoll. The editor let out a huff of air. He inspected the flaccid form. It was just a suit of clothes stuffed with old newspapers. A silly prank. Nothing more. He picked up the dummy and tossed it into the dumpster next to the recycling bin. He shook his head at his own skittishness and headed home. He had a hard time falling asleep, but eventually he forgot about the dummy and drifted off.

The next day, the editor nearly jumped out of his skin when he jogged up the steps of the newspaper office and discovered the same beige apparition slumping limply against the front door.

"Dammit!" the editor muttered. He grabbed a leg and roughly dragged the floppy thing back to the alley. He chucked it into the dumpster and went about his business irritably. Nervously. Fearfully, even. This innocent prank gave him the willies for some reason. It made him feel like he felt when the newspaper phone used to ring, before he silenced it forever.

The dummy came back. And it kept coming back. That summer, the editor found it leaned up against his car, seated at a table in the Burger Bower when he went out for lunch, and sagging on a bench at the back of the courtroom when he covered the sheriff-mayor's latest indictments. It was reclining against a cage filled with kittens when he arrived at the Vet 'n' Pet Shop to report on the recent escape of Dr. Barney's prize parrot. It listed against a pallet of Skåp Och Lådor units when he showed up unexpectedly at the Fack Sex Furniture Distribution Warehouse to investigate reports of a parrot infestation. It was discovered lurking in the background of a photo that ran on the front page above the heartwarming story of Dr. Barney's tearful reunion with his wayward parrot.

Upon each maddening discovery, the editor grabbed the bedeviled poppet and flung it into the nearest garbage receptacle. Often with an enraged shriek. Sometimes followed by a fit of uncontrollable shaking. He began to doubt his sanity.

Had Daddy stopped at this point, perhaps things would have gone back to normal and the dreadful fate of the editor could have been avoided. But like me, Daddy can't stop when boredom overtakes him.

The editor resolved that he would destroy the dummy the next time he encountered it. He began to carry a lighter and a canister of gasoline everywhere he went. The citizenry of

Somwärin had no doubts about his sanity.

Two whole weeks went by without the dummy making an appearance. After a solid fortnight's reprieve, the editor began to feel hope. Perhaps it was all over. Perhaps he could breathe again.

Then one night, as he stepped back into his office after dumping yesterday's newspapers in the recycling bin, he caught a glimpse of something beige out of the corner of his eye. He stopped dead in the middle of the darkened newsroom. There, seated in his very own chair at his very own desk, was the dummy.

The editor was overcome with fury.

"Goddammit!" he shouted into the empty newsroom. "Oh, that does it. That really does it!"

He marched over to his desk. He glared at the figure dressed all in beige that sat slumped in his chair. He would finally do what he should have done that first terrible night. He would burn the thing and set himself free.

The editor reached for the dummy. The dummy reached back for him.

"BOO!" it shouted.

The editor screamed, tripped over a wastepaper basket, fell to the floor, and covered his face with his hands as Daddy, disguised by the all-concealing sweatsuit, scampered out of the newspaper office, cackling with mirth.

A year passed. The editor suffered fits of anxiety and episodes of nervous collapse. Summer returned, and so did Daddy, and so did his boredom. He took a stroll into town one evening. He encountered the editor carrying several old newspapers to the recycling bin behind *The Somwärin Sentinel.*

"Howdy, friend," said Daddy. "How about I take a few of those?"

The editor froze. This had happened before. This was more than déjà vu. The man standing before him was a malevolent manifestation of the supernatural.

"It's old news," cried the editor hysterically. He clutched the newspapers to his chest frantically. "Go away! Leave me alone! Go away! GO!"

Daddy shrugged.

"Whatever you say," he replied. "Have a good one, amigo."

The editor watched him as he ambled away. When he had vanished from sight, the editor let out a shaky breath. His shoulders relaxed slightly. He felt as if he had dodged a bullet inscribed with his name by the hand of fate. He glanced at the recycling bin, clasped the newspapers tighter to his chest, and took them home with him. He set them in a stack by the head of his bed and refused to let them out of his sight until dawn.

The next day, the editor, having slept not a wink all night, was too drowsy to notice what Daddy and his buddy had done.

It was exactly a year, in fact, before the editor discovered what Daddy had done. And when he did, his mind broke completely.

Now, some eight summers after Daddy first took it into his head to torment the editor of the now-defunct *Somwärin Sentinel*, I lay sprawled flat on the sofa like roadkill, idly watching TV. My little sister, Pearl, sat on the floor with her back pressed up against the front door, guarding me grimly. Pearl's punishment for fighting with Perdee Dora was to supervise me while I cleaned the trailer. It was a heavy task, I'll own, and I had sorely tried Pearl's patience throughout the day. Finally, around the four o'clock hour I'd given up trying to:

1. Escape
2. Learn to smoke cigarettes
3. Quit smoking
4. Teach Pearl to smoke cigarettes
5. Escape again
6. Convince Pearl that I'm a wizard and can levitate her with my mind
7. Prank call the Swedish ambassador
8. Prank call the King of Sweden

9. Prank call myself

10. Escape yet once more

And I had buckled down to clean. That lasted seventeen minutes. Then I betook myself to the couch and clicked on the TV.

"Why not give up your state of eternal vigilance?" I wheedled, for the twenty-third time. "Join me on the couch. I promise I won't dart out the door."

"Ha," Pearl replied. "I wasn't born yesterday. You best hurry up and scour this trailer, or Mama's gonna be mad at you when she gets home."

"I've got the matter well in hand," I said, gesturing at the scene I had staged.

A large aluminum bucket sat in the middle of the gold shag living room rug. It was filled to the very rim with pungent cleaning fluid. A scrub brush floated languidly in the chemical soup, which perfumed the air with pine forest freshness.

"I can see fumes coming out of the bucket," said Pearl. "I'll bet they're bad for us. I'll bet they're making us high. Mama'll be really mad if you get me high, Ruby. You know how opposed she is to recreational drug use."

"The fumes are good for you. They'll clean out your mind."

"Mama says a clean mind is a fertile field for planting bad ideas."

That sounded biblical, so I dared not argue.

"It's all part of my grand plan," I said. "As soon as I hear Mama's car pull up, I'll fall to my knees in the middle of the floor and begin scrubbing the rug. She'll open the door to a clean-smelling trailer and the sight of me in a penitent pose, and I'll be forgiven."

I was quite pleased with my scheme. By the time Mama made a tour of the trailer to inspect my housework, it would be well after the dinner hour. Sated by a fine repast of Lutefisk Helper, she would be sluggish of mind and mellow of temper, and I could blame the mess that I hadn't cleaned on my sisters. It was a fine plan and I was surprised it hadn't occurred to me sooner, considering the years of trailer-cleaning punishments

I'd endured.

Yes, Mama would forgive me by nightfall. Pearl, for her part, had forgiven me after a mere hour of grouching and grumping. But Opal was another matter. I couldn't be certain she'd let me off easy. Last night's feeling of self-righteousness was gradually being replaced by a sense of self-wrongeousness. I'd had my reasons for saying mean things to my big sister, but maybe they were bad reasons.

"I wonder if Opal will ever forgive me," I said.

"I wonder what Perdee Dora's gonna do to me," Pearl replied.

Suddenly, we heard a little *plap!* as something struck the front door. Pearl's face lit up.

"Is it the paper? Do you think it's the newspaper, Ruby?" she said, jumping to her feet.

She wrenched open the door, letting in a beam of dust-motey sunlight that spilled across my supposedly clean rug.

"It *is* the newspaper!" she exclaimed. "This will shed some light on our fate."

Pearl shut the door and scampered to my side, clutching a diminutive packet in both hands. The arrival of *The Somwärin Soothsayer: A Not-Yet-Newspaper* always incurred excitement when it mysteriously arrived on doorsteps around town. This latest edition was printed on day-glo orange copier paper, the pages folded this way and that until it was the size of a deck of cards. Somwärin's only form of journalism contained no news. Instead, its doll-sized pages were filled with fearsomely accurate predictions of the future written by the paper's staff of deceased astrologers, biblical prophets, and mythic beasts.

Pearl sat down on the floor next to the couch and scanned the tiny six-point font.

"Listen to this!" she exclaimed, waving the eye-scorching neon sheets close to my face. "The Soothsayer says, 'Girl who labors in penitence: June 15 is not your day.'"

"Tell me about it," I grumbled, listlessly shifting so as not to join the loose change in the unfathomable purgatory between the cushions.

"It says your unlucky letters are C and B. I wonder why?"

"You shouldn't read that thing. Mama says it's just hints and nonsense that make you gullible to being sold crystals and milagros and other magical doo-dads."

"Nah-uh! Remember last week? It warned, 'Avoid the drunk, smoky woman, lest your summer commence with tears and woe,' didn't it? Had you heeded the not-yet-newspaper's advice, do you think you'd be in your current predicament?"

True, I had imprudently made Opal cry in front of our drunken, chain-smoking Mama. And thus, I found myself enjoying the worst first day of summer vacation on record.

"Well," I said uneasily. "Maybe."

Pearl suddenly began to bounce with excitement.

"Ruby, listen to this! I can't believe it! For Taurus—that's me and Opal both—it says, 'Your unlucky letters for June 15 are C and B.' Same letters, C and B, for all three of us! Isn't that incredible? What can it mean?"

"Lemme see that," I said, snatching the not-yet-newspaper out of Pearl's hands.

I scanned the patchwork of blotchy images of stoned-looking Virgin Marys, perhaps affected by the fumes in our trailer, and columns of miniscule text.

"Look, here's something about Perdee Dora," I said.

Pearl bent over my shoulder and ran her bubble-gum colored fingernail along the wee prognostication.

"'Queenie-meanie, blond and cruel, who dares reveal what you will do? Not I,'" she read. "Stupid Nostradamus! How'm I supposed to prepare to defend myself if I don't know what she's scheming?"

"Say, Pearl," I said. "What did Perdee Dora call you last night? Sounded like 'silly spaceship,' but that don't make sense at all."

Pearl's brows knit and her eyes darkened.

"Don't wanna talk about it!" she thundered between gritted teeth.

I was taken aback by her rage.

"But," I said. "But—"

"Look here," she interrupted. "Here's one for Dr. Dick. 'Doctor, dacta, new in town, in your future, what is found? Nothing.' What's that mean, d'you suppose?"

I had no answer. Was it a bad omen? Did it mean Dr. Dick had no future in Somwärin? Or did it mean the Soothsayer was unable to predict the unpredictable Dr. Dick's actions? Was our new physician the only person in town whose future was not already written?

"Ruby…" Pearl said. Her trembling finger hovered over Hot 'n' Sexy Leos of a Certain Age, Mama's very own subsection of the zodiac. "Ruby, look!"

"What? What's it say?"

"I can't! I'm too scared!"

"Come on, read it!"

Pearl gulped, and her quivering lips formed the words, "The Virgin of Guadalupe says unto you, sparkling crystal lady, 'Your disbelief shall be stained with an immutable sign; look upon it if ever you doubt the power of the Soothsayer. Trials and tribulations come in threes: Three daughters, three sheets to the wind, three Js. And beware the letters C and B!'"

"Ah!" we shrieked in shrill duet.

"What're you two doing?" barked a voice from the front door.

"Ah!" we shrieked again, clutching each other desperately.

What the editor never noticed all those years ago, and what no one had the heart to tell him, was that while he spent all night vigilantly staring at the stack of newspapers in his bedroom, Daddy and his pal were busy stealing every single copy of *The Somwärin Sentinel* in town. Earlier that evening, while Daddy distracted the panicky editor out back by the recycling bin, his dumb, good-natured buddy had darted out of the shadows and slipped through the open door leading into the newspaper office. There he hid until the coast was clear, then he unlocked the front door and let Daddy in.

The pair ransacked the newspaper office for every copy of *The Somwärin Sentinel*, which they loaded into Daddy's semi truck parked a block away. They even took the proofreading copy that the editor had left on his desk. They drove away through the night, unloaded the towering stacks of newspapers, and locked them up tight in Daddy's storage locker.

The next morning, the adolescent delivery boys found no bales of newspapers awaiting them, and nobody in Somwärin received a copy of the *Sentinel* on their front stoop. When folks beheld the crimson-eyed and twitchy editor upon his arrival at the newspaper office, they tacitly decided to say nothing.

Summer passed with agonizing slowness for the editor. He spent every waking moment waiting for the hammer to fall. Daddy, for his part, went whistling about town, smiling and waving at the editor whenever their paths crossed. And their paths crossed very, very often.

The editor grew paranoid. He refused to leave the newspaper office, which effectively ended the newspaper's coverage of local news. On the day of the Trucker Jamboree, he spied Daddy sauntering slowly past the newspaper office, and at that moment his nerves snapped. He threw open the window and leaned out so far he nearly toppled into the bushes below.

"Just get it over with!" he screamed. "I can't stand it—just do it! DO IT!"

Daddy simply grinned and said, "Howdy, friend!" then continued on his way.

The next day, hungover and weary, the truckers climbed into their trucks and vanished down the highway. The editor should have breathed easy. But he could not relax. He spent the next year in a daze of unease and suspicion. He was jumpy. He was sleepless. He trusted no one. He began consulting horoscopes and tarot cards, astrology charts and tea leaves, trying to predict what Daddy would do next. *The Somwärin Sentinel*—bereft of journalistic reportage since the editor took no phone calls, received no visitors, and no longer went outside—began to reflect his prophetic bent.

One year to the day after Daddy and his buddy stole all the newspapers, they struck again. In the gray hours before dawn, Daddy gathered several dozen snickering truckers, outlined his plan, and threw open the door of his storage unit.

As the yawning delivery boys were stuffing papers into their bicycle baskets and canvas carry-alls, Daddy and his junta crept into town. A stealthy army of grown men stalked the youngsters, scooping up the just-tossed newspapers and replacing them with carefully folded objects concealed beneath their shabby beige uniforms.

When the editor awoke from the nest of blankets beneath his desk and arose that fateful June morning, he sensed something was amiss. What was it?

He could hear a sound, ever so faint, coming from the Main Street. What could it be?

Cautiously, suspiciously, he raised the blinds covering one of the windows that faced the thoroughfare. What he saw devastated him completely.

In the middle of Main Street stood dummies. Dozens of dummies, their beige hoods pulled tight to render them faceless. The editor grasped the window sill, his heart and lungs freezing solid in his chest.

As one, the dummies raised their right hands and jangled sets of keys. Then they raised their left hands and waved copies of the newspaper. The editor screamed and dropped into a fetal position on the cold floor. Who can say how long he remained there, jibbering and jabbering hysterically? Eventually he uncoiled his body and dared to peer out the window again. Sunny, empty Main Street met his gaze. Hesitantly, he stepped outside for the first time in months.

The dummies had been real. He knew this because they had dropped their newspapers in the street. He bent and picked them up, one by one. His mouth fell open as he beheld the dates on each copy. They were last year's papers, published this very day twelve months ago. He began to run up and down

Main Street, snatching papers from the front steps of businesses and homes. Every single newspaper was from last year.

The editor dashed back into the newspaper office, desperate to find a copy of today's paper. On his desk sat the proofing copy he'd worked on last night. Hands trembling, he picked it up. It was last year's proofing copy. He began to shriek.

"Old news! It's old news! It's all…old…news!"

The editor staggered around town for a while. Dr. Flo tried to coax him close to shoot him up with sedatives, and the sheriff-mayor tried to lasso him from his cop car to decompress behind bars, but the editor was having none of it. Eventually he made his way to his abandoned home. He wandered through the stuffy, long-sealed rooms until he reached his bedroom. He fell to his knees by the stack of papers that had remained, gradually yellowing and accumulating a layer of dust, by the head of his bed. He gasped in horror. Instead of the familiar, grungy pile, a neat stack of pristine papers met his eyes. They were the very same year-old papers Daddy and his beige-bedecked brethren had distributed around town.

There was only one thing to do under such circumstances, and that was to drive to Big City, buy every piece of security and surveillance equipment in town, and take up residence in a junky Airstream trailer on the outermost edge of the Somwärin Trailer Park and RV Pleasure Garden with the other delusional kooks.

The erstwhile editor, now known as the Soothsayer, hadn't been seen in the flesh since. According to legend, the lunatic spends his days hunkered down in his tricked-out trailer, monitoring his spy gear and editing contributions from Nostradamus, a groundhog from Pennsylvania, the Virgin of Guadalupe, and three or four lesser demons from the Old Testament.

Daddy, for his part, was placed under *EXTREME!* indictment by the sheriff-mayor, which meant he was forbidden from entering Somwärin for the rest of his natural life; the only exception being the hour or two it took him to drive his semi up to the loading dock of the Fack Sex Furniture Distribution Warehouse to receive his cargo each summer. That meant that my sisters and I hadn't seen him for years.

That Daddy could no longer swing by at random times of the day or night to visit his ex-wife and children was fine by Mama. She'd long since had enough of his shenanigans. But it made me feel queer and lonely sometimes. I couldn't actually remember what Daddy looked like. All my memories of him were from the back: Daddy fleeing from the sheriff-mayor, Daddy dodging a flaming pack of Mexican cigarettes hurled by Mama, Daddy on the run from an angry mob after absconding with all the books in the library. I wished, just once, I could see him face-to-face.

"I said, what're you two doing?" the voice at the front door repeated.

The hungover, smoky woman flung the front door wide open, allowing a gust of fresh air to enter the solvent-addled trailer. Before our heads could clear, she stumbled over the bucket, sending chemical-fouled water cascading across the rug.

Mama scowled at me as she kicked off her sodden lime green high heels and tossed her cigarette-laden purse onto the couch.

"What's this mess here on the rug, Ruby? You better not have spent the day on that sofa watching the TV. You better have cleaned this trailer from top to bottom. I remember telling you to do it last night—I wasn't that far gone, so don't you try to trick me into believing that I just thought it loudly in your general direction."

"No, Mama—I sure did clean every inch, but see, um, then, and—"

"Your word games make my head hurt. Just fetch me the aspirin bottle and a soda and the black pepper and don't chat at me anymore," Mama said, sinking into the fåtölj and waving me away with an acrylic-spiked hand.

By this, I knew I was forgiven.

I scurried into the kitchen as Mama rubbed her forehead with both hands.

"What a day," she moaned. "I'm getting too old to party in the super-cool way of my youth. There was a time I could drink me a bottle of the rankest hooch and eat me a whole chocolate chip ice cream cake, and go forth the next morning with nary a sign of hangover or weight gain. That was my heyday; my twenties. My early twenties," Mama amended.

"Mama, is there any significance to the letters C and B?" Pearl ventured in a small voice.

Mama glared up at me as I, butler-like, proffered her hangover remedies arrayed on a dinnerplate.

"What? CD? What're you trying to get me to buy you now, Pearl? You know I don't get paid till next Friday, and seeing how your grades came out this year, I wouldn't be counting on no rewards if I was you."

"No, Mama—look. The not-yet-newspaper…"

Pearl held out *The Somwärin Soothsayer* in an unsteady hand.

"What's this? Gimme here—don't be waving it to and fro to make me seasick."

Mama whipped her narrowed, kohl-lined eyes back and forth over the text.

She snorted in agreement as her strawberry lips outlined the part about "three daughters."

She paused at "three Js," flicking her gaze ceilingward in brief contemplation.

Then she shrugged and tossed the newspaper aside. It came to rest next to her purse on the shabby sofa.

"That's just nonsense that don't make sense," Mama stated as she took the dinnerplate from my impatient hands and balanced it on her knees.

She cut herself a line of pepper, leaned down, and snorted

deeply. She held her breath, her face reddening alarmingly, and popped four aspirins in her mouth, then guzzled half the soda.

"Ah-cha! Hoo-choo! Help me, Lord Jesus! AHHHHH-CHOO!"

Mama sneezed, belched, and prayed her hangover away for seven solid minutes, in the traditional manner. She then groaned thrice and sank deep into the fåtölj to dig sharp fingernails into her temples and mutter to herself.

"Lordy, lordy, I'm so old. It's y'all girls' doing. Years of motherly heartache and worry brought on by your antics have prematurely aged me, eroding my ability to hold my liquor."

Mama's eyes drifted to the abandoned copy of *The Somwärin Soothsayer: A Not-Yet-Newspaper* and she abruptly stifled her remonstrations. She snatched it up and turned the pages, searching for something.

"Will you look at this. Here's a prediction for the whole town. About your daddy."

Mama's voice grew pinched and sour at the word "daddy."

"Groundhog Phil, Nostradamus, the Virgin of Guadalupe, demon Halphas, demon Morax, demon Jessie Garon Presley, the chupacabra that lives outside Southernmost Sweden, and the Soothsayer HIMSELF caution all of Somwärin: BEWARE the coming of the Great Evil One this summer, as he and his eighteen-wheeler bring naught but darkness and desecration. His tailpipe is the burning tail of SATAN, and the exhaust billowing in his wake is smoke from the fires of HELL,' yeah, yeah, same ol' song."

She skimmed on.

"'We pundits of prognostication predict that this year's Trucker Jamboree shall bring MISFORTUNE and CHAOS on a scale never before seen in Somwärin. Mark our words: This year ALL shall cry out in CONSTERNATION and DISMAY! Flee while you have the chance."

Mama tapped her chin thoughtfully.

"Can't imagine it could be any worse than the summer when the truckers bought moonshine off Farmer Bill, and come to find out he brewed it outta hallucination-making ergot grain. I still haven't gotten the teargas outta my blue pleather skirt. I should've gone ahead and sent it to the fancy cleaner in Big City, then mailed your daddy the bill. Though Lord knows he wouldn't have paid it. Who pays for everything around here? Me! I put the lights on, I put water in the tap, I put food on the table—and where is dinner, anyway? Why haven't you started it, Ruby? Do I have to do everything around here?"

I had a moment of Cinderella-ish indignation, considering I'd slaved away all day pretending to clean. Then I recalled that it was Saturday, which meant dinner was effortless TV dinners.

"That no-good daddy of yours better just keep himself outta trouble this summer," Mama said. "Listen to this: 'And it shall be HE, the PRINCE OF LIES, Mr. Don Reginald Bejou, Esq., who will ringlead the riot. His intentions are FALSE—do not believe his slippery promises and slushy lies.' He better not trouble us like the not-yet-newspaper says he will. I can't afford to lose any more clothes. It's hard to find quality pleather nowadays. I'll never be able to replace that skirt. Never. That was my man-getting skirt. Notice how there ain't been no men for me since the incident?"

"Yes, Mama," Pearl replied too quickly. Mama's glare was audible, even a room away.

"Ain't my fault! I'm saddled with three daughters. Three pieces of evidence that my outwardly girlish figure lies in ruins beneath my clothes. Men don't like that. Nor do they like being reminded that a woman can get knocked up, if fed rum and Coke on the first date. Not that any of you girls came about that way," Mama added.

"Oh Mama, I'm so a-feared now," Pearl moaned. "This summer's gonna be worse than ever before."

"Bosh," Mama either said or belched. "Hysterics and hoo-hah to make you buy things like hairspray and CDs. Don't you girls fall for it."

As I reached into the freezer for our cardboard encased meals, the side door leading to Mama's gravelly parking space banged open.

"Ah!" I cried.

"Ah!" cried Pearl from the living room.

A pair of enormous fun bags wrapped in red spandex floated through the doorway, like twin Hindenburg blimps. Moments later, Opal herself joined them in the kitchen. Home from a day of dates, her cleavage was uneven and doubtless contained sundry lost retainers, toothpicks, wads of Juicy Fruit gum, cigarette butts, and gold fillings.

I forced a smile of reconciliation.

Opal's knockers bobbed past me, then Opal marched past, her head held high. Her rack sailed swiftly into the living room, the rest of her body gliding behind in its wake.

By that, I knew I was not forgiven.

Lucky for me, I had a sister in reserve.

"Can you believe it? *The Somwärin Soothsayer* is filled with significance for us Bejous today! I'm all creepy-feeling up my arms," Pearl said, darting into the kitchen, glancing around nervously, and shuddering.

"Opal's still mad at me."

Pearl shrugged.

"You two bicker all the time."

"But she cried last night. I didn't mean to make her cry."

"Well, then you shouldn't have said mean things."

Pearl was always full of helpful advice.

"That's the problem with you CD-wanting girls nowadays," Mama breezed in, a fresh cigarette bouncing between her lips as she spoke. She flicked a dead lighter over the tip repeatedly and added, "Y'all ain't mastered the ancient arts of our foremothers."

She gave up on the lighter, snapped on the gas burner of the stove and stuck her head into the blue flame, whisking her blond hair out of the way at the last possible moment.

"What y'all need to do is learn to cook and keep house. Then I can get down to the serious business of earning a living, unencumbered by domestic concerns. Learn to fix things around the home," she commanded, tossing the broken lighter at Opal as she passed by the doorway. It hit my sister in the largest target on her body and settled somewhere within her hammock-sized bra. Opal rolled her eyes and thrust her arm down her shirt up to the elbow. She fumbled the lighter out, leaned against the doorjamb, and began to tinker with it.

"If only I'd had me three strapping sons. Alla y'all would've been farmed out to work by now, earning solid, boyish incomes to chip away at the awesome cost of your collective upkeep. Three landscape-business-running boys I could've had me, if your daddy's sperm would've cooperated. Instead, y'all bankrupt me daily with demands for hairspray and CDs," Mama puffed her way out of the kitchen, shaking her peroxided head.

"It's not CD, it's C and B, Mama! It's prophesy. *The Somwärin Soothsayer* is never wrong," Pearl dogged Mama out of the kitchen, followed by Opal. I, the kitchen slave, could go no farther than the doorway.

"It's a bunch of hogwash and frippery," Mama said, as she settled onto the sofa and reached for the remote.

Opal jounced her traffic stoppers over to Mama and planted a hand on her disproportionately tiny hip.

"Pearl's right, Mama. Many's the time you've consulted the not-yet-newspaper for guidance in your dark hour of uncertainty."

"Y'all girls are getting witchy and pagan," said Mama. "Y'all need Jesus."

"Everyone knows *The Somwärin Soothsayer: A Not-Yet-Newspaper* is not a substitute for religious practice. It tells of things to come and leaves it up to the reader to utilize their God-given free will to pursue their goals and live their lives," Opal retorted, flicking the repaired lighter on, then tossing it to Mama with a flourish.

Ordinarily, I would have been impressed with my big sister's oratorical skills. However, she had simply read aloud from the disclaimer on the back page of *The Somwärin Soothsayer*. I was torn. Was Mama right, or was the not-yet-newspaper? Was my future already written, or was it in my own hands?

We four settled in for our customary Saturday night meal of

TV dinners eaten in the living room whilst *The Wild World of Wrasslin'* was broadcast live from Big City to our TV. Pearl forgot the omens in *The Somwärin Soothsayer* and her anger at Perdee Dora. Mama forgot her hangover and her perpetual irritation with Daddy. Whoops and cheers issued from their mouths at every piledriver, half-nelson, and paramedic intervention. It should have been a perfectly pleasant evening spent in the warm embrace of my family, but Opal's silence chilled me. I dared not look at her for shame.

"Now, that was some quality sportsmanship," Mama said, as the credits rolled. She ground out her cigarette butt in her empty TV dinner tray and clicked on the lamp. "Wonder what movie's coming on next? I could go for something spooky tonight."

Suddenly, a loud banging came from the side door in the kitchen.

We four screamed.

"It's the C and the B come to kill us all!" Pearl shrieked, as she dove behind the sofa.

The banging sounded again.

"Someone's at the door. Go open it, Ruby," Mama said in a voice that wasn't quite steady.

"No way!"

"Maybe it's Dr. Dick," said Pearl.

Nobody made a move to open the door.

"Opal, maybe it's one of your many admirers come a-courting," said Mama.

Opal's low wattage eyes brightened.

"Be right there, hon!" she called, giggling and jiggling her way into the kitchen.

We waited, listening hard, each of us holding tight to each other's hands.

"Oh my God!" we heard Opal exclaim. "3-J!"

"*The Somwärin Soothsayer* was right! My baby girl's being sucked away into the Supernatural Somewhere!" Mama cried, springing to her feet.

Mama, Pearl, and I dashed into the kitchen, and what to

our wondering eyes should appear?

Why, it was Daddy's dumb, good-natured buddy, he of the many pranks, known to his fellow truckers as 3-J. This nom de route was on account of how his real name was the tongue-twisting John Jesse James Whitehead, and calling him J.J.J. tended to make one sound drunk, drugged, or dopey.

3-J, back-shadowed by the gathering twilight, grinned at us from the back steps. It had been years since any of us had lain eyes on him. He was just as unshaven and unwashed as I remembered. He ducked his baseball-capped head at Mama respectfully.

"Evening, Crystal-Lynn. Hope I didn't startle y'all none."

"What in the nine circles of hell are you doing here, 3-J? Well, come on in."

Mama herded him into the living room hospitably, but with a cautious glint in her eyes.

3-J settled himself into the much-favored fåtölj and heaved a great sigh.

"Sure is good to sit on a quality piece of furniture. Soothing to the butt-bones after so many days and nights and afternoons in the driver's seat."

"Well, it's Swedish," Mama replied. "So, what brings you by outta the blue?"

"Well," he drawled. He crossed one leg over the other and gazed at each of us in turn. "I'm here at the request of your husband, Crystal-Lynn."

"Ex-husband. Ex," Mama corrected.

"Don sends you…" 3-J dug into the front pocket of his worn blue jeans and withdrew half a paper napkin defaced with a scrawl of blue ink and several maroon blobs of barbecue sauce. "He sends you his tender greetings on this, the eve of his return to his family," he read haltingly.

"What?" Mama sat bolt upright on the sofa next to me, her face all a-shock. "What do you mean, the eve of his return? Don's under *EXTREME!* indictment. And even if he weren't, there ain't no family as far as he's concerned. That man's on his own, now 'n' forever."

3-J shook his head.

"Don has a plan for y'all. He received a message from The Great Beyond."

"Plan? What plan?" Mama bleated. "What message?"

"Listen," said 3-J, reaching out to switch off the lamp and cast the living room into eerie shadows. "I'll tell y'all the tale."

Pearl and I clutched each other tight, because we could tell it was going to be a ghost story. Even Opal eased herself closer to me.

"It was late one night in the cold, dead heart of the desert. Me and Don was doing a straight run through the Southwest with several other rigs in convoy. Yet in that bleak, blackest night, it seemed like each of us was driving alone through the very fathoms of our souls."

"Huh? What the hell are you talking about?" Mama blared in a mood-killing voice.

"Shhh!" we girls hissed, watching 3-J with great intensity.

"I was driving fifteen miles over the speed limit, as is my habit, listening—as is also my habit—to the familiar voices of my fellow truckers on the CB radio."

"Oh! Didja hear? CB radio! CB! Ruby—C and B!" Pearl bleated, hiding her face against my shoulder.

"Suddenly, all the channels began to go quiet. First one, then another and another and another, till I could hear nothin' at all."

We girls gave a communal shudder, rocking the sofa on its uneven legs and drawing an exasperated glare from Mama.

"Then, it happened! The CB crackled back to life…only I didn't recognize the voice that spoke. 'John,' it said, and I shuddered, for it seemed to mean me. 'John, listen to me and listen good. I got something to tell you, and it ain't pretty.'"

"Is there some point here?" Mama grumbled, as she inspected one of her very long, very false nails.

"I got the heebie-jeebies," 3-J continued, unruffled by Mama's impatience. "Coz that voice wasn't distorted in the least—not like usual over my CB radio. No sir, it was just as clear as if the fella was sitting right there beside me in the passenger seat of my truck."

"Oooh!" we girls squealed.

"'John,' the voice said. 'I was once just like you. A shiftless trucker roving the wild highways with nary a care for where the road might lead me…and nary a care for the family I'd left behind.' That voice had a fear-makin' tone of doom. I kept on driving, but my eyes were glued not to the road, but to the CB."

"Beware the CB," whispered Pearl.

"The voice continued, 'It was on a night just like this one, in a dull month of winter just like this one, when last I drove down the very road you're driving on right now: Route 40. And I was pulling the very load you're pulling: perishable goods.'"

3-J paused.

"Now, lemme tell y'all, I just about screamed, coz it sure was night, it sure was winter, I sure was driving on Route 40, and I sure as a great goddamn was pulling perishable goods! How could he know? How, I ask, could he possibly know?"

"He was probably part of your convoy," Mama replied dryly.

"Hush, Mama!" Opal said, since even she was aware that it had been a rhetorical question.

"The voice gave a low moan and said, 'John, on that terrible night, the night wind was like the breath of death, and I heard the banshee call three times, but I ignored it. I ignored everything but the road. Fool, fool that I was!' And the CB went silent. I thought the fella had signed off. I shook my head a bit to clear it and kept on driving."

"That sure was some story, 3-J. You want a beer? We're about to take in the Saturday night movie."

"All at once," 3-J resumed, ignoring Mama. "The voice let out a wail. 'Listen to me, John! When you ain't there to protect your family in the traditional masculine fashion, what woe can befall y'all! When I finished my run that deadly winter so long ago, I wandered home carelessly and slowly. Do you know what I found when at last I returned to the bosom of my family? Do you?'"

3-J swept his gaze over each of us.

"What? What did the voice find?" Opal asked in a low, fearful voice.

"'John,' the voice said. 'When I set foot in that home of mine, no one was there. Them offsprings of mine, that wife— all were nowhere to be found. I went to the fridge for a beer to ease the sting of a lonely homecoming, when I noticed a strange smell. I followed it like a bloodhound, all the way to the basement. I flicked on the light, and—OH SWEET JESUS!'" 3-J shrieked.

"Damnation!" Mama exclaimed, jumping. "Dial it down, we ain't deaf."

"What? What was it?" we girls cried.

"'There they lay, all four of them! All four sprawled at the foot of the stairs below. All four dead, dead, DEAD!'" 3-J declaimed, his head tipped back to the ceiling, his eyes closed. "'I went mad with shock and grief for a spell. When I returned to my senses, I realized what had happened. My wife had been doing a load of laundry in our washer. Having no dryer, she'd piled the wet, weighty clothes into a basket to lug up to the clothesline. But the load was too heavy for a mere woman. On the top step, she'd lost her balance and fell to her death on the stony basement floor below. Hearing her mother fall, my oldest girl had rushed to her aid. In her haste, she slipped on a wet sock and plunged to an equal death beside the woman who'd given her life. Then, unsupervised, the toddler had toppled down the stairs and met her end. I don't know how my middle girl fell, since she always had herself a good sense of balance. In any event, my family was dead, all to a one, because of my absence. Because there had been no protector male to lift loads and rescue the fallen and supervise the unsupervised. Now…I rove the road alone. I sure hope you heard this, John, and you understand what you must do.' And with that, the CB went silent for good."

3-J sat back and fetched a deep sigh, his face alight with anguish. Pearl and I were near tears, while Opal sniffled and shook her head sympathetically.

"That is so much horseshit!" Mama exclaimed. "What kinda fool do you think I am? Don's coming back here because you heard some stupid story on the radio? Hell, Don knows we do our laundry in the laundry trailer, and that's on the ground floor—not that he ever lifted a finger to—"

"But there's more, Crystal-Lynn! So much more. I radioed your husband as soon as—"

"Ex! Ex-husband," Mama snapped.

"I radioed Don, but before I could say a word, do you know what he said? 'Great God, 3-J! I heard a wise and terrible voice on the CB just now, speaking directly to me! Told me the road I'm on, called me Don, and knew I'm hauling parachute hoods!'"

We girls gasped and shuddered with uncanny chills. Mama made a disparaging hacking sound in the back of her throat.

"So he heard wrong. Don always was one to hear just what he wants and nothing more."

"But Crystal-Lynn, listen to this: Don and I got Big Bobby Watson on the CB and asked him if he'd heard the voice. Know what he said? He'd heard it all right, but it said the name 'Shawn,' his own middle name, which his daddy called him in years gone by! And not only that—it knew he was hauling parish hall roods! That's what Methodists call crucifixes. So then we called up El Señor Poco Loco, and he said he'd heard the CB call him 'Juan,' which is his Christian name sure enough. And while he didn't recall the voice mentioning his load, his CB *hadn't been on*, yet the voice came through loud and clear!"

"Oh God! Like the *Twilight Zone* show!" Opal cried.

"Then we got Rockin' Ron on the horn, but he hadn't heard nothin' on account of him being in the midst of a caffeine pill binge at the time, rendering him incapable of sending or receiving coherent communication. The point is, we each heard the CB call us by our right name! Sending us a message! From The Great Beyond!"

We girls screamed and fell back in fear-swoons on the

couch. 3-J switched on the lamp, his tale concluded.

"So, to summarize, Don's coming home to organize some masculine protection and influence for y'all."

"The hell he is! When I kicked that man out ten years ago, I had enough reasons for a hundred divorces. I ain't taking him back."

"Don has thought of that, and requires no marital comforts from you. He will sleep in his truck, so he can listen to the CB for messages from The Great Beyond. In the evenings, he will carve the meat at the family meals in the traditional patriarchal way, dispense wise advice, and take his pleasures out Motel Way with dainty ladies of easy virtue."

"And what about the *EXTREME!* indictment? The minute Don hits town, the sheriff-mayor's gonna slap him in jail," Mama said with satisfaction.

A sly smile curved 3-J's chapped lips up and up and up until they formed an uppercase U.

"Don's got a clever plan to deal with that," he said. "A devilish clever plan the likes of which even the most bold and foolhardy trucker would never dare imagine."

"What about money? Does he plan to work at all?"

"Providing masculine protection and influence for a family is a full-time job. You will serve as the wage-earner, and he will serve as the figurehead. Like the King of Sweden."

"In other words, he wants to loaf around my home all day, eating up my food, corrupting our daughters, and bossing everyone around, just like he did when we were married?"

3-J shook his head with pity.

"Don warned me that you would resist enlightenment. One day soon, you will see the light, Crystal-Lynn."

"How come Daddy didn't just tell us this himself?" I ventured.

"He's up doing the Canada run at the present moment. But I wasn't busy, so he sent me to serve as stopgap in the protector and influencer role."

"You?" Mama exclaimed. "You think I'm gonna let you hang around here, after what you just told me? It was all probably just a trucker joke or something."

"It weren't no joke," 3-J replied. "It was a message from The Great Beyond, and it must be obeyed."

Mama jumped to her feet and began to stalk the living room like a caged lioness.

"Dammit, I ain't taking Don back, you hear?"

"Nevertheless, he's a-coming."

3-J was implacable and irritatingly placid. Mama was speechless, her cheeks puffing and puffing until they looked as if they would pop.

"I'm gonna—I'm gonna—girls, y'all go to bed! I can't deal with you three right now."

We rose and tiptoed into the kitchen to eavesdrop. Unfortunately for us, 3-J decided it was time for him to guard our sleep from the subtle blind of his truck cab. Mama pursued him outside and out of our hearing.

When we returned to the living room, I happened to look down at the rug. A vast stain had settled into the shag where the cleaning bucket had spilled. The toxic concoction had bleached a wide section of the carpet, transforming it from bold gold to a sickly mushroom hue.

"Lookit!" I gasped, bounding backward in shock.

Blurry but unmistakable, a hooded figure in a beige sweatsuit leered up at us from the middle of our living room rug.

"Oh my," Pearl breathed. "'Your disbelief shall be stained with an immutable sign!'"

"*The Somwärin Soothsayer* was right," I marveled.

"It always is," Opal replied.

Then she realized she had spoken to me even though she was no longer speaking to me. She huffed away to our room and slammed the door.

By this, I knew I was still not forgiven.

Chapter Five
The Sissy Spacek Movie Marathon

Sunday, June 16

10:30 a.m.
Badlands (1973)
A teenager from Texas (Sissy Spacek) is corrupted by an older man with a penchant for criminal acts and cross-country driving.

Every summer, the local TV station out of Big City, Texas, aired the Sissy Spacek Movie Marathon for the entertainment and edification of rural children like myself. Three months of *Coal Miner's Daughter*, *Badlands*, *Crimes of the Heart*, and *JFK* made for an instructive and relevant alternative to summer school. Instead of being overtaken with idleness, we learned how to accept the oppression of poverty, how to run away from home with a hooligan boyfriend, how to shoot a cheating husband, and how to assassinate a standing president. All useful skills for a girl of my social standing.

I arranged myself on the couch bright and early on the first day of the marathon, just like every summer. I positioned a box of Lucky Charms on the coffee table, placed a carton of milk beside it, and clicked on the TV. *Badlands* was the first film of the summer, which was not a movie to be tardy for.

"My mother died of pneumonia when I was just a kid," Sissy Spacek began. "My father had—"

At this precise moment, a scruffy, unwashed man wandered into the living room.

"Morn," he yawned, his jaws gaping. He scratched at the crotch of his much-worn blue jeans, then beneath his crusty baseball cap.

I froze. For a heartbeat, I had no notion who this stranger in my living room might be. Then I recalled the high drama of the previous evening.

3-J's eyes swept the living room, then the coffee table, then my breakfast.

"Hey, Gaelic good fortune grub," he crowed. "Gimme here."

He loped over to the couch, plopped himself down next to me, propped his road-grimed cowboy boots on the coffee table, and grabbed the box of Lucky Charms. He poured the entire carton of milk directly into the box, then began to grope at the front of his jeans, fumbling first to the left and then to the right of the zipper.

"There's my tool."

He withdrew an elaborate Swiss Army knife from his right pocket. I was torn between relief—thank God that's what the bulge thereabouts had been!—and alarm at seeing Daddy's none-too-sharp pal wield a weapon.

3-J extended a spork utensil, thrust it deep into the box, and began to shovel cereal into his maw.

"Nothing like home cooking!" he crunched, grinning appreciatively at me and the demented leprechaun on the box in turn. "What-all's on? Is that Sissy Spacek? Is this *Natural Born Killers*? Turn 'er up, I love Rodney Dangerfield! And how's about you run and fetch me some coffee while you're at it?"

For an unwelcome guest, 3-J seemed to be making himself right at home.

"Are you still here? I thought Mama kicked you outta her home," I retorted.

"Naw, naw, she said I couldn't stay in the house, so I slept in my truck. I take my role as y'all's temporary guardian very seriously. Your mama will come around in time. So," 3-J mumbled, spraying his boots with a rainbow of marshmallows bits. "What-all are we doing today?"

"Are you still here?" came a wrathful voice from the hallway leading to the bedrooms.

Mama entered, her eyes fiery with sleeplessness. She beheld 3-J seated on her couch, devouring her hard-earned vitals, his truckerly feet uglying up her furniture. With five decisive stabs of her stiletto heels, she was upon him.

"Well, hi there, Crystal-Lynn. How's about some coffee?"

Mama snatched the Lucky Charms box out of his hands and shook it menacingly beneath his nose.

"You lookie here, 3-J. Don ain't moving back here now or ever, and that's that. You best long-haul your ass outta my home right now and don't come around here no more. You hear?"

"Oh, well, I can't do that," 3-J drawled sheepishly. "I wouldn't be much of a friend to Don if I abandoned his family. Womenfolk need a male protector in the house at all times. Don is firm on that point."

"Male protector! I know what Don means by that. He wants to lie around the house all day 'protecting' it while I support us financially. What if I lost my job? Is he gonna up and drive away to parts unknown, like when we were married? Hell, if that's all it takes to get rid of him, I'll give notice at the warehouse this very minute, I swear I will."

3-J shook his head.

"You don't understand The Great Beyond, Crystal-Lynn. Don has realized that his sacred marriage vows are binding, now and forever. Don is your temporal and spiritual husband on earth, in the heavenly hereafter, and beyond into the Beyond."

3-J tipped his disheveled head back to gaze at the ceiling, where he seemed to see a vision of Mama and Daddy, all decked out in celestial nightgowns and feathery wings and amicable smiles. I looked up, too. I tried, I really tried, but I just couldn't see it myself.

"Don't you feed me that foolishness!" Mama snapped. "I know Don—he's always got something up his sleeve. Well, this time I won't be bamboozled by his flowery words and fancy notions. This is all just a ruse so's I'll let him hide out here while the Feds hunt his lawless ass, isn't it? I watch *America's Most Wanted* show every week, and I ain't seen Don on it yet, but three weeks ago I remarked to my girls that a fat Alabama woman bore quite a passable resemblance to their father. Is Don hiding out in drag for trafficking Mexicans over the border encased in life-sized Scooby-Doo piñatas? You can tell me, 3-J."

Mama softened her eyes and nodded encouragingly in the tricky manner she used to interrogate us girls about our misdeeds.

"The only thing Don is trafficking right now is a load of canned sweet corn up to Saskatchewan. He told me he just passed through Oklahoma this morning, and is speeding due north just as fast as he can so's he can return to the women who need him."

Mama threw the Lucky Charms box clear across the room and shouted, "Oh, for the love of Jesus H. Chr—wait. You're in contact with him?"

3-J nodded solemnly.

"Via the CB radio. Don is diligent about heeding his CB, what with the mystical messages it sends."

"In that case, you go right out to your truck and send this mystical message to that crazy ex-husband of mine: We don't need him. I'm a fine protector of our girls, so he can just keep trucking his sweet corn, all by his lonesome, till the day he dies."

"Nah…nah, I don't think that's right," said 3-J. "A woman can't be the protector of a family. It's unnatural."

Mama sighed loud and long and hard. She rolled her head around a full circuit on her slim neck, her vertebrae popping like BB gunshots, in preparation for an extended rant.

Suddenly, she froze. Her head circled back to neutral. Her face was alight with cunning.

"We need us a *male* protector, is that right? Well now, this home already has itself a male protector. Yes, sir, it sure does. My boyfriend, who is a man—a big, burly man—he protects the hell outta us. He could throw Don clean out the door and down the road with one hand, oh yes, he could."

I stared at Mama in shock, but I dared not make a sound.

3-J reached under his baseball cap and scratched his hair contemplatively.

"Well…that may or may not be true, Crystal-Lynn. The thing I'm wondering is, how come I ain't seen a man hereabouts? And no signs of male habitation neither?"

Our bra-ridden shower rod and always-down toilet seat must have tipped him off.

"He's out of town. On a trip," she said. "A business trip. For his business, where he works as a businessman. But he'll be back any day. Isn't that right, Ruby?"

Mama rounded on me, her eyes sending telepathic messages that I couldn't decipher. I gave an indeterminate squeak. Apparently, that was sufficient for 3-J.

"Well, if you say so, I guess it must be true. I don't know what Don's gonna think about it, though."

Mama's voice became low and her eyes grew intense as she leaned close to 3-J.

"Don's gonna think," she intoned. "That he'd best high-step it outta our lives for good. My boyfriend's powerful jealous—I hate to think what he'd do to Don if he came within smelling distance of this-here trailer."

"Hmm," said 3-J. "I gotta mull this over a spell. Got any beer?"

"Not for your ass at crack of dawn o'clock; no, I do not."

3-J rose, hitched at his jeans, and shambled out of the trailer.

"This is a brainteaser for sure. I wish Don was here…he'd know what to do…"

The instant the front door banged shut behind him, Mama deflated with a loud hiss.

"Oh, dear Lord! What a mess!" she wailed, covering her face with her hands.

"Mama, why did you tell him such a lie? He's gonna find out the truth—everyone in town knows you ain't got a boyfriend!" I exclaimed tactlessly.

Mama moaned and shook her head in dismay.

"I know that, but what else could I say? You heard him: Your daddy's not gonna leave us in peace unless I got me a man, but I ain't got a man, and now I'm trapped in my web of lies! I ain't had me a boyfriend, not even a casual one-nighter, since—never you mind! The point is, there ain't no man I can call on to help me in my time of need. Oh Christ Almighty!" Mama tore at her high-sprayed blond hair and attempted to rend her low-cut pink spandex top in grief. "Show me the strength, Jesus! Show me the strength!"

She repaired to the kitchen. I was torn. The TV beckoned. With a sigh, I followed Mama.

She sat slumped at the table, her tousled blond head in her hands.

"Maybe everything will be okay after all," I said, sitting down across from her. "Maybe 3-J will take you at your word and tell Daddy not to come home. Or maybe Daddy'll get distracted by a new scheme, as is his way, and we'll hear no more of this notion of his."

"Well," she said. "Maybe—"

The front door banged open. Mama jumped to her feet and dashed out of the kitchen. A brief murmuring came to my ears, then Mama's mighty shout echoed through the trailer park and all the way into town.

"WHAT THE HELL DO YOU MEAN, HE'S STILL COMING?!"

I hopped up and ran into the living room, where I found Mama had backed 3-J up against the TV. He leaned against the screen, watching with a look of mild bemusement on his face as Mama swung her arms in gestures of futile rage.

"Like I said, I radioed Don and relayed your message. Now he's coming for sure."

3-J shoved his hands into his too-tight jeans pockets and gazed hazily into the distance.

"Don was mighty distressed to hear of your faithlessness to the holy marriage vows y'all took nigh on eighteen years ago. He said—"

"Faithless? Faithless! Who ran around porkin' every stripper in the county, while my own self was occupied with three babies and two jobs?"

"Nevertheless, Don has formulated a new plan on the fly. He will return and check out this new fella of yours. If he meets with Don's approval as protector of the Bejou women, he will permit your adultery and leave y'all in peace. But if Don finds your man lacking, he's gonna kick his ass three ways to Sunday and re-install himself as the Bejou family patriarch."

Mama staggered backward and grasped my arm for support.

"Why didn't he accept my word? I said we don't need him here."

"Don has certain responsibilities—"

"Bullshit out a cannon! Don's got the responsibility of a chickenhawk in a hen coop! I—I—oooh, lordy! Get out! Go on, get out! GET OUT!"

3-J shrugged and removed himself from the trailer. Mama gave a hop of wrath, then sagged to her knees in the dead center of the carpet stain shaped like Daddy's dummy disguise.

She was awfully still for a long time.

"Mama?" I said hesitantly. "Mama…"

She shook her head weakly. She was the very picture of woe.

"What about…" I began, searching for something that would wipe away her hopelessness. "What about…"

A fabulous notion bloomed in my mind.

"What about Dr. Dick?"

"What about him?" she mumbled.

"Think, Mama," I said. "3-J doesn't know him, Daddy doesn't know him, nobody in town knows him. Tell 3-J that Dr. Dick is your boyfriend!"

Mama snorted and started to laugh.

I knelt beside her on the rug and grabbed her hand. She looked up at me with dull eyes.

"He's perfect, Mama. He's new in town, so nobody knows anything about him. The only fact everyone agrees upon, besides his status as a hootchie doctor, is he's spent the night here—slept with you, technically speaking. There's not a person in town who'll deny he's intimately acquainted with this household and its inhabitants, should Daddy go inquiring."

"True that," said Mama slowly. "But what about Dr. Dick himself? Your Daddy's sure to ask him if he's…*known* me in the biblical sense, like a proper boyfriend."

I thought a moment.

"What if you got yourself one of his hootchie exams? Then, between him staying in your home overnight and sexaminating you in the back closet of Dr. Barney's shop, he'll practically be your common law husband. There's no way this plan can fail!"

Mama stared at me. Her eyes and mouth were wide.

"You," she said, with measured deliberation. "Are a genius, child, and that's a fact!"

She rose unsteadily and I followed suit. She gripped me by the shoulders.

"This is a glorious plan," she said, a smile dawning on her formerly bleak face. "It's a plan worthy of your no-good daddy himself!"

I smiled back. I turned to sit down on the couch and watch Sissy Spacek and Martin Sheen hit the open road as outlaws, my work done. Mama grabbed the remote and clicked the TV off.

"Not so fast," she said. "We've got work to do."

12:30 p.m.
Coal Miner's Daughter (1980)
A teenager (Sissy Spacek) dreams of escaping her life of household drudgery and poverty.

That sticky afternoon, we three daughters (a.k.a. servants) of Crystal-Lynn Bejou found ourselves, as was our wont every Sunday, hard at work within the laundry trailer of the Somwärin Trailer Park and RV Pleasure Garden.

Pearl stood folding freshly laundered clothes on the three-legged card table in the middle of the trailer, while I hunched over the utility sink and scrubbed a week's worth of the Bejou household's delicate hand-launderables. Grumpily, I cast frequent glares at my sister—not Pearl, but Opal. As I sieved soapy water through the ten-gallon cups of her soiled bras, she sat atop the washing machine, feigning work. Supposedly, she was holding down the unstable old washer with her considerable ballast. As her jumbo jugs jiggled and jounced with each rotation of the washer drum, she squinted at the orange sheets of *The Somwärin Soothsayer: A Not-Yet-Newspaper*.

"My! Oh my! News!" she exclaimed in a vibrating voice.

"Your horoscope says you're gonna get pregnant! I'm too youthful and overworked to raise a grandbaby," Mama wailed, as she sorted our dirty clothes into various shades of hot pink, powder pink, neon pink, and bubblegum pink.

"No, it's *news*! In the newspaper—an actual news article," Opal replied.

Mama, Pearl, and I gasped in astonishment. *The Somwärin Soothsayer* hadn't contained a legitimate news article since its inception. We dropped our laundry and crowded around Opal. Dodging her eldest daughter's undulating udders, Mama snatched the not-yet-newspaper and scanned it.

"It's true! It's a news article," Mama exclaimed.

Buried amid the usual horoscopes, astrological charts, prophecies, interpretations of omens, tarot card spreads, and photos of the uncanny appearance of the god of mischief in stains on gold shag carpets, which constituted the regular content of *The Somwärin Soothsayer*, we saw an inch-wide column of text purporting to predict the future without supernatural assistance.

"'Miss Somwärin: Can she be Miss America?'" Mama read aloud.

Pearl and I glanced at each other, shocked.

"'The answer to this apparently rhetorical question," Mama read. "'Is yes, she can! This summer, our township's annual beauty pageant will, for the first time ever, comply with all rules and regulations set forth by the Miss America Organization, rendering it an official qualifying competition for the title of Miss Texas. Should Miss Somwärin defeat Miss Dallas, Miss Houston, and Miss Big City, she will be granted a shot at the Miss America crown. In accordance with Miss

America's guidelines, this year's Miss Somwärin pageant will not include the following elements:

1. Wet paper bikini competition
2. Naked lingonberry wrestling match
3. Judge kissing contest
4. Swedish history exam

Local women who wish to compete must be between the ages of 17 and 24, must never have married (common law, Vegas, or otherwise) and must be of good moral character [*HA! They can't be serious—fact-check this later.*] Any female human residing within Somwärin town limits who is eligible and interested must submit an application, in writing and on paper, to the Celestial Temple of Psychedelic Truth and City Administration on Wednesday, June 19. Bribes in the form of legal tender or sexual favors will no longer be accepted by officiants.'"

"Such news!" Pearl breathed in wonder.

"Monumountainous news," Opal agreed.

"I've heard me some news in my day, but never anything of this magnitude," Mama marveled, handing the not-yet-newspaper back to Opal.

"Yeah, it sure is something," a masculine voice concurred. "What're we-all talking about?"

3-J pressed himself through a chink in our wall of womanhood, a garbage bag stuffed with reeking clothes dangling from one hand. He stared in wonder first at Opal's bouncing Buddhas, then at the bright pages of *The Somwärin Soothsayer*.

"Ah!" he exclaimed.

He yanked the not-yet-newspaper out of Opal's hands. He held it aloft and pointed to a final line of text at the very bottom of the article.

"This is indeed great and awesome news: 'Mayor Häri Härison of Härisverige, Sweden, which is Somwärin's sister city, will attend the Miss Somwärin pageant and tour the Fack Sex Furniture Distribution Warehouse in June.' Wow!"

"That's just a horoscope or something," Mama snorted,

returning to her piles of pink womenswear.

"Can you imagine if someone from our own town won Miss Texas?" said Pearl.

"Or Miss America," I enthused.

"Just imagine…" Opal and Mama breathed in unison.

We four females sighed as we pictured the glistening gowns and glittering crown atop the head of an-as-yet faceless Somwärinite. 3-J scratched beneath his Mountain Dew baseball cap and re-read the presumed astrological addendum at the end of the article. He raised his head and squinted. His trucker's speed-trap-avoiding eyes were keen.

"It's a sign. A profound sign," he announced in a voice larded with awe. "Two great men will arrive in Somwärin at the same time, Crystal-Lynn: the King of Sweden and your excellent husband."

"The Mayor of Sweden and my ex-husband! Ex!" Mama snapped. "I don't see why they wanna come around here, anyway. There ain't nothing for neither of them in Somwärin, that's for sure."

"All's I know," said 3-J. "Is if you ain't able to produce this male-boyfriend fella you claim to have by the Miss Somwärin pageant, your once and future husband and His Royal Emperorness will find themselves sharing a companionable pint of grog to toast Don's return to the Bejou household."

3-J gave Mama a firm nod and dumped the stinking contents of his garbage bag atop our girlish garb.

"Gah!" Mama shrieked, raking the motor oil-streaked jeans, T-shirts bearing obscene slogans, and unspeakably zesty underpants to the floor with her long fingernails. "Go on, get away with this nastiness of yours! Opal, take that newspaper away from him. It's getting him high somehow. Pearl, you finish up this sorting."

Opal bestirred herself from the jostling washing machine, hypnotized 3-J with her titanic teats, and withdrew the newspaper from his hands.

Distracted, 3-J didn't notice as Mama turned to me and jerked her thumb imperiously.

"You," she said in a low voice. "Come with me."

2:30 p.m.
Raggedy Man (1981)
A divorced Texan mother (Sissy Spacek) scandalizes her neighbors when she takes up with a young man from out of town.

"What? What did I do? I didn't do anything yet," I yelped, as Mama dragged me out of the laundry trailer. She kicked the tattered screen door closed behind us. Out in the bone-bleaching heat, she shaded her eyes with a slim hand and surveyed the brown sugar landscape of the trailer park. Her eyes sought something among the mobile homes, which dotted the ground like partially-sucked lumps of candy.

"I need protection," she said. "It's time for me to do the deed that'll set us free from your daddy for good."

I perked up pugilistically. I gave the terrain a rapid reconnaissance of my own and spied a two-by-four lying abandoned in the dust. I raised it to my shoulder at parade rest, then swung it about in intricately interconnected arcs. I gave Mama my best ninja-nod to indicate my readiness.

Mama drew in a profound breath, clenched one hand into a fist and plunged the other deep into her cleavage. She drew out a shining quarter. It winked once in the sun. She braced her shoulders and raised a glossy, grape-hued high heel above the dun dirt.

"Pay phone," she said.

Mama stepped cautiously off the laundry trailer porch and aimed her three-inch elevated stride at the public telephone booth located on the other side of the trailer park. Instantly, there came a growl as if from the depths of hell itself. Mama froze. I raised the two-by-four like a baseball bat and whipped my gaze to and fro.

The growl sounded again, closer, raising the hairs on the

back of my neck. An ominous silence fell as we picked our way between the rows of trailers. Just when the phone booth came into sight, a great ball of scabrous fur and flashing fangs flew at us.

I spun around and held my weapon aloft.

"It's her!" I cried. "Run, Mama!"

Mama took off in a tottering sprint for the phone booth as Bitch-Girl, the feral thing-that-may-once-have-been-a-dog, snarled and sank her finger-length canines into my two-by-four. She shook it fiercely, nearly tearing it from my hands, then released it to gallop after Mama.

Slowed by her too-tall shoes and her nicotine addled lungs, Mama shrieked as Bitch-Girl closed in on her. I dashed after the beast, the two-by-four raised over my head in both hands like the Viking battle-axe carried by the Fack Sex Employee of the Year during the opening ceremony of the Miss Somwärin pageant. Mama made a desperate leap and landed on her knees inside the phone booth. She fumbled with the sliding door and slammed it on Bitch-Girl's greasy muzzle.

Bitch-Girl yelped with rage and began to gnaw the Plexiglas door. Panting, I reached her mangy side and swung the two-by-four with all my strength. Buffeted aside, Bitch-Girl skidded a good twelve feet through the dirt, throwing up a wall of dust in her wake.

Safe within the phone booth, Mama let out a sigh. She shut the door firmly, stood, and ran a long, red fingernail down the Somwärin Yellow Page taped above the phone.

"Let's see…Vet 'n' Pet Shop. I don't guess Dr. Dick has a phone in that back closet of his," I heard her say, her voice distorted by the phone booth's walls and Bitch-Girl's ferocious barks.

Mama lifted the receiver, inserted her quarter, and pecked out the phone number with the tip of her pinky fingernail. She pressed the sticky receiver to her ear. Sensing her tension, Bitch-Girl circled the phone booth. I hovered by the door, my two-by-four primed to defend my mama with deadly force. The brute lowered her head, her gnarled lower lip tracing a curve in the dust. She and I had spent years studying each other's fighting tactics; I knew what this posture meant. Bitch-Girl's gluey, yellow eyes met mine through the scratched Plexiglas. Her lip curled up as if in a smirk.

Mama wrapped her free arm around her middle and shifted from one foot to the other as the phone rang.

"It's ringing," Mama reported, her voice extra shrill with anxiety. "It's—oh, hello there, Dr. Barney!"

Mama painted on a fake smile, as if the town veterinarian could see her.

"How're you doing? Oh yeah? Yeah? Yeah. Yeah. Yeah? Look, Dr. Barney—yeah. Yeah. Dr. Ba—yeah. Actually, Dr. Barney, I need to speak to that Dr. Dick fella. That's right. Well, I'm thinking about giving him—it—what he does a try. Yeah. Is he around? Well, no, I don't guess I know what I'm getting myself into. Yeah. Yeah? Like a what—a duck bill? Yeah? He sticks it where now? Yeah? But—what for? He peeps where now!? Yeah? Yeah…yeah. Well, I guess I gotta do what I gotta do. Yeah…"

Mama's face was pale. She covered the mouthpiece with her hand.

"He's getting Dr. Dick," she called.

Her hands were shaking. She looked stricken. What terrors had Dr. Barney described to her?

I gave her a hasty thumbs-up as Bitch-Girl stalked this way and that around the phone booth, seeking to bust into the clear box, disarm me, or accomplish both in one fell swoop.

"He ain't come to the phone yet," Mama reported.

Bitch-Girl sprang at me. With an echoing volley of barks, she sank her thick fangs into my two-by-four and shook it, using all the weight in her muscular body. Like an overwhelmed fisherman, I clung desperately to my pole and sought to plant my feet securely in the powdery trailer park grit.

"He still ain't come to the phone—will you shut up that damned dog, Ruby! I don't want him to think we're some kinda dog-fight-gambling trailer trash—oh, well hello, Dr.

Dick."

Mama's voice morphed from rawhide roar to petal-soft purr in a bare half-second.

"I—I—well, how're you doing?"

"Bitch-Girl, prepare to meet the wolf-witch that whelped you," I screeched, as I charged to do battle, my weapon raised on high.

"Will you tone down that Nordic nonsense! No, no, Dr. Dick, I was just, some crazy kid, I don't know her…um…listen. I called to ask you something."

As I swatted and swung, I saw Mama's mouth work, though no sound came out. Her face went from pasty to dead white. Her shoulders began to shake. Her eyes began to dart. I had seen this before.

Mama was losing her nerve.

Her free hand unclasped itself from her waist and began to grope blindly about the interior of the phone booth. It alighted first on the Yellow Page, then the ancient Schlitz beer can superglued to the top of the phone as a cigarette butt repository. Her index finger crept to the duct tape festooned cradle.

"Um…um…the thing is…" Mama bleated.

Her sharp nail hovered a millimeter above the cradle. She was about to hang up, ending both the call and any chance of preventing Daddy's disastrous return.

"I need to…um…get a—an exam. Your exam. That hootchie thing you do."

She slapped her hand over her face in horror at her vulgar phraseology.

"Yes. That's right—only—only it's not for me. It's for my daughter, Ruby."

"What?!" I shouted.

I dropped my two-by-four just as Bitch-Girl made a leap to take out my throat. In my outrage, I slammed a mighty roundhouse punch square into her ribs. The scabby dog sailed through the air a good three feet, then came to ground. Yelping in fear, she dug in her scaly paws and fled into the depths of the trailer park.

Within the phone booth, Mama blurted out, "I need it as soon as possible. She does, I mean. Hell—heck, tomorrow will be perfect."

"Mama!" I hollered, banging on the door with my dog-mashing fists. "No, no, no!"

She flapped a hand at me, avoiding my eyes.

"It's spelled R-U-B-Y, last name B-E-J-O-U. No, I don't guess it's French. It's the husband's name anyway—ex-husband! Ex."

"Cease, Mama! Desist!" I shrieked desperately.

"Three o'clock? Alrighty, I'll see you then. We'll see you then, I mean. Bye, Dr. Dick."

"Noooooo!" I wailed.

I collapsed to my knees as Mama hung up the phone, flicked her hair out of her face, and licked her front teeth to remove any nervously smeared lipstick.

"Hoo, Lord!" she hooted, as she slid the phone booth door open.

She fanned her face with a limp hand and rolled her eyes up to the non-judgmental sky, to avoid looking at me lying prostrate in the dirt.

"Goddamn the pusher man! I've lost my booty call making skills, and that's a fact. Ain't that right, honey-muffin? Ain't your mama out of practice? Ain't she lost her touch with the menfolk?"

She gave forth an awkward laugh that faded to a burble of unease when she encountered my horizontal glower.

"I couldn't help it. I panicked," she said. "What else could I do?"

I emitted a Bitch-Girl-style growl and sprang to my feet. I crossed my arms over my chest.

"What?" she protested. "I didn't mean to, but now it's done. You understand, darling-heart, don't you?"

"I ain't amused, Mama," quoth I, using one of Mama's pet phrases against her.

I scowled at Mama until she lost her shifty evasiveness and

scowled back.

"I'll give you a dollar to do it," she said.

"Ha," I brayed, turning away. "Do you think I'm so cheap?"

"Four—six. Ten?"

I paused and contemplated my current state of bankruptcy.

"Very well, Mama. You got yourself a deal. But I want the cash in hand before the exam. Cash—no personal checks from the likes of you."

Mama tossed her hair haughtily and eyed me up and down.

"Oh, Ruby. You think your mama would play you false? Cruel daughter! After all your mother has done for you, working herself to death to give you sustenance and shelter. You might have wanted to do her one little service gratis. But there's no such thing as a free favor from the likes of you, is there?"

Having turned the tables on me, Mama pivoted and minced away, her high heels leaving rejecting little punctures in the dirt.

"I heard what you were saying to Dr. Barney," I shouted. "Dr. Dick's gonna poke all around my Place. I ain't letting no man do that for less than the cost of a Coke and a drive-in movie. You taught us girls to value ourselves better than that."

Mama paused and turned back to me. Her narrowed eyes revealed that she was pondering whether to allow me to perform my first act of prostitution, or to revise reality as she knew it.

"It's just a doctor's examination, Ruby," she replied with great difficulty. "Dr. Dick is a…legitimate medical professional who performs…legitimate medical procedures in an illegitimate medical setting."

She drew in a shaky breath and pressed her hand to her heaving bosom.

"It…ain't…sexual…" she gasped out, shattering both logic and the natural order with just three words.

Reeling within this new paradigm, she staggered away from me.

I tipped my head up to the humid, cloud-hazed sky and drank deep of the novelty. Then I hurried to follow Mama back to the laundry trailer before Bitch-Girl could sense the vulnerability engendered by my new worldview.

4:00 p.m.
Carrie (1976)
An unpopular teenager (Sissy Spacek) is relentlessly bullied, has a hideous liquid dumped on her, and plots revenge.

The laundry cycle was a little over halfway done when Opal cleared her throat in an announcement-making fashion.

"I remember the first time I saw the Miss America pageant on TV. All them girls flashing white teeth and saying smart stuff about how to fix up the world at large. I wonder if the girls in the Miss Somwärin contest will make speeches about how to improve the town?" she mused.

"I'll tell you who ought to make a speech on that topic: the one and only Don Bejou. Girls, your daddy's one wise fella. Wise, with wisdom. Wise-dom. Wise-Don. Ha! That's clever," 3-J chortled as he scrubbed his Teamster duds with a nailbrush and a slimy bar of Irish Spring soap.

"Pure gibberish. I ain't heard no wisdom from Don since I was seventeen and drunk on corn whiskey and he suggested that we head to Motel Way to—never you mind," Mama said, as she hauled a heaping handful of salmon socks, coral cutoffs, and blush bras out of the washer.

Opal wandered away from the pile of ironing she was supposed to be attending to and sat down on the lint-covered floor, her back pressed against a drier door as it thumped busily. She gazed moonily at the newspaper. I scowled at her and roiled both hands through the garment brew fermenting in the utility sink to keep from rolling my eyes in like manner.

"Do you suppose Miss Somwärin will get a real crown and

sash this year? Not that nasty pair of pasties and the Viking helmet like usual?" Opal wondered.

She traced her fingertip around the article, smearing the cheap ink. She lifted her eyes to the grimy window that looked out on the vast Texan sky, where she seemed to see better things.

"You shouldn't disparage tradition, Opal. Tradition's crucial to the functioning of Somwärin. For example, the pasties incite the good menfolk to lust, which encourages the making of babies. They in turn grow up to follow the example of our Swedish employers and send the dead bodies of their sires floating into The Great Beyond in Fack Sex brand funeral ships, some assembly required. As you girls will do when your daddy kicks the bucket."

"We gotta do what?" Pearl squeaked.

"Will you shut up, 3-J!" Mama said exasperatedly, releasing a shower of rosy panties into the washing machine, followed by a blizzard of laundry detergent. "You know how squeamish girls are about corpses and death rites and such."

"Well," 3-J drawled. "All I know is Don has often emphasized how important it is for a man to have plenty of descendants to see his soul out of this world and into That Which Lies Hereafter. Y'all girls ought to start producing Don some grandsons if you're scared to handle his decaying corpse yourselves."

Mama shook the detergent box menacingly at 3-J.

"I swear, I'll pour this straight down your chatty gullet and shut you up myself."

"Let's just agree to agree that Don's a true prophet. Since receiving the mystical message from the CB, he's been enlightening me good, telling me all about the glorious future of mankind and the true path to enlightenment and how to crack sunflower seeds in your mouth without swallowing the shells. Don is a king among men."

"King? King?!" Mama choked back five degrees of profanity to spare our tender, girlish ears. "Balderdash!"

"I wonder if that king from Sweden will crown Miss

Somwärin?" Opal rested her chin in her hand and sighed, her eyes filled with bright dreams.

"There ain't gonna be no king or nobody from Sweden at the pageant, I can promise you that," Mama snapped irritably. "The only Swedes that ever come to this town are from Fack Sex Corporate Headquarters, and their coming ain't never announced. They just show up, all unexpected, and you can't seem to get them to leave. Like that one over there," she added, pointing at 3-J.

"I like the Viking helmet. I hope they keep it," Pearl offered.

"Well, it *is* a historical relic," Opal agreed.

"In nineteen-hundred and eighty-one," 3-J sang. "They put their horny helmets on. They put their horny helmets on, to conquer Boscoe Counteee! With quality home furnishings at affordable prices…"

"You think we need a history lesson? You think we won't hear that stupid song a thousand times before the summer's out?" Mama said.

"Now we are Somwärin town, Somwärin town, Somwärin town," 3-J persisted melodically. "Now we are Somwärin town, instead of Boscoe County! Thanks to Fack Seeeeeeex…."

"For the last, final, and ultimate time, shut up" Mama barked, banging her fist down on the washer for emphasis. She cranked the machine's cycle knobs and added, "Get on up here and hold this sucker down, Opal. Quit ruminating on that stupid newspaper."

Opal rose slowly, still clutching *The Somwärin Soothsayer* with a faraway look in her eyes. She raked her fingers through her long, blond hair and tossed it over her shoulders. She arched her back, gave forth a grunt that could be mistaken for a moan, parted her knees, and mounted the washing machine like a porn star straddling a lucky lad.

"You know something?" she said. "I think I might enter Miss Somwärin myself this year. Wouldn't it be something if I actually won and got to try for Miss Texas?"

She sighed dreamily.

Leaden silence fell upon the laundry trailer and all who dwelt within it. I glanced at Pearl. Pearl glanced at Mama. Mama glanced at 3-J. 3-J glanced at Mama's cleavage, then at me.

I let out a loud, derisive snort.

Opal swung eyes flashing with anger to me.

"You got something to say, Ruby? Just spit it out instead of making like a pig."

Pricked by her choice of barnyard animal, I piped up when I should have piped down.

"You'll look a fool prancing around that stage. Worse than a fool—you'll be a spectacle."

Opal leaned toward me from her perch atop the washing machine, her two top-heavies nearly unbalancing her.

"I know what you are: jealous, pure and simple. Because I'm old enough and pretty enough and idea-having enough to enter, and you ain't."

I opened my mouth to retort, then recalled what had happened to me the last time I'd found myself in such a situation with my big sister. Now, as then, Mama was present and unsympathetic to either my witty wordplay or my side of things.

I held my tongue and lowered my eyes.

Triumphant, Opal hopped down from the washing machine and strode toward me. Her vast chest was puffed with pride.

"I'm right, aren't I, Mama? Ruby's envious coz I'm gonna do good up on that stage and make you proud."

Mama hesitated.

Opal's gleeful grin flickered.

"You think I can win, don't you, Mama?"

"Um, ha, laundry, er, well…"

Opal spun around to study each of our faces, her boobs sloshing together and asunder and together again like two great buoys.

Pearl stared at her shoes.

Mama shifted her eyes to the window.

3-J leered at Opal's hood ornaments.

"What? What's the matter with y'all?"

"Well…Opal, honey," Mama replied. "You can't go and enter that pageant."

"Why not?"

"Well, sugar baby…" Mama bit her tawdry lower lip, her well-plucked brows ratcheting close enough to form a unibrow.

With everyone else avoiding her eyes, Opal met mine. Hers were desperate. Mine were resentful.

"It's them gazongas of yours!" I blurted out. "The pageant is classy now. It's Miss America. The likes of you ain't Miss America material."

Opal went pale. Her eyes grew nearly as huge as her boobage.

"Mama?" she whispered.

"It's true, babydoll. Everyone will laugh at you," Mama admitted.

"Is that what y'all think? That I'm a joke?"

"No, no, lovey-dove, sugar—"

Opal stomped her foot, making her gargantuan globes lurch skyward, which sent a corresponding jolt through the rest of her body that knocked her off balance. She staggered and grabbed the washing machine with both hands to steady herself.

"I hate alla y'all!" Opal cried.

She dashed out of the laundry trailer. Her breasts parted the air before her, leaving a stiff breeze in their wake. The ragged screen door banged loudly behind her. A difficult silence overtook we who remained in the laundry trailer. After a moment, 3-J could contain himself no longer.

"Gazongas!" he hooted and collapsed into guffaws.

Two hours later, the laundry cycle was complete. We lugged the overflowing baskets home, put the clothes away, and still Opal had not returned to us.

I lolled on the couch with Pearl, dissolutely watching the Sissy Spacek Movie Marathon. My heart was barely in it.

"I wanna be normal," Sissy Spacek was imploring her mother on the TV. "I wanna start to try and be a whole person before it's too late for me—"

These fine words were abruptly cut off when her mother flung her beverage straight in Sissy Spacek's face.

"Go hunt up your big sister," Mama commanded Pearl and me from the doorway of the kitchen. "Like as not, she's out sulking shotgun in the Oldsmobile."

Mama sounded unconcerned, but I noticed she was fretfully gnawing on her nails and had smoked nary a cigarette since Opal's departure.

Pearl gamely trotted outside. I trailed her grudgingly.

"Nope," Pearl proclaimed, peering through the Oldsmobile windshield, which was tangled with a fisherman's net of cracks. "Let's take a turn around the trailer park. Maybe someone's seen her."

"Such melodrama," I grouched. "You wouldn't catch the likes of me flying off and worrying folks. I've got greater maturity."

Pearl glanced at me with undisguised skepticism as we rounded the back end of our home on wheels. Parked smack dab in the midst of our well-pruned whirligigs, procession of pink flamingos, and colony of stately gnomes, we encountered 3-J's semi. Pearl and I pulled up short in astonishment. By my finger calculations, 3-J had arrived at the Bejou abode less than ten hours ago. Somehow, in that time, the long-haul semi had attained the look of a venerable monument erected in our lot thirty summers ago.

I gaped at the knee-high weeds that had sprung up around the tall tires, the rusted beer cans that formed hefty hillocks beneath the undercarriage, the two-inch thick spackling of dust that obscured the crimson paint job emblazoned with cavorting blue devils and the legend, "3-J outta the FIRES OF HELL YEEEEEAH!!!"

From within the primordial hulk came a low rumble, then a massive belch split the air, sending a cluster of crows roosting on the hood soaring skyward.

Having no desire to learn how our daddy's bestest buddy was occupying himself alone in his truck, Pearl and I shuddered and scurried away.

"Let's go back home. She ain't worth the trouble of hunting high and low," I complained, as Pearl diligently scouted behind and beneath our neighbors' metallic homes.

"Why're you so down on Opal lately?"

"I'm not!"

"You are. You've been radiating a specific hostility toward and regarding Opal for two whole days. Why?"

"Because I'm sick of her ways and means! She's sly and false. Mama's still angry with me for calling her a name or two, but everyone forgets it was Opal who insulted me first."

"When did she insult you? I don't remember that happening," Pearl frowned as we passed the McMayberry brothers' school bus.

"See! No one ever recalls her misdeeds, but everyone remembers mine. It happened when we were walking home from Perdee Dora Dolan's Superior Summer Shindig and Smörgåsbord—you were there! Opal insulted me in terms I can no longer precisely recall and incited me. She's crafty. She pretended to cry so I'd be the one to be punished. It's all just a big-boob-having, pageant-wanna-be-entering act!" I railed.

Pearl shook her head in a zenful manner as we gave a wide berth to the Tooth Witch's sinister trailer.

"You should let go of your grudge, Ruby. It's wrong to stay angry over a petty quarrel. Take me for example. I, too, was insulted at the Superior Summer Shindig and Smörgåsbord—and by Perdee Dora herself. She insulted me most bitterly. But I've chosen to forgive her rotten, bratty, spoiled, snotty self."

My little sister's face was clouded by a harsh scowl, just like the one she wore after cleaning Perdee Dora's clock at the Superior Summer Shindig and Smörgåsbord.

"Say, what exactly did Perdee Dora call you that night?" I inquired. "It sounded like 'silly spaceship.'"

Pearl's chest swelled like a puff adder beneath her pink teddy bear t-shirt.

"I…won't…discuss…it!" she growled.

All at once, it dawned on me what Perdee Dora's words had been.

"Did she…did she call you 'Sissy Spacek?' The Greatest Insult of Them All?" I gasped.

Pearl swung killing eyes at me as we passed Quentin Keeton hosing his two-foot-square patch of imported Iberian lawn. The sight of his pale, fishy flesh covered by aught but zebra briefs and a pair of sparkly red cowboy boots caused her to regain her calm via revulsion. She sucked in all the air she could hold, then exhaled with the force of a hurricane.

"I have chosen to forgive and forget. You should too, Ruby. There's nothing to be gained from seeking revenge."

At this precise moment, the sheriff-mayor's patrol car roared into the Somwärin Trailer Park and RV Pleasure Garden, its dozens and dozens of red and blue lights ablaze, its falcon-shriek siren blaring. Casting up great sheets of dust, it careened to a stop and narrowly missed running over Bitch-Girl, who had been stealthily stalking us girls. She bolted as the car's front bumper halted a bare inch from our shins.

My interior went cold and clammy when I spied a female head in the back seat.

Was it Opal?

I grabbed Pearl's hand in alarm. Had X-rated Opal been arrested simply for expressing an interest in entering the now G-rated Miss Somwärin pageant? Worse yet, had she fallen into the hands of a prowling trucker of 3-J's ilk, who had been compelled by lust to lay siege to her big kahunas? In my fear for my big sister, I forgot to be angry with her.

The driver's door of the police car swung opened. With a grizzly grunt, the sheriff-mayor of Somwärin hefted his formidable layers of fat and muscle out into the overheated atmosphere. He hitched his bullet-studded belt to a business-doing position and leveled his fearsome gaze upon us.

"You," he barked, aiming a meaty finger at Pearl. "I've got a bone to pick with you, missy."

Sheriff-Mayor Dolan strode with marrow-melting

deliberation to within kissing distance of Pearl. With much creaking of firearm-associated leather, he leaned down and locked his flinty eyes on hers.

Pearl gulped, then steadied herself impressively. I, for my part, collapsed in utter terror at the sheriff-mayor's feet, my martial ways replaced by abject cowardice.

"After that disgraceful ruckus you caused at my little girl's party, I was of a mind to arrest you. What do you think of that? A day and a night in the Somwärin Public Jail for disturbing my peace. But Mrs. Dolan informed me that young girls delight in fighting amongst themselves during their teenage years, so I decided to let you run free. However…"

Sheriff-Mayor Dolan formed his face into its most menacing sneer. It was the one reserved for the wretched, pleading criminal caught in the act. To my surprise, Pearl remained tear-free, erect, and silent.

"However," he continued. "My little Perdee Dora has been so mightily undone by the quarrelsome violence you enacted upon her tender person that I've been unable to console her with either presents or cash money. Therefore, we're gonna take care of things old school style."

The sheriff-mayor straightened to his full height. He turned to his cop car and opened the back door. Out pranced Perdee Dora wearing a smirk as broad as a canyon.

"My daddy says this is perfectly legal," she declared.

Perdee Dora took a deep breath, placed both hands on her hips, and cocked her head into a belligerent angle.

"You, Pearl Bejou, are a no-count pasty ol' Sissy Spacek looking scrap of trailer trash that don't no one in town like and your sister right there is the ugliest and troublemakingest girl anyone ever laid eyes on and your daddy is a crazy lawless whoring maniac and your mama's a cheap unschooled warehouse Swede-slave and probably a whore for them Swedes too and she can't even support her family right and alla y'all Bejous ain't nothing but bottom of the barrel poor white trash!"

Perdee Dora turned away. I thought she was finished. But

no.

She reached into the cop car, pulled out a filthy paper cup, and lobbed a lukewarm chocolate milkshake straight at Pearl. It hit my sister full in the face, running in thick brown rivulets down her cheeks and hair to soak her shirt and shorts and sneakers like sticky fingerpaint.

"Now you got trash on you, white trash! I took that outta the dumpster behind the Burger Bower where that slutty, illiterate, stripper-titted big sister of yours is gonna be working like a dumb dog this summer."

Perdee Dora daintily wiped her unsullied fingers on a Burger Bower napkin, tossed it at Pearl's feet, and climbed back into the police car.

"Now y'all are even-steven," declared Sheriff-Mayor Dolan.

He got in the driver's seat, tipped his Smokey Bear hat at us, and pulled away.

As the car sped off, I slowly unclenched myself from the fetal position I had assumed. I lifted my eyes to Pearl. The milkshake oozed earthward in thick, runny drips that took refuge in the dry dirt like worms. Pearl was terribly silent. I could hear each *plop* as it hit the ground.

"Oh, um, can I, should I…" I stammered.

"You best just leave me be, Ruby."

Pearl pronounced each word carefully. She stood straight as a steel girder, blocking out the sun with her ramrod profile. She turned stiffly and began to walk away. Bitch-Girl, having recovered from her brush with death by automobile, sprang at Pearl. She pulled up short, whimpered, and ran away full-tilt when she beheld my little sister's lethal aspect.

I remained seated in the dirt until fire ants began a linear march to the gummy puddles of milkshake, stinging me for impeding their progress. More painful than their stings was that of my conscience. Perdee Dora's cruel invectives against my entire family rang in my ears, making me acutely aware of how hurtful my bad-tempered words must have been to Opal. Guilt, more cloying than the chocolate ant feast, betook me and made me feel sick.

Once, not so very long ago, Opal and I had been close. Then at the age of nine, Opal's bosom had commenced its uncontainable expansion. By age eleven, she was beyond a DDD cup and was discovered by the boys of Somwärin. Away she drifted, leaving me behind. In my heart of hearts, I was still waiting for her to drift back to me.

8:00 p.m.
Crimes of the Heart (1986)
Three sisters overcome their differences when they face an unexpected crisis.

Night fell around the Bejou family trailer, all spangly with stars and shimmery with moonbeams that served only to taunt the miserable souls within.

Pearl remained locked within the bathroom, showering again and again, and muttering something that sounded like, "Revenge! Revenge!"

Mama sat at the kitchen table, still not smoking, still ruining her nails with her gnawing, still looking pained and worried.

I lurked in each room for brief, restless minutes. In the living room, the TV blared away. I passed it and paused.

"I'm having a bad day," Sissy Spacek tearfully confessed to her sister.

I ached to see Opal. I switched the Sissy Spacek Movie Marathon off.

Around nine, there was a commotion at the front door.

"Go on, then! I gots important business to conduct yet tonight," a male voice boomed.

I crept through the kitchen and peered into the living room.

3-J was hustling Opal through the front door as Mama, with nicotine-deprived agility, sprang forward to hug and shake her.

"Home at last! Where you been? Near killed me with wondering what'd become of you. Where'd you find her, 3-J?"

3-J released my sullen sister and stuffed his hands into his tight jeans pockets.

"Well…I might have been heading out Motel Way for a variety of purposes that I won't detail at this point. And who do you suppose I came upon, hitchhiking all half-hearted? This one."

"What?" Mama gasped, pressing her hands to her well-rouged cheeks.

"Maybe I was on my way to seek female companionship for the night. Ain't none of your business what I do," 3-J sputtered. "Ya ain't my wife, Crystal-Lynn! I ain't got nothing to be ashamed of with my male urges. See—see—this is why Don's a-coming! Womenfolk ain't capable of keeping their nubile young daughters at home where those of us with a six-pack of Lone Star won't mistake their hitchhiking thumb for a come-hither hooker wave. Ain't my fault—it was dark!"

He threw up his hands and banged out the front door in defensive disapproval of Mama's lax parenting.

"Why?" Mama exclaimed, as soon as he was gone. "Why on earth did you pull such a foolhardy stunt? Don't you realize what a degenerate, lawless stretch of road Motel Way is? Don't you realize you could've been snatched by a horndog trucker—one just like 3-J, only untroubled by uncle-ish feelings toward you? Why would you do such a thing?"

Opal fetched a great, shattered sigh from her very depths. Her chest inflated to prodigious proportions, then deflated to drag her spine into a Quasimodo hump.

"Coz Ruby's right. I won't never be a beauty queen. All I'll ever be is a trucker toy out Motel Way."

Opal drooped her chin onto her wide-spreading love-ledge and gave a miserable sob.

"I'm a freak. Why, Mama?"

Mama pulled Opal into her arms. She cradled Opal's head as she was unable to reach around her back.

"You stop such talk! You just got yourself some big boobies. It ain't nothing to be ashamed of."

"Yes, it is," Opal wept, laying her head on Mama's own

moderate-sized bosom. "Why ain't I normal, Mama?"

"Coz—coz—I dunno, baby. Cause your titties just grew in real big, and ain't nothing you can do about it."

Opal gave another sob.

"Ruby predicted my future better than the Soothsayer. I'm gonna end up a stripper or a hooker…or worse. Nobody in town likes me, Mama. No one ever looks me in the eye. I got no friends."

Unseen in the doorway, I began to sniffle.

"And now Ruby hates me, and soon Pearl will too, and then I'll have no sisters. No companionship. No man's ever gonna feel genuine love for me—what'll I do when I ain't got no sisters to care about me?"

I let out a wail and rushed into the living room.

"I don't hate you, Opal! Love ya! I do!"

I threw myself onto the rug at Opal and Mama's feet and sobbed.

"Sorry I said mean things! You're right, I'm jealous of you."

Opal bent down to me. Her heavy hooters caused her to tumble awkwardly onto the rug by my side. She clutched me in her arms, smothering me in the deep crevasse between her chest pillows.

"I'm jealous of *you*! I wish I was normal like you."

"Love you!"

"Love you more!"

"My babies!" Mama descended upon us, embracing our already embracing selves. "I knew my girls couldn't be hateful to each other forever. I knew you'd reconcile."

Our weepy hug-fest continued for a good ten minutes, then I wiped my face on my shirtfront and sat back on my heels. Opal's sobs eased and she scrubbed at her tears with both hands like she used to when she was a little girl.

Mama smoothed back the dishwater-blond hair from our foreheads. She put a hand on each of our shoulders and we turned our faces to hers. Mama gave both of us a bracing shake and looked deep into our eyes.

"Don't neither of you girls give up. You go on and enter

any pageants you want, and if anyone dares laugh, well, you'll think of some way to fix 'em. You get out there and make your lives just how you want 'em to be, my jewel-babies!" Her face grew determined. "I know I'm a-gonna."

Chapter Six
The Pubic Library

Monday, June 17
9:02 a.m.

Three summers ago, my daddy stole all the books from the town library. He was bored that Friday evening, as was his best buddy, 3-J, with whom he committed the larceny. No one knows how they got the hundreds and hundreds of books out of the library in a single night, nor what they did with them. Being truckers, it was supposed they strapped the load onto a flatbed and made tracks for the Mexican border to fill the nearest canyon, arroyo, or dry oil well with the misappropriated prose.

Pricked either by regret or further mischief the following evening, the two broke back into the Somwärin Public Library and laid a literary donation on the bare shelves: eight copies of *Playboy*, three issues of *Hustler*, one Swedish edition of *Healthy Outdoor Nude Lifestyles*, a beat-up videocassette of *Debbie Does Dallas*, and an old Polaroid of my own mama exposing her good 'n' plenties.

When the townsfolk saw the daring new direction in which their staid library had swerved, they embraced the literary institution as never before. Similar donations came flooding in. Every citizen signed up for a library card. The sparsely attended book club swelled beyond capacity, with enthusiastic bookworms meeting every day of the week and twice on Sunday. By the time I was fourteen, the shelves of the rechristened Pubic Library were crammed to bursting with every flavor of pornography known to man, and the high school cancelled the sex-ed program as redundant—every kid in town was thoroughly self-taught.

Every kid except me: I was banned for life from setting foot in the Pubic Library.

Monday morning found me dreaming of a sugarloaf cake

covered in rainbow candy sprinkles. Suddenly the sugarloaf formed a mouth and bellowed, "Today your magic kingdom shall be invaded, Ruby! On guard!"

I opened my eyes. Confusion clouded my brain until I remember that today, at three o'clock precisely, Dr. Dick was going to ply his trade on my V-spot. I groaned and rolled over, stuffing my head under my pillow. How had I let Mama talk me into this…thing I was about to undergo?

What *was* I about to undergo, exactly?

I withdrew my head from beneath my pillow and cogitated for a spell. I had no notion what it was Dr. Dick did for a living. If I was inexperienced in the "Ways of Luv" on account of my overall lack of appeal to the boys of my peer group, I was doubly ignorant on account of my lack of access to the Pubic Library.

I got out of bed and wandered into the living room, then the kitchen. The trailer was sunny and silent. Every member of my household had gone their separate summer ways: Opal to her first day of work at the Burger Bower, my unwitting porn star mama to toil in the Fack Sex Furniture Distribution Warehouse, and Pearl to…somewhere.

I withdrew a frozen waffle from the freezer and chawed upon it, unthawed. If only I could follow the normal course of maturation in Somwärin and waltz into the Pubic Library to leaf through a few dirty magazines that would familiarize me with the mechanics, then saunter into the Masters 'n' Johnson Reading Room to gain knowledge of theory, and finally settle in to browse the dusty archive of sex toy instruction manuals to learn practical methods applicable to daily life. All these educational resources were denied me forever just because of a simple error in judgement on my part.

I scowled defiantly.

I cast aside my icy breakfast.

I stood.

I refused to accept my banishment any longer! I would sneak into the Pubic Library and gain access to the knowledge so long withheld from me. And I knew exactly how to do it.

I hied to my bedroom and assembled a cunning disguise: oversized heart-shaped sunglasses raided from Pearl's collection; semi-obscene Daisy Dukes courtesy of Opal; Mama's blue and yellow "Bra Handling, God Fack Sex!" T-shirt, which she wore to mandatory morale-building work events; and the long-haul trucker's indispensable beer-themed baseball cap—"If U can read this, I ain't drunk E-NUFF"—which 3-J had left unattended under the kitchen table. I strapped on a sturdy pair of highway-grade high heels and gave myself a nod in the bathroom mirror.

Now unknowable to all familiar with me, I set out for the library.

As I marched into town, I steeled my resolve.

When you got right down to it, it was altogether unfair that I'd been banned for life from the library. My misdeed had been minor. And not entirely my fault.

Three years ago, in the inaugural month of my final year of elementary school, my lack of a chronic reading habit was noted by my fifth-grade teacher, who sought to remedy the situation by pawning me off on the town librarian. Per orders one sunny afternoon in September, I'd slogged across town to the Somwärin Public Library, former home of *The Somwärin Sentinel* editorial office. Inside the noiseless, book-brimming chamber of knowledge, I stood stock-still and stared stupidly at the shelves.

At that point in my young life, I was not yet a fan of the written word.

The librarian, eager to ensnare an unsullied soul within the oubliette of literature, came hustling up to me.

"Welcome!" she said. "What brings you to the library?"

"I'm supposed to pick a book and read it," I replied in a surly tone.

"Wonderful!" enthused the librarian. "What do you like to read?"

I shrugged sullenly.

"Don't you like to read?" the librarian inquired, a note of dismay creeping into her voice.

"It's boring," I replied.

The librarian gasped, placed a hand upon her bosom, then shook her head sternly.

"Reading is not boring," she admonished. "I'll prove it to you."

She stepped briskly across the worn hardwood floor, upon which the erstwhile editor had once cowered in fits of paranoia. She ran a finger along a shelf of children's books and let it rest on a slim hardcover volume. She tapped the title decisively and withdrew it.

"This," she said, walking back to me with a firm step. "This is the book for you."

She stepped behind the checkout desk, stamped the book, and slid it across the polished wooden surface to my indifferent hands. I glanced at the cover. A slavering, fearsome dog snarled back at me. *White Fang*, it read.

I brightened. Clearly this book recounted Bitch-Girl's origin story. By reading it, I would gain valuable insight that would give me the upper hand over my mortal enemy.

"Thanks!" I said with genuine enthusiasm.

"Take a great adventure with this book!" the librarian sang out, as I skipped out of the public library with my prize.

My gusto was short-lived. That evening, I tossed the text aside with a growl of contempt. It was not Bitch-Girl's biography after all. Worse, it was boring.

I sighed.

Then I reconsidered.

Maybe I was approaching the book in the wrong manner. What was it the librarian had instructed me to do?

Take a great adventure with this book.

And so, that's exactly what I did.

I took *Wild Fang* with me on a rollicking adventure through the trailer park that night. Thanks to the power of imagination, Jack London's early twentieth-century novel was transformed into:

A toboggan to slide down the steep roof of the Bejou family trailer.

A shovel to dig in the hard-packed earth on the outskirts of the trailer park in a quest for black gold.

A source of fuel for a lonesome explorer's campfire under the stars.

A shield to fend off Bitch-Girl, upon whom the tedious tale was not based.

The book and I had a great adventure together indeed.

When I returned *White Fang*—shredded, smashed, singed, streaked with soil, and scarred by the real White Fang—the librarian did not congratulate me.

"Ruby," she said in dismay. "That…that was not what I meant. You've ruined this book beyond repair. I'm sorry, but I must ban you from the library for a month."

I didn't set foot in the library again until my degenerate first-semester report card was exposed to Mama's displeased eyes.

Now, three years later, my steps slowed as I reached the outermost edge of Main Street. I would have to be cautious in my approach to the innocuous-looking brick building that housed the Pubic Library. If Daddy, 3-J, or myself were ever caught on the property, dastardly retribution would befall us.

The slate roof was spiked with towering antennas and platter-shaped listening devices that twirled hypnotically like the gaudy whirligigs that surrounded my trailer park home. The pristine outer walls were blemished by an array of dark, glistening surveillance hubs, like the blackheads that bedecked the faces of the teens of Somwärin who so loved their local library.

I swallowed hard and sought to rein in my trembling. All the wisdom of the adult entertainment industry lay just beyond the electronically monitored threshold. All I had to do was summon the courage to approach, and I'd be able to stuff my brain with the knowledge I needed to face Dr. Dick's exam with dignity and fortitude.

I took a deep breath, drew myself up tall on my plastic high heels, and took a step toward the Pubic Library. A hand instantly grabbed my arm.

I yelped as a bizarre figure tugged me into the concealing shadows of the fearsome Tree of Contemplation.

"Shhh! If we're reconnaissanced, we're done for."

A man—I think—hissed at me from beneath a familiar foam hat in the shape of a horned Viking helmet. Cinched around his neck was a purple feather boa that shuddered in the breeze, while a faded aqua mu-mu whipped around his jeans-clad thighs.

"Hey!" I barked indignantly. "That's my Miss Somwärin pageant commemorative helmet. Is that you, 3-J?"

"Shhh!" he hissed again. "Maintain radio silence, Ruby. Radio sil—hey, what're you doing with my baseball cap? Gimme here!"

As 3-J scrabbled his cap from my head, I wrested my Viking helmet off his and clutched it to my underdeveloped chest. He settled his cap on his skull with finicky precision, then his farsighted trucker eyes returned to the Pubic Library's all-seeing façade. He pressed a finger to his lips.

"What are you doing here?" I demanded in a whisper.

"I'm gonna reclaim my old *Playboy* from the shelves within. I need a little private time with Miss November 1998. It's sensual nostalgia that's pressing down on me and there's no denying it. But look," he said, pointing at the varnished walnut front door.

A neat little hand-lettered sign taped to the door read, "Open in one hour."

"When did you get here? How much longer do we have to wait?" I said.

3-J waggled his finger in my face.

"You misunderstand the message of the sign, Ruby. Many's the time I've seen my fellow truckers defeated by 'Free Beer Tomorrow' signs within bars along our great nation's highways. Ya gotta come on the *right* tomorrow, not just any tomorrow. I've been waiting here four straight hours. When the right hour has passed, the door will open."

"What? That don't make no sense," I said.

"It makes all the sense in the world," 3-J retorted.

"Eventually the right hour will pass, and that door will swing open, and I'll steal my favorite dirty book back. I ain't budging from this spot until that happens."

Suddenly I understood.

Clearly word had gotten around: 3-J was in town, and I was in need of sexual education for the first time in my young life. Gossip ran swift in Somwärin, and with equal swiftness a trap had been laid to catch us.

I sighed, plunked my foam Viking hat on my head to shield myself from the pounding beams of summer sunshine, and turned away from the Pubic Library.

"Well," I said. "Good luck, I guess, 3-J."

"Shhh!"

I wandered away, leaving 3-J squatting in vigil beneath the formidable arms of the Tree of Contemplation.

Now what? The day was young and I was still ignorant.

Where else in town could I learn the intricacies of the sexual anatomy of the human female?

Of course!

Planting my three-inch heels sharply in the tidal dust surging along Main Street, I marched straight to Dr. Flo's clinic. As I reached for the shining doorknob, I chanced to glance over my shoulder. I thought I spied a familiar girlish figure that bore a strong resemblance to Pearl darting into the Swedish Embassy & Beauty Parlor & Coffee Shop. I shook my head. Surely I was mistaken. Pearl would never betake herself to our favorite hangout without me.

Inside Dr. Flo's clinic, I found a long line of patients ahead of me. I plopped myself onto a tall kitchen stool and proceeded to count the ceiling tiles until my turn came.

Dr. Flo was harried and unwilling to humor me when I finally got her alone in the exam room. She glowered at me as I sat on her non-equine examination table, swinging my legs nervously.

"What are you asking me, Ruby? Are you asking me for advice on how to obtain sexual favors from some unnamed male? I've been asked nine foolish questions today, but this one is the topper."

As Dr. Flo was the sworn opponent of Dr. Dick, I had not informed her of the real reason I wanted to know how my tweedle-dee worked.

"Sexual intercourse has ever and always been the primary tool used to subjugate womankind. If it's not untimely pregnancy forced upon an unwitting young female, it's disease. If it's not disease, it's rape and sexual abuse. Or the looming threat of all these things, wielded by oppressor males to keep 'their' women in line. Witness the veiled Saudi Arabian woman, swathed in suffocating robes which lead to vitamin D deficiency and the debilitating disease of rickets. Why is she veiled? To prevent skin cancer from the merciless Middle Eastern sun? No! She is told that men will lust after her body and assault her if she does not hide herself. Rubbish. I myself have had no time to see the sun today. I will have no lunch break, no vitamin D fortified dairy products—and why? Because of the superfluity of sexually transmitted diseases that the men of the world have begun to inflict ahead of schedule on the benighted female population of Somwärin. And by men, I mean truckers."

Fatally, I suggested, "You could send them to Dr. Dick. He's not busy."

Dr. Flo's face transformed to pale dragon scales and fire began to shoot from her nostrils.

"I will rot in a chill grave in the heart of the Alaskan tundra before I refer even one of my patients to that ridiculous charlatan! There is no greater medical fraud than the practice of obstetrics and gynecology. I have more faith in the efficacy of acupuncture! Or the ludicrous myth that is chiropractic medicine! Get out! GET OUT!"

I scampered out of Dr. Flo's wrathful presence.

And again, now what?

The sun had ascended to a crabby, feverish zenith above the town, bringing sweat and a lust for soda to my person. Frustrated and dry-throated, I wandered along Main Street. If only there was a way to quench my thirst while simultaneously consulting a sexually savvy soul.

Of course!

I turned on my towering heel and aimed my stride for the Burger Bower.

Opal was the best person in town to impart a solid sexual education. The bulbous boobies that graced the space between her head and her Golden Womanly Palace had rendered her man-bait from a most tender age, meaning that as soon as she became aware of the charms of the male of the species, she Knew those charms in a biblical sense. And indeed, she Knew and Had Been Known By nearly every boy in town at least four times by her seventeenth year, which had no small part in landing her a fabulous summer job at the Burger Bower.

As I approached the Burger Bower, I was surprised to find the parking lot jammed with vehicles of all makes and models, from pickups and motorcycles to semis and skateboards. There was a line of waiting patrons strung out the door and down the block. From the four corners of town, a steady stream of pedestrians was wending its way to the entrance.

I wondered briefly if the Burger Bower had changed its plebian menu of so-so grade beef burgers and substandard fries. I ran my eyes over the folks in line and the figures marching toward the fast food joint. To a one, they were all of masculine bent. I frowned in confusion. Then I spied Opal: the titty twiddler on the roof.

My big sister was on glorious display in broad daylight, clad in a bikini shaped like a pair of cheeseburgers that barely covered her mega muchachas, which swelled out of her comestible bikini top like a pair of over-inflated basketballs. She waved a sign that read, "Burger Bower: The Breast Burgers in Town!"

"Buy a burger!" she called down to the panting males. "If you buy two, I'll blow you a kiss!"

In the sea of testosterone that surged through the parking lot, I shone forth like a lighthouse. Opal's face brightened when she spotted me.

"Hi-ya, Ruby!" she called over the gutter. "Come on up—

I'm bored outta my gourd."

I mounted the roof via a series of vaults and squawking leaps from dumpster to fire escape to drain spout, flailing and hooting in a manner that drew more attention than Opal's bronzed bazooms. Panting, I collapsed on the hot tar beside Opal's plastic deck chair. Opal settled into the chair, sighed delicately, and kicked off her high heels in a Mama-ish way. She thrust a giganto-size soda at me to plug my parched mouth-hole.

"Worn out already, what a day!" she informed me before I could ask. "Life of a working woman, Ruby. I tell ya, you best don't go into the fast food industry when you're old enough to go out for a job. Ain't nothing but grease and grills and ultraviolet rays that'll age you before your time."

"Sha," I slurped desperately at the straw, my hands and knees becoming one with the sun-liquefied tar.

Opal leaned over alluringly, displaying her cheeseburgers for the benefit of the drooling crowd in the Burger Bower parking lot, and began to rub her bare feet. She grinned at me.

"So…how was the exam? Did Dr. Dick do you good with his magical medical fingers? Did he crank you open and peer inside with a flashlight, like Dr. Barney said his kind do?"

"I ain't had the exam yet," I said.

Opal, perceptive to aught generally, perked up as she caught a whiff of the venereal trepidation that emanated from me like a skunk's musk. She uncorked the life-giving beverage from my suckling lips and peered into my eyes.

"What's ailing you, Ruby?"

"I got the dread," I said. "I'm scared of the exam. I wanna know where and in what manner Dr. Dick's planning to jimmy his fingers before he commences doing so."

Opal narrowed her eyes.

"No," she said. "I think there's something else troubling you."

"No, that's really what I—"

"Ah ha! I understand the situation completely," crowed Opal. "You harbor certain feelings for a certain boy in your bosoms, am I right?"

I sighed. My big sister wore a gleeful, mulish smirk on her lips. I'd encountered this smirk before. The only thing to do was concede the point.

"Sure, okay, why not," I replied. "I am enamored of a boy. Tell me: Once I force him to become smitten with me as well, what can I expect him to do…to me…down below?"

Opal's lips and brows pursed in confusion as she pondered this inexplicable question.

"Don't you know?"

"Uh," I replied.

"You don't mean," she gasped. "That you've never…"

She shrieked and fluttered her hands in horror. Then she recalled that she was at work and ought to comport herself professionally. She tossed her hair, shook her chi-chis, and flashed a dazzling smile at the lusty lads down in the parking lot who were wildly waving wads of cash at her.

She turned back to me and snagged my borrowed Fack Sex shirtsleeve.

"You really ain't never, ever…*ever*?! Oh sweet, merciful God! How do you live, Ruby? How…*how*?"

Ever-so-cheered by the stricken shock on my sister's face, I stood and prepared to throw myself from the roof, either to meet my maker on the hot asphalt below, or to find ravishment at the hands of one of Opal's randy fans.

Opal retained her hold on my sleeve and reeled me back in.

"Now, now. Let's not panic," she said. "You and I will never again speak of your late blooming. We'll swear a blood oath under the next dark moon to tell no one of your crushing shame."

"Can't you just tell me what, y'know, goes on when a person, y'know…"

"Well—" Opal began.

A loud crash cut off her words.

She glanced down at the riotous mass of men in the parking lot. They were attempting to batter down the front door of the Burger Bower with a variety of improvised siege implements, ranging from yesterday's greasy sporks to a loudly revving tow truck. She sighed and rose.

"There's no time. I gotta get back inside and sell some burgers before they launch another insurrection and try to steal me away in the confusion again. If you get nervous, just…just keep your eyes closed and try to divert your mind."

Opal gave me a weak smile, hoisted her cheeseburgers securely over her fun bags, opened a small trapdoor in the roof, and slithered down a fireman's pole that had been installed for her to make a grand entrance behind the Burger Bower cash registers. I knew that I wouldn't be welcomed should I make a similar entrance, so I flopped myself back over the drain spout, skidded down the fire escape, and landed unceremoniously in a pile of soggy onion rings at the bottom of the dumpster.

Now reeking of tar and rancid side-dish, I stumped off in the direction of the Vet 'n' Pet Shop. It was time to meet Mama out front.

My steps were as sluggish and my heart was as filled with anxiety as they were three years ago when I trod this very sidewalk toward the Public Library, the threat of a summer of remedial reading looming over me.

When I crossed the threshold of Somwärin's hallowed hall of prose and prosody for only the second time that school year, the librarian gritted her teeth, forced the corners of her mouth up into a smile, and came to greet me.

"Hello, Ruby," she said. "Do you have a book in mind that you'd like to read?"

"There's nothing I want to read," I said. "I'm a terrible reader."

"No!" said the librarian, in a tone of sympathetic outrage. "Who told you such a thing? Children are never terrible readers, they just need practice."

"Teacher says I'm not reading books the right way."

The librarian's face went mock-stern and she planted her hands on her hips.

"Nonsense," she said. "You go pick out three books that

look interesting, read them in your own way, and I'll bet you'll see that you're a wonderful reader."

I perked up.

"Okay!" I said.

I scampered off and seized the three books with the brightest covers in the library. I piled them on the checkout desk. The librarian stamped them and handed them over.

"Remember, there's no wrong way to read a book," she called out, as I scooted away with my trio of tawdry tomes.

I read each and every one of those books cover to cover. In the interest of variety, I read each book in a different way. The librarian had assured me there was no wrong way to read a book, after all.

I read *Slaughterhouse-Five* with a black permanent marker in hand, crossing out every instance of the phrase "so it goes" because it annoyed me. By the time I'd finished the book, it looked like Al Capone's redacted FBI file.

I read *Watchmen* with a companion volume: Pearl's discarded copy of *The Cat in the Hat*. I assiduously cut out Rorschach's dialogue and glued it over the cat's, to augment the nihilistic overtones of the feline protagonist's worldview. Then I snipped every image of Doctor Manhattan's wang from the graphic novel and glued them on Thing One and Thing Two, which made me giggle. Tee-hee—*things*.

I read *Catch-22* in the shower.

When I returned the books, the librarian was apoplectic.

"There *is* a wrong way to read a book!" she sputtered. "In fact, you've discovered three wrong ways. You are a terrible reader, Ruby Bejou, and you are banned from the library for the rest of the school year!"

I departed in disgrace and didn't set foot in the library again until summer.

"What kinda get-up have you got on, Ruby?" a voice cawed, calling me forth from my reverie.

The Bejou family Oldsmobile roared up to park half-on, half-off the curb in front of the Vet 'n' Pet Shop. Mama, on her break from the "bra" and "god" handling of the Fack Sex

Furniture Distribution Warehouse, was sitting behind the wheel. She appeared tense and testy.

"Climb in," she said. "We're gonna ride 'round a bit before the appointment and get our stories straight."

As I was sliding into the passenger seat, I spied Pearl darting out of the Vet 'n' Pet Shop. What a coincidence. I hailed her, but she scampered down a side street and vanished.

Mama, unaware and unconcerned that her youngest daughter was Up To Something, drove us down Main Street with stern resolve. Fine, hot dust sifted like cocoa powder through the open window to coat my arms, which were crossed tight over Mama's borrowed T-shirt.

"Today's the day a sexy, sophisticated woman of the world ensnares Dr. Dick," was Mama's open salvo.

"That woman you, Mama?"

"Damned straight. Dr. Dick didn't see us Bejous at our best when he boarded with us the other night. Today, I'm gonna convince him I'm real classy."

"That right, Mama?"

"Yep. I'm gonna make him lust after me, so when your daddy takes it upon himself to go right to the source and ask the horse, Dr. Dick'll confirm, yes indeedy, he gots the hots for me. Then your daddy'll give up and hit the open road again, and I'll be free of his nonsense for good."

"You sure it'll work?"

"Of course it'll work," Mama snorted. "I'm still super-hot. Crystal-Lynn Bejou's always been able to get any man she sets her cap for. My man-getting powers have only increased with age and experience."

"Mama," I said hesitantly. "I've been thinking. Maybe I can't do this after all."

Mama sighed impatiently.

"Ain't nothing to it—just like going to the dentist. Only at the other end."

"I hate the dentist and I don't wanna do it, Mama! Why don't you just ask him to pretend to be your boyfriend for a couple days, and see if he won't play along? I'll do it for you, if you're scared."

Mama's cheeks went white under her circular rouge job.

"This-here was your plan, Ruby! Don't you double-cross me this late in the game, girl! You keep that troublemaking mouth of yours shut. You hear me? Or else I won't give you the ten dollars I promised you."

"But Mama, when I devised my clever scheme, this wasn't how it was supposed to go—"

"Shut it! I'm on a short fuse. Shorter than normal."

Mama glared at me from under her sky-blue eyelids, unmindful of the road. She pulled a U-turn and we jounced back up Main Street in silence. After a prolonged pause, Mama cleared her throat in a way that I recognized as her Prequel To Serious Sexual Discussion. I squirmed as close to my door as I could.

"Ruby," she said. "I was thinking about this last night. We need a reason why a young girl like yourself'd be needing an Obee-Gee-Why-N visit. I hear that in Big City, a girl'll go get herself an exam after her first roll in the hay…"

Mama gave me a significant glance. I wriggled on the hot vinyl seat and clutched the armrest.

"Quit staring at me, Mama!"

"Well, can we tell him that's the reason I'm bringing you in?"

"No!"

"Damn. Your big sister could've used that excuse eight times over at your age. What's the matter with you?"

"Mama!"

"Ain't none of my business," Mama seemed to realize that she had been advocating promiscuity and snapped her candy-apple lips shut. After a moment, she began again. "Well, they look into mens-troo-al problems, that's for sure. Any mens-troo-al problems, Ruby?"

"No."

"You sure? You ain't spotted blood at the wrong time of the month? You ain't had no weird mucus—"

"Dear God in heaven, take me up!"

135

I rolled down the window and prepared to leap to my salvation.

"Stop that melodrama and blasphemy!" Mama commanded. "Think now: There's gotta be something wrong with a girl like you."

Mama frowned and went silent, hip-deep in gynecological thought. I retracted myself back into the car, watching her suspiciously.

"Oh well, something'll come to me," she said at last.

We pulled up in front of the Vet 'n' Pet Shop and Mama applied the brake. She sat stock-still and sucked in a deep breath. She turned the key in the ignition, shutting off the motor. Her hand was trembling slightly.

Suddenly it hit me that it was really going to happen—Mama wasn't going to back out.

"Mama," I said faintly. "I don't think I can go through with it. Let's just go on home, okay? Please?"

"You're just having an attack of womanly nerves," Mama said in a not-quite-steady voice.

"But Ma—"

"I'll give you twenty dollars."

I hesitated as greed made me consider how many bottles of nail polish this would net me.

Mama perceived my mental dithering and withdrew a crisp twenty-dollar bill from her purse. She waved it to and fro before my eyes, hypnotizing me.

"Just think what you can do with such a fortune," she crooned. "Why, you could treat yourself to an ice cream sundae with the works, and purchase yourself the finest hairspray in town, and buy a whole bag of Söderberg's Suckable Sucrose, and still have the financial resources to bribe your sisters into doing your weekend chores."

Dreamlike, I reached for the bill. Mama withdrew it from my grasp and tore it down the middle. She stuffed one half down her cleavage and handed me the other half.

"You get the rest after the exam," she said.

Weak of will, I nodded. Mama gave me a decisive nod in

return, grabbed my arm, yanked me from the car, and hauled me to the front door. She steadied her home-manicured hand and arranged her face into the sultry, purse-lipped lines of a fancy woman at a fancy nightclub sipping a fancy drink in a fancy soap opera. She took a deep breath and turned the knob.

We crept into the bestial gloom.

"Dr. Dick? Yoo-hoo? You here?" Mama called.

Birds began to shriek at us from cages hanging from the high ceiling. Rodents squeaked on all sides. Mama flinched around the boa constrictor's spindly wicker cage and tiptoed timidly into the depths of the Vet 'n' Pet Shop.

Unsure what to do, I drifted past the rows of kennels and percolating fish tanks, then bumped smack dab into a small cage in which a decorative lizard lay sunning itself under a wee tanning lamp. The cage crashed to the floor and cracked open like a plastic Easter egg. The lizard skittered across the floor on tiny claws, whipping its tail about in alarm.

Mama turned to yell at me, then instantly let out a scream. Mama had a deathly terror of scaly things. She set herself to shrieking and tried to climb the rat cages that lined the wall, until she realized what was in them. She screamed louder and began to jitter-dance around the lizard, which was darting back and forth across the linoleum in a panic.

"Ooooh! Hoooo-noooo!" she hooted, arms pinwheeling as she recoiled to and fro.

Dr. Dick emerged from the obscure door of his office-closet at the other end of the room.

"Is everything alri—"

Mama leapt at him, throwing her skinny self into his arms like a bride going over the threshold.

"Hoo lordy! It's a-comin'! Ooooh Jesus!"

Dr. Dick made to set Mama on her feet, but she clung desperately to his neck.

"Mrs. Bejou—could you—um—ah—"

"Ooooh vile!" Mama screeched.

He staggered, grunted, protested briefly, then gave up and bent to scoop up the lizard with his free hand, deadlifting

Mama's dead weight with one strong arm in the process.

My, my. What a strapping young man. That's what Mama would've appreciatively murmured, had she been coherent.

Mama hopped out of Dr. Dick's arms when the writhing lizard came near her fly-away hair. She wavered to me on jelly legs and clutched me to her special occasion pushed-up bosoms, wheezing and mumbling madly.

Dr. Dick righted the cage and set the lizard inside. Then he turned to us, ever-so nonplussed and well-groomed, like a befuddled newscaster on the TV.

Mama quivered all over like some kind of vibrating dildo, made a great steadying effort, and forced her face to assume a merry mien.

"Hi there, Dr. Dick! We're here for Ruby's appointment, just like we spoke about on the phone," she trilled shrilly.

Maintaining her bright beam of teeth, Mama released me, flicked her hair out of her face, and hissed in my ear, "I'm fixed to die! Go talk to him. I—I—I gotta settle my nerves."

I wasn't sure what to say, but I sauntered up to Dr. Dick and opened my mouth obligingly.

"My sister Opal can belch the song of your choice," was what came out.

Dr. Dick looked more befuddled than ever.

"Uh. Yes. Mrs. Bejou?"

Mama's face came up from the depths of her purse, in which she was rooting for a restorative agent, edible or inhalable. Her eyes were sharp.

"Nobody calls me that, Dr. Dick. I ain't married to that no-good man anymore. You call me Crystal-Lynn."

"Ah," he replied. "I see. Are you two ready?"

"Of course!" Mama forced that gleaming grin again. "Why wouldn't we be? Come, Ruby."

Mama grabbed me by the hand, gave it a quick squeeze of either support or threat, and pulled me into Dr. Dick's carnal cabinet.

I could hear Mama chattering away, but I couldn't see anything, as I had squeezed my eyes shut to avoid glimpsing the sexual torture devices that awaited me.

"And that's when the Lord Himself appeared and said to me, 'Crystal-Lynn, you'd better take that wild child to see Dr. Dick. He'll tell ya what she's been up to with all those boys out back of the school yard.' So here we are, as was commandedeth."

I opened my eyes and my mouth to gape at Mama, and found that I was in a room about the size of our shoebox bathroom back home. It had fake wood paneling on the walls like our bathroom, too. I was standing in the only free floor space. Mama had perched herself on the edge of the utility sink, while Dr. Dick was wedged uncomfortably—but striving for dignity—up against the sharp corner of a menacing metal table. Was it meant for me? It looked cold and mean. I inched—or rather, millimetered—toward the door.

"But," said Dr. Dick, his face all creased up in confusion. "But I'm not sure I undastand what brings you in today. Is Ruby engaging in—"

"Acts of mortal sin! That's right, uh-huh! With a mess of boys. That's what Our Lord and Savior Himself has informed me, so it must be true."

I opened my mouth again, this time to protest the slander upon my good name. Then I reconsidered. To be the town trollop required a heaping helping of good looks and personal magnetism, which I demonstrably didn't have. Perhaps my loose reputation would spread and I would become much sought-after by the boys of Somwärin for the first time in my life. I beamed and tried to cock my hip alluringly, but only succeeded in clocking it on the end of the table.

"So, you...people are very religious, I take it?"

"Everyone's got the spirit of God in them, Dr. Dick," said Mama, solemnly yet somehow sleazily, as she dexterously uncrossed and re-crossed her legs.

"Of...of course. Well. I'll just excuse myself and Ruby can get into a gown."

Dr. Dick limboed under the table, ducked around Mama's legs, and rustled a paper exam gown out of a cardboard box beneath the utility sink. I wrinkled my nose in distaste, but Mama snatched it up eagerly.

"Great, yes, you just step on out and I'll see to this one. Gonna stay in here with y'all for the exam—"

"No!" I bellowed.

"Coz I gotta keep you honest, huh Dr. Dick?" Mama winked lewdly.

"Uh…yes. I'll give you a couple minutes of privacy before I knock."

"Yessirree! You do that! You—oh lordy, I'm looking a fool," Mama wailed the very instant the door closed, leaving us alone. "I can't go on. I'm looking worse with each and every second that passes. Help me, Ruby! Help—"

"I ain't wearing that paper-thingy!"

"Oh yes, you are! Oh yes. You're gonna put this right on, and you're gonna think of something classy and sophisticated to say, coz I got nothing. Oh, God—Dr. Dick doesn't look at all enraptured with me, does he?"

Normally I might attempt a soothing lie, but Mama had me by the shirt and was tugging mercilessly.

"No, Mama, he sure don't," I said from the depths of the cotton T-shirt.

Mama stripped me, cinched me into the paper gown like it was a corset, glanced me over critically, and positioned herself back on the rim of the sink. I stood awkwardly in the middle of the floor, waiting for the tightly tied paper to tear and leave me utterly naked.

"Get up on that table and stop looking so hangdog, like he's some kinda skeevy pervert—"

Dr. Dick's knock sounded, cutting off Mama's imperious—and surely audible—command. I struggled up onto the enormous table.

Mama called graciously, "Come on in, Dr. Dick."

Dr. Dick had pulled on his official white doctoring coat and was looking more composed and in-charge.

"Alright, Ruby. Have you had any physical problems lately? Any symptoms of—"

"No, no, she ain't got any womanly problems at all. I questioned her in the car. I said, 'There must be *something* wrong with you!' But she said…"

Dr. Dick gave Mama a blank look and she shut up. For nearly six whole seconds.

"So, tell me, Dr. Dick," she resumed. "Are we your very first patients?"

"In this particula town, yes, as a matta of fact, you are," replied Dr. Dick, as he tried to get at the sink to wash his hands. Mama just kept on perching and swinging her crossed legs coquettishly.

"Ya married?"

"Could I have you hop down offa the sink for a second?"

"Oh my, yes," said Mama. She leaned in and peered at Dr. Dick while he soaped and scrubbed up. "So, you got a wife?"

"No."

"How fascinating! You got a girl?"

"Mrs. Be—Crystal-Lynn, this is really not an appropriate—"

"How old're you—'bout twenty-eight? Twenty-nine?"

"Did you happen to bring Ruby's medical recads?" Dr. Dick countered.

Mama hesitated. I was impressed that he'd managed to confound her.

"No, those're over at Dr. Flo's. She been Ruby's doc ever since she popped outta me," Mama blurted out, then grimaced at me over Dr. Dick's shoulder, horrified by her own gaucherie.

"So, no wife and no girl," she persisted in a voice spiked with a sliver of desperation. "You aren't gay, are you?"

Dr. Dick shook off his hands and seemed, from the set expression on his face, resolved to ignore Mama and speak only to me. He gave me a reassuring smile and stepped to the end of the terrifying table.

"Okay, Ruby, why don't you scoot on ovah to the edge and lie down. We don't have the usual stirrups yet, I'm afraid."

"Stirrups!" Mama guffawed, then caught Dr. Dick's eye and

muted whatever she'd planned to say next.

I lay back on the hard, chilly table. I heard a *snick-snick* as Dr. Dick pulled on latex gloves. I clenched my fingers around the edges of the table, my arms and legs all spread-eagle and defenseless.

I felt a prodding on my abdomen. I let out a yelp of surprise.

"Does that hurt?"

"No."

"Cold hands, huh?"

"What?"

"The sink only has cold watah," Dr. Dick said. "That's one thing we've got plenty of—cold watah."

I refused to fall for his attempt at folksiness. I gritted my teeth and kept my eyes closed and my muscles tensed.

Suffice it to say, it was nothing like going to the dentist.

Opal's advice echoed in my ears, "Just keep your eyes closed and try to divert your mind."

With nary a transitional sentence, my internal monologue began to recount the sorry story of how I got myself banned for life from the library.

It was Midsummer Eve. Since the day school let out, I'd spent every one of the interminable daylight hours of my summer vacation trapped in the blasted library, plodding my way through the remedial reading caseload that had so long been threatened by my teacher. Because of my previous errors in judgement, the librarian would not permit me to check out any of the precious volumes within her charge. I was required to do my reading under her watchful eye at an empty table, seated upright in a bare chair, with both hands in plain view at all times.

The boredom was driving me mad.

But then Midsummer Eve rolled around: the day before Somwärin's foremost holiday of the year, thanks to the insightful influence of our Nordic nabobs. Everyone grew a bit languorous on Midsummer Eve. Everyone relaxed whatever guard they might normally have up, as visions of hardcore drinking from sunup to sundown on the longest day of the year danced in their heads.

Before I left for a day spent digging literary ditches as a chain gang of one, Mama bade me buy her an essential Midsummer cake-making ingredient at the Fack Sex employee grocery store. Mama's Midsummer cakes were drab, utilitarian affairs. *What if*, I suddenly thought, struck with inspiration in the middle of the Fack Sex employee grocery store. *What if, instead of buying Mama the five-pound bag of workaday* socker *(translation:* sugar*) that she requested, I bought her the five-pound bag of* glitter *(translation:* glitter*) I'd noticed sitting on a shelf two aisles over?*

Not only would Mama discover a lustrous Midsummer surprise when she tore open the bland white bag, her cake would astonish and delight all who partook of its sparkly goodness. She would be thrilled and I would be rewarded.

It was a flawless idea, so I acted on it at once. Off to the library I skipped, my glitzy prize tucked under my arm.

The sight of me bopping into the library with an unmarked paper sack in hand and a gleeful grin on my face would ordinarily have set off all of the librarian's alarm bells. However, woe unto her, when I entered and took my customary seat at the table closest to the checkout desk, she was seated across the room on the floor, surrounded by a gaggle of little kids decked out in their Midsummer Eve finery. She was reading aloud from the world's dullest book, *Pippi Longstocking and the Midsummer Murders*. Many's the time I'd been forced to sit through a recitation of the seasonally-appropriate tale of a plucky young girl, a grizzled police detective one day from retirement, and a brutal serial killer stalking a small Swedish village determined to celebrate the summer holiday in spite of the slayings.

"Books are filled with magic," the librarian was telling the whippersnappers. "The words inside sparkle. They *sparkle!*"

I felt bad for the gullible tots. They were being heartlessly hoodwinked. My eyes drifted to the shelves, which slogged along every wall of the library from north to south and east to west. A barren wasteland of tedious tracts returned my gaze with flat indifference. I'd explored a sufficient cross-section of the locally available canon to avow there was not a single book in the public library that "sparkled." Every one of the tiresome tomes was crammed with spiritless sentences that crab-walked interminably toward the horizon of the page, leaving behind inky footprints like dead runes, not sparkly glitter like…like my five-pound sack of glitter.

Slowly, my eyes slid from the mendacious librarian to the bulging bag of glitter, which leaned, portentous with promise, against my left sneaker.

With a glint in my eyes as gleaming as the glitter (a glint that I couldn't see, but could feel most distinctly beneath my narrowed eyelids), I surreptitiously rose from my chair. Over the course of the storytelling hour, I roved from shelf to shelf with great stealth, sprinkling liberal pinches of rainbow glitter between the pages of romance novels and cookbooks and dictionaries and memoirs and picture books and biographies. The citizens of Somwärin, including the innocent tykes clustered around the librarian (whose eyes never wandered from the page during the course of my escapade), would crack the covers of these bleak books and discover unanticipated enchantment within. It was my Midsummer gift to the town.

"'If you hadn't killed my partner, I wouldn't have to kill you,' Pippi Longstocking growled. She raised the Colt .45 semi-automatic and aimed the gore-spattered barrel. All mercy drained from her ice-blue eyes and she pulled the trigger, sending the Stockholm Slasher careening into the churning depths of Hårsfjärden Fjord. And with that, the Midsummer sun finally sank beneath the blood-red horizon. The end," read the librarian.

With satisfaction, she closed the book and the library, informing us that it would not reopen until the day after Midsummer. I slipped out with the bored-to-catatonia children, my empty glitter sack balled up in my fist. I promptly forgot all about my stunt during the wild bacchanalia that ensued the following day. I extracted a rash Midsummer promise from Mama during her inebriated euphoria: I would be allowed to take three whole days off from my remedial reading duties. As Mama gradually crawled out from under her hangover the day after Midsummer, I happily lounged around the trailer, watching the Sissy Spacek Movie Marathon and losing all the literacy I'd gained over the course of the summer.

But the next day, right as *A Private Matter* was beginning, Mama suddenly stormed home from work, her eyes wide with news that had stunned her into full sobriety. She grabbed me by the arm and dragged me into town. Straight to the library.

Inside we found a howling librarian encircled by a swirling storm of glitter. Sparkly drifts lay along each shelf, shimmery dunes were piled in corners, the very air was filled with scintillating clouds. The librarian stood mired in the middle of it, shaking book after book from which glitter showered.

"You did this!" she shrieked. "I don't know how or when, but I know it was you! I vacuum and dust, but it keeps coming. Who will clean out the library? You," she howled, pointing a sparkly finger at me. "Are banned from the library for life. Banned…for…life!"

Word of my disgrace swept the town with record speed. It was all anyone could talk about. I was the only person ever to be banned for life from the public library. It was the greatest humiliation of my life. In fact, th—

"Well, Mrs. Be—Crystal-Lynn, she hasn't been having vaginal sex," Dr. Dick interrupted, ungloving and turning to Mama.

Mama cocked her head.

"How's that again?"

"Her hymen is intact."

"Looks like Jesus was way off base yet again," said Mama, hopping off the sink. "Get up and back into your clothes, Ruby."

"But don't you want me to finish the exam? Just because there's no evidence of vaginal intacourse, it doesn't mean—"

"Whoa-ho! Hold it now. Ain't no girl of mine take it in the mouth or the pooper. I raised 'em right."

Dr. Dick watched in speechless shock as Mama swooped

my T-shirt and shorts on over the paper gown, thrust her purse at me to hold, and began a slow and somewhat abbreviated sashay across the brief expanse of linoleum.

Toward him.

"Thanks a bunch, Dr. Dick. You sure are some doctor."

She had him in her sights; she was bearing down on him.

"I'll be seeing you around town plenty, I expect. In fact," Mama fluttered first her dagger nails, then her stiletto eyelashes. "Maybe you and me could step out for an evening. Show ya the lively nightlife hereabouts."

"Um…" Dr. Dick's eyes darted wildly.

He was treed and without recourse. I'd have me a new stepdaddy within a month.

"Shall—shall I…" he fumbled.

"Yes, Dr. Dick?"

Mama leaned in, her hand poised to adjust his necktie, or worse.

"Shall I bill you directly for the exam? Or your insurance?"

"Bill?"

Mama froze. Her eyes took on an alarmed gleam. She had underestimated the wits and wiles of young Dr. Dick.

"You *are* insured, aren't you?"

Uninsured-Mama hadn't counted on having to fork over hard cash for this spurious appointment. She'd assumed Dr. Dick would fall under her spell and the exam would be but an unpaid traffic ticket on the road of love.

She burst out, "I see, I see! Send the bill to Fack Sex Corporate Headquarters in Stockholm. It'll take a while for them to see to it, but don't you worry—them Swedes are a thorough and contentious breed."

"But—"

Mama darted out of the exam room, dragging me by the wrist, pursued by Dr. Dick.

"Goodbye, see ya around, Dr. Dick!" she called. "You really are some doctor!"

And with that, Mama fled the Vet 'n' Pet Shop, towing me urgently behind her. She dashed to the car, jumped in, and threw the lock on the passenger door before I could get in.

"Mama!" I wailed, pumping the handle.

"Ain't no time for that! I gotta get to work—gotta hide my lie from the supervisory staff across the Atlantic. Find your own way home. Oh lordy, what a disaster!"

Mama blew away in a cloud of dust, exhaust, and muffled curses. I was left standing in the middle of Main Street with the paper gown crinkling under my clothes and my shoes on the wrong feet.

I stood alone in the street for a spell. The exam had left me supremely underwhelmed. I felt prodded and passed over, like an unripe cantaloupe in the grocery store. It was barely any different than when Dr. Flo gave me my yearly check-up. Except Dr. Dick hadn't muttered about the machinations of the feminine hygiene industry or come at me with a terrifying booster shot needle.

What to do now?

Disillusioned, I wandered down Main Street in the direction of home. As I neared the Pubic Library, I saw 3-J still hunkered down in his hiding spot across the street, his face rapt as he stared at the sealed structure.

I wondered if that was the exact spot he and Daddy had hidden while waiting for darkness to fall so they could break into the glitter-fouled space. As the sun set that night three years ago, the town had been a-buzz with gleeful gossip about my misdeed. I would never be able to hold up my head in Somwärin again. The librarian's words were on everyone's lips: "Who would clean out the library? *Who*?"

I never figured out why Daddy chose that particular night to carry out his daring after-dark raid. I hadn't caught a glimpse of, nor heard a word from, Daddy for a couple years, due to the *EXTREME*! indictment. Surely it was a coincidence that he took it upon himself to bedevil the library mere hours after I was banned.

Daddy certainly "cleaned out" the library, leaving not a single, solitary volume on a single, solitary shelf. That was bad enough, but the following night, after discovering the library was now supplemented with a smattering of porn, the townspeople spied Daddy loitering beneath the Tree of Contemplation and chuckling at their consternation. They pursued him in a mob. Daddy was lucky to escape with his life, making a flying leap like an impala into 3-J's fast-moving rig as it barreled up Main Street just ahead of the furious horde.

Within a week of the incident, the town had a collective change of heart. Everyone was delighted with the library's new collection. The town council called a general meeting to discuss the issue with the populace. A vote was held, and it was unanimous: The books were gone for good, and the porn was here to stay. The librarian quit in a huff on the spot and the sheriff-mayor, raising both arms above his head, declared to the assembled citizenry, "We are ALL the librarian now!"

A blow-up sex doll was placed behind the checkout desk as a cheeky mascot to remind the good people of Somwärin of their duty. Everyone in town took it upon themselves to sort and catalog the library's materials, order new stock, enforce due dates, initiate reading programs for youngsters, and keep out the enemy, which unfortunately was me. After the library received its X-rating, I tried to slip inside to see what the fuss was all about. I was immediately set upon by friend and foe alike, and cast roughly out into the street.

My steps slowed. I glanced at the Pubic Library, then at 3-J.

I paused.

I considered.

I took a step toward 3-J.

A black cat darted across my path.

I took another step toward 3-J.

An ominous roll of thunder sounded in the distance.

I took another step toward 3-J. Then another and another and another.

A flock of ravens took flight.

I tapped 3-J on the shoulder. I opened my mouth. I said, "I'm bored."

A mirror within the Swedish Embassy & Beauty Parlor & Coffee Shop spontaneously shattered.

Thus, it began.

Chapter Seven
The Tooth Witch

Tuesday, June 18
6:17 p.m.

"Girls! Get on out here—I have news."

Mama exploded through the front door of the trailer. Her arms were laden with cartons of food from the Fack Sex cafeteria and her eyes were aglow with mingled confidence and cunning.

Her arrival roused me. I lifted my heavy head from the flattened cushions of the sofa and squinted at her. I'd spent the entire day awash in apathy, staring with glazed eyes at the Sissy Spacek Movie Marathon, and waiting for 3-J to turn up. By the time *Missing*, the final movie of the day, came on, I was so thoroughly steeped in a honey-thick sludge of ennui that I couldn't concentrate on the film at all. Much as I ordinarily enjoyed any account of the 1973 Chilean coup d'état, all I could think about was 3-J's package.

After our disastrous bid to breach the formidable defenses of the Pubic Library the day before (immediate discovery, alarm bells tolling on high, a throng of angry citizens descending upon us, a harrowing flight into the wilderness, and a grim trek home unencumbered by pornography), 3-J had attempted to cheer me up with an intriguing promise.

"Tomorrow I'll show you something that'll put a smile back on your face. It always does the trick for me," he said. "I'll show you my package."

Instantly my curiosity was piqued and my disappointment over our failure was forgotten.

"It's real unusual," he continued. "You've never seen anything like it before. And if you promise to be real, real gentle, I might even let you touch it."

Well, that sealed the deal. From the moment I awoke at the mature hour of nine this morning until the present moment,

I'd been on pins and needles to get 3-J alone and take a gander at his package.

Unfortunately, he'd made no appearance as yet.

Mama marched past me into the kitchen. I rolled myself off the couch and followed her.

As she deposited the cartons on the table, Pearl emerged from our bedroom and Opal strolled in from the yard, fanning her sweaty tank top away from her yum-yums.

"We're going to Big City to see the Wild World of Wrasslin's Man Versus Beast exhibition match tonight!" Mama announced, brandishing a brace of tickets.

My heart surged.

"For real, Mama?" I said.

"Oh, Mama, what a treat!" Opal clapped her hands and beamed.

Pearl began to hop up and down.

"Oh wow!" she cried. "Oh wow, oh wow, oh wow!"

The Man Versus Beast exhibition match had been long-anticipated 'round these parts, and had just as long been sold out. Among other rarefied entertainments on the docket, there was to be a no-holds-barred fight between a man in a bear-suit and a bear in a man-suit. Before my sisters and I could caper away, giving physical expression to the excitement this unanticipated windfall warranted, Mama added portentously, "Yes, I've formulated such a scheme as has never before been conceived by the female mind."

She laid the tickets out on the tabletop like a winning poker hand, placed her hands upon her hips, and looked at each of us in turn.

"I got to thinking today while I was toiling to provide the three of you with home and hearth. I realized that my former plan to enrapture Dr. Dick through general flirtation while he's plying his trade will never work. My subtle ministrations haven't hit pay dirt and time is running out. Then, like a bolt from the blue, a foolproof plan came to me. Follow!" she ordered, hustling out of the kitchen toward her bedroom.

We three girls obediently dogged her as she threw open the

door to her closet and began to reap armloads of garments made of synthetic fibers. She threshed those unripe in hue to the floor, winnowing the shiniest, tightest, and unsubtlest into piles on the worn coverlet of her bed.

"My plan, which hatched full-grown in my brain a mere three hours ago, is as follows. Step one: I acquired us six tickets to tonight's wrestling match."

"How'd you ever get 'em, Mama?" I asked.

"I have my ways," Mama replied cryptically.

"Why six tickets, Mama?" Opal inquired.

"Four are for you girls and myself. One is for 3-J," Mama made a sour pickle face. "If he's hell-bent on serving as your daddy's in-house spy, I'll be blamed if I won't put him to work as a double agent. The sixth and final ticket is for Dr. Dick."

"Dr. Dick agreed to go to a wrestling match?" I said incredulously. "With *us*?"

"He doesn't know he's going to a wrestling match yet," Mama replied.

She stripped off her work uniform of regulation blue and yellow Fack Sex Furniture Distribution Warehouse T-shirt and non-regulation black micro-mini skirt. She snatched up three low-cut blouses and hung them about her shoulders, scrutinizing herself in the warped, cardboard-backed mirror that hung askew on the back of her closet door.

"Step two," Mama went on. "After I obtained the tickets, I called Dr. Dick up and invited him to a friendly family dinner."

"And he actually accepted?" Opal gasped in shock.

"Well, not at first. But he was plumb fascinated by the Tooth Witch, so—"

"The Tooth Witch?" Opal shuddered. "How on earth did he find out about her?"

"I told him about her."

"Why?" I cried. "Why would you tell him about the source of ultimate horror?"

"The subject came up in casual conversation," Mama replied.

"But how?" Pearl demanded.

"That's neither here nor there. The upshot of my phone call was I managed to plant an interest in the Tooth Witch in Dr. Dick's mind, pried outta him the fact that he likes Chinese food, and maneuvered him into accepting an invitation to our home tonight, coz we're having his favorite food *and* the Tooth Witch to dinner."

"What?!" we girls shrieked.

"It's not true, is it, Mama?"

"Is it?"

"Mama?"

Mama tossed the blouses aside and reached for a trio of see-through crop tops. She held them up one by one, studied her reflection critically, and teased her blond hair with her long fingernails.

"While he's dining with us, I'll initiate step three: Casually mention the exhibition match and the extra ticket, and invite him to come along. He can't turn down a neighborly invitation without being rude, and he seems averse to being rude. While we're at the match, I'll launch step four: Ply him with domestic beer, let the bestial passion of the man-on-beast aggression enflame his blood, then make my move. That's my foolproof four-step plan."

I saw how it was. The entire evening, start to finish, was itself to be an exhibition match—an exhibition match designed to convince 3-J (and, by proxy, Daddy) that Mama was enmeshed in a torrid love affair. Mama turned away from the mirror and pointed a sharp fingernail, pistol-style, at the lineup of us girls.

"Now it's time to put my plan into action. Pearl: You go find 3-J and tell him to get in here for dinner—and in a respectable, non-intoxicated state, if possible. Opal: You use your fast food prep skills to make that Fack Sex fare seem Oriental in origin. And Ruby: You trot off and invite the Tooth Witch to dine with us."

I let out a wail of terror.

"Mama, no! She gives me the heebies. She's demonic."

"The only reason Dr. Dick agreed to set foot in our home

again is because I told him she's a good friend of ours. You best get friendly with her quick."

I looked to my sisters for support, but both had darted away, only too happy to let me be damned forever while they escaped scot-free.

"Mama, please," I said. "Think of my immortal soul!"

"Go on, hurry now, I'm losing patience with you!" Mama blared, coming at me all wild-eyed and draped with violently swinging sleeves.

Fearing the immediate peril of an enraged mama slightly more than the impending perdition that awaited me, I dashed out into the orange heat of early evening. With a gulp of dread, I began to walk toward the hauntedest trailer in all of Texas.

As I approached the dust-enshrouded, cobweb-ensconced caravan in the darkest corner of the trailer park, I began to tremble. The Tooth Witch was Somwärin's most ancient resident—not simply in age, but in length of residency. Some said she and her trailer had lain buried beneath the Texan soil since the beginning of time, just waiting for unsuspecting mortals to migrate into her gnarled grip. Legend had it, when the rag-tag gaggle of burned out ex-hippies pitched their tents on the grounds of what would one day be the Somwärin Trailer Park and RV Pleasure Garden, her caravan had pushed its way up through the soil into their midst, like a tooth cutting through the resisting gums of a sobbing child.

She was the reason no one, but *no one,* in Somwärin ever left spare change lying around.

It was known that if you casually scooped a handful of coins out of your pocket and dropped them on your dresser, or deposited a jingling tip on your table as you left the Swedish Embassy & Beauty Parlor & Coffee Shop, or saw a penny and did not pick it up, all day long you would have worse than bad luck. You would be visited by the Tooth Witch.

Loose change attracted the Tooth Witch just as her fairy counterpart was attracted by loose teeth. But where the beneficent fairy would discover your discarded tooth and replace it with a shiny new nickel, the Tooth Witch would fall upon your dull dimes and burnished bicentennial quarters and replace them with teeth. Many had been driven to the edge of eldritch insanity by the discovery of a collection of yellow horse molars or a handful of lethal rattlesnake fangs or a scattering of shrew incisors like grains of spilled salt where they'd tossed their vending machine change just last night.

She was rarely seen, but when she was, everyone in the trailer park ran for their lives emitting crazed cries, one hand flashing heavy metal devil horns to ward her off, the other balled in a tight fist around their wallet or coin purse. She had been the terror of my days and the star of my nightmares for as long as I could remember.

I edged up the creaking metal stairs of the decaying trailer with its peeling curls of red paint and air of abomination. I raised my fist. Swallowing hard, I knocked. From within came the sound of scuffling little steps—terrible scurrying sounds that brought to mind rats scampering behind thin walls.

I nearly ran. I was scared out of my skin.

The door swung inward on howling hinges, raising the hair on my arms. A dense cloud of silver smoke billowed within the night-black doorway. It coalesced to frame a tiny, wizened human form.

The Tooth Witch abruptly poked her head out into the bright sunset glow, robbing me of my breath. She was smoking a thick cigar, her steel-gray hair wound into a tight bun, her broad face as crinkled and cracked as a sun-dried riverbed.

"I…I…I…" I stammered.

The Tooth Witch regarded me blandly, one wee claw of a hand perched on her hip, the other working the cigar around her knife-slash mouth in a slow circle.

"I…I…I…"

Oh, how I wanted to turn tail and flee screaming for the safe space under my bed! But, though the undercarriage of my sleeper was a haven from monsters and bogeymen, it wouldn't protect me from the wrath of Mama.

"Dinner," I managed to gasp out. "With us. Your neighbors, the Bejous. Come."

The witch cocked her head and shouted, "*UH?*"

I yelped and nearly fell off her decrepit porch.

"Dinner," I repeated in a quavering voice. "At my house. Come with me, please?"

"Uh?"

I bit my lip, steadied my nerves, and grabbed the old woman's leaf-dry hand. It crunched unnaturally within my palm. I shuddered.

"Come," I said.

I tugged gingerly, and to my surprise and alarm, she stepped out of her trailer to follow me.

Fully committed to my unholy task now, I led the Tooth Witch through the trailer park under the shocked and horrified eyes of the other residents. Children ran. Dogs yelped and dragged their bellies in the dust. Grown men fell to their knees and sobbed.

Inside the Bejou family trailer, I steered the Tooth Witch over to the couch, released her hand, and pointed at the dented cushions.

"Sit," I said. "Okay?"

I edged away. The Tooth Witch extinguished her cigar in Mama's askkopp ashtray and pursued me like my wicked shadow as I made for the kitchen. At the table, I found Opal dumping soy sauce liberally over the gravlax, gubbröra, and kroppkakor that Mama had gathered for our evening meal.

"Hey, Ruby, did you—ah! AH!"

Opal screeched when she beheld the Tooth Witch standing right there on our very own linoleum, her squat form exuding occult power all over our clean countertops and dishware. Opal brandished the half-empty bottle of soy sauce, clearly meaning to break it as seen on TV and fend off the Tooth Witch with the jagged, salty shards.

At this moment, Mama sashayed in, clad in aught but bra, panties, and mismatched neon house-shoes, a skimpy dress draped over each arm.

"Opal, you got the pipeline into what men find sexually provocative these days. Which one of these—oh my!"

When she beheld the Tooth Witch, instinctive fear caused her to forget that the unholy necromancer was our invited guest. Mama held up the two skin-tight frocks like a pair of shields.

Then she remembered her Foolproof Four-Step Plan.

Slowly Mama lowered the dresses. She drew in a shuddery breath. She beamed a tremulous smile at the Tooth Witch, carefully avoiding the hypnotic eyes that had not blinked even once since she opened the door to her haunted trailer.

"Yes! Good, yes!" Mama bleated. "Welcome, we're gonna enjoy us a neighborly dinner tonight, that's right. Well! Have a seat in the living room; dinner's almost ready but we got us another guest to wait for. Ruby, why didn't you offer…*her* a seat on the couch? Make yourself at home, Mrs….um…ma'am."

Mama booked it for her bedroom. She slammed the door, leaving the three of us alone in the kitchen. Opal gradually lowered the soy sauce bottle, her eyes lost in the midnight orbs of the Tooth Witch.

"Ruby," Opal spoke in a serpentine hiss between gritted teeth. "I think she's put a spell on me. I can't move."

The Tooth Witch angled her head slightly at the soy sauce bottle, which steadily dripped black liquid onto the linoleum, forming a murky pool around Opal's bare feet. Her mouth twitched and seemed about to shape itself into a malevolent grin. Clearly, I would have to intervene, but I was too frightened to stir.

Fortunately, at this point, there came a desperate pounding on the front door.

"Help! Help me, someone—she's got my wrist! Someone call her off, fathalovagawd!"

That would be Dr. Dick.

I hustled into the living room and threw open the front door. Our town's young ob-gyn lunged at me. His hair was astray and his tweedy jacket had been rent asunder in many places.

"Wicked hell!" he cried, desperately shaking his left wrist, to which Bitch-Girl had attached her teeth.

I grabbed our scraggly corn-husk broom, which was always close at hand for such occasions. By means of three judicious jabs, I managed to extract Dr. Dick's wrist and send Bitch-Girl yipping away into the depths of the trailer park.

"Mama!" I hollered gracelessly. "Dr. Dick's here. Ya best put some clothes on."

Ordinarily, Mama would have hollered back at me: something pejorative, something loaded with four-letter words. But she wanted to make a good impression.

"Be right there, sweetness!" she called musically. "Did you offer Dr. Dick a cold beverage?"

"Would you like a cold beverage?" I offered.

Dr. Dick's face was the color of a rain-soaked raspberry. He crouched with his hands on his knees in the middle of our golden shag rug, panting desperately.

"I think the teeth broke the skin! I think I'm bleeding. I should go to the hospital—what if that dawg is rabid? It must be rabid!"

"Naw, Dr. Barney has captured Bitch-Girl many times to vaccinate and de-worm her for the good of Somwärin and the beast herself. Some say her bad-tempered meanness is natural. Others," I lowered my voice, glancing around cautiously. "Others say the Tooth Witch stole Bitch-Girl's favorite fang and used it in a spell that turned her evil. *She* is abiding in our kitchen as we speak. Don't look toward the kitchen, Dr. Dick. You'll lose your soul."

As is the way of witches, now was the time that the Tooth Witch chose to materialize within the doorway. I cried aloud and leapt back. Dr. Dick, ignorant Yankee that he was, reacted not with dread but with embarrassed courtesy. He drew in a self-composing breath and stood up straight. He smoothed his shredded jacket and extended his unmauled hand to the Tooth Witch.

"It's a pleasah to meet you," he said. "I apologize for my appearance. I'm afraid I had a little run-in with a dawg. I undastand you're a specialist in orthodontics. I'm sorry, but

Mrs. Bejou neva did tell me your correct name...?"

The Tooth Witch regarded Dr. Dick and his outstretched hand. The silence between them grew uncomfortable, then taut, then epic. Dr. Dick's smile and hand began to waver. The Tooth Witch abruptly slapped his palm in what might have been a curse-activating act of violence, or a sideways gimme-five.

I didn't want to find out which it was. I availed myself of the distraction and fled to the kitchen, where Opal was hiding. Just as my big sister and I had settled ourselves into a comfortable cower under the kitchen table, Mama breezed in. She was poured into her tightest, pinkest, spandexiest halter dress, which featured yellow racing stripes down both sides and a checkered flag on the rump, inspired by the hide-no-secrets bicycle shorts of the Tour de France.

"Girls! What-all are you doing? Quit crouching down there on the linoleum. Opal, are you done fussing with the food? Where are them nice paper plates you ripped off from the Burger Bower? Ruby, you go bring our guests in to supper."

I rose and tiptoed into the living room. The Tooth Witch and Dr. Dick were seated side-by-side on the couch, eyeing one another in silence.

"Dr. Dick," I whispered. "Break free! Release yourself from her spell. Come hide in the kitchen with me. Dinner's ready; we can eat while we take refuge beneath the table, where *she* won't be able to get us."

I held out my hand beseechingly.

Just then, a hot-pink-and-yellow freight train roared into the living room.

"Howdy, Dr. Dick! Welcome back to my home. Knew you couldn't stay away for long. Can't keep any man away once he gets a taste of Crystal-Lynn!"

Mama came to a high-heeled halt within kissing range of Dr. Dick. She leaned down to give him a preview of her cleavage, then made to brush at the flying threads of tweed to which his jacket had been reduced by dog attack.

Dr. Dick attempted to rise: perhaps in gentlemanly dinner-guest fashion, perhaps to get his face out of Mama's hooters. Blocked on one side by our supernatural visitor and head-on by Mama's jigglies, he hesitated, then feinted adroitly to his left and slid over the arm of the couch.

"Um, yes. Thank you for inviting me. I wonda," he lowered his voice with a tactful glance at the impassive yet searing face of the Tooth Witch. "I wonda if our dinna companion is a bit hard of hearing? I asked her if she has retired from her dentistry practice, where she went to dental school, what her area of orthodontic specialty might be, but she hasn't said a word."

Mama planted her hands on her hips and frowned in confusion at Dr. Dick.

"What're you talking about? Oh, you mean the Tooth Witch! She ain't deaf, she's just diabolical."

Dr. Dick glanced at the Tooth Witch, then at Mama.

"I beg your pardon?"

In lieu of elucidation, Mama opted for high-class manners.

"Dinner is served, Dr. Dick."

She made a deep bow at the waist, gesturing with wide arms like a figure skater finishing up a routine.

Dr. Dick uneasily stepped past my even-more-cleavage-revealing mama. She waited until he'd gotten a good look, then popped upright and was hot on his trail before he could gain the sanctuary of the kitchen. I made to follow.

"Ruby! Our guest," she hissed, jerking her head at the Tooth Witch.

I, the caretaker of Satan's octogenarian bride, timidly took the bloodless hand and tugged the witch to yet another location she didn't necessarily care to visit.

In the kitchen, Mama was boob-a-liciously shoving Dr. Dick into a chair at the head of our meager table.

"Best seat in the house; it's a genuine Kafé Köksstol courtesy of the Fack Sex Furniture Distribution Warehouse's Employee Discount Product Purchase Program—or F.S.F.D.W.E.D.P.P.P. for short. Guaranteed ergonomic and easy to assemble."

At this moment, young Pearl bounded through the side door into the kitchen.

"Mama! I finally found him!"

My sister was leading a scruffy man by the hand.

"He was passed out beneath his truck amongst the weeds and dozens of empty beer cans. I splashed oily puddle water on his face and he perked right up, so I think he ain't too drunk after all."

When Pearl beheld who I myself was leading by the hand, she squealed and hid herself behind Mama's slickery, checkerboard-plastered rear.

I was much-cheered to see 3-J, mellowed as he was by a day spent drinking downmarket American beer in the shade beneath his semi truck. He waved at each of us in turn with sleepy eyes. When his gaze fell upon my quadrant of the kitchen, it brightened considerably.

Before I could become flattered, he exclaimed, "Well! Threes and eights, good to be layin' an eye on ya—am I comin' out the windows?"

The Tooth Witch's raw-wound mouth spread to resemble the gaping maw of hell itself. Her ruddy gums were completely devoid of teeth. She yanked her hand out of mine and whip-cracked one of her sideways-fives against 3-J's outstretched palm.

"Threes 'n' eights 'n' all good numbers—I'm readin' ya! Been gobbin' the barley pop?"

"That's a big ten-four and affirmatory, got your ears on?"

"Ten-ten on the side."

"What's the good word on the buffalo?"

"Darktime on my end," the Tooth Witch replied, shrugging. "Wrap it up an' take it back."

3-J spun one of our guaranteed ergonomic and easy to assemble köksstols around and settled in with the back of the chair snugly secured against his crotch. He planted both elbows on the tabletop and leaned across to leer at Dr. Dick.

"Howdy and greetings, stranger. I can't say I know you. I can't say I was expecting to find a man in my good buddy's house, that's for sure."

"3-J," Mama put in hastily. "This-here's Somwärin's new physician of womanly anatomy and feminine functions. He's the one I told you about. Remember? The…*one*…I told you about?"

Mama was replete with winks and elbow nudges. 3-J let his eyes fall half-closed. He appeared to be reaching back into the murky depths of his memory, shuffling through a variety of intoxicated recollections. His eyes abruptly flew open and he pointed an accusing finger first at Mama, then at Dr. Dick.

"Ah-ha! This is the guy! This is the guy that you—"

"Yes, yes, I told you various things concerning him and his presence and whatnot and so forth. Yes, indeedy!"

Mama's voice was at bellow-level, a volume with which she could have masked the sound of an incoming 747 jumbo jet.

"Then you're the guy I must study," 3-J concluded, inclining his head to peer speculatively at Dr. Dick, his eyebrows perched high on his forehead, his eyelids at half-mast.

Poor Dr. Dick shifted uncomfortably.

"Um," he said. He extended his hand warily, in light of the palm-slapping that had prevailed throughout the evening. "Pleased to meet you. I'm Dacta Richard Grant."

3-J contemplated the outstretched hand, then took it in his and shook it.

"Good to know you, Dick," he replied. "John Jesse James Whitehead's the name, 3-J's the handle. Best not get too comfortable in this palatial abode. When Crystal-Lynn's magnificent ex-husband is restored to his seat of honor at this-here table, there'll be no room for the likes of you. But I'm glad enough to share a meal with ya tonight."

Mama's tightly-contained body shot sizzling lightning bolts of disapproval in 3-J's direction as she dished up the Asianized Swedish food.

"You get your elbows off my table, 3-J. God knows where they've been."

3-J sniffed the air like a bloodhound.

"What-all's on the menu tonight? It smells different-like."

"Elbows!" Mama barked, then shoved her head under the table. "Opal! You get on out here and be sociable."

My big sister shakily crawled out from under the table and mounted the köksstol next to Dr. Dick. She glanced across the table at the silent Tooth Witch, who sat next to 3-J. She moaned and glommed her globular goodies up against Dr. Dick's upper arm for protection. Dr. Dick cleared his throat awkwardly and fiddled with his fork.

Mama thunked a flimsy paper plate in front of 3-J. Within the circular geography of the plate, islands of food swam in lakes of noxious black fluid. He leaned down and obtained himself a big whiff. He immediately recoiled.

"Rank as a ten-day roadkill left to marinate in a flooded ditch outside El Paso," he opined.

Mama leaned close to 3-J's ear.

"You shut your goddamned pie-hole right here and now, or I'll take out after you with a pair of metal tongs and a steak mallet all up and down the trailer park, you hear me?" she ordered in a perfectly audible whisper.

Mama seemed to sense Dr. Dick's eyes on her. She turned her head and flashed him an overboard smile of reassurance, exposing a rack of drugstore-whitened teeth all the way back to the molars. She placed Dr. Dick's paper plate before him with deft ceremony, then spread her hands in a gracious gesture that encompassed the exotic repast before us.

"Please, I encourage y'all to dig in," she proclaimed.

We did so and, as one, immediately spat our mouthfuls back onto our Burger Bower plates.

"Oh, holy pal Jesus!" 3-J sputtered.

"Could, please, watah, please?" Dr. Dick clutched at his throat, his face redder than it was following Bitch-Girl's vicious attack.

"What did you do to this stuff, Opal?" I cried.

"Manners! Manners! Elbows!" Mama exclaimed, her saran-wrapped body jouncing as she clapped her hands together to put a stop to our antics.

The Tooth Witch rose on stubby legs and gathered up our plates.

"Worse'n a choke 'n' puke outsida Shaky-Town," she said. Shaking her head disapprovingly, she pitched the plates into the garbage pail and shuffled to the cupboards.

"Hag-bag done whipped out the inheritance powder! Keep it between the ditches, coz I'm gonna die in a short-short, that's a Q.S.L.," 3-J groaned.

"Ten-four," the Tooth Witch replied, as she began to rummage amongst our canned goods.

"See," 3-J wheezed, turning on Mama. "This-here's why the sage Mr. Don Bejou says womenfolk should only learn that which can be put to use within the confines of the family home. Cooking, for instance."

"Don't you start with that nonsense," Mama choked out, warring to contain both 3-J's reminiscences of her ex-husband and an unladylike gag as she tasted the meal before her.

"Your once and future husband would never accept such poisonous cuisinery on his dinner table. You best beware, Dr. Dick. This may ever and always be your fate come suppertime, lest you take measures."

Mama jumped to her feet and began to laugh maniacally.

"Ha-ha-ha, yes—anyway! Anyway! Let's change the subject, shall we? How's your new job going, Opal-baby? I hear sales are up four-hundred twenty-three percent since they put ya up on the roof at the Burger Bower. Takes all kinds to make the economy roll along, don't it, Dr. Dick? I mean, look at what you do for a living! Couldn't pay me enough to stick my digits into the secret holes of my friends and neighbors. I've been meaning to ask: How much do you make?"

"Gaelic good numbers, steer ya right," the Tooth Witch declared, thunking a box of Lucky Charms and a stack of bowls onto the table.

"Oh, what humiliation! Cereal, and not even the nutritious bran kind!" Mama wailed sotto voce, before picking up her spoon and flashing a falsely confident smile at Dr. Dick. "How fun! Breakfast of Champions, but for dinner so's we can be champions in the afterhours, oh yes, enjoy!"

With more than a little suspicion, Dr. Dick accepted the milkless bowl of magical marshmallows that the Tooth Witch handed him. Our loud crunching filled the small kitchen; a locust-like munching that made conversation impossible. When Pearl rose to fetch the milk, the Tooth Witch flailed a stout arm and jabbered alarmingly, sending Pearl into a dry-sobbing cower beneath Opal's massive left boob.

Thus far, the evening was not delivering the pleasurable entertainment and sense of discovery I had anticipated when I awoke this morning. I wondered if 3-J had forgotten about his promise to show me his package.

"It's funny colored," he'd told me yesterday, as we made the final mile roundabout the backway to the Somwärin Trailer Park and RV Pleasure Garden. "And if you shake it, the sucker makes a peculiar noise."

I sighed and gazed across the table at him.

3-J raised his eyes and frowned back at me quizzically. Then he broke into a knowing grin, held out his hands about eight inches apart, and nodded.

I was filled with joy. He hadn't forgotten!

"Ah…" he sighed as he pushed his empty bowl away. "That leprechaun can kidnap me and sell me as a seven-year slave to the Emerald Isle any day of the week."

Mama took this as a sign that she could end the ill-fated dinner.

"All done, everyone? Good!"

She snatched away our bowls. She dared not reach for the Tooth Witch's dish, however. It stood denuded of marshmallows, which the witch had rapidly and methodically sorted by shape, then deposited into various pockets on her person.

"Shall we adjourn to the living room? Not you three!" Mama snapped over her shoulder as my sisters and I rose.

She took Dr. Dick forcibly by the arm.

"Come and relax in the fåtölj, Dr. Dick. I remember how you enjoyed it during your recent sojourn in our home."

3-J took the fast lane into the living room, swerved around the pair, and parked himself in the fåtölj before Dr. Dick could reach it.

"Can't beat the Swedish for their knowledge of the human buttocks and the support thereof," he said, wallowing luxuriously.

A scowl darkened Mama's face; then, in a psychotically rapid reversal of expression, her features became wreathed with delight.

"Sit here next to me on the sofa," she urged, seizing Dr. Dick by the hand and pulling him down to lose himself among the saggy cushions with her.

We three girls clustered in the doorway to spy upon the adults in their postprandial repose. A hush, not altogether peaceful, fell over the living room. The Tooth Witch, seated primly on the sofa to Dr. Dick's left, opened her toothless mouth wide. She began to sing in a high voice.

"It's your nickel; I'm monitoring," 3-J enthused, slapping his thigh along to the tuneless, wandering melody.

"Interesting," Dr. Dick ventured. "I expect that's some form of Chinese opera? The Met commissioned an intriguing reinterpretation of *General Chao and the Ninety-Six Featherless Roostas* several seasons ago. I was too busy with my surgical rotation at the time to make it down to New Yawk, but I heard—"

The Tooth Witch abruptly broke off her song. She turned her head impossibly far to the right, as if castors were embedded within her inhuman neck. She stared at Dr. Dick.

"Chow?" she inquired. "Wanna smokemup?"

"Um," Dr. Dick replied.

"That's a big ten-four!" 3-J said eagerly.

"What—um—"

"Ignore those two," Mama said, clutching Dr. Dick's hand relentlessly within hers. "So, you were telling about surgery on roosters to make them featherless? That'll be so convenient! No more goose-bumpy skin on the fryers at the market. I wonder why we don't call 'em chicken-bumps? I personally can't recall the last time I saw a goose, much less one plucked bare of its plumage."

"I seen a goose get into a fight one time with a squirrel, and that honker lost a whole clean sweep of feathers right offa his butt-region," said 3-J. "Them's was goose-bumps, alright."

The Tooth Witch reached into one of her marshmallow-ridden pockets and pulled out two strips of white paper. She laid them across her knees and withdrew a silken pouch from another pocket.

"What I've always wondered is why chickens still got wings nowadays. The damned things can't fly worth two beans, and the wings ain't the meatiest part on their bodies. Why ain't they being bred with four fat drumsticks?"

"A four-legged chicken," 3-J marveled. "I'd buy me one of them at any price!"

The Tooth Witch sprinkled a thick line of olive-green herbage down the middle of each piece of paper. 3-J watched with salivating enthusiasm. Dr. Dick watched too, but with growing alarm. Mama chattered on, oblivious.

"The suckers would sell like wildfire. It's a million-dollar idea, I'm telling you."

"I'd enter my four-legged chicken in the Saturday night cockfight out on Farmer Bill's back acre, and just see if we didn't take home the prize pot in three seconds flat."

3-J thrashed his arms and legs violently, emitting a series of clucks, crows, and karate cries to demonstrate the fighting form of the mutant chicken.

The Tooth Witch rolled up the paper taquitos on her lap and dragged a stumpy pink tongue over the edges of the papers.

"If you ask me, a featherless chicken might be just as deadly as a four-legged one. You could dress it up in a little suit of armor and ain't no talons could hurt it," Mama speculated.

"Armor's against the rules. So are geese. I tried to enter that squirrel-brawler last summer, but Farmer Bill said nothing doing."

The Tooth Witch rose and presented 3-J with a fat, paper-wrapped "cigar."

"Smokemup," she proclaimed.

"Preesheaydit. You got a light, Dick?"

Dr. Dick's eyes were saucers.

"Never mind, I got me a scrap of flint here in my pocket."

"Smokemup," the witch said, presenting the other super-joint to Mama, who at last took notice of the impending drug use in her living room.

3-J dug deep within his painted-on trucker jeans, but before he could withdraw his caveman fire kit, Mama jumped to her feet and snatched the smokemup from his hand.

"You give me that! You know well and good I don't allow narcotics within these four walls of mine. I've a good mind to kick you sky-high towards the state penitentiary!"

Mama cast the joints across the living room in impressive spirals worthy of a pro quarterback. They came to rest under the ändbordet upon which the TV stood, looking like two fat grubs nesting beneath a log in the forest.

3-J assumed the tragic face of a little boy whose ice cream cone has been grabbed by a bully.

"Oh!"

He struggled to emerge from the fåtölj and fetch his goodies, but was sucked down by the relaxing Swedish lifestyle-technology. Mama commandeered the floor, both hands held above her head.

"We're getting off track, here," she said. "We need to stick to the plan, and the plan is this: We're alla us gonna head, right this very minute, to Big City where we will take in the Wild World of Wrasslin's Man Versus Beast match. Once-a-year event, sold out for ages, but I used my connections to secure us tickets. And you will be our very special guest, Dr. Dick."

"Hey, right on, Crystal-Lynn!" 3-J whooped, pumping his fist in the air.

"Four on that!" the Tooth Witch said, her chubby body wriggling within the sausage casing of her floral housedress.

"Ah, well, that's very generous of you," said Dr. Dick. "However, I must regretfully decline. But thank you."

Mama, having just fished the six tickets from the depths of her cleavage, turned to gape at him. Her expression was crestfallen.

"What?" she said.

"What?" 3-J exclaimed.

"Ten-nine?" the Tooth Witch growled.

Dr. Dick glanced at the stricken countenances around him.

"I can't say I'm a great connoisseur of professional wrestling," he said.

3-J's indignation sent him vaulting from the grasp of the fåtölj to loom over Dr. Dick. He poked his square-nailed finger thrice into Dr. Dick's chest.

"Wrasslin's a man's sport. Are you a real man? Then you're a-coming with us," he said. "You think you can deny the brotherly code and send me by my lonesome all the way to Big City with this passel of clucking hens? You damned well *are* coming! Besides, if you wanna woo Crystal-Lynn, you gotta—"

"3-J! Ix-nay!"

This came not from the Tooth Witch, but from suddenly bilingual Mama, goaded by desperation to recall the pig Latin of her childhood.

"And you're hookin' onto our convoy, too, ya ol' lot lizard. Copy that?" 3-J informed the Bejou family's drug dealer, who clapped her wrinkled hands.

"Copy, copy!" she said happily.

Mama stretched her thickly painted lips into a grimace that pretended to be a smile.

"Now, 3-J, we only got six tickets, and the match is clean sold out. You understand?"

As 3-J commenced a befuddled count on his fingers, Dr. Dick rose.

"Well, that settles it. I wouldn't dream of taking a ticket away from a true aficionado of the…sport," he said.

"I'll stay home, Mama," Pearl piped up.

Both Opal and I stared at her, agog. She was the most ardent fan in the entire town.

"I got business to conduct tonight," Pearl said, her eyes

filled with sinister intrigue and dark plotting. "Serious business."

"Then that's that," 3-J replied gleefully, slapping his thighs with both hands.

"To the Oldsmobile, y'all!" Mama blared, clamping a hand over Dr. Dick's bicep.

We piled into the family roadster, and off we set for Big City: population eight-thousand. Visions of funnel cake and violent men in tiny briefs filled my head as Mama drove us up the highway through the gloomy, gloamy evening haze.

Upfront with Mama and her supposed lover, 3-J clapped a buddy-buddy hand on the shoulder of his default best friend for the evening.

"So, how many wrasslin' matches have you taken in, Dick?"

"Well," he said. "None."

Our gasps drowned out the coughing motor of the Oldsmobile.

"What sort of cultural backwater do you hail from, man?" 3-J sputtered.

"Bean Town," the Tooth Witch snorted.

"Don't worry, Dr. Dick. We'll see to it you're educated properly so as not to embarrass yourself," Mama put in, anxious to ameliorate the ignorance of her presumed beloved.

"First match of the evening's man versus cat in a bathtub full of water," Opal said.

"Then it'll be man versus kangaroo, with a twist. Instead of the traditional boxing match, they gotta wrestle their way out of a big ol' pouch," said Mama. "Like a giant kangaroo pouch—you following me?"

"This you'll never believe. It'll blow your mind. Seriously— it's never been done before, anywhere, ever," said 3-J. "Are you ready? Man versus bull. Ha! Can you believe it? A man's gonna fight a bull. A bull!"

"Three years ago, they had a man versus dog match, and they entered Bitch-Girl, and she maimed so many competitors, referees, spectators, paramedics, and SWAT team officers that she was banned from ever competing again," I said. "She won a hundred bucks, though."

"But here's the best part: They're gonna give the man a cape to wave at the bull, to encourage it to fight. And what color do you suppose that cape's gonna be? You'll never guess. Never. Can you guess? Red! Waving a red cape at a bull—how did they ever come up with that?" said 3-J.

"The Soothsayer put the word out that the chupacabra that lives outside Southernmost Sweden is fixing to fight this year, but I don't know if I believe that," said Mama. "He's mythological. And a pacifist."

"And here's the even better best part: The man's gonna have him a sword, and he's gonna try to stab the bull! By gum, who thought of such an original idea?" said 3-J.

"The final match of the night's gonna be man versus man," said Opal.

"Coz who among us can say he ain't truly a beast?" insinuated 3-J, nudging Dr. Dick in the ribs and waggling his eyebrows up and down.

"Man," said Mama. "The deadliest prey."

"You best watch your back, Dick, or you might end up Crystal-Lynn's prey—"

"Ix-freakin-NAY, 3-J!"

"Oh…dear…Gawd," Dr. Dick whispered into his dog-mangled tie.

The jam-packed parking lot of Big City Arena was lit like the outskirts of heaven by ultra-intense floodlights. Mama maneuvered our land boat into a compact slot in the remotest corner of the lot. Even at such a distance, the din of patriotic warm 'em up songs and the bouquet of deep-fried wrestling comestibles were intoxicating.

"You take our tickets and go on ahead with Opal, Dr. Dick. She'll get you good and comfortable in your seat."

Mama took me by surprise, offering Dr. Dick the chance to revel in the charms of her bustiest—and nearest-to-legal—daughter, all alone and unsupervised. As soon as Dr. Dick had staggered off with my big sister jouncing on his arm, the reason for Mama's bequest of the ever-distracting Opal became clear.

"Now you listen good," Mama snarled, seizing 3-J by the front of his raggedy T-shirt and dragging him down to go nose-to-nose with her. "Me and Dr. Dick have been quarreling as of late. That's why us-two are acting all stiff and unfamiliar with each other. East Coast men pretend like they ain't in a relationship when they're having a disagreement with their girlfriend. It's their queer custom."

"Ahhh," 3-J said, nodding sagely. "I sensed that something was afoot."

"You respect Dr. Dick's bizarre upbringing and don't allude to his and my state of couplehood again, you hear me?"

"Mums."

3-J made a complicated gesture around the area of his lips.

Mama gave him a fierce nod and set out with purposeful, pavement-wrecking stiletto heel strides toward the main gate.

When we reached the ticket turnstiles, however, we were in for a rude shock.

"There seems to be a bit of a problem," Dr. Dick offered in a discreet voice.

"These-here tickets are crap, Mama!" Opal wailed at top volume, thrusting the brace of rainbow-emblazoned cardstock strips at Mama.

Mama examined the tickets for the first time, squinting at the fine print.

"These-here tickets are base counterfeits!" she cried. "Says so right here: 'Fake tickets for Crystal-Lynn Bejou.' My underworld connections have once again done me a false turn."

There was nothing to do but decamp and troop dispiritedly back to the car. Dr. Dick for his part had a relieved spring in his step.

"I…I…such a situation!" Mama stammered. "How can I rightly apologize for such a profound disappointment?"

"Don't mention it," he replied cheerfully.

"Yoink!"

Taking advantage of Mama's embarrassed bewilderment,

3-J yanked the car keys from her hand.

"I insist upon driving," he said.

Mama was in such a tizzy that she didn't protest. She merely climbed through the passenger's side door and pressed herself close to Dr. Dick.

"Such a tragic letdown!" she murmured, plucking at Dr. Dick's frayed sleeve as 3-J pulled out onto the highway with truckerish swivels of his head and the mandatory leaning of his elbow out the open driver's side window.

"The night is cool and clear. Smokey Bear's hibernating this p.m. and the city kitty's takin' a nap. We got us a happy hunting ground running straight down the gray ribbon," 3-J announced, perplexing me until I realized he was habitually chatting as if into his CB radio.

"Ten-four," replied the Tooth Witch, who was seated between Opal and me in the backseat.

"Dr. Dick, how can we Bejous ever rectify this awful tragedy?"

"Don't worry about it."

Dr. Dick's voice was positively chipper as he none-too-subtly glanced at his wristwatch and smiled about the unmissed TV show that surely awaited him back at his apartment.

Bitter disappointment was coursing through my veins. I had so longed to see the man-on-animal carnage!

But there was one silver lining to our communal misfortune. Once we regained the homefront, I could get 3-J away from the prying eyes of my nosy family and satanic neighbor, and finally look upon—and possibly handle—his much-vaunted package. "Sometimes," he informed me yesterday. "When I'm feeling blue, I like to sit in the cab of my truck and hold it in both hands. That always puts me back in a good mood." I hoped it would do the same for me.

In his element on the open road, 3-J sped faster and faster, his sandy fringe of hair fluttering beneath his baseball cap. Under the sheltering tent of the stars above, his eyes took on a proprietary gleam. They darted from side to side across the windshield, then sharpened as they beheld a speck of steel roosting in our lane barely a mile up ahead. The shape gradually resolved within the twin cones of our high beams into a slow-moving motor vehicle.

"One side! Down in front," 3-J hollered into the whipping wind, flashing his brights and honking the horn in the familiar rhythm of a 1980s power ballad.

The little car in our lane simply slowed down further. 3-J's eyes narrowed and he clenched down on the hand lotion scented steering wheel.

"I'm gonna tailgate that no-cylinder comedian," he announced.

With professional efficiency and a disturbing lack of hesitation, 3-J swerved to ride the double yellow lines separating our car from on-coming traffic. He held the wheel with one hand, and jabbed the other out the window to display his middle finger. Blaring horns from carloads of wrestling fans on their way to the arena provided a lively soundtrack as 3-J swiftly closed in on the bumper of the brilliant green hatchback, whose dumbly staring taillights, bemusedly smiling bumper, and low-hanging tongue of a license plate brought to mind a Mr. Yuk sticker.

"That unaesthetic make and model don't deserve to dwell upon the highways of the great U.S. of A," 3-J growled. "I'm gonna clear him off the road for the good of my fellow Americans."

"Perhaps you would care to dine with us tomorrow, under more intimate circumstances that I can assure you you'll enjoy better? I just gotta find some way to make this up to—what the hell're you doing, 3-J?" Mama shrieked, returning to reality when her gaze chanced to alight upon the speedometer, then the bare arm's-length distance of our car from the enemy vehicle before us.

"Don't you squall, now," 3-J commanded into the night, his head thrust entirely out the window. "This is how we professionals keep the flow of traffic steady on our country's thoroughfares. It's a public service."

"Ten-four on that," said the Tooth Witch.

"You get off his ass right the hell now, 3-J! If you wreck my car, don't even entertain the notion that you're long for this life! I will tear you five new ones and thread the remainder of your sorry ass through 'em like I'm lacing a shit-kickin' boot, I swear to almighty Christ!" Mama screamed, deafening and dismaying Dr. Dick.

Undeterred, 3-J took both hands off the wheel to wave them, drowning man in a lake style, at the lollygagging car. He knelt on the driver's seat, with nary a foot on the gas or brake pedal.

"Off the road!" he shouted. "Clear off!"

Somehow, untouched by human hand, the Oldsmobile's engine revved and we edged to within a hair's breadth of the green car's bumper. I glanced at the Tooth Witch. A shudder of uncanny understanding shook me when I saw her tiny foot pumping vigorously against an invisible gas pedal, while her tiny hands mimed the handling of an unseen steering wheel.

Alas for us all, a sleek Cadillac suddenly appeared on the horizon. It bore down upon us in the oncoming lane and, fatally, 3-J ignored it. He redoubled his catcalls, infusing them with scraps of profanity in an array of highway tongues, and banged his fists against the body of the Bejou family roadster to emphasize his wild disapproval of the obstructive vehicle. And at that very moment, the strangely familiar black Cadillac was upon us.

In a symphony of brake shrieks and powerhouse engine whoops, the Cadillac hauled itself in a U-turn out of oncoming traffic and planted itself on our tail. A palpable rush shuddered through our car as the outer surface of the Cadillac lit up with dozens of flashing red and blue lights of varied size, shape, and shade.

"It's the sheriff-mayor!" Opal cried.

"Oh sweet, handsome, erotic Jesus," Mama moaned, covering her eyes with both hands.

"I can outrun him," 3-J declared.

He pulled himself through the window and back into the car. He gripped the wheel with the rigid arms and white knuckles of one who has done this many times before. Both he and the Tooth Witch floored the gas and jerked the wheel, sending us into oncoming traffic where we were met with a seagull-like choir of squawking horns.

We darted around the little hatchback, unwitting cause of our lawless state, and attained ninety-eight miles per hour in the wide-open lane. Behind us, the sheriff-mayor followed suit.

"Stop, 3-J! Are you out of your ever-lovin' mind?" Mama cried.

"Pull ovah! Pull ovah for the police offica! He's not a reasonable man," Dr. Dick pleaded.

"Breeze it!" hooted the Tooth Witch, perhaps in alarm, perhaps in elation.

"Dear God, don't let me die before I get my chance to try for Miss Somwärin," Opal wailed.

"You still harping on about that?" said 3-J.

"I got me the entry form in secret. I was gonna sneak over and file it tomorrow," she said. "I think I can win. I gotta at least try. Even with my…assets."

3-J craned his head around to stare at the assets in the backseat, inadvertently letting up on the accelerator. The sheriff-mayor used the opportunity to speed around us and halt his Cadillac lengthwise across the road a quarter of a mile up, blocking our lane.

"Stop!" Mama and Dr. Dick chorused.

3-J managed to tear his eyes away from Opal's ovoids and yelped at the sight of the cop car. He rammed the brake to the floor and skidded to a stop barely a foot from the blue-and-red Christmas tree of justice.

"Oh Gawd, oh Gawd," panted Dr. Dick, his eyes closed, his hand unconsciously squeezing Mama's knee, much to her pleasure. So delighted was she that she was hard-pressed to look away from Dr. Dick's terror-stricken face, even as the sheriff-mayor of Somwärin exited his vehicle and angrily huffed in a circle around our overheating car thrice, whacking at the hot metal with his nightstick in wordless disapprobation.

The sheriff-mayor sputtered a chain of vowels that didn't

quite resolve into a word, then drew his revolver and pointed it at 3-J.

"License! License now!" he bellowed into the open driver's side window.

3-J withdrew a worn card from the inner brim of his baseball cap and offered it with a calm lack of contrition that turned the sheriff-mayor's face red. When he read the text printed thereupon, his face darkened to purple.

"This-here's a CDL! You're a trucker! A trucker running from The Law. Reckless road hogging at its worst—I should have known. Wait…wait just a minute and a half. I recognize you. You're that troublemaker buddy of Don Bejou. And you," the sheriff-mayor peered into the car and leveled both his eyes and his revolver at the hyperventilating Dr. Dick. "You, sir, are under indictment in Somwärin! If you were just six-point-two miles up the road, I'd run you into jail and lock you in the fatalest cell of all, from which no man has yet emerged whole of limb or sane of mind, don't you doubt me none!"

The sheriff-mayor puffed and flapped with frustration as he scanned each of our faces.

"Speeding! Tailgating! Tooth Witch on board! If you were within my jurisdiction, there ain't no end to the arrests I'd make and the tickets I'd issue. I'd radio for the Big City sheriff, but she and I got us a mutual dislike and general feud going, so there ain't nothing to be done about you law-breaking hooligans. If only this-here car was six-point-two miles up the road!"

The sheriff-mayor kicked the front tire wrathfully.

"What I oughta do is drive ahead and lie in wait at Somwärin town limits, then fall on y'all like Thor's hammer when ya try to slink home. However, I got me a ticket to tonight's wrasslin' match, and it's been sold out for months."

His revolver drooped against his thigh in impotent rage. With a parting roar, the sheriff-mayor stomped back to his Cadillac, killed the colorful lights, and pulled back into the lane leading toward Big City Arena.

The silence within the Oldsmobile was thick and heady.

"Give me the keys," Mama ordered in a dreadful voice. "Lest I perform homicide and dump your body here in the lawless outskirts of Big City."

Mama drove us at a cautious clip back to Somwärin. She halted on Main Street in front of Dr. Dick's apartment above the Vet 'n' Pet Shop. She turned to him with appealing eyes.

"Dr. Dick, I just wanna apologize again—"

Before she could get any further words out, Dr. Dick had fled in a genuine run up the steps to his front door. He yanked it open and slammed it behind him. A light dawned in his front window and he pulled the curtains firmly closed. He did not peep out at us even once. Fully deflated, Mama pointed the Oldsmobile toward the Somwärin Trailer Park and RV Pleasure Garden.

"Another wacky adventure for me," 3-J laughed.

Mama sank five false fingernails deep into his thigh, warping his chuckle into a scream of pain.

"What kind of madman are you, 3-J? Ain't you got the basic ability to be present in society for more than half an hour without breaking the law? Such a disaster of a night—and it's all your fault."

"What harm did I do? The ticket snafu was your doing. Your car and Dr. Dick are just as they were at the outset of the evening. Meanwhile, we all learned Opal's ridiculous secret, which will amuse us for days to come. Seems like everything's copacetic to me, ten-four?"

"Big ten-four," the Tooth Witch replied, eyeing Mama pointedly.

As she pulled the Oldsmobile into our gravel-covered parking space, Mama threw up her hands in defeat.

"At least Diamond Don Desmond's Highway Lawbreakers show wasn't filming! Dr. Dick would never speak to me again if he had to appear on courtroom TV and be shamed for his reckless conduct within a motor vehicle."

We got out of the car with sighs and dour faces. Mama tugged her man-trap dress down to a respectable level and rubbed a hand over her flamboyantly made-up face.

"Well, Mrs. Whatever, Ruby here will conduct you home…"

But when she turned to the spot where the Tooth Witch had been standing, there was nothing but an ankle-high swirl of dust. We peered into the darkness, but she had utterly and mysteriously vanished.

Inside, the ganja cigars had also vanished.

"Oh no," 3-J intoned. "My smokemup!"

He settled on his knees on the carpet, disappointment clouding his face.

"Suddenly the tragedy of this night is becoming clear to me," he said sadly.

"Opal, honey," said Mama. "You really serious about entering that pageant?"

Opal nodded.

"I gotta at least try," she said.

"Right about now, that bullfight's probably happening. I was so keen to see that," 3-J sighed. "Man stabbing a big ol' bull with a sword. What a sight. But…I don't guess that would feel nice to the bull, would it? Probably might hurt a bit. Probably might hurt a lot. Probably might even…kill the good ol' bull, wouldn't it?"

"Well, if you're set on competing for the crown, let's make hay of this debacle and find you a suitable outfit from my haute couture. There's a sequin-studded fanny skirt that'll knock them judges dead," said Mama, putting an arm around Opal's shoulders.

"That poor bull! All he wanted to do was wrestle a man for the joy of the sport. Now he's likely dead. I feel myself falling into a funk," said 3-J, rising and shambling toward the front door. "There's only one thing that'll pull me out of such a blue frame of mind."

"Beer," scoffed Mama, as he pulled the door open and exited.

Twenty minutes later, I found myself seated in the cab of 3-J's semi. Behind the front seats was a sleeper compartment with a narrow bed spread with dingy sheets and a battered pillow. Up front in the driver's seat next to me sat 3-J. With a secretive smile, he reached down and pulled out his package.

"Here it is," he announced proudly. "Wanna hold it?"

I nodded and held out my hands.

"It's smaller than I expected," I said.

3-J frowned in admonishment.

"It ain't the size that matters, it's how you wrap it."

I took the package, which was a perfect cube about eight inches on each side. It was covered with yellow and red striped wrapping paper. I held it in my hands for a moment, then shook it gently. A funny sort of jingling sound came to my ears.

"What's inside?" I asked.

"Dunno," said 3-J. "Your daddy gave me that-there package nigh on five years ago for my birthday. Nobody ever gave me a birthday present before. I've been trying to guess what's inside ever since."

"Why don't you open it?" I said.

3-J shook his head.

"That would spoil the surprise. Many a lonely night, when your daddy and I are driving long-haul through some desolate stretch of flatland, I get on my CB with him and I try to guess what it might be. He says I got close once about two years ago, but I can't remember what I guessed. All I know is it's something amazing. Let's guess together right now, Ruby. What do you suppose is inside my package?"

Chapter Eight
The House Of Man-Catching Beauty

Wednesday, June 18
3:03 p.m.

"Now the trick is," whispered 3-J. "To get in and out without anyone seeing us. If we're caught…"

He didn't need to finish; I knew how dreadful the consequences would be. Hunched behind a shopping cart in the parking lot of the Fack Sex employee grocery store, we held in our hands capacious sacks and wore on our persons many-pocketed jackets, the better to conceal things in.

"Remember, this-here's a Class-D criminal violation we're about to commit," 3-J said, pulling his baseball hat down low over his eyes to conceal his too-recognizable visage. "The store employees've been warned not to pursue or attempt to detain those what commit this all-too-common retail crime. But that don't mean they won't call the sheriff-mayor, who will surely apprehend and frisk us within an inch of our lives. The key is to ditch the goods before he nabs us."

I hadn't woken up this morning with the intention of committing a petty misdemeanor with an experienced felon, but circumstances had led me inexorably down this path.

Though word had reached all Fack Sex employees that the truckers would arrive en masse today, and though Mama had warned us girls not to set foot outside the trailer for our own safety, Opal awoke bound and determined to turn in her Miss Somwärin entry form. Bright and early, Pearl and I had accompanied our big sister into town to lend moral support and bodily protection as she signed on for what would surely be the greatest humiliation of her life. Our familial altruism quickly evaporated, however, when we beheld the sprawling herd of women milling about out front of the Celestial Temple of Psychedelic Truth and City Administration.

Young and old, married and unmarried, of good moral

character and not so much, it seemed as if every woman in town had lined up to put her name in the hat for the illustrious title of Miss Somwärin. The lowing of the ladies was deafening.

Nervous but excited, Opal took a deep breath, gripped her entry form tight to her chestuses, and took her place at the back of the line. When the crowd sighted her and her rotund rack, a wave of guffaws and grumbles swept from one end of the feminine flock to the other.

I reluctantly sidled in to stand beside her.

At a small folding table beneath the Tree of Contemplation sat the Gentleman Gym Teacher, emcee of the pageant. One by one, each prospective beauty queen stepped up and presented her entry form—and herself—for his inspection.

"This is gonna take hours," I muttered to Pearl.

I received no response. I swiveled my head from side to side, but my little sister had mysteriously vanished, as was her wont these days.

After fifteen minutes of sighing and shifting, I wandered away, too. As I prepared to roam the town aimlessly, aim abruptly struck me in the form of 3-J, who was skulking around the dumpster behind the Vet 'n' Pet Shop. And the rest was about to go down in history as the greatest act of third-degree criminal mischief ever committed in Somwärin.

"You ready?" said 3-J.

I nodded.

"Pure stealth," he whispered out of the corner of his mouth. He straightened up and assumed a casual posture, his hands thrust deep into his capacious jacket pockets. "You hit the makeup aisle, I'll take the produce section."

I gripped my sack filled with outlandish artifacts, which 3-J and I had spent hours collecting: an empty Burger Bower French fry carton stuffed with dry grass, an annotated copy of *The Somwärin Soothsayer: A Not-Yet-Newspaper*, three crow's feathers stuck together with a piece of dried-out Wrigley's chewing gum, and a plaid scrunchy with mud in the seams and a few stray blond hairs still tangled around it.

We were about to engage in the act of "shop-laying," a

retail transgression invented by Daddy some years back. After obtaining our precious detritus from the garbage cans and gutters of Somwärin, 3-J and I had laboriously counterfeited wildly inflated price tags, which we affixed to each objet de trash that swelled our pockets and bulged from our bags. Now was the moment to carry out the scheme whose prep work had consumed the better part of the past four hours. We would saunter casually through the Fack Sex employee grocery store, lay our unauthorized items on the shelves at random, and wait for mayhem to ensue.

"Six-hundred and thirty-five dollars for a cigarette butt smeared with Cherries in the Snow lipstick? I can get that for half as much in Big City! This is outrageous," the shoppers would be heard to say.

3-J took one step toward the Fack Sex employee grocery store, then froze. The automatic doors slid open, revealing Mama, a fresh pack of cigarettes in one hand, nothing at all in the other. She raised her eyes, then her free-to-strike hand when she beheld 3-J.

"Just what are you—" she began.

3-J let out a yelp of terror and fled. I made to do the same, but Mama whipped out that unencumbered hand and snagged my upper arm.

"What're you up to? Why aren't you safe at home? Didn't I warn you them truckers are on the very outskirts of town?"

"I—I—I—" said I.

"No time for your cunning wordcraft," Mama said. "I guess I'll just have to take you along on my daring after-work enterprise."

Holding me firmly by the arm to prevent absconding à la 3-J, Mama marched us up Main Street, past the line of would-be Miss Somwärins in which Opal was still patiently waiting, straight to the Swedish Embassy & Beauty Parlor & Coffee Shop.

"You gonna get a cinnamon bun?" I inquired hopefully.

"Nope," Mama replied.

"You gonna get another ambassadorial pardon for showing

up late to work?"

"Nope."

"You ain't gonna get…a haircut?" I said incredulously.

"I'm gonna," Mama said grimly. "Get gossip. The best gossip. And not just get—I'm gonna give gossip as well. In order to accomplish this substantial task, I gotta let the Swedish ambassador do something unnatural and abhorrent to me. I gotta let him give me a haircut."

I gasped.

Mama never let the Swedish ambassador cut her hair. Though my sisters and I adored the rare luxury of getting our locks stylishly snipped by our town's foreign official, Mama was adamant that not a strand of the teased blond umbrella that shaded her head would ever be hewed by his sharp shears. She preferred to maintain her mane herself, clipping the split ends periodically whilst seated in front of the TV, a 1970s-era episode of "The Lawrence Welk Show" blaring at full volume.

As ambassador, our town's only hairdresser-cum-restauranteur had three duties: assist his fellow Swedes when they found themselves stranded in Somwärin; represent the motherland at social shindigs; and keep abreast of cultural, economic, and political developments within his host realm.

The Swedish ambassador carried out the first of these duties never, although a sad, dust-covered desk topped with a tarnished brass plaque reading "Svenska Ambassaden" stood in a corner of the Swedish Embassy & Beauty Parlor & Coffee Shop, should a straying Swede someday become shipwrecked on Somwärin's soil-locked shore.

He enacted the second of his duties with formal Nordic efficiency on a daily basis within the coffee shop. As Somwärin's only public gathering place, besides the jail, it was the citizenry's preferred site for regular meet-and-greets, goodwill receptions, and milestone celebrations. The Swedish ambassador always proved himself a discreet, polite host.

But it was as backdoor governmental informant that the Swedish ambassador truly shined. His lips were sealed when serving coffee and sorting the yellowing embassy forms that were never deployed on behalf of his countrymen. But as soon as he stepped across the invisible barrier that separated the embassy and coffee shop from the beauty parlor, he blossomed into an espionage operative worthy of the CIA, MI5, and the KGB combined.

"I need to get the good word on what the town's saying about me and Dr. Dick," said Mama. "If the gossip's turned in my favor, I can rest easy and let the damned truckers and your damned daddy roll into town when they damned well please. But if news of last night's fiasco has caused folks to doubt the authenticity of our romantic relationship, I'll have to do damage control and plant the seeds of better rumors for the Swedish ambassador to sow."

As I wondered how a person could sow seeds that had already been planted, Mama gave my arm a yank and made a gimme-here motion with her free hand.

"I'm gonna need that half-twenty back from you."

"No way!" I cried. "I earned that fair and square with my bathing suit region."

"I need cash to pay for the haircut, and I'm fair short right now."

"Nah-uh! I ain't giving up my fee for services rendered."

"I see that you drive a hard bargain," said Mama, fishing her half of the torn twenty-dollar bill from the fathoms-below of her cleavage. "Tell you what. I'll make each half of this-here twenty-dollar bill become whole come payday. Yes, that's right—your twenty-dollar fee for undergoing Dr. Dick's queer exam will be transformed into forty dollars! Just for loaning your poor, selfless mama some cash when she's down on her luck."

I was thrilled. Forty dollars! What a fortune.

"Okay, Mama!" I said, pulling my half of the twenty from the sweaty bowels of my left sneaker and handing it over. I was a smooth operator. Perhaps I could go into loan sharking when I came of age.

As we entered the Swedish Embassy & Beauty Parlor & Coffee Shop, a grape-shaped cluster of bells above the door gave forth a silvery dingle. Like a pair of landed aristocrats, Mama and I strolled through the coffee shop, past the forlorn embassy, straight into the candy-pink and gilt-gilded décor of the beauty parlor. Crystals winked translucent rainbows from all surfaces. Magic mirrors and luminous light fixtures flattered our faces. Dreamy fairy windchimes tinkled in a faint, unseen breeze. The beauty parlor promised splendor and romance, and it did so in gold script that hung framed on the wall above the elegant cash register.

Man-Catching Hairstyles
The Borgholm Bob: Responsible for 18 marriage proposals
The Falköping Flip: Inspiration for 32 love letters
*The Stockholm Starlet: 27 ex-boyfriends left speechless and
heartbroken when unexpectedly encountered at the
Fack Sex employee grocery store*

On and on it went, chronicling the real-world success of each hairstyle. At the bottom of the list was an asterisk—an asterisk of shame for we Bejous.

*We refuse to provide the Somwärin She-Mullet, as this was the hairstyle with which Crystal-Lynn Bejou attracted Mr. Don Bejou, miscreant.

The Swedish ambassador was alone in the Swedish Embassy & Beauty Parlor & Coffee Shop, curled up in one of the salon chairs, listening to "Dancing Queen" by ABBA and reading a Wallander murder novel. Mama cleared her throat. He looked up. He jumped to his feet. He shoved the book under the chair cushion and switched the music off.

"Välkommen till Konungariket Sverige: För Sverige i tiden," he said, his face red. "What may I do for you ladies this fine afternoon? A coffee?"

"No, no," laughed Mama, the very picture of docile surrender and coy supplication. "I finally realized, after all these years, that I can't hold out any longer. My hair is, as you've so often pointed out, a raging disaster of outta style feather-cut malfeasance. I need your help. Will you cut my hair?"

Mama gave the Swedish ambassador the puppy dog eyes and he clapped his hands together with delight.

"Such wonderful news!" he exclaimed. "How long have I waited for this day!"

Then his face darkened.

"But lest we forget what happened the last time you were here."

"Oh that," Mama said lightly. "Lookie here: I only got one daughter with me this time. And she ain't prone to bickering disruptively, not like those other two."

The Swedish ambassador did not appear convinced. He turned to the cash register and retrieved two crisp sheets of paper from a drawer beneath it.

"Please fill out this simple form attesting to your acquiescence of culpability for last week's expulsion from Swedish soil, as well as this petition for readmission to the country of Sweden."

"Oh, now, can't we just forget alla that?" said Mama.

"Please to fill out the paperwork," he replied sternly.

Mama swallowed her grunt of exasperation, choking slightly as it went down, and forced a willing smile.

"Anything you say," she replied, glancing illiterately at the tangle of Swedish gobbledygook and scrawling her name at the bottom of each page.

She handed over the forms. The Swedish ambassador scanned them intently. Then his scowl melted into what was, for him, a radiant smile.

"Now we may begin our great work," he said, whisking Mama into a salon chair and draping her with a sheet of shimmery rose satin fringed with scarlet lace.

"Which is the man-catching hairstyle you have in your mind?" he inquired.

"Oh," said Mama, with faux helplessness. "You know I ain't got a speck of taste when it comes to the topiary arts. I'd be tickled to death if you'd pick out what you think would suit me best."

The Swedish ambassador looked tickled to death himself.

"Of a certainty!" he said.

He opened another drawer beneath the cash register and pulled out a thick album of hairstyles. He opened it and began to peruse, his lips slightly pursed.

"I'm surprised there ain't no other customers today," said Mama, watching him as he turned the pages with brisk decisiveness.

"Indeed, this is the first moment of peacefulness I have seen all day," he replied. "So many ladies have become infected with the Miss Somwärin pageant fever. Uncounted dozens thronged my door this morning to have their hair done before queuing to submit their paperwork. So many braids and curls did I make today. Such excitement in the air!"

"You must be all kinds of excited about the pageant yourself," said Mama.

"Ah!" said the Swedish ambassador ecstatically. "The idea is beyond your fathoming. What an honor it is that a great political personage shall be in attendance at our humble pageant!"

"Come again?"

"Mayor Häri Härison of Härisverige," said the Swedish ambassador. "For our sister city's mayor to journey so far, simply to pay a visit to our town—ah! I am standing beside myself."

"Sure, yeah, that's gonna be great," said Mama. "So, how's about that new doctor in town? You seen him around lately? Talked to him?"

"Oh yes," replied the Swedish ambassador in an ominous tone. "In truthful fact I saw and spoke with him in the early hours today. And most shocked I was by what he—ah!" he interrupted himself, turning the album around and holding it out to Mama in triumph. "Here I have found the very hairstyle for you."

"What? What did you and Dr. Dick talk about? What did he say?" Mama demanded.

"This is known as the Piteå Pageboy," the Swedish

ambassador replied. "It shall showcase your cheekbones."

"Was it about me? Did Dr. Dick tell you he—oh lordy!" Mama exclaimed when she got a load of the trim, sleek style that the Swedish ambassador intended to inflict upon her. "Ain't—ain't that a helluva lot shorter than it oughta be?"

"Hush-hush," said the Swedish ambassador, spinning her salon chair around to face the mirror. "You are in my best hands."

Mama bit her lip.

Oh, I could see the future more clearly than the Soothsayer! Mama was gonna walk out the door of the Swedish Embassy & Beauty Parlor & Coffee Shop looking like a fright. On the sidewalk, she would run into Dr. Dick, who would be horrified by her hacked hair. She would flee in tears, but I would stick around and inform Dr. Dick that she had done it to prettify herself for him, which, while not strictly the truth, would delight him. He would seek her out, speak sweet words to her, and fall head over heels in love, just like a flick on the Sissy Spacek Movie Marathon. I began to silently craft wise and comforting things to say to Mama to console her for the obliteration of her blond mop as the Swedish ambassador picked up his spray bottle and pointed it like a pistol at her temple.

"So," bleated Mama. "You were saying how you spoke to Dr. Dick today?"

"Yes, but before that I spoke with the sheriff-mayor about the impending visit of Mayor Häri Härison," said the Swedish ambassador, putting down the spray bottle and taking up his sharp shears. "I very much hope that the sheriff-mayor will take a role in the many ambassadorial functions and receptions that I must plan for the visit. My first political delegation from Sweden! I am most nervous, yet I relish this opportunity."

"Yeah, it'll be something," said Mama. "Whoa, whoa! How much hair are you fixing to cut off?"

"But I am also afraid," said the Swedish ambassador, snipping away unperturbed. "For the not-yet-newspaper foretold more than this auspicious visit from Sweden. Have you heard about the coming of the truckers? The Soothsayer warns us they will bring mayhem more than the usual. What if their mischief disrupts Mayor Härison's visit?"

"I hear they're right outsida town," replied Mama. "Miz Jackson in the shipping department caught wind of 'em before dawn. My own ex-husband is on his way with nefarious intent, as I'm sure you heard."

The Swedish ambassador nodded.

"Speaking as we are of the wind, it also carries rumors that your young daughter is up to something this summer."

In the mirror, Mama swung her eyes to meet mine.

"I knew it!" she exclaimed in rage. "Palling around with that no-good 3-J, getting up to who-knows-what hijinks while I'm at work!"

"Not that young daughter," the Swedish ambassador hastily amended. "The smallest one of all, little Pearl."

Mama's expression instantly went from outraged to dismissive.

"Oh," she said, flapping her hand. "She probably just got herself a summer hobby or something."

I was indignant at Mama's instant absolution of Pearl—and gnawingly curious to hear the gossip. I'd been unable to get a word out of my little sister regarding her secretive sneaking around, tease and wheedle as I might.

"What're folks saying about Pearl?" I asked.

"Never mind that," said Mama. "Have I got some gossip for you. It's about me. And that new doctor in town."

The Swedish ambassador turned her salon chair away from the mirror and took her by the shoulder.

"First the dryer," he replied, guiding her to a pink plastic hairdryer chair against the wall. He seated her, lowered the glass hood over her head, and turned on the air, which roared like a lawnmower. Mama's mouth continued to work, but no sound was audible over the racket.

I aimed my gaze out the big plate glass window at dusty, dry Main Street, which was baking in the sweltry sunlight like a strip of pizza dough. Suddenly a small semi-truck cab, like 3-J's but painted black with dark red racing stripes down each side, whizzed up Main Street as quick as the flash of a camera.

"He's going awful fast," I murmured.

Zip! There he went again, back down Main Street. I'd never seen a truck go so fast. It moved more like a high-adrenaline hot rod than a stoic tugger of Nordic loads.

"What is it you are looking upon, Ruby?" inquired the Swedish ambassador.

"An impending crash," I prophesized.

The Swedish ambassador joined me at the window. The truck flew back up Main Street.

"He is going 120 kilometers per hour at the least," said the Swedish ambassador.

"He's like to kill someone out there."

"Perhaps himself."

"No loss there."

"I wonder where could be the police at such a moment as this?" said the Swedish ambassador.

The truck zigzagged back down Main Street again. From behind the thick plate glass we heard a most evocative sound—one that sent shivers through both of us. The shriek of a falcon, interspersed with static, rent the overheated air.

The sheriff-mayor was coming.

The Swedish ambassador and I pressed our noses against the window and ceased our breathing so as not to fog up the view.

The truck started to fly up the street yet again. It abruptly veered and swerved into a U-turn, throwing up clouds of dust. The falcon siren screeched again, punctuated by the scream of tires braking on hot road. The driver took off in the opposite direction, with the sheriff-mayor's car in reckless pursuit. Every inch of its exterior was plastered with red and blue lights that flashed in complex patterns, dazzling our eyes. The sheriff-mayor's awesome vehicle sped out of sight. Suddenly we heard a squeal of brakes and our law enforcement officer sped by, pursued by the truck.

Zip! They were gone again.

"Them fools are gonna crash straight into someone, and it's probably gonna be us," I said.

"They shall crash through this very window, most likely," said the Swedish ambassador.

Like the experienced tiny tornado watchers we were, we didn't bother to budge. Danger had to be quite literally on top of us before we'd bestir ourselves to do more than speculate about it.

We heard the shriek of the falcon siren again.

Zoom! The truck was hightailing it back down Main Street with the sheriff-mayor bearing down upon him.

"I think he's gonna—"

CRASH!

The truck slammed right into our town's one and only stop sign. The red octagon went spinning like a Frisbee through the air, straight for the Swedish Embassy & Beauty Parlor & Coffee Shop.

It was heading directly towards our window.

The Swedish ambassador and I hit the floor. There was a dull *thunk!* as the sign struck the wooden siding of the Swedish Embassy & Beauty Parlor & Coffee Shop just above the window. We cautiously rose to our feet and peeked out. Smack dab in the middle of Main Street, the sheriff-mayor was dragging the trucker out of his truck cab. The man flipped and flopped like a fish pulled from the depths of the sea. Hooting with misplaced merriment, he shook off his captor and initiated a dash for the untended cop car and grand theft auto. The sheriff-mayor made an impressive leap, considering his great girth, and landed on the trucker, flattening him.

His mouth working vigorously, the sheriff-mayor straddled the trucker like a rodeo steer and cuffed his wrists behind his shirtless back with a flourish. He then rubbed the defeated trucker's face in the dust a few more times than was strictly necessary, hauled him up by his belt, and tossed him into the back of the Cadillac. The sheriff-mayor spit, glanced at the window from which we gaped, tipped his Smokey Bear hat at us, and climbed behind the wheel. With a wave and a shriek of the falcon siren, he and the trucker were gone.

There was nothing more to see, so the Swedish ambassador crossed the room and switched off the dryer.

"And that's how Dr. Dick and I came to be, as I told you, a couple," concluded Mama, who had been chattering away the entire time.

"Dr. Dick, you say?" the Swedish ambassador replied. "It is a great coincidence that you are mentioning him, for he came to see me the first thing this morning."

"Is that a fact?" said Mama, as the Swedish ambassador led her back to the salon chair and began to work globs of mousse into her hair.

"It is so. The very minute I opened my door for business, Dr. Dick stormed himself in. He had many things to say, but to our joint misfortune I cannot understand his strange dialect of English. At last, in desperation, I telephoned his medical colleague, Dr. Barney, to provide translation. He arrived shortly, bringing with him three young parakeets who caused much mischief among my saucers and cups.

"The moment Dr. Barney arrived, the young gentleman loosened his tongue and said, 'Ayherrdabout you bein anotha publikaffical othahthan tha sherrifmayah. Nawt theddaye dawn't awpreciate tha communiteean this pahticyalah pahdah Texas. Buddaye wanna discussa transfah.'"

I giggled at the Swedish ambassador's imitation of Dr. Dick.

The Swedish ambassador shook his head.

"As you can imagine, I was perplexed. But Dr. Barney has learned the doctor's dialect and he translated easily. 'He says he heard that you're a public official here in town, and he wants to discuss a transfer out of Somwärin,' said Dr. Barney. And I replied, 'As I am given to understand, you signed a contract stipulating that you would work in any locale, however exotic, specified by your federal government for a period of five years. In return, your medical school loans were expunged. Is this not your understanding?'

"And he replied, 'Smaye undastandin swell, buddaye can't

wahk inna town wheah thaotha dactas openly hastile. Annaye havven gadda proppa clinic!'

"Dr. Barney most graciously interpreted for me at this point, explaining, 'Dr. Dick here says that he just can't work with our Dr. Flo, and he isn't too thrilled with the office I set up for him over there in my veterinary practice.'"

"What did you say to that?" asked Mama. She had a worried look on her face.

"I most regretfully told him if he wishes to leave Somwärin, there are many arduous steps that he must undertake. I explained to him that the Swedish government, under the auspices of the Fack Sex Corporation, bought out his contract from the United States federal government to bring him here, and now Sweden owns his medical school loans. 'It will require an act of international negotiation,' I informed him. 'You will be obliged to travel to Stockholm to initiate the process, provide an immediate payment of one hundred thousand dollars in forfeiture fees for early release from the debt, and return the full amount of the loan within a fortnight. To that must be added ten years of taxes and interest to cover the healthcare, road maintenance, and social infrastructure that your loan was expected to generate, payable to Skandinaviska Enskilda Banken, which is the bank that assumed your debt on behalf of the Fack Sex Corporation. And there would be so much paperwork…' At that moment, the young man began to vocalize in great distress.

"'Ahmtellinya aykanttayekit wahkin innatown wheah ayeohnly gaddasingle patient innaholweek! Wikketpissah!'

"Even Dr. Barney could not discern his meaning," concluded the Swedish ambassador. "I had much sympathy for the gentleman and his frustrations. I told him that I myself have been stranded in this forsaken burg for seven long years. And in the last three, I have been unable to leave the embassy, the sheriff-mayor having placed me under indictment for the international incident that befell us all during that unlucky year's St. Lucia Day. I explained that the sheriff-mayor pays me the occasional diplomatic visit, but I know it is but his attempt to lure me outside the embassy so that he can arrest me. Even so, I told the doctor, 'I have learned to endure the unending trial that is my existence in Somwärin. As I am certain you shall. We are all ultimately marking time in an undesirable posting from which we shall never be released, save by sweet death, are we not?' Dr. Barney heartily agreed with me. The young doctor, however, did not appear consoled."

"This is a disaster," Mama exclaimed, aghast. "He can't try to leave! I need him to stay here."

"Indeed," said the Swedish ambassador, whipping the satin drape off Mama's shoulders with a flourish. "And here is your haircut, fröken. Surely you are pleased."

Mama caught sight of her reflection in the mirror. Her mouth fell open. It stayed open as she stood up and went to the cash register, forked over the two halves of the twenty-dollar bill, collected me, and walked stiffly out the door.

Outside in the hot sun, Mama finally closed her mouth. She stood very still on the sidewalk for a long time. She kept blinking and reaching up to fondle her shorn head. A smooth cap of unfrizzled, unteased, unpuffed hair lay lightly against her face in natural waves. Having always seen her topped by a vast flaxen hood, this short, sleek cut was confusing to me. I couldn't stop staring at her.

Mama, to her own surprise, was not dismayed by her hair.

"Feels nice," she said. "Feels soft and light. I dunno…I think I like it. I think I like it a lot."

She turned to me.

"Does it look good?" she said. "Not too short?"

"No, Mama, it looks nice," I grumbled, profoundly disappointed that her hair indeed looked foxy. There would be no cinematic speeches from me.

But even her brand-new coiffure couldn't distract her from the distressing knowledge that Dr. Dick was trying to skip town at the very moment when she needed him the most.

"He can't leave me in the lurch," she said. She drew in a deep breath. "I gotta initiate the nuclear option. I gotta tell Dr. Dick that I'm in love with him. Then he'll have no choice but to fall in love with me and my plan will be back on track."

"But you ain't in love with him," I said.

"True that," agreed Mama. "I hate to lie to him. And I'll feel right bad when I cut him loose as soon as he's served his purpose, leaving him to pine lovelorn for me. But desperate times call for desperate measures."

With a decisive nod, Mama marched herself straight up Main Street, straight into the Vet 'n' Pet Shop, and straight out again.

"Nooooo, noooooo, it's slithering!"

She was wringing her hands, shaking her head in vigorous negation, and doing a full-body shudder.

"It's outta its cage, roaming free," she said. "Forked tongue flicking away, beady eyes staring at me."

She steeled herself.

She re-entered the Vet 'n' Pet Shop. She immediately re-exited.

She repeated this maneuver four times before I grew bored and glanced across the street. Opal had at last reached the Tree of Contemplation and was next in line to present her forms. I trotted across Main Street to join her.

Fresh from booking the stop sign slaying trucker, the sheriff-mayor was on hand doing crowd control.

"Keep to the line, hens! Keep your order, now," the sheriff-mayor bellowed, savoring the king-sized serving of breasts and thighs before him. "There's no need to shove, no need to bounce about, yes indeedy, lookit you bopping around, all energetic and flexible!"

Opal welcomed me with a smile, grabbed my hand, and squeezed it.

"Here goes," she said, as the girl in front of her was conducted away by the Gentleman Gym Teacher to join the other approved entrants, who stood milling about with excitement in their eyes and official Miss Somwärin pageant rulebooks in their hands.

Opal stepped up to the little table and watched eagerly as the Gentleman Gym Teacher, crisp and immaculate in a white suit cut in the style of an old-timey Kentucky plantation owner, forced his way through the unwashed masses while giving every appearance of strolling easily through a lush field of clover. He sauntered nobly up to the little table and smoothed his lapels before resuming his seat. Notoriously loath to despoil either his pure, snowy suits or his gracious dignity with the déclassé push-and-shove of a crowd, he was making an exceptional exception for this significant ceremony.

Opal leaned over the table, smiling and unintentionally presenting the great gully of her cleavage.

"Hi there, Mr. Ryker."

"Well, hello, Miss Opal," said the Gentleman Gym Teacher. "A fine day it surely is, and a fine day to you."

"Here's my entry form," Opal said, thrusting the paper across the table.

"Well, I thank you, and I shall review this ever-so-briefly…yes, everything seems to be in order. You've taken the time to peruse the fine print, certainly?"

"Hmm…mmm…" Opal pursed her lips and half-lowered her lids with an expression that men generally assumed was lust, but which was in fact confusion. "Sure," she lied.

"Well, I do most appreciate your diligence in completing this important paperwork, Miss Opal. And…" he glanced around, then leaned across the table to speak confidentially to her. "I do hope you are enjoying this fine, warm summer we seem to be having."

"Oh yeah, it's the best," Opal said, glancing over her shoulder at the impatient women waiting in line behind her.

"So," he continued. "You've graduated this fine summer into the world of adult responsibilities, and I hope…pleasures?"

Opal's face blanched.

"Oh no, not me—not yet! I just finished eleventh grade. I'm only seventeen," she said.

The Gentleman Gym Teacher's face fell.

"Is that so? I was certain you were in the graduating class this year, since only Seniors are exempt from gymnastic instruction. Why, if I may ask, didn't you attend my gym class this year?"

Opal leaned closer, her eyes at half-mast. She looked like she had a sensuous secret to share, but I could tell she was desperately trying to conceal her embarrassment and prevent anyone from overhearing her.

"There are…certain things that make it difficult for a girl like me to…to undertake the jumping and jogging and what-all."

It took the Gentleman Gym Teacher a bare three seconds to apprehend that the "certain things" were her humongous headlights. When he did, he made a manly grin and started to adjust his black string bowtie. It was at this point, however, that he noticed me staring up at him, agog. He flinched and cleared his throat.

"Good afternoon, Ruby," he nodded at me.

"Hi," I croaked.

The Gentleman Gym Teacher became shifty and nervous under my eyes, so unlike his dignified self. Fortunately for him, a sophisticated-looking blond woman interrupted—no wait, it was Mama.

Dragging Dr. Dick by the hand, she mounted the steps of the Celestial Temple of Psychedelic Truth and City Administration. It was obvious from the look on her face that she had employed something other than a declaration of love to lure Dr. Dick from his hidey-hole in the back of the Vet 'n' Pet Shop.

Mama waved her arms over her head.

"Attention!" she called to the crowd. "Attention, y'all! Dr. Dick here's got something to say!"

The sheriff-mayor glanced up from the bare midriff he was interrogating and threw a menacing glare at Dr. Dick.

"Indictment! I'm a-gonna hog-tie ya and drag ya right up them steps, straight into my jail…I'm a bit occupied at the present interval, though," the sheriff-mayor's eyes, dazzled by the female flesh that surrounded him on all sides, drifted away from his quarry. "Why don't you make an appointment with one of my deputies, turn yourself in, go easy on ya, my, you are a frisky, firm young thing, ain't you?" he chuckled, chucking one of Opal's classmates under the chin, triggering a boob-bouncing barrage of giggles.

"Listen up, y'all!" Mama shouted again, waving her arms harder. "Dr. Dick's got an important announcement."

The Gentleman Gym Teacher, relieved to see a lady in distress, beat a hasty retreat from Opal and me to join Mama on the steps. He cleared his throat, doffed his wide-brimmed hat, and raised his voice.

"Ladies! Good ladies…may I beg the honor of your attention?"

The crowd continued to chatter, ignoring the three on the steps.

"SILENCE, SKIRTS!" the sheriff-mayor bellowed.

The crowd went silent.

"Our new physician of the feminine arts would like to request the privilege of offering an announcement to your indulgent ears," the Gentleman Gym Teacher said.

"Shut your traps and listen to the hootchie-healer, y'all!" the sheriff-mayor shouted.

An intimidating silence fell as the crowd stared up at Dr. Dick. Mama gave him a little shove and he opened his mouth.

"Good aftanoon," he began. "It has been brought to my attention that…perhaps I have not propaly introduced myself to the majority of my potential patients. So…my name is Dacta Richard Grant. I'm from Bwastin, as I'm sure you can tell. I earned my medical degree from Bwastin Univasity School of Medicine. I completed my obstetrics and gynecology residency at Mass'chusetts General Hospital, which is also in Bwastin. Contrary to what…a certain individual may have said, I am a real dacta. I'm certified by the American Board of Obstetrics and Gynecology, I'm a memba of the American College of Obstetricians and Gynecologists. I'm fully qualified to perform obstetric procedyas, gynecological surgery, and oncology treatment."

He trailed off. Mama gave him another shove.

"Does anyone have any questions?"

The crowd was still. Too still. A ripple of uncertainty undulated through the assembly. Little watery whispers began to sluice back and forth.

"What'd he say?"

"Can't understand a word."

"That accent of his—it's Swedish, ain't it?"

"Someone get the Swedish ambassador out here to translate."

"Ain't no way I'm spreading my legs in the back of the Vet 'n' Pet Shop."

"I hear he's banging Crystal-Lynn."

"He's a fast one. Probably got a gal in every port."

"He's one good-looking fella. Tell him to take his shirt off."

"No! You do it!"

"Not me, no…hee-hee-hee…take your shirt off!"

And that's when the catcalls began.

As the taunts were turning from mild vulgarity to scatological obscenity, a slow clapping began at the edge of the mob. The women shushed as Dr. Flo strolled into their midst, applauding sarcastically.

"Advertising your services with a common huckster's speech, like the snake oil salesman you are," she said. "Maybe the time has come for you to face the fact that you just aren't cut out to be a doctor."

Dr. Dick's face went red.

"Maybe the time has come for you to face the fact that I'm more qualified than you. You're just a general practitiona, afta all."

There was an audible intake of breath from the crowd.

"Uh-oh. You've done it now, Dr. Dick," said the sheriff-mayor.

He and the Gentleman Gym Teacher abandoned Dr. Dick on the steps. Mama fidgeted fearfully but stayed by Dr. Dick's side as Dr. Flo advanced on him, her eyes snapping sparks.

"You claim you're a real doctor?" inquired Dr. Flo, with the frostiest pause before "doctor," as if icicle-shaped quotation marks hung around the word. "Then come with me on Motel Rounds."

The crowd gasped.

Mama trembled and gripped Dr. Dick by the elbow.

"No," she whispered.

"Good gracious," said the Gentleman Gym Teacher.

"May God have mercy on your soul, sir," said the sheriff-mayor.

"I'm not familia with the term 'Motel Rounds,'" said Dr. Dick.

"Just a little old-fashioned country doctoring," smiled Dr. Flo. It was a cruel, reptilian smile that sent a chill down my spine.

"Don't do it, Dr. Dick," Mama said.

"It's a death sentence," said the Gentleman Gym Teacher.

"Even I don't dare go out there," said the sheriff-mayor.

"I'll do it," said Dr. Dick. "I interned in an emergency ward in South Bwastin. It was no cakewalk. I've handled more than my share of trauma cases."

Dr. Flo's wicked smile spread until I thought it would split her face asunder.

"I'll fetch you in the ambulance at seven tonight," she said. "Wear waterproof shoes. And a bulletproof vest, if you have one."

Dr. Flo departed. Dr. Dick glanced at Mama, then stepped off the stairs. The women parted to let him through, murmuring in wonder.

"Going on Motel Rounds!"

"He's so brave."

"I guess he's a real doctor, after all."

"Must be a damned good doctor if he can handle Motel Rounds."

Their audible admiration put a faint glow of color in his cheeks as he walked across Main Street, pursued by Mama. I scooted after them, eager to eavesdrop.

Out front of the Vet 'n' Pet Shop, Dr. Dick halted and waited for Mama to catch up.

"You were right," he said.

He smiled at her for the first time ever.

Mama smiled back—one of her real smiles, not a seductive smirk—also for the first time.

"You changed your hair," he said. "It suits you. Well. I'd betta go put togetha a paramedic kit. I doubt Dacta Flo will share her medical supplies."

After the door to the Vet 'n' Pet Shop closed behind him, Mama turned to me. Her expression was unusually lighthearted and joyful.

"You know something?" she said. "Your daddy ain't never once told me I was right about anything. Nor has he ever noticed a change in my appearance. And he sure as shooting never paid me a compliment unbidden. What a day!"

We strolled to the Oldsmobile, the sun warm on our shoulders. Mama unlocked the doors, Pearl spontaneously materialized from wherever she'd been, and the three of us got in. As we drove past the Tree of Contemplation, Mama waved at Opal, who stood with the other competitors, awaiting the pageant orientation.

"I'll meet you back home tonight," Opal called.

Mama pulled the car off Main Street and aimed the front bumper for home.

"Everything seems to have worked itself out," she said.

But no!

Three hours after leaving an optimistic Opal on the front lawn of the Celestial Temple of Psychedelic Truth and City Administration, she returned home in tears.

"The other girls made fun of me," she wailed. "They said the pageant's too classy for the likes of me. They said I oughta quit before I embarrass myself, coz of my boobs. They said my posture is unacceptable, coz of my boobs. There ain't a Miss America approved swimsuit on earth that'll fit me, coz of my boobs. And on the way home, a gang of truckers hollered at me and threw empty beer cans, coz of my boobs!"

Three hours after that, 3-J, soaked in milk and vigorously pedaling a child's bicycle, came whooping into the trailer park.

"He's stateside!" he shouted. "Don's crossed the border into Texas! Yeeeeee-haaaaaw!"

Just then, the patrol car of the sheriff-mayor of Somwärin skidded to a dust-spewing stop behind 3-J and the lawman leapt out. He, too, was drenched in milk. The sheriff-mayor gave pursuit on foot and swiftly ensnared 3-J within the bear trap of his meaty arms.

As 3-J was wrestled into handcuffs, he hollered at Mama.

"Crystal-Lynn! Your ex-husband is coming!"

The sheriff-mayor threw scrappy 3-J over his shoulder in a fireman's carry and carted him to the Cadillac. 3-J latched both hands onto the doorframe and let out another whoop.

"He's coming *imminently*!" 3-J shouted, clinging like a burr as the sheriff-mayor struggled to pry him free. At last he succeeded, slammed the door, and jumped into the driver's seat.

The sheriff-mayor gunned the engine and sped away into the dark of night, 3-J's cries bounding and rebounding off the trailers that surrounded our home.

"Imminently…imminently…*imminently*!"

Three hours after that, at precisely midnight-thirty, I awoke to a commotion outside our trailer. Somewhere in the great, wild night, I heard a squeal of brakes and a thud, like a body hitting the ground.

I rose from my bed and peered out my bedroom window. High-wattage headlights swerved to paint the neighboring trailers yellow. Dr. Dick, unceremoniously tossed to earth from a moving car, was struggling to regain his feet. As soon as he did, he staggered in the direction of the side door leading into the kitchen.

Dr. Flo rolled down the window of the wood-paneled Brady Bunch station wagon turned ambulance.

"Mrs. Bejou," she called out. "I'll task you with returning this one to town. I have no time to spare. I have patients waiting."

She paused long enough to give Dr. Dick a disgusted up-and-down with her eyes.

"You, sir, are no doctor."

With that, she spun the steering wheel, revved the engine, and allowed the night to swallow the makeshift medical vehicle whole.

I found the kitchen ablaze with buttery light. Mama, skanky in see-through summer nightwear, had Dr. Dick buttonholed in a chair at the kitchen table.

Dr. Dick was bedraggled, a ravaged mess. Coated head to toe with beer, dirt, paintball spatters, dog hair, and some unidentifiable powder, his face was as white as the full moon and his entire body shook so hard the kitchen table rattled on its uneven aluminum legs.

"At first, it was alright," he was saying. "Rough, yes. Primitive, certainly. Intoxicated men by the droves. Trucks as fah as the eye could see. I did a stint with Dactas Without Bordas during medical school—I know the drill. Alcohol poisonings, caffeine pill ovadoses, sex toy extractions. The truckas let Dacta Flo treat them without hesitation. But they were suspicious of me. Narc—that's what they kept saying. Narc, narc, narc!"

"Let me get you a drink," said Mama. "To settle your nerves."

Dr. Dick shook his head.

"As the evening wore on, they seemed to accept that I really am a dacta. Then the *incident* occurred."

Mama folded her arms under her boobage, pushing said boobage up so high it nearly popped clean out of the top of her naughty nightie. Dr. Dick, his eyes blank, saw nothing as he gazed upon the hellish memory from Motel Way.

"Dacta Flo found herself ovaburdened with several spinal complaints of driva's slouch. So she sent me alone to a dakened motel room to treat a man suffering from left-ear deafness brought on by driving with an open window. But I went to the wrong room. And I'm afraid I…blundered into an illicit business dealing."

Mama let out a little groan of dismay.

"The…Mrs….that orthodontist neighba of yours was

standing on top of a nightstand surrounded by a group of truckas. As I stepped into the room, she held up a freeza bag full of white powda and said, 'Oh-pee-YUM—y'all ten-four? You wanna smokemup? Three Jacksons.'"

Dr. Dick turned utterly shocked eyes to Mama.

"I was utterly shocked," he said.

Mama groaned again.

"I was about to back out of the room, when she caught sight of me. She pointed and said, 'Y'all eyeballin' that buffalo? That-there hard to pull out sawbones outta Bean Town's shackin' up with the first sergeant of Don Bejou, copy that.'" Dr. Dick shuddered. "Everyone turned to look at me. Such hard, glassy stares! I have no idea what she said, but all the truckas jumped to their feet and started to chase me. I ran and ran…but they caught me. Dacta Flo was unsympathetic when she rescued me an hour and a half later."

Mama placed her hands on his shoulders and gave them a squeeze.

"Don't fret, now," she said. "You just relax here with us, and see if a week or two of peaceful repose in the Bejou home don't put you back in good spirits."

Dr. Dick stared at Mama in horror. His eyes drifted from the greasy walls festooned with glittery nail polish smears to the battered cupboards defaced with Swedish bumper stickers to the line-up of empty Almond Roca tins that marched from one end of the counter to the other. His last nerve gave out and he dropped his forehead onto the kitchen table with a keening moan.

Mama fluttered about him, unsure how to respond.

"I am a broken man," he said. "Dacta Flo is right. Maybe I'm not cut out to be a dacta afta all. This is my first medical practice—I've failed at my first and only practice. In less than a week!"

"Now, don't you dare take on so," said Mama uneasily, herding him to his feet. "You come on with me and get yourself cleaned up, and you'll soon see things in a whole new light."

Her eyes fastened upon my silent self, hovering as I was in the doorway.

"Go on, git!" she hissed. "You'll spook him further."

I slid out the side door, wrapped my arms around my chest to ward off the chill midnight breeze, and tipped my head back to look up at the stars. They were hidden behind a thick encrustation of soot-gray clouds.

This was indeed the bitterest of days.

I turned my head toward town. A strange glow was coming from Somwärin. It was a singular shade of orange that I'd seen every summer since I could remember: a melange of semi truck headlights, police lights, and riot fires.

The truckers had arrived at last.

Chapter Nine
Midsummer Eve-Eve

Thursday, June 19
7:02 a.m.

Dawn dawned.

When I awoke, the bedroom was peaceful and pooled with fresh morning light. I yawned. I stretched. I got out of bed.

I walked down the hall toward the living room. A niggling thought worked its way to the forefront of my mind. Wasn't there something I was supposed to do? Something pertaining to Pearl? Something I had vowed to do, when sleep was overtaking me?

As I stepped into the empty living room, the phone rang.

Suddenly it all came rushing back to me. At an hour most wee, 2:38 in the morning to be precise, the phone rang just like this. I'd groggily opened my eyes, then raised my head from my hot pillow at the sound of Pearl vaulting from the top bunk above me to the darkness below. She had tiptoed out of our room. Within seconds, the telephone's piercing cries had ceased, to be replaced by the low sound of my little sister muttering confidentially in the living room.

Drowsily, I had decided that I would confront Pearl as soon as she returned. I would demand to know, once and for all, what she was up to.

My head had dropped back onto my pillow. My eyes had closed. Back to dreamland I had drifted…

Now, nearly five hours later, I pounced on the phone and picked up the receiver.

"Hello?" I said.

"This is Perdee Dora," the receiver replied.

"Really?" I stammered.

"Yes, really, you dummy," said Perdee Dora, confirming with her staccato sarcasm that she was, indeed, Perdee Dora.

"Really?" I repeated, my inchoate thoughts racing from one

end of my noggin to the other.

She sighed so hard it knocked birds off the telephone wires three miles outside of town.

"Meet me outside the Swedish Embassy & Beauty Parlor & Coffee Shop at ten," she said. "Don't you dare be late, Ruby."

She hung up.

I listened to the dial tone for a good minute and a half before I hung up as well. I stood, mystified and uneasy, in the middle of the living room.

What could the town's greatest living villainess want from me? It couldn't be good.

One never attributed good intentions to Perdee Dora Dolan. That fact was driven home six summers ago by the awful incident that occurred at Fun Time Swedish Language Learning Camp for Little Youngsters.

I shuddered at the memory, then went cold as I considered what it might mean for Pearl, who was Up To Something— something I was beginning to believe began with vengeance upon Perdee Dora and ended with the unthinkable.

I set out to find my little sister in the 840-square-foot labyrinth that was the Bejou family double-wide.

I poked my head into the bathroom. Empty.

I glanced inside Mama's bedroom. Deserted.

I made my way down the hall to us-girls' bedroom. Only Opal, curled up in a fetal position in her bed, was in residence. Her eyes were open, beseeching, and bloodshot from crying.

"I'm doomed," she announced when I entered. "I'm gonna be a freak and social outcast for the rest of my life. I'm tired of never finding clothes that fit, being leered at by men, getting glared at by women. I just wanna be normal!

"Now, Opal," I said in a Mama-ish tone. "The best cure for doom is hard work. Ain't you supposed to be at work now?"

"I don't wanna go to work!" she sobbed. "They call me Jiggle Jugs and holler at me to take my top off and throw fries between my cleavage—and them's my co-workers! You can't imagine what the customers do. I can't take it anymore!"

"Now, Opal," I said again.

She looked at me expectantly.

"I…dunno," I concluded lamely.

My big sister groaned and hid her head under the covers.

I sensed I was making the situation worse. I backed out of the room and continued my search for Pearl. In the kitchen, I rediscovered Dr. Dick exactly as I found him last night. He sat slumped at the kitchen table, his head cradled in his hands like a forty-pound burden. He didn't look up as I entered.

I pressed in close and peered at him. In the harsh light of day, his condition appeared to have deteriorated.

"Dr. Dick?"

No response.

"You okay?"

No response.

"You want some breakfast?"

No response.

"Should I poke you a bit? To rouse you to sensibility?"

"You leave him be," Mama ordered as she breezed into the kitchen, clad in her day-off clothes, her new haircut, and a thick cloud of cigarette smoke. "You go on and play while me and Dr. Dick have us a grown-up chat."

She gave me a broad wink, which notified me that she was going to put the moves on him. Half the battle was won: He was installed in her home, held captive by his depressive catatonia. But as her eye unwinked, I perceived that she was not entirely delighted with the situation. A worried little crinkle remained around both her eyes as she bent over Dr. Dick and put her lips close to his ear.

"Dr. Dick?"

No response.

"You okay?"

No response.

"You want some breakfast?"

No response.

I had seen this scene play itself out already, so I departed to look for my little sister alfresco.

Powdery clouds dusted the hot sky like spilled talcum. As I

209

roamed the trailer park, swinging a Bitch-Girl-repelling stick and scanning my neighbors' grass patches for Pearl, I considered the potential ramifications of a counterattack against Perdee Dora.

Perdee Dora's ghastly response to direct opposition was unveiled to the public during her first summer at Fun Time Swedish Language Learning Camp for Little Youngsters. The enormity, which took some parties years to recover from and scarred others for life, was committed on Midsummer Eve-Eve when she and Pearl were six, I was eight, and Opal was a DDD cup.

Fun Time Swedish Language Learning Camp for Little Youngsters was held in Mexico, just outside the town where the Fack Sex Furniture Manufacturing Factory was located. The Fack Sex Corporation had informally christened the town "Sydligaste Sverige," meaning "Southernmost Sweden." But what the Mexican townspeople heard was, "Si Le Gustas...Es Varían," roughly translated, "If You Like It...It's Different." The hijos and hijas of If You Like It...It's Different were forced to spend their summers at the camp with their hapless American visitors. Together, we resided in cabins named not for flora, fauna, or indigenous native groups forced out by the encroachments of Spanish colonialism, but for departments and facilities found at Fack Sex Corporate Headquarters in Stockholm.

Aside from hours upon hours of Swedish grammar, spelling, and conversation practice, we lucky kids were treated to all manner of corporate retreat activities, including mission statement memorization, slogan brainstorming sessions, trust falls, and sexual harassment awareness training.

We were also given the mandatory opportunity to enjoy a story hour each business day after lunch. The story in question was always the same, and it was always read to us live from Sweden via two-way video conferencing by the founder and CEO of the Fack Sex Corporation, a severe, testy gentleman in his late sixties with eyes as blue and cold and unfathomable as Mälaren Lake in the home country.

After reiterating that he considered each and every one of us to be his future employees, and after moralizing at us for a good twenty minutes in the impenetrable Skånska dialect of his childhood in the Deep South of Sweden, the founder and CEO of Fack Sex would clear his throat and crack the covers of the seminal business memoir and professional leadership manual he authored some years back. The book, *Lust för Smak: Sex Affär Planen för Sex Män*, chronicled the founding of the Fack Sex Corporation, its early days of operation, its rise to prominence throughout the globe as a Swedish lifestyle tastemaker, and its bitter rivalry with the much larger IKEA Corporation—all told through six business plans designed by six business leaders the founder and CEO of Fack Sex most admired and held responsible for his success.

From her first moments at camp, little Perdee Dora Dolan was on her worst behavior. She was willful and surly and combative and sardonic. Even as a six-year-old, her talent for immediately discerning a person's greatest area of insecurity and mercilessly mocking them for it was incredible. We kids—taunted in fluent English, rudimentary Spanish, and pidgin Swedish from sunup to sundown—acquiesced to her abuse without a fight. The Fack Sex camp counselors, however, did not. Leia From Accounting and Lykee From Sales caught on to her tricks immediately and were not awed. By the end of Day One, Perdee Dora had been marked as a problem child and was publically shamed by being demoted from the highly desirable Executive Boardroom cabin to the miscreant-filled Human Resources cabin, where she became my bunkmate and a massive thorn in my side.

That the Swedes paid no heed to her imprecations, were not stung by her insults, and laughed at her invocations of her father's municipal power enraged Perdee Dora. Their refusal to be cowed by her tried-and-true torment techniques provoked her to greater and greater outrages, which garnered harsher and harsher punishments as the summer wore on. Nothing she said to the Fack Sex camp counselors, no matter how cutting, drew blood. Until, that is, she figured out the one thing they were all fatally self-conscious about.

Having failed to pinpoint Pearl in the outside world, I turned back toward home. When I stepped back inside, I discovered that the situation had degenerated severely.

Dr. Dick had graduated from slouching at the kitchen table to lying flat on his back on the linoleum beneath it. His hands were pressed over his face and he moaned like a wounded animal in a trap. Opal and Mama were shrieking at each other off-camera.

What was going on? I waffled between coaxing the supine gynecologist out of his none-too-clean place of retreat and throwing myself into the fray with my pugilistic relatives.

Suddenly, Opal charged into the kitchen, pursued by Mama.

"Give me a knife and I'll take care of it myself," Opal yelled.

"You stop these hysterics this instant," Mama yelled back.

"I wanna cut 'em off! I hate 'em!" Opal cried, slapping her hands against her breasts, which shuddered like enormous bags of gelatin. "I hate 'em, I hate 'em, I hate 'em!"

Mama grabbed Opal's wrists as she lunged for the butcher knife to finish her attack upon the treacherous love melons.

"Stop it, stop it, you hear me—stop it right now!" Mama screamed, so harsh and shrill that Opal was stunned to stillness. Tears began to flow down my sister's face. She fell to her knees and began to sob.

Not a sound came from any of us. Even Dr. Dick was silent beneath the table.

"I wish I could cut 'em off," Opal declared at last, in a broken voice. "They're lumpy and bumpy and they hurt all the time. My back is sore every day from lugging them around. They swell up even bigger when it's my time of the month until I can't stand it. And they leak. They ain't normal and I don't want 'em anymore."

"Don't say such a thing," Mama said. "You ain't got no—"

"Fosberg Syndrome!" Dr. Dick exclaimed.

Emerging like Dracula from his coffin, he slithered from underneath the kitchen table and sat bolt upright, his face alight with epiphany.

"At first," he said. "I thought it was a case of pubertal mammary hypertrophy—most likely juvenile macromastia causing excessive growth of the breasts in adolescence. But those are the symptoms of Fosberg Syndrome."

Opal's tears stopped. She turned to Dr. Dick with an avid look in her eyes.

"What do you mean?"

Dr. Dick crawled across the linoleum to sit beside her.

"Fosberg Syndrome is a cystic condition," he said. "It's not unusual to find small, fluid-filled cysts in the breast. They're harmless. But with Fosberg Syndrome, the breasts become overrun with multiple cysts that contain an inordinate amount of fluid. The breasts enlarge to accommodate the cysts, mimicking breast growth. To reverse the condition, the cysts simply have to be drained."

"How?" Opal demanded. "How do you do that?"

"Needle aspiration," Dr. Dick replied. "A syringe with a very fine needle is inserted through the skin into each cyst and the fluid is drawn off. It takes seconds. It's a very simple procedya. Minor outpatient surgery."

"It's gruesome!" Mama cried. "Sticking needles in my baby girl—surgery, my God!"

"How do I find out if that's what's wrong with me?" Opal asked.

"A basic breast exam would indicate—"

"No!" Mama said. "Dr. Flo says there's nothing wrong with her. She says Opal's just been overly blessed, that's her lot in life, there's nothing to be done about it."

"The thing about Fosberg Syndrome," said Dr. Dick gently. "Is it can cause complications the longer the patient lives with it. Regula breast cysts are harmless. But the fluid in these cysts tends to calcify ovah time. That means the cysts harden and become painful and very difficult to remove. And there's some indication they have a risk of becoming cancerous afta menopause."

Mama blanched in horror.

"A breast exam would tell us one way or the otha," Dr. Dick concluded. "Opal's only seventeen, so she'll need your permission—"

"Oh God," Mama moaned. "I don't know. I don't like this. I don't like this one bit."

"If you'd prefer, Dacta Flo can perform the exam. The condition's not difficult to diagnose," Dr. Dick said.

Mama stared at him. Then at Opal. Then at him again.

"No," she said at last, with a quaver in her voice. "You do it. Dr. Flo's been tending to Opal for years and ain't never once said there could be something wrong that can turn into cancer. And…and…I trust you."

It didn't take Perdee Dora long to discover that the one thing that Fack Sex, as a corporate entity, was self-conscious about was its subordination to that other ready-to-assemble Swedish furniture behemoth, IKEA.

This inferiority complex was woven like a tarnished gold thread through the tapestry of our summer. During arts and crafts, we were tasked with designing print advertisements more visually compelling than those of IKEA. The evening campfire skits performed by each cabin were on the theme of "A commercial for Fack Sex that demonstrates the company's unique selling proposition relative to IKEA." At bedtime, Nils From Marketing asked us to pray for the fall of the IKEA Corporation's stock price.

Absorbing this information like El Cactus de Contemplación in the town square of Si Le Gustas…Es Varían absorbed water, Perdee Dora pivoted from mocking the hair, posture, accents, and clothing of her adult overseers and began to needle them about the superiority of IKEA.

It worked. Their annoyance became visible, audible, and, increasingly as the days passed, palpable. Perdee Dora was delighted. She doubled her efforts to plague, pester, and provoke.

Then she went too far.

On that fateful Midsummer Eve-Eve, the boys were sent to sit out in a field where they were made to weave and wear wildflower crowns, which gave them much displeasure. The girls, meanwhile, were tasked with assembling the maypole, a Fack Sex product that came in sixteen baffling parts. Perdee Dora spent the entire time reciting, in a sing-song voice, scraps of Swedish that made the camp counselors' faces turn red with fury.

"Fack Sexs midsommarstång är dålig."

"IKEAs midsommarstång är bra."

"IKEA gör bra möbler."

"IKEA är bättre än Fack Sex."

"Jag älskar IKEA!"

One dares not translate her formidable taunts. By the time we girls had brought the maypole to full erection, the counselors were livid and Perdee Dora was beaming smugly.

Sweaty and satisfied, we girls trooped into the Employee Breakroom cabin for story hour. We were joined by the boys, who returned from the field bedecked with sullen scowls and fragrant flower crowns they were under strict orders not to remove. Juan Tomás de la Vega, who had been crowned Queen of the May by his confrères, trailed the group with a particularly stylish floral corona on his cabeza and an aggrieved glare etched into his brow just below the quivering petals. On Midsummer proper, he joined me in the Human Resources cabin after confirming his lack of corporate spirit when he refused to place seven flowers from his crown under his pillow so that he might dream of his future wife. Juan Tomás and I became great friends.

Though normally we kids loathed story hour, we were looking forward to it on Midsummer Eve-Eve. This was because the founder and CEO of Fack Sex had reached the section of his book that described the establishment of the Fack Sex Furniture Distribution Warehouse in Somwärin.

The Somwärin chapter contained several words in English,

to give it an international flavor. We eagerly listened for, and cheered upon hearing, the precious syllables from home. Even our friends from Si Le Gustas...Es Varían joined in the shouts of jubilation. Our counselors misunderstood the anti-Swedish foundation of our joy, and reveled in the favorable light our attentive enthusiasm shone on their counseling in front of the head honcho in the home office.

Even the humorless founder and CEO of Fack Sex seemed charmed to see us leaning forward, cross-legged, from our positions on the floor as he solemnly read the words:

"Texas…'rednecks'…North American Free Trade Agreement...Swedish-Texan corporate commonwealth… incompetent…'Fack Sex Distributionslager, *som är in Texas*'... 'Fack Sex Furniture Distribution Warehouse, *which is in Texas*'… 'Somwärin'…idiots."

When he reached the end of the chapter, the founder and CEO of Fack Sex broke character and allowed a tiny smile to invade his chilly countenance.

"Har ni några frågor?" he inquired, as he always did at the end of story hour.

Ordinarily we kids declined to ply him with questions. But on this day, to our collective surprise, Perdee Dora raised her little hand.

She wore an evil smile upon her evil face.

Within the minuscule back closet of the Vet 'n' Pet Shop, Dr. Dick was pressing one of Opal's massive breasts between his latex-gloved palms, a frown of concentration on his face. Mama was holding Opal's hand, a frown of apprehension on her face. The space was far too small to accommodate me, so I waited out in the hall and peeped through the crack between the door and the jamb.

"There's a good one," Dr. Dick said.

He swiped Opal's skin with a cotton square soaked in

rubbing alcohol and picked up a syringe with a long, silvery needle.

"On three," he said. "One, two…"

He inserted the needle.

Opal winced and squeezed Mama's hand. Mama winced too, but not from pain.

Dr. Dick withdrew the needle and smiled reassuringly at her.

"All done."

He put a protective cap on the end of the needle and opened the exam room door.

"I'm going to run a quick analysis of the fluid to see what we're dealing with. You can put your shirt back on and relax. I'll be back in a few minutes."

I trailed Dr. Dick as he walked briskly down the hall to the veterinary lab. Inside, Dr. Barney stood over the centrifuge, a vial of blood in one hand, a ham sandwich in the other.

"Mind if I borrow your microscope?"

"Be my guest," said Dr. Barney, not taking his eyes off the whirring centrifuge. "Say, Dick. I sure could use a second set of hands on that poodle ovariectomy this afternoon—"

"We're not having this convasation again, Owen," Dr. Dick replied, as he squeezed a drop of cloudy fluid from the syringe onto a glass slide, slipped it under the lens, and bent down to peer into the microscope's eyepiece.

"Aw heck, Dick, Perdita Fluffington is the sweetest little dog you ever—"

"I'm not a veterinarian. And I have no desiya to run afoul of the American Board of Veterinary Practitionas."

"Who's gonna tell 'em? Perdita Fluffington?" Dr. Barney quipped, pushing a button on the centrifuge, which slowly ground to a halt.

"There we go," Dr. Dick murmured intimately to the microscope. "Just what I thought."

"Whatcha got there?"

"Mammary cystic fluid."

"Mind if I take a gander?"

Dr. Dick straightened up and moved aside so Dr. Barney could hunch over the microscope.

"No blood cells," said Dr. Barney. "That's good. You get it all?"

Dr. Dick nodded.

"Lump collapsed?"

"Fully," said Dr. Dick. "And no inflammation of the surrounding tissue in evidence."

"Any others?"

"Several dozen."

Dr. Barney whistled.

"You thinking needle aspiration for the whole shebang?"

"That's the standad treatment."

"Same's we do for bovine mammary cysts. Can't fool me—you're a vet!"

Dr. Dick shook his head and pitched the syringe into a sharps container, then returned to the closet where Opal sat on the big exam table waiting tensely.

"Well?" she demanded.

"The fluid presented as cleah, which is a good sign. I'm going to confirm my original diagnosis. The treatment is basically the same as the diagnosis. Each cyst is drained of fluid with a syringe. Given the unusual numba I've found, the procedya would take longa than usual—maybe a couple hours. But there aren't likely to be any complications," he smiled. "I think this is, overall, a fairly uncomplicated case."

Opal's eyes gleamed.

"Can you do it right now?"

"No!" cried Mama.

No," said Dr. Dick. "The procedya needs to be performed in a propa clinical environment."

His expression grew dark.

"Wait here," he said. "I'll see what I can do."

Dr. Dick marched out the door of the Vet 'n' Pet Shop. I had to jog to keep up with him. He didn't notice I was following him as he walked up Main Street to Dr. Flo's clinic. He pushed the door open and strode straight to the reception desk, past the waiting patients. Without hesitation, he reached around the astonished receptionist and pressed the troublemaker button.

Dr. Flo instantly emerged.

Without preamble, without salutation, he said, "I have a patient in need of a minor outpatient surgical procedya. I would like to request the use of your clinic space, at your convenience, to perform multiple cystic fluid extractions via needle aspiration."

"I see," said Dr. Flo. "And what condition, precisely, do you think you're treating?"

"Fosberg Syndrome."

Dr. Flo narrowed her eyes.

"I have an idea who you've mistakenly diagnosed with that particularly rare condition," she said. "And I can tell you now, you're way off base. The patient in question has been under my care since she was born, and the disorder she suffers from is juvenile macromastia. The only treatment is cosmetic breast reduction once she's an adult."

"Respectfully," Dr. Dick said, with very little respect in his voice. "I disagree with your diagnosis."

"Of course you do," Dr. Flo replied. "You have no experience, just a head crammed with obscure conditions and rare disorders you spent weeks desperately trying to memorize for your licensing exam. But this is the real world, not a textbook."

The anger radiating off Dr. Dick was tangible.

"Again," he said. "I formally request the use of your clinic facility to perform the procedya. Will you grant my request?"

"No."

"In that case, please release *my* patient's medical recads. I'll perform the procedya at the outpatient surgery centa at Big City General Hospital."

Dr. Flo laughed dryly.

"You are green indeed," she said. "You can't just waltz into any hospital you please and start performing surgery."

She stepped closer to him and raised her voice, as if

speaking to an unusually dense child.

"You must have admitting rights," she enunciated.

"I do have admitting rights," Dr. Dick enunciated back.

Dr. Flo's left eyelid gave a little twitch of surprise.

"What do you think I've been doing all week, with no patients to care for?" Dr. Dick said. "I applied for and obtained admitting rights at every hospital within a three-hundred-mile radius of this town."

Dr. Flo drew her head back and seemed about to retort.

She hesitated.

"Very well," she said coldly.

Dr. Flo snapped her fingers at the receptionist, who opened a large file drawer and pulled out a manila folder. She stood and walked around the desk with a look of loathing for Dr. Dick on her face. She gave the folder to Dr. Flo, who handed it over to Dr. Dick.

"Thank you," he said.

He turned to go.

"Poach my patients as you wish," Dr. Flo said. "You can't build a practice on my coattails."

"You keep misdiagnosing your patients and you won't have a practice," he countered. "Much less coattails."

He turned on his heel and exited, his white doctoring coat billowing behind him like a cape.

Back at the Vet 'n' Pet Shop, Dr. Dick ducked into Dr. Barney's office, sat at his desk, and opened the file containing Opal's medical records. I took a stroll down the hall to the clinic-closet, in which Mama and Opal were waiting. Opal was chattering away a mile a minute, gung-ho with hope. Mama was uncharacteristically silent. I sat down on the floor to await Dr. Dick's return.

Twenty minutes elapsed before he emerged from Dr. Barney's office. He stepped around me, knocked lightly on the half-open door to the closet, and entered. I jammed myself in the doorway to listen.

"Based on fluid analysis and a review of your medical recads," he said. "I'm going to recommend drainage of all palpable cysts. I found an unusual numba, of unusually large size, which would account for the atypical enlargement of your breasts and the severity of your symptoms."

Opal looked pleased.

"So that means after you drains the cysts, my boobs'll shrink down real small?"

"I can't predict what sort of change in size you'll experience," he said. "But it's likely you'll see a significant reduction in overall mass. More important, it should relieve your back pain, the aching and periodic swelling you're experiencing, the leakage, and the majority of otha symptoms that have been troubling you."

Mama gritted her teeth and refused to object, though it was obvious she wanted to.

"Since Dacta Flo is unwilling to let me use her clinic, I took the liberty of contacting the outpatient surgery centa at Big City General Hospital. They actually had a cancellation late last night that opened up a procedya room for noon. Today."

"Really?" Opal exclaimed.

"That's too soon!" Mama said.

"The next available opening is sixteen weeks out," Dr. Dick replied.

"Today is perfect," Opal said. "If we wait, I'll have to miss school."

"I don't know, I don't like this," Mama dithered. "This is all happening too fast."

Dr. Dick looked discreetly from Opal to Mama.

"If you decide to have the procedya today, I'll call the hospital and tell them to reserve the clinic space. I won't need nursing staff or an anesthesiologist since the procedya is so minor. We can drive ovah togetha—it's just 45 minutes away—and you'll be home in time for dinna."

Mama said nothing.

"Please, Mama?" Opal begged. "Just think: I'll be all fixed up in time for the pageant!"

"That damned pageant again!" Mama exploded. "I won't have you go risking your life over that stupid pageant, you hear me?"

"But Mama—"

And then Mama did something that shocked Opal and me alike.

She burst into tears.

Opal met my eyes. Hers were wide. I knew mine were, too. I couldn't recall the last time I saw Mama cry.

"Girls," said Dr. Dick in a low voice. "Would you mind stepping outside for a moment?"

Opal and I beat it for the hall. Dr. Dick shut the door firmly behind him. Immediately, murmuring began within the little room. I'd like to say we granted Dr. Dick and Mama the privacy a closed door commanded, but curiosity got the better of us. Opal stealthily worked the door open a crack and we peered in.

Mama and Dr. Dick were seated side-by-side on the big silver exam table. Mama was crying softly and Dr. Dick was awkwardly patting her shoulder. Suddenly she let out a great sob and threw her arms around his neck. He held her, stiffly at first, then naturally, his left hand rubbing her back as if she were a child.

"I've been playing you false," Mama sobbed. "I've been using you like a gadget or a gizmo that ain't got no free will. I told 3-J and the Swedish ambassador and every-danged-body in town that you're my new man, as a ploy to keep my ex-husband from coming home and ruining everything I've worked so hard to build up for my girls. It was a mean, low scheme and I ought never to have done it. You're a nice man. But it's a terrible time I'm having these days, and I'm sore a-feared for my girl right now, and I'm just at sea—I don't know what to do."

Dr. Dick looked baffled, but he nodded anyway.

"I know you'd never let anything happen to my Opal," Mama said, wiping her cheeks with the back of her hand. "I trust you. But I can't go on making a puppet outta you. I'm sorry I used you, even if you didn't know."

Dr. Dick opened his mouth. He looked terribly confused.

He closed his mouth. Then he opened it again.

"I forgive you," he said.

"Thank you," Mama said.

Opal, Mama, and Dr. Dick left for Big City at ten o'clock on the dot, at which time I trudged up Main Street to meet Perdee Dora.

Downtown Somwärin was in modest disarray. A slender rivulet of broken glass streamed along the sidewalk in front of the Fack Sex employee grocery store. Three cars had been flipped, their tires pointing helplessly skyward, like beetles stuck on their backs. A rosette of lewd graffiti bedecked the front door of the Swedish Embassy & Beauty Parlor & Coffee Shop. But no newly minted widows wailed for justice in the middle of Main Street, which was a good sign. It was a restrained riot, as summer riots went. The truckers had stormed the town around midnight, carousing and cavorting until they were arrested, dispersed, or rendered unconscious by their own crapulence around 3 a.m.

Perdee Dora was leaning against the outer wall of the Swedish Embassy & Beauty Parlor & Coffee Shop, tapping her jewel-studded sandal impatiently.

"You're late," she said, when I sidled up to her. "I told you not to be late."

"Sorry, Perdee Dora," I said. "I was—"

"Word around town is your sister, Pearl, is up to something," Perdee Dora said. "Something that may involve a scheme against me. You tell me what it is."

"I don't know, Perdee Dora."

"Yes, you do."

"No, I don't—honest!"

Perdee Dora narrowed her eyes and studied me for a long moment.

"In that case," she said. "You tell Pearl she better think

twice if she *is* up to something. Because anybody—and I mean *anybody*—who crosses me winds up wishing they were never born."

Then she smiled an evil smile.

It was the same smile she wore at summer camp all those years ago. Recent kindergarten graduate Perdee Dora smiled and waved her hand in the air eagerly. From the video screen, the founder and CEO of Fack Sex squinted into our midst and pointed at her.

"Ja, min söta flicka?"

He looked almost kind, beguiled by her enthusiasm.

"Varför…" she said in a honey-sweet voice. "Varför är din bok…"

"Ja?" encouraged the founder and CEO of Fack Sex.

"Sämrrrrrrrre," she rolled the R cruelly, eliciting gasps of horror from the counselors. "Än Ingvar Kamprads bok?"

The silence that fell in the Employee Breakroom cabin was horrific, the stuff of night terrors.

Perdee Dora—clever, vicious brat that she was—had masterfully twanged the tenderest nerve of the founder and CEO of Fack Sex.

Just months earlier, Ingvar Kamprad, founder of the detested IKEA, had released his own business memoir and professional leadership manual, *Historien om IKEA*, which chronicled the founding of the IKEA Corporation, its early days of operation, its rise to prominence throughout the globe as a Swedish lifestyle tastemaker, and made no mention whatsoever of its lowly competitor, Fack Sex. It was being hailed throughout Sweden, the UK, and the Northern and Southern Americas as superior in every way to *Lust för Smak: Sex Affär Planen för Sex Män*.

The founder and CEO of Fack Sex was most bitter about the whole affair. And Perdee Dora had just asked him, "Why is your book worrrrrrrse than Ingvar Kamprad's book?"

On the video screen, the founder and CEO of Fack Sex's face clouded with a species of wrath one never sees outside the Old Testament.

"Vad?" he barked, making every adult and kid in the Employee Breakroom cabin—except smirking Perdee Dora—flinch.

"Varför är din bok—" she repeated, bold as brass, before a counselor clapped a hand over her mouth.

Pointing his finger as if at a leper, the founder and CEO of Fack Sex let forth a string of Skånska-infused execrations the likes of which we innocent kids had never heard. The normally inexpressive counselors kept repeating, "Ja, ja, ja," with an obsequiousness we had thought them incapable of.

The founder and CEO of Fack Sex abruptly cut off his own tirade when he slapped the video conference camera to the ground in rage, ending the video feed. Perdee Dora was hustled out of the Employee Breakroom cabin and immediately extradited to the U.S.

She was never allowed to return to Fun Time Swedish Language Learning Camp for Little Youngsters, which was fine by her. No one had ever been kicked out of Fun Time Swedish Language Learning Camp for Little Youngsters as a six-year-old. Heck, it was rare for anyone to be kicked out of Fun Time Swedish Language Learning Camp for Little Youngsters at all. It took Juan Tomás and me two more summers and a whole lot of troublemaking to get ourselves politely asked not to enroll in our final year of camp. Perdee Dora had made herself a sworn foe of the Fack Sex Corporation in general, and the founder and CEO of Fack Sex in particular, in mere days.

Now, six years later and 'round about dinnertime, I cornered Pearl at the stove, where she stood stirring a simmering pot of kalops.

"You tell me what you're up to, Pearl Bejou," I commanded.

"I'm cooking the kalo—"

"Don't play dumb with me," I said. "I invented that trick. You tell me what you're up to with regards to Perdee Dora."

"Who says I'm up to something?"

"My very own brain," I replied. "It says you're seeking revenge on her for dumping that nasty ol' milkshake on ya. I did a bit of contemplating and concluded you're on a quest for revenge. I, with my very own eyes, have seen you sneaking all over town as of late. You've become uncharacteristically sly and secretive. And you accepted a mysterious phone call at zero dark o'clock this morning. Taken altogether, it's irrefutable proof that you're plotting a vendetta most dangerously intricate. Tell me what it is. I will help you carry it out."

"Mind your own business," she replied.

"I am minding my own business," I countered. "Perdee Dora herself has caught wind and has made it my business by ordering me to warn you off. You tell me what you've got up your sleeve, and I'll tell Perdee Dora, and then I'll attempt to shield you from her fury."

"I won't tell you a thing," said Pearl. "In fact, I'll neither confirm nor deny that there's anything to tell."

"Consarn it, Pearl!" I cried. "You confess to me right now or I'll—"

But my threat, which was empty, was interrupted by the sound of the front door opening. I abandoned Pearl forthwith to pop off to the living room, where Dr. Dick was helping Opal over the threshold. Opal's face was pale and pained. She moved with excruciating slowness, leaning heavily on Dr. Dick's strong arm. Mama fluttered from one side of the pair to the other, flapping her hands and fussing.

"Don't jostle her," she said. "Don't jerk her too fast. The floor's riddled with humps and holes—don't let her stumble."

"Everything's fine," Dr. Dick said. "Let's get her settled in bed for a little rest and we'll see if she's ready to eat in an hour or two."

I stared at my big sister's chest like a common masher, but her back was hunched so acutely that it was impossible for me to catch a glimpse of her goodies.

"How come you look so sick, Opal?" I said.

"Surgery is hard on the body," Dr. Dick replied. "Even minor surgery. The procedya took longer than expected. But Opal was a real troopa."

"How come it took longer than usual?" I demanded, dogging the pair down the hall to our bedroom, with Mama on my tail.

"You want that cold compress Dr. Dick gotcha at the hospital pharmacy, baby?" Mama asked. "You want a couple aspirins? You want your old teddy bear that you told me to throw out when you were fourteen but I saved in the back of my closet?"

"She just needs to rest and hydrate," Dr. Dick replied, easing Opal into her bed. "Do me a favah? Get a large glass of watah for her."

"Right!" Mama said, darting off with alacrity.

"How come the surgery took longer than you expected?" I asked again, as Dr. Dick pulled a shabby crocheted afghan up to Opal's chin. Her eyes were closed and her forehead was knit in discomfort.

"Well," he said. "The cysts were larger and more numerous than I anticipated. As I drained the superficial cysts, more and more became palpable deepa in the breasts, which had to be drained with a longa needle. If the symptoms persist, ultrasound-guided aspiration might be appropriate. But I think I got the majority of them."

"When can I see the new chestuses?"

"Here ya go," Mama said, dashing into the bedroom with an enormous glass of water slopped up to the very rim.

Dr. Dick took the glass and gently lifted Opal's head from her pillow. She sipped the water, then let out a long, slow breath and unwrinkled her forehead a bit.

"I want to see the new chestuses," I insisted. "Can I see 'em?"

"You leave your sister alone so she can rest!" Mama said. "Don't you dare pester her at a time like this—you get on out and let her be."

"Let's all give Opal a little space," said Dr. Dick.

"Yes, that's exactly what we oughta do," Mama said. She ushered us out of the bedroom and shut the door. She hissed at us to be quiet, ordered us not to walk so loud as we made our way down the hall, insisted we were breathing too noisily, and grew apoplectic when I dared to crack my knuckles.

"She's fine," Dr. Dick assured her, as we regained the living room.

"No, no, she's not," Mama fretted, running a trembling hand through her short blond hair. "She don't look like my Opal at all. She's wan and drawn. What if she's fixing to turn feverish? What if she's bleeding to death under her skin?"

"There's very little risk of infection with needle aspiration," Dr. Dick replied. "And the odds of significant blood loss are practically zero—"

"Oh God!" Mama moaned. "I just know something's gonna go wrong and she's gonna slip away, right under my eyes!"

Dr. Dick reached out and gripped her left shoulder, which brought a surprised look to her face and an abrupt halt to her nattering.

"Crystal-Lynn," Dr. Dick said. "Listen to me. She's fine. I promise. Now, I'm going to go, but if anything—"

"Go? Go where?" Mama demanded.

"Back to town," said Dr. Dick. "To my apartment. It's nearly seven."

"No, no, you can't do that, no!" Mama cried. "You have to stay here in case something happens to her."

"Nothing is going to—"

"Don't go! Just—just stay for a little while. Just until I'm sure she's alright. Just—please just stay for dinner at least," Mama said.

Dr. Dick let out a sigh. I suddenly perceived that he was nearly as tuckered out as Opal. It must have been exhausting, surgerizing Opal's gigantic breasts for hours and hours.

"Alright," he said at last. "Just for dinna."

"Thank you," Mama said, letting out a shaky breath. "Thank you—you're a nice man. And you're the best doctor in Somwärin."

Upon Mama's invocation of "the best doctor in Somwärin," there was a knock upon the front door. When I yanked it open, there stood the devil herself, conjured by the incantation of Her Name.

"Good evening," said The Best Doctor in Somwärin. "I thought I'd stop by and check on the patient."

Dr. Dick's face went from tired to stony as Dr. Flo stepped into the living room.

"Well, well," she said, her hands clasping an old-fashioned doctor's bag. "I must say I'm surprised to see you here. House calls are not usually the provenance of your breed of…doctor."

She pronounced the word "doctor" as if it was the punchline to a dirty joke.

"Doctor" Dick's face went from stony to furious.

"Your consideration is noted," he replied. "And your consultation is rejected. You can leave."

"Mama, there's something wrong with the stove!" Pearl hollered from the kitchen.

"You hush that yelling!" Mama yelled. "Your sister's trying to rest."

"You forget that Opal is my patient, too," Dr. Flo replied. "As her primary care provider, I have an interest in how she responds to any medical treatment."

"But Mama, it's smoking! Not like usual—it's smoking green!" Pearl cried.

"I sincerely doubt you're here out of concern for Opal's well-being," Dr. Dick retorted. "I'm in charge of the young lady's treatment and recovery in this particula case. You will neitha evaluate nor participate in her care at this time. Please go."

"Throw the baking soda on it," Mama shouted to Pearl. "Don't let it sweep up into flames and burn the whole danged trailer down!"

"I have no interest in bandying words with you," Dr. Flo snapped. "And I'm not going anywhere."

"You listen to me," Dr. Dick said in a dangerous voice, leaning down close to Dr. Flo's antagonistic little face. "If you don't leave immediately, I'll—"

But his threat, which was dire, was interrupted by the front door banging opening.

Into our midst swooped 3-J, whooping.

"He's here! He's here!" he proclaimed. "Y'all's father and your husband has hit town!"

Mama let out a scream.

"Don…has…arrived!" he shouted, raising his arms above his head. "Yeeeee-haaaaaw!"

Pandemonium ensued.

Emerald green smoke spilled out of the kitchen, Dr. Dick and Dr. Flo shouted at each other, 3-J emitted six ear-splitting rebel yells, Pearl shrieked, Mama pounded into the kitchen, and a deafening sizzle announced that the fire had been doused.

Then a hush descended as Opal staggered into the living room.

"Behold!" she said, grinning.

She opened her button-down shirt and flashed us all.

As one, we inhaled in surprise. Her chest, while heavily bandaged, was normal in size.

Normal.

Average.

A C-cup at most.

Our mouths fell open.

"And this is with the swelling. Soon they'll be even smaller," Opal announced triumphantly. "I'm hungry—is dinner on yet?"

There was nothing to do but repair to the kitchen to share the evening meal, friend and foe alike. We ate in silence. 3-J squirmed with excitement at the head of the table while Mama frowned at him from the other end, her eyes shifty with terrorized thoughts. Dr. Flo sat on my right, glaring across the table at Dr. Dick, who glowered back at her through the silvery steam wafting up from his bowl of beef stew. Pearl and I goggled at Opal's chest, and Opal beamed at all of us contentedly.

Suddenly, we each jumped a foot in the air as a soul-bleaching white light blasted through the window. An earth-shaking horn blared, rattling the dishes on the table and the very bones within our bodies.

"Them aliens've returned to take me!" Pearl shrieked, diving under the table.

"He's here, he's here!" 3-J exclaimed, jumping to his feet. "It's Don, come home to his women at last!"

He flew out the flimsy side door into the hellishly illuminated yard.

Mama stood, her eyes huge, her lips trembling.

"What's all this? What sort of nonsense is transpiring?" Dr. Flo demanded.

"My—my—my ex is here," Mama said in a faint voice.

Dr. Flo pursed her lips in disapproval.

"I thought you extracted that troublemaker from your life years ago."

"I thought so, too," Mama said. "But he's back."

Dr. Flo daintily pressed a paper napkin to her mouth and stood.

"This is a convalescent house," she said. "I won't have my patient disturbed by truckerly shenanigans. Not while she's recovering from questionable surgery."

Dr. Dick stood too, his lips parting to make an irate rejoinder. But Dr. Flo simply stepped around him and marched out of the kitchen into the supernova in our yard.

We clustered at the window, watching as her teeny-tiny silhouette glided up to the two hulking forms that loomed in the white glare of the truck headlights. Like Javanese shadow puppets, the little black outline of Dr. Flo gesticulated as the two rangy male shapes jumped and jerked and pointed and pivoted. The truck's powerful engine thrummed like a gamelan. One of the shadow-men threw up his arms and galumphed away. The other followed. The bright high beams swung aside to reveal red taillights that drenched the kitchen like a blood-bath. The engine revved and the taillights shrank into the darkness, then vanished completely.

Presently Dr. Flo re-entered the kitchen.

"Your ex-husband and that semi-moron friend of his will return tomorrow. He was imprecise as to the hour. When he does show up again, you had better plan to clear him out once and for all, Crystal-Lynn."

"I…don't know how," Mama said.

Dr. Flo picked up her black medical bag and clucked her tongue in censure.

"If you require assistance, send Don to my clinic. I will give him a thorough talking-to. But I can't fight your battles for you indefinitely. Once Opal has healed from this dubious procedure, you're on your own."

And with that, she nodded and departed.

Opal looked upset. Pearl took her by the hand.

"The Sissy Spacek guest appearance on 'The Waltons' is about to start," she said. "Lemme make you a snug burrow on the couch and we'll watch together."

I, the less considerate of Opal's little sisters, remained in the kitchen to spy on Mama and Dr. Dick, who both appeared to be in distinct distress.

Dr. Dick paced back and forth, a dark scowl casting impenetrable shadows over his eyes. Mama huddled up against the refrigerator, chewing her fake fingernails and twitching apprehensively.

"It's maddening," Dr. Dick muttered. "Every step of the way, she undamines me, she intaferes…house call…primary care provida, my foot…meddling in the relationship of a patient's motha and fatha!"

Mama tugged at the strands of her sophisticated hairdo and sighed. She looked worn out. Beleaguered and beat.

"She thinks she's the quintessential old-fashioned country dacta," he scoffed. "She thinks she's the only one who can handle your ex-husband."

He stopped.

He turned to Mama.

"She's wrong," he said. "I can do it betta than she can."

"What?" Mama said weakly.

Dr. Dick strode across the kitchen. He grabbed her shoulders. He looked into her face, his eyes intent, his jaw set.

"Remember in the cah, on the drive back from Big City?

You explained that plan you came up with to get rid of your ex-husband. Let's do it. Let's tell him I'm your boyfriend."

Mama made a little meep of protest, but Dr. Dick shook his head.

"No, it's a wicked cleva idea," he said. "It's simple, it's harmless. And it's the least I can do afta you got me my only patients. Besides, I'm curious to meet this famous guy. They talk about him all the time in town."

Mama shook her head, dazed.

"I…" she said. "I…alright."

I scurried to the living room to report this momentous happening to my sisters. They squealed. We three were giggling and gabbling when Dr. Dick entered. We fell silent and gazed at him with devilish mischief.

"So," said Opal. "You want us to call you 'Dad?'"

"Or 'Uncle Dick?'" Pearl suggested.

"You do that and folks'll think he's *my* live-in lover," Opal snickered in disgust.

"Now, girls," said Uncle Dad in a serious voice. "I know your motha told you three all about that plan of hers, so let's be mature about this. It's just for a day or two, and just to convince your fatha that he's not welcome here."

He hesitated.

"He isn't welcome…is he?" Dr. Dick said. "Am I doing something inappropriate?"

Opal and Pearl sobered up and pondered Dr. Dick's question.

"No," said Opal slowly. "He ain't welcome. We miss him and all, I guess. But every time he comes around, everything goes topsy-turvy. It's much better with just Mama."

"We don't want Daddy to come home to stay. We're glad you're helping Mama," said Pearl.

I said nothing. All of a sudden, I wasn't sure how I felt.

"I'm tired," Opal said.

Dr. Dick bent down and helped her to rise from the couch.

Mama, spying on us from the kitchen à la me, sprang forward to assume the tucking-in duties.

"You just lean on me," she said, guiding Opal away to our bedroom. "Don't you think of lifting a finger tomorrow—you call in sick to work and make your sisters do your chores."

"Hey!" I exclaimed indignantly.

Dr. Dick grabbed his jacket from the back of the couch and made for the front door.

"Hey!" I exclaimed indignantly again. "Where do you think you're going?"

"Home," he replied.

"Oh no, you don't!" I said. "You're Mama's live-in lover. That means you live here."

"Just for pretend, Ruby," he replied.

"Ruby's right," Pearl said, seizing his left arm. "3-J or Daddy could return any minute of the day."

"Or night," I said, seizing his right arm. "He could be turning that truck of his around as we speak and high-tailing it back here."

"You gotta be here when he shows up, or he'll know it's all fake," Pearl insisted.

"Okay, fine," Dr. Dick sighed, looking with antipathy at the fåtölj, his bed in nights of yore.

We giggled, absconded with his coat, and tugged him to sit on the carpet.

"Goodie!" Pearl squealed. "But since it's just for pretend, you can't sleep with Mama—you gotta sleep with us."

Dr. Dick looked disturbed by this.

We giggled harder and flew away to gather the necessary implements.

While we fetched armloads of blankets and pillows and nail polish and playing cards and soda and chips to form a barricade around Dr. Dick, Mama returned from our bedroom. As she watched us hurrying to and fro, the tight-ratcheted tension in her shoulders loosened. An amused smile crept over her lips. She kicked off her high heels and sat down on the carpet beside Dr. Dick.

"What are they doing?" he said in a bewildered voice.

"They're making you a slumber party," Mama replied.

Opal seemed to be alright after all, Dr. Dick was staying to look after her, and Daddy was waylaid for the moment at least—the relief these facts brought Mama was apparent as she good-naturedly rolled Pearl's hair on rags and cooked up a mess of s'mores on the stove and allowed me to paint her nails bright orange when Dr. Dick flatly refused to permit such an activity to be performed upon his.

We four played card games and gorged on junk food and joked and laughed until first Pearl, then I dropped off to sleep late into the night.

Maybe I was already asleep and dreaming, but I swear that around midnight I saw Mama and Dr. Dick murmuring quietly in the flickering blue light of the TV. Then slowly, slowly he leaned in and kissed her on the lips.

At an hour most wee, 2:42 in the morning to be precise, the phone rang. I groggily opened my eyes, then raised my head from my hot pillow at the sound of Pearl skittering across the living room in the darkness. Within seconds, the telephone's piercing cries ceased, to be replaced by the low sound of my little sister muttering confidentially.

I sat up. In the faint light from the mute TV, I saw Mama curled up on the couch, snoring. Dr. Dick was sprawled in the detested fåtölj, fast asleep.

Pearl was cradling the phone to her ear.

"Hey," she said softly into the receiver.

She listened for a moment, then said, "God."

She hung up. She looked supremely satisfied.

She turned and saw me looking at her.

"The wheels have been set in motion," Pearl whispered.

Chapter Ten
The Day Before the Longest,
Drunkest Day of the Year

Friday, June 20
6:01 a.m.

As the sun was preparing to pull his Peeping Tom routine in the Bejou family living room, I was roused from my blanket fort on the floor by the clamorous cries of a teaming multitude. Shouts from hundreds of voices were superimposed with a cacophony of honking horns, pounding feet, and the offkey squawks of a brass band.

Instantly awake, Pearl and I jumped to our feet and dashed for the front door.

"Put some shoes on!" Mama said, as she staggered to verticality from her couch of repose and pursued us to the trailer's egress.

From his roosting place within the fåtölj, Dr. Dick raised himself on one elbow. He scrutinized us with bleary eyes as I hunted for my sneakers, and Pearl simply stuffed her feet into the first shoes she encountered and sprinted out the door.

"What's going on?" he said.

"It's Midsummer Eve," said Mama, hooking a pair of blue high heels with yellow pinstripes over her bare feet. "Hurry, we've got to go!"

"But—"

There was no time for such prevarication. She snatched up his brown leather Oxfords in one hand, grabbed him by the elbow with the other, and hauled him out into the wide world. I followed, leaving my shoes untied and the front door wide open behind me in my haste to evacuate my home.

The four of us hustled to the edge of the Somwärin Trailer Park and RV Pleasure Garden, where dead grass met dirt road. Dr. Dick hopped from one foot to the other as he slipped his shoes on, then his mouth fell open when he beheld the spectacle that was approaching.

From one horizon to the other, the road was filled with people in various stages of undress. They were advancing toward us from the direction of Somwärin proper, like a colossus with many legs and many mouths. Every member of the mob shouted at us at the top of their lungs as they closed in on us.

"Vakna! Vakna, vakna, vakna!" the crowd bellowed.

All around us along the edge of the road thronged the four dozen denizens of the Somwärin Trailer Park and RV Pleasure Garden, clad in their questionable nightwear. The moment the horde was upon us, we threw ourselves into the thick of it and began to shout in like manner.

"Vakna!" Pearl and I hollered, waving our arms over our heads to emphasize that we were serious about our command.

"What's happening?" Dr. Dick shouted at Mama over the clamor.

"It's Midsummer Eve!" she shouted back. "Vakna!"

"But—what—why…I don't undastand!"

When the last trailer park stragglers scurried into our midst, we ceased our shouting and started to march up the road, singing the timeless traditional Swedish folk song, "Crying at the Discoteque."

Dr. Dick's head swiveled as the crowd surged around us, swallowing us to become part of the monstrous millipede. To his right, Dr. Flo scooted along in a white nightgown. To his left promenaded the Gentleman Gym Teacher, looking most distinguished in his velvet dressing gown, Morocco leather slippers, and hair curlers. Shoving his way to the head of the parade, the sheriff-mayor was unmistakable in his stained wife-beater undershirt, long john bottoms, and silver-studded holster. The high school band, all in pajamas, was scattered hither and yon throughout the crowd, providing unsynchronized accompaniment to our singing.

Dr. Dick stared in shock as Dr. Barney ambled past wearing nothing but sky-blue boxers and a pair of loafers.

"Howdy, Dick!" he said. "You look like you're dreaming—vakna!"

As we passed by a tangle of cottages, the shouts of "Vakna!" resumed until groggy but eager indwellers in nightclothes emerged to join the parade.

"What is the point of this?" Dr. Dick yelled into Mama's left ear.

"It's what we do every year," she replied. "We circle Somwärin, hollering at folks to wake up, until everyone's marching in the parade."

"But…when do we stop?"

"When we've circled back to town. Vakna! Vakna, vakna!"

On and on, we marched and marched, singing and shouting and periodically cheering for no reason until we were hoarse. Along the way we collected the inhabitants of shacks and trailers and bungalows and survivalist compounds. The only lodging places we would not deign to approach were the pay-by-the-days out Motel Way, where the truckers slumbered in hungover indolence.

At last, 'round about the hour of eight, we reached Main Street. By now, every ambulatory resident of Somwärin was part of the crowd. We massed up, shoulder-to-shoulder, at the bottom of the steps leading to the Celestial Temple of Psychedelic Truth and City Administration. Our collective civic body vibrated with excitement. The sheriff-mayor climbed the steps and raised both hands over his head.

"Midsummer Eve has officially be…GUN!" he shouted, pulling his revolver from its holster and brandishing it.

The citizenry laughed appreciatively and let out a cheer. Then, when the sheriff-mayor began to enthusiastically fire said gun, the laughter was transformed to cries of alarm and the crowd abruptly scattered.

As the population of Somwärin split into twelve tribes and fled to the four corners of the earth, Dr. Dick stood like a pillar of salt and gaped until Mama gave him a shove in the right direction.

"Now where are we going?" he demanded.

"Now," Mama replied, puffing as she hustled him along. "We gotta get home and get dressed and get our asses to work so tomorrow we can dive head first into the bottle for a rare reprieve from the burdens of gainful employment and family life."

On the hike back to the trailer park, Mama and Dr. Dick joined forces to put her (my!) daring plan into action. In between huffing breaths, she loudly informed any and every individual who had the misfortune to be hoofing it in our shared direction that she and Dr. Dick were lovers.

"We even slept together last night, right there in my own living room," she announced.

"Technically," Dr. Dick awkwardly corroborated.

For the first time, I began to doubt the probable success of the plan.

Back on the home front, we four fought over precious and swiftly diminishing resources including hot water in the shower, the contents of the cereal box, and the ever-dropping level of the coffeepot. Dr. Dick showed surprising spunk in jostling for supremacy at the bathroom mirror. And then suddenly, everyone had up and gone. I found myself alone with the still-sleeping Opal and my thoughts.

I stepped outside to sit at the little weather-beaten picnic table that marked the border between our property and that of the Disgraced Modern Poetry Professor. I dropped my chin into my hand and fell to brooding.

After a good night's sleep, I still wasn't sure how I felt about Mama and Dr. Dick running Daddy off for good and all. Even though I had conceived the plan, niggling little doubts were beginning to gnaw at the edges of my conscience. Daddy was a source of endless vexation for Mama, true enough. And he'd riled up the townspeople both severally and collectively more times than I could count. But it had left me feeling nonplussed when my sisters, without hesitation, joined the general consensus and voted to oust him. Daddy was a troublemaker, that was certain. But did he deserve to be exiled from the family forever? Wasn't he worthy of a second chance?

Would I one day find myself in Daddy's shoes, banished for my troublemaking ways?

My increasingly glum musings were interrupted by the appearance of Opal. When she sat down next to me on the splintery bench, I leaped to my feet in astonishment. Herselves no longer preceding herself by a good yard, her arrival was a thing of pure stealth.

I stared and stared at her torso. I doubted I'd ever get used to it. She looked so ordinary. A regular teen you might glance at once and then forget. She was smiling a three-hundred-watt smile that was pretty unforgettable for its pure bliss, though. I don't think I'd ever seen a happier smile in all my born days.

"I feel so light," she said, swinging her arms in wide arcs. "Every time I take a step, I feel like I'm gonna rise up off the ground and float around. Dr. Dick said he took a liter of fluid outta each of my titties. How much is that?"

"I dunno. Maybe a gallon jug of cleaner's worth?"

"Maybe. Feels like it. Wheeeeee!" she said, jumping to her feet and twirling in a circle. "Lookit—I can stretch out my arms and join my hands in front of me! I ain't been able to do that in years. I've really got a shot at my dreams now. I can dance, go jogging, swim, lie flat on my stomach—all kinds of things I never been able to do. I can even win Miss Somwärin."

I was only dubious about the pageant.

"You sure? It's just three days away. You think you can be ready by then?"

"Yes," she said with determination. "I'm gonna write a really good speech and find me a talent and work day and night. I won't go out with any boys or watch TV or do anything fun until the pageant."

"Well," I said. "Then I guess you've got a shot, if you want it that much and are fixing to work that hard. Heck, you know what? Maybe I'll help you—"

But my uncharacteristic sisterly generosity was cut off by a commotion on the outskirts of the trailer park. From the dirt road leading to town came the sound of squealing tires and hissing air brakes. All at once, a semi truck, sans trailer, came careening through the Somwärin Trailer Park and RV Pleasure Garden. It veered hither and thither, narrowly missing mobile homes, parked cars, unemployed residents out gathering the morning rays, and Bitch-Girl. It swerved, cutting a hard line in the dust with its skidding tires.

Then it happened: craaaaaaaash!

Screams rang out: some male, some female, some bestial.

The truck had crashed into a trailer.

And not just any trailer.

The Tooth Witch's trailer.

Opal and I leapt atop the picnic table to bear witness to the carnage. As we watched, the Tooth Witch emerged from her front door, which now pointed skyward like a trapdoor because her venerable caravan had been knocked clean onto its side.

As the trucker dragged himself out of the twisted cab of his truck, she set upon him, shrieking and beating about his beer gut with her wizened hands. He tried to stagger away from her, but she threw herself at his spine and clamped both arms around his neck, dangling down his back like a possessed rucksack. The trucker flailed his arms in the manner of a bee-stung bear and spun this way and that, trying to dislodge her. She sank her toothless gums into the back of his neck, bringing a screech of horror from the intoxicated Teamster.

A crowd gathered to observe these happenings. Just as the menfolk were beginning to make rumblings about who among them ought to gather his courage and extract the Tooth Witch from the trucker's hind side, the sheriff-mayor arrived. The red and blue lights on his car were in full vigor of operation, which indicated that he had been in hot pursuit of the self-same semi that had just crashed, and that this pursuit had directly or indirectly (but probably directly) caused the crash.

The sheriff-mayor strode into the loose circle of gawkers and hitched at his belt importantly.

"Well, well, well!" he announced, sounding pleased to find himself knee-deep in a genuine Situation. "And just what've we got here?"

He took in the tilted trailer, the smashed semi, and the floundering driver with equanimity.

"Looks to me like somebody's starting the Midsummer mayhem a whole day early."

The man to which the Tooth Witch had affixed herself gabbled in distress until the sheriff-mayor stepped astern and discerned the she-demon clinging to his back. The sheriff-mayor bent down to confer with her. Her nipping and kicking ceased as she cocked her head to listen, her little legs dangling like a puppet's. The sheriff-mayor pointed at the semi, then at her upended trailer, and shrugged.

The Tooth Witch opened her mouth and made a strident reply, "Yahoo with a triple digit ride done played the bear bait, ain't backed off the hammer, gone and broke the crayon! Broke my crayon!"

The sheriff-mayor scratched beneath his Smokey Bear hat, a sure sign he was puzzled. He considered the Tooth Witch for a moment, then reached out and prized her from the trucker's back. He held her uncertainly under the armpits. He glanced around. He espied Opal and me atop the picnic table. His beady eyes lit up.

Within a dozen paces, he'd closed the distance. He held his charge out to us like an antique ragdoll.

"This-here neighbor of yours done got her trailer totaled. Since you Bejous are known to be friendly with the likes of her, y'all can put her up until she secures new accommodations."

"What—no! We can't—" Opal began, but the sheriff-mayor cut her off with a stern, "You hush now!" and set the Tooth Witch down at our feet.

He turned to leave, then pivoted and stared at Opal's chest. He shook his head.

"Them rumors was true," he commented. "This is a dark day for alla Somwärin."

He stomped back into the ring of lookie-loos, seized the trucker by the collar, and hauled him to the waiting cop car. Away he drove, leaving the Somwärin Trailer Park and RV

Pleasure Garden once again devoid of law enforcement. The crowd regrouped around the picnic table to stare at us with slack jaws for a moment, then grew bored and dispersed.

Opal and I were left alone with the Tooth Witch.

We climbed down from the picnic table. We gazed at her. She gazed back at us.

She let out a little huff of air, sat down on the dusty ground, and opened her toothless mouth.

She began to wail.

Alarmed, we reached out and patted her about the head in an ineffectual, apprehensive style.

All at once, she ceased her lament. She looked at Opal. She pointed at my sister's chest. She cackled merrily.

Opal proudly smoothed her T-shirt.

"Dr. Dick fixed 'em for me," she said.

The Tooth Witch got a faraway look in her inky, wrinkle-framed eyes.

"Bean Town sawbones," she said.

She shot up and toddled into our trailer, just like it was her own home. Which, per the sheriff-mayor, it now was.

Curious, we followed.

She plucked a slightly soiled paper napkin from the kitchen table, snagged one of Mama's abandoned lipsticks, and scrawled a series of fire engine red characters thereupon. She held out her handiwork to Opal.

"Bean Town sawbones," she proclaimed.

Opal disdained the napkin.

"You take it, Ruby."

"No way! She wants you to have it."

"You two are bosom acquaintances. It must be for you."

"You're the oldest. You take responsibility for it."

"I'm the oldest, so I'm ordering you to take it."

"You take it!"

"You!"

"Bean Town sawbones!" the Tooth Witch shrieked, stamping her foot and glowering like the nightmare Tooth Witch of my most terrifying dreams.

I seized the napkin and dashed out of the trailer.

I hurried along into town and betook myself to the Vet 'n' Pet Shop. To my surprise, the door to Dr. Dick's clinical closet was closed.

Dr. Barney poked his head out of the reptile exam room, a lime-green anaconda of alarming girth coiled in figure eights around both arms.

"Got himself a patient in there," he said. "And not one of your relatives!"

Well, you could've knocked me over with a feather. I held out the napkin, my hand trembling.

"A message for him," I said. "From a fearsome master of the occult."

Dr. Barney grasped the napkin between the middle and index fingers of his left hand, which were the only free appendages granted him by the serpent.

"Okie-dokie, I'll pass 'er along," he said.

I didn't reply, for I had already fled.

Back home, I opened the door cautiously. A piercing, keening sound pervaded the air, along with the scent of burning evil.

I froze. If I didn't move, I would be unseen. As I played statue, Pearl scurried into the living room from the kitchen, sporting the one and only apron our household possessed. She was accessorized by a sloshing bucket of cleaning fluid and an expression of indignant servility.

She spied me and mouthed, "Save yourself!" before continuing on her path to the bathroom.

I sidled along the living room wall, intent upon attaining the outer world unnoticed. However, I was unsubtle.

"Twelves?" demanded the Tooth Witch, hearing my T-shirt scraping along the fake wood paneling.

Instantly, she manifested in the kitchen doorway.

I froze, my hand upon the front doorknob.

"Goin' through the woods?" she said. "Got us an expressway boogie. Quitcher dead keying 'n' convoy it."

She jerked her head at me to follow her into the kitchen. I

dared not. But I dared not-not more.

In the kitchen, I found a pot of something foul roiling on the stove, and Opal lying spread-eagle on the table. The Tooth Witch was mumbling and rubbing black stuff on my sister's bare feet.

"She killed Opal!" I screamed.

But it was not so. Opal sat up slowly, a relaxed smile on her face.

"I feel great," she said. "My back's all loose where it always aches, and the spots where Dr. Dick stuck the needle yesterday ain't sore no more."

Opal made to get off the table, but the Tooth Witch chattered at her sternly. Opal obligingly flopped back into her attitude of repose.

"Bean Town sawbones?" the old woman said.

I mimed passing the note along and she nodded, satisfied. She turned away from Opal, reached around the pot of boiling guck, and grabbed her kind's customary mode of transportation.

"Do it to it," she ordered, thrusting our Bitch-Girl-repelling broom into my hand.

"Uh…" said I. "But—"

"Dead pedalin'? Dig you out!" she barked.

I cowered and began sweeping.

As evening drew on, Pearl and I grew mighty tired of the Tooth Witch. She set us to scrubbing and dusting and vacuuming and bed-making and stirring various and sundry pots on the stove. Opal for her part was made to remain flat-out on the table the whole time, dozing and getting her feet rubbed, which I found unfair.

At last, upon the hour of six, a set of keys jangled outside the front door. Pearl and I dropped our tools of domestic servitude and ran to greet Mama.

"Mama! Mama, Mama, thank Thor you're home!"

"It was awful!"

"She keeps calling me 'little beaver.' What if that's a spell?"

"She made me clean the toilet! The *toilet*!"

"What if I wake up tomorrow and I'm a beaver? There ain't no creeks hereabouts where I can build a dam. Where will I live?"

"Wha…" said Mama.

The Tooth Witch strolled into our midst and gave Mama a gummy grin.

"Stack them eights," she said. "How about ya, concrete blonde?"

"Howdy," ventured Mama, adding in a whisper, "What's she doing here?"

"She lives here now."

"Sheriff-mayor says so."

"A trucker ran over her trailer."

"She makes us clean things!"

"We don't like her."

Mama blinked six times. She put her hand to her forehead. She closed her eyes.

She shook her head with resignation.

"Where's Dr. Dick?" she said.

"Bean Town sawbones!" the old woman insisted.

Pearl and I shrugged.

"He's supposed to be here. What if your daddy shows up?" Mama said.

She crossed the room and picked up the phone. She pressed the makeup-stained receiver to her ear.

"I'm a bundle of nerves," she announced as she dialed. "All day long, I ain't had a thought in my head but 'twas about your daddy. What if he shows up and Dr. Dick ain't here? What if—hey there, Dr. Barney. Yeah. Yeah? Yeah. Yeah. Lookie here, is—yeah. Dr. Barney, is Dr. Dick there? Yeah? A real, live patient? Yeah? Well, I'll be."

She hung up.

"He's working," she said in wonder. A smile crept over her lips, then immediately faded as unease got the better of her. "Hope he gets off soon. Hope he makes it here before your daddy. What if he don't?"

She jittered across the worn shag rug, her high heels

catching on the stain shaped like Daddy.

"I ain't got no backup plan," she fretted. "What if I'm caught off guard? What if—"

The front door swung open.

Mama jumped five feet in the air.

3-J strolled in.

"What're you doing here?" she demanded as he sauntered to the couch, plunked himself down, and grabbed the remote. "Where's Don? Ain't he with you?"

"Don," quoth 3-J in a mellow voice. "Is settin' up a three-ring strip club in a big-top tent in the parking lot out front of our lodgings on Motel Way. But even in the throes of his labor, he was a-thinking of his womenfolk, so he sent me here to guard y'all until his great and glorious arrival."

"So he's coming tonight?" said Mama, snatching the remote out of his hand.

"He's going," said 3-J. "To come when the time is right."

Mama threw up her hands.

"He's comin', he's goin'! Tell you where he's going—he's going insane and he's trying to take me with him!" she cried.

Deprived of the televised arts, 3-J rose and shambled in the direction of the beer.

Mama pointed a bright orange fingernail at him.

"You stay put so I can keep my eye on you," she commanded. "There's so damned many people here that I don't even know who's who and what's what no more!"

The Tooth Witch uttered a string of soothing sounds and led Mama into the kitchen. 3-J followed and made a bee-line for the fridge, but was snagged mid-air by the strong paw of the Tooth Witch.

"Let the channel roll," she ordered, thrusting a wooden spoon into his hand and giving him a shove toward the simmering pots on the stove.

"Aw—"

"Quit rakin' the leaves—get 'er going!"

3-J began to stir.

The Tooth Witch seated Mama beside Opal's head, which

hung off the edge of the table.

"G.B.Y.," she said consolingly. Mama was not consoled.

"And who's she? Why's she gotta live with us? We have her over for dinner once, and now we're kin?" Mama fussed at Opal's upside-down head. "And why're you upside-down? What in God's name is happening around here?"

For forty solid minutes, Mama fretted in like manner. At length, her jeremiad was interrupted by a commotion outside. Mama let out a yelp, 3-J let out a hoot, and the Tooth Witch let out a growl. Pearl yanked the side door open and we mashed ourselves into the doorway. Straight down the narrow alley between the trailers ran a man. He was pursued by a salivating beast, which sprang after him at top speed.

Mama gasped.

"Run!" I shouted. "Run for your life, Dr. Dick!"

"Hammer down, buffalo!" the Tooth Witch yelled.

"He's done for!" 3-J wailed.

Dr. Dick sprinted faster, his legs jacking up and down, his arms pistoning in and out.

Bitch-Girl stretched forth her drool-dripping jaws and took a chomp out of the air a mere inch from Dr. Dick's Achilles tendon. He made a mighty leap and landed within the embrace of our ten welcoming arms.

Dr. Dick slammed the door. Panting, he leaned against it to hold it closed as Bitch-Girl commenced a last-ditch, full-body assault upon the flimsy particle board.

Dr. Dick grinned.

"I had the best day," he said. "Well, except for the dawg-incident just now. Is that kung pao chicken I smell?"

He stepped to the stove, took the lid off one of the pots, and inhaled deeply.

"It was incredible," he said, withdrawing a bowl from the cupboard and the wooden spoon from 3-J's hand. "I had three patients today. Three! I'd almost forgotten what it's like to have a good day at work. All of them had heard about Opal's procedya. You were right about word-of-mouth advatising, Crystal-Lynn."

He dished himself a bowlful of the Tooth Witch's brew, plucked a fork from the dishrack, and sat down at the table next to Opal's hip.

"I figga," he said, chowing down heedlessly on the supernatural slop. "If I can get ten to fifteen loyal patients within the next month, I can build a secure medical practice. Big City doesn't have a women's health clinic. There's only a part-time gynecologist at the family medicine centa associated with the hospital. Dacta Flo was completely wrong about the distribution of medical personnel in the area. I'm the only full-time ob-gyn within a two-hundred-mile radius of this town. There are plenty of potential patients. This might not be the biggest disasta of my life afta all!"

Dr. Dick sat back in his chair and smiled at all of us, his dinner consumed. We stared at him, waiting for him to turn into a toad.

"Ah…" he sighed.

He was still in human form.

The Tooth Witch took his empty bowl.

"Thank you," he said.

She stood, bowl in hand, looking at him expectantly.

"That was delicious," he added.

She waited.

"I appreciate it," he said.

She stared at him.

He stared back at her.

"What?" he said.

"Sawbones," she said.

He frowned.

"What does she want?" he asked.

"Lil beaver motored for ya in the big hole. Nailed ya down—catching you on the flip-flop here. Us-all havin' a negative contact?"

"Says she sent ya a note today," said 3-J. "Didn't you get it?"

Dr. Dick fished in his jacket pocket and pulled out the smeary napkin. He handed it to the Tooth Witch. She took it.

She held out her other hand eagerly.

She waited.

She frowned.

Dr. Dick frowned back.

She stamped both feet.

"You hanging my needle? Come on back!" she shrilled.

Clearly they had reached an impasse. Mama lit a cigarette and began to smoke with conviction. 3-J, seeing how Dr. Dick had not become amphibious, dished himself a helping of grub and began filling his maw.

"Mr. Clean ain't jack jawing at ya," he informed the Tooth Witch. "Coz y'all're on the skip."

"Negative!" snapped the Tooth Witch.

She held up the napkin and read aloud, her eyes locked on Dr. Dick's face.

"Prince Harry plumbing, Mickey's pal junior, kennel juice, buffalo bawlin'. Four-ten?"

"I'm sorry, I don't undastand," said Dr. Dick.

"Me neither," said 3-J with a frown. "Ten-one on a ten-ninety-two, come on back?"

"I'm walkin' in blowin' smoke!" the Tooth Witch replied.

She grabbed Dr. Dick by his jacket lapels and began to root through his pockets.

"What's she doing?" he said.

Finding nothing but his wallet, a set of keys, and some lint, she let out a holler of frustration.

"Probably was a shopping list. Can't never trust a man to get a damned thing you sent him out for," Mama commented between nervous puffs of her cigarette.

"Affirmative!" the Tooth Witch crowed, pointing her finger at Mama. She seized Dr. Dick by the hand and dragged him out of his chair.

"Ten-ten me in the wind," she commanded.

She dug through the cupboards and found a decades-old tin of powdered ginger.

"Ginja?" Dr. Dick said.

The Tooth Witch nodded. She set the ginger on the

counter, opened the refrigerator, and rummaged through the produce drawer. She pulled out an antediluvian carrot.

She pointed to the first line on the smudged napkin.

"Prince Harry plumbing. Prince Harry," she said, holding up the ginger. "Plumbing," she concluded, thrusting the carrot under Dr. Dick's nose.

"Ginja…carrot?" said Dr. Dick.

"What the hell's a ginger carrot?" Opal blurted out from the table.

"No wonder he couldn't find 'em. Fack Sex employee grocery store don't carry foreign stuff like that," Pearl said.

The Tooth Witch shook the two blameless comestibles threateningly at Dr. Dick and pointed again at the first line of characters on the napkin.

"Prince Harry plumbing!" she shrieked.

3-J slowly raised his index finger.

"Ah ha! I gets it! It ain't ginger carrot. It's ginger *root*. A root's a plant's plumbing, and a carrot's a root, right? Ha!" he crowed.

"Ah!" we chorused.

The Tooth Witch nodded approvingly at the lights of comprehension dawning in our faces.

"Hold on, let me write this down…gin…ja…rooooot. Okay, got it," Dr. Dick said as he scrawled in his illegible doctor's handwriting on a piece of paper that was, unfortunately, Mama's latest paycheck, and a small one at that.

The Tooth Witch set the carrot and ginger tin on the counter. She pointed to the next item on the list.

"Mickey's pal junior," she said.

She pulled a carton of eggs from the fridge.

"Eggs!" we all yelled

"Yeah, eggs!" 3-J piped up, too late.

"Mickey's pal," said the Tooth Witch.

We gave her nothing but blank looks.

She stuck her hands under her armpits. She squatted and stumped around the kitchen, saying, "Wak! Wak-wak-wak!"

"Pelican!" hollered 3-J.

"Chicken!" I said.

"If she wanted chicken eggs, she'd just take one'a those. Turkey!" said Pearl, and I couldn't be sure if she was guessing "turkey" or calling me one.

"Duck?" Dr. Dick ventured. "Quack-quack? Like Donald Duck—Mickey Mouse's friend?"

"Ten-four," she said, then patted his cheek so hard it was a slap.

"So….duuuuuck…eeeeeggs. That'll be hard to get," Dr. Dick wrote and opined.

"Naw, just go on out Dark Mile Road and Farmer Bill'll sell 'em to you four bucks a dozen," Opal said, looking both inverted and pleased to know something.

"What's next?" 3-J asked.

"Kennel juice," read the Tooth Witch.

"Whiskey?" said 3-J.

"Negatory."

"Vodka?"

"Negative."

"Gin? Beer?"

"Ten-seven, 3-J!"

3-J shut up.

The Tooth Witch pondered for a moment. She slowly approached Dr. Dick and took his hand tenderly in hers. She splayed it and stroked the palm. Then…

"Ta!"

She stabbed his palm with a hairpin drawn from her own silver bun.

"Ow!" he exclaimed, trying to yank his hand away.

She held tight and pointed to the little drop of blood that had beaded up.

"Blood!" we all proclaimed, except Dr. Dick, who maintained a mute and wounded expression.

"That was cool," said 3-J.

The Tooth Witch released Dr. Dick's hand and got down on all fours. She crawled around the kitchen floor, declaring, "How-how-how!"

She abruptly snarled and swung to take a bite out of my ankle. I jumped away in the nick of time.

"Dog!" we all yelled.

"That was easy!" Pearl beamed.

"Dog's blood?" said Dr. Dick. "That's not going in food, is it?"

"Where are we gonna get dog's blood at this time of night?" said Mama.

"Bitch-Girl!" Opal, Pearl, and I chorused.

"Serves that beast right. She drew my blood enough times," said Opal.

"No, this isn't sanitary," said Dr. Dick. "Let's substitute something. Like red food coloring—"

The Tooth Witch slapped Dr. Dick about the chest and arms.

"I guess it's gotta be dog blood and no other, Dick," said 3-J.

"Anything else ya need?" I asked helpfully.

The Tooth Witch consulted her list.

"Hng…" she mused.

She covered her face with both hands.

"Wah!" she sobbed.

"Musta finally hit her about her state of homeless indigence," Opal observed wisely and horizontally.

We rushed to console her.

"Negative!" the Tooth Witch snapped, dry-eyed. "Wah…" she mimed, wiping at her cheeks.

"Tears?" Pearl said.

"That's a Q.S.L.!"

She looked from Dr. Dick to 3-J and back again. She pointed at 3-J.

"What? Whatchoo want?" 3-J protested.

"I guess she wants you to cry for her," said Pearl.

"Well! Nah-uh, ain't gonna happen! Negatory, no way. Let one'a them girls do it," he said, hands on hips, cock-a-walking huffily over the linoleum with his head bobbing in and out.

The Tooth Witch shook her head and reached out to grab

Dr. Dick's and 3-J's crotches.

"Hey, hey!" exclaimed Dr. Dick.

"Buffalo bawlin'," the Tooth Witch said.

"Looks like it's gotta be man-tears. Figures," Mama snorted, smoking madly and joggling her knee in a spasm of nerves and nicotine.

We looked expectantly at the Tooth Witch. She folded her arms and walked into the living room.

"Now what?"

"What's she trying to tell us?"

We followed her and crowded around as she settled onto the couch and turned on the TV.

"Y'all make like bear bait," she ordered, whisking us away with a shooing motion. "I gotta ten-six it."

We wandered back into the kitchen. Mama peeped paranoidly out the window thrice until Dr. Dick gently guided her away and pulled out a kitchen chair for her to sit in. Pearl and I joined her to cluster 'round the fleshy hearth that was our supine big sister.

"Tell y'all what," said 3-J, settling in to sit with us as Dr. Dick brewed a pot of coffee. "Games of chance ain't got nothing on the rigorous intellectual delights of an ol' fashioned game of charades."

"That was fun," said Pearl.

"It certainly was a challenge," said Dr. Dick.

"I wonder what she wanted with alla that stuff," Mama mused, reaching for a fresh cigarette with which to stoke the fire of her anxiety.

"Prolly just a way of passing the time during her sojourn as a displaced refugee in this-here home of yours," 3-J replied, handing around half a dozen stale donuts that he withdrew from some secret place on his person.

"Y'all monitoring?" called the Tooth Witch from the living room. Dr. Dick brought over three cups of coffee for the grownups and settled into the chair next to Mama's. We sat around Opal, nibbling our folksy snack and chatting.

"Y'all ten-seven on me?"

We didn't respond.

Presently the Tooth Witch entered the kitchen. She looked at us, aghast.

"Y'all ain't ten-eight! Y'all glugging the hundred-mile, hangin' it in the ears? Motor it to the skipland!"

"Lemme check my eyelids," protested 3-J.

"Gimme a shout," she ordered. "Prince Harry plumbing, Mickey's pal junior, kennel juice, buffalo bawlin'. Final-final!"

"She says we gotta fetch them exotic vittles right now," said 3-J.

"Are you serious?"

"I done worked a full day—I ain't aiming to go finding and fetching at this hour!"

"I really don't think those items are sanitary."

"Y'all cheese it!" bellowed the Tooth Witch.

And cheese it we did. But most reluctantly.

Grumbling sourly, Mama grabbed her car keys and Dr. Dick, and together the duo set out for Dark Mile Road. Pearl was conscripted to scour every cauldron in the house. Opal remained on the table.

As for 3-J and me, we were granted the deadly mission of exsanguinating Bitch-Girl.

We drew in steadying breaths and threw back our shoulders. We stepped out into the Prussian-blue night. With the stealth of big-game hunters creeping through the African savannah, we tracked the beast through the trailer park, following her deep, raggedy-edged paw prints.

There she was. Tethered to the drainpipe of her owner's run-down single-wide.

We froze. We held our breaths.

She was asleep.

We edged closer to the huge, inert canine form. As we edged, I whispered, "How're we gonna do this?"

"Cut'er open?" 3-J hissed between his gappy front teeth.

"Who's got the knife?" said I.

3-J and I looked at one other. I raised my eyebrows and held out my hand expectantly.

"Why I gotta be the one walking around armed?" he said.

"Alright," I conceded. "And how're we gonna carry the blood home?"

"Cup?" said 3-J.

"You got a cup?" said I.

"No."

We stopped edging.

"Let's pause a moment and consider this," said 3-J.

We formed a two-person huddle.

"So we need to run home and get a knife and a cup," I said.

"Yeah, but that-there's one mean dog. She ain't gonna sit still and let us cut her," 3-J said.

"What if we drug her?" I said.

"Yeah!" 3-J said. "With what?"

"Mama's got some Russian vodka left over from the Cinco de Mayo fiesta she held with her lady friends," I suggested.

"No good. Bitch-Girl's got herself a mile-high alcohol tolerance from her six-pack-a-day habit. You know that," 3-J said.

"Maybe the Tooth Witch's got something druggy," I said.

"Nah, alla her narcotics and recreational pharmaceuticals are currently upended, as is her trailer," said 3-J, and he shook his head with profound regret.

"Let's think logical," I said, frowning in thought.

"How do you get blood outta something without killing it or spilling it all over?" mused 3-J.

"A syringe!" I exclaimed.

"Yeah! Good thinkin', Ruby!"

"Where're we gonna get a syringe?" I asked.

"Dr. Dick?" 3-J said.

"Him and Mama left already," I said, casting an eye across the trailer park to the empty spot where Mama's car usually stood.

"Hell, there're tons of 'em out Motel Way where we truckers hold congress," said 3-J.

It was the reasonable choice.

We hopped into 3-J's truck and sped out to Motel Way.

I'd never been to the truckers' preferred crash pad before. As we pulled up in the lot of the largest of the motels, I goggled and gaped at the enormities that met my eyes.

Dozens upon dozens of semis stood in a ring around the center of the parking lot, like restive bull elephants surrounding a watering hole. Behind them slumped a dull driftwood-gray tenement of two feeble stories, its roof sagging and its windows drooping and its siding shedding like the scales of a decrepit lizard. Betwixt the motel and the trucks towered a gigantic tan and yellow tent, which glowed from within. Several vigorous bonfires leaned in to kiss the canvas sides of the tabernacle, which inflated and deflated like the flanks of an unholy beast.

Music that was all bass resounded from the tent, taking the easy route from the concrete through the tires of 3-J's truck and straight up my sneakers to rock my entrails. Slinky shadows slithered across the magic lantern sides of the tent. All around it, truckers were making mayhem: yelling, punching, cursing, fondling, puking. Firecrackers popped, bottles shattered. A gang of bikers roared up on their motorcycles and joined the fray.

"Behold the modern and most-righteous Sodom and Gomorrah," 3-J said reverently. He hopped out of the truck, calling, "Be right back!"

I sat in the truck. I stared out the windshield. I didn't believe for a minute that he'd be right back.

I began to talk to myself.

"Can't believe Daddy's here somewheres!" said I.

I was silent for ten minutes.

"Y'know, 3-J ain't never coming back till morning," I said.

"I don't wanna stay here till morning!" I wailed.

"I best go find him—he can't have gone too far," I advised.

I agreed with me.

I hopped out of the truck. Immediately, I was enveloped in chaos. I was swept fore and aft by the throng until I washed ashore within the tent. It was sweltering. All around the edges stood rickety bleachers of questionable soundness. They were packed with scruffy-faced, baseball-hatted, flannel-shirted men. At ground level, three rings had been demarcated by orange traffic cones. Within them twirled fancy ladies with no clothes on. The men in the bleachers cheered and carried on, flinging fistfuls of low-denomination currency from seven sovereign nations at the ladies. The stench of sweat and diesel fuel and testosterone was unbearable.

I had to flee.

Alas, I was not as graceful as the naked circus nymphs. As I turned to make my escape, I tripped over a nondescript bungee cord attached to a guy rope. The bungee cord shot away like a rubber band released from the thumb of a mischievous Sunday school lad. While it struck neither strippers nor truckers in its flight, it did release the guy rope from its moorings, which caused the tent to ominously sag first on one side, then another. After shrugging louchely like an Italian playboy for a spell, the top of the tent began to sink earthward in slow motion, eliciting screams and a mad stampede.

I made it out easily enough, but the denizens of the titty teepee weren't so lucky. As the canvas settled softly upon them, they were ensnared. In the light of the bonfires, they wriggled like worms beneath the fabric, which now lay flat on the concrete. Their yells of displeasure filled the night air. One of the first to emerge was 3-J.

He staggered to his feet, shaking his head to clear it. He spied me. He commenced a stunned shuffle in my general direction. He tripped and fell against one of the bikers' motorcycles, knocking it clean over.

"He laid hands on my hog!" the biker screamed in a high, womanish voice.

The entire gang, which had wisely remained outside the doomed circus tent, crowded around 3-J and me.

"I—I—I'm Don Bejou's kid," I shouted. "And this-here's Don's best buddy. So no one better hurt us!"

"Don Bejou!" chorused a clutch of strippers who had just wrested themselves from their cloth cage.

"He stiffed us for our services!"

"Owes over five hundred bucks to me!"

"That's a felony in Somwärin!"

"And Sweden!"

"International criminal!"

A faction of irate truckers joined them.

"Don's deep in arrears to us for erecting that danged tent of his. Owes us a whole stack of Jacksons."

"And a bottle of Jägermeister."

"Ain't seen a dime nor a shot."

Truckers, bikers, and strippers were accreting into an impenetrable ring, encircling 3-J and me.

"We—we done called the sheriff-mayor, so you best scatter," I ventured.

The ring tightened and its constituent parts burst out laughing.

"The sheriff-mayor don't dare set foot here after dark."

"Both of ya's done for. Burn 'em!"

"Into the bonfire!"

The crowd surged forward.

"Daddy, why ain't you coming to save us!" I wailed.

"Dr. Flo!" shouted 3-J.

The crowd froze. In the flickering firelight, their faces were slack with fear. Then one of the bikers spoke up uncertainly.

"Bullpucky. It ain't Saturday. She don't make her rounds until then."

"That's right!"

"She ain't here—burn 'em!"

The crowd surged toward us once more.

I gripped 3-J's hand in wild panic.

Suddenly everyone stopped dead as Dr. Flo, her very self in the very flesh, stepped into the center of the ring.

She looked unamused.

"What's all this?" she barked. "I get an emergency call from a woman stating that she's giving birth, and I find only a welder-by-day with an unnaturally high voice and a poor sense of humor."

The soprano biker grinned sheepishly.

"How often must we go through this? Is this how you people occupy your time? Callow pranks…and a medieval witch burning ceremony?" she accused.

The truckers, strippers, and bikers hung their heads.

"And why," Dr. Flo proclaimed, spinning on her sensible heel. "Do I find a child in this den of iniquity? Must I remind you once again of the five flaws of the hedonist lifestyle? I believe I must. Don't you try and slink away—get back here!"

"Yes, ma'am," a gaggle on the periphery replied meekly, inching back into the circle.

Inspired by their example, 3-J and I edged into the circle proper, then into its midst, then to its outer edge as Dr. Flo declaimed, "One: The life of the flesh is a life of corruption that takes as its founding principle the subjugation of the female."

As Dr. Flo rounded third base with, "Three: The hedonist takes for his—and he is always a male—personal philosophy a solipsistic worldview that admits no possibility of wrongdoing on his part. Yet he is always doing wrong. Always," we made a break for it.

Unfortunately, Dr. Flo noticed.

"You two need to hear this informative lecture more than all of these moral blunderers combined," she shouted. She turned to her obedient auditors and pointed at us. "Bring them back."

3-J and I dashed to his truck, chased by the mob. We clambered aboard, 3-J ignited the engine, and we roared off. But woe unto us, the rest of the crowd was equally equipped with automotive transportation. Behind us, semis and motorcycles and even Dr. Flo's makeshift ambulance rumbled to life and ground the concrete beneath their tires in pursuit of us.

3-J humped us up onto the highway and put the hammer down. The semi surged forward, the needle laying in close to 80 mph. Behind us, our pursuers did likewise.

"Never have I seen my brother truckers so riled," 3-J said in a desperate sort of voice I hadn't heard emerge from his mouth before. "We ain't likely to get outta this in one piece."

Meanwhile, Mama and Dr. Dick were traveling peacefully along the pastoral backroad that led to Farmer Bill's place. Dr. Dick turned on the radio as Mama drove. He scrolled in vain through the stations.

"We ain't got no Chinese opera channel around here," Mama teased.

"I'd settle for any sort of music," he replied, as the stations shouted:

"Jesus!"

"The Lord commandeth you!"

"Santo Dios!"

"Odin, reach down from Valhalla—"

He gave up and switched the radio off. Mama laughed.

"It just seems so quiet out here," said Dr. Dick. "I don't know if I'll evah get used to how quiet it is in the countryside. It's like you're all alone in the world."

"Well, ya are all alone. With me," said Mama.

"True," said Dr. Dick.

"It's nice being alone with you," said Mama. "I like talking to you."

"I like talking to you, too," said Dr. Dick. "I can't get enough of your accent."

"Accent? I ain't got an accent."

"You most certainly do."

"Nah-uh, mister, you're the one with the accent. Ask anybody in town."

Dr. Dick sighed.

"You may have a point," he said. "Half of them can't undastand a word I say."

"I understand you just fine," said Mama, taking her eyes off the road to give him A Look.

"I undastand you, too," he replied, giving her A Look of his own.

The two were silent for the rest of the drive.

They pulled up out front of Farmer Bill's darkened farmhouse at the romantic hour of 8:43 p.m., when the sky had gone velvety and the moon had become shimmery and the stars had turned glittery. Mama parked the car on the crisp, dead lawn and got out. She shivered as the chill night air wafted through her filmy Fack Sex T-shirt and up her short skirt. Dr. Dick got out as well, stepped to her side of the car, and put an arm around her shoulders to warm her.

They took three steps toward the lifeless farmhouse.

They stopped.

Mama plucked a cigarette from her pocket and thumbed her lighter to life. She raised the cigarette and the flame to her cherry-red lips. Dr. Dick pushed her hands down gently. She dropped the lighter and the cigarette. Her eyes became trapped in his as he gazed tenderly at her. He leaned down and kissed her.

As he pulled back, he shouted, "Wicked pissa!"

A small fire was burning in the dry grass where the lighter—repaired by the altogether too effective Opal—had fallen.

Mama yelped and jumped back.

"I'll find watah!" Dr. Dick said, dashing off.

Mama toe-tapped at the flames with her high heels, trying to stamp it out. But her meek ministrations only served to fan the flames.

"Hurry, Dick!" she cried. Then, "Oh lordy!" The fire hit an oil patch and flared into a blazing column that towered ten feet in the air.

Mama ran to the front porch and pounded on the front door.

"Farmer Bill! Open up!" she shouted. She tried the knob, but the door was locked.

As Mama was failing in her duties as volunteer firefighter, Dr. Dick was feeling his way around the exterior wall of the house, searching for a hose. The lack of artificial illumination hindered his progress. His citified eyes were not accustomed to nocturnal scavenger hunts conducted in a rural milieu. At last his fumbling fingers made contact with a small shed. He battered at it with both hands until he discovered a door. He pulled it open. There sat Farmer Bill, reading a book by candlelight, as was his preferred pastime when visiting the outhouse after dark.

"ARRR!" Farmer Bill bellowed.

"Excuse me!" Dr. Dick exclaimed, slamming the door.

Dr. Dick reopened the door. "Are you Famma B—"

The business end of a shotgun confronted him, and Dr. Dick fled, screaming.

Meanwhile, resourceful Mama had jimmied open a window and was trying to climb into the house. Unfortunately, she had overestimated her slenderness and had gotten herself wedged between the sill and the sash, leaving her hanging half-in and half-out.

"Help! Dr. Dick! Farmer Bill! Stuck!" she called.

Dr. Dick had no time to render assistance. He dodged her kicking legs as he fled from Farmer Bill.

"Mista Bill, sir, I think we misundastood each otha!"

Farmer Bill let out a roar of alarm in reply.

"Far! Far! There's a far on m'land!"

He abandoned his pursuit of Dr. Dick and veered to the front door. Suspicious rustic that he was, he insisted upon triple-locking his doors in the time of truckers, which led to a good deal of fumbling with his key ring and bucolic cursing.

The fire surged voraciously upward and outward.

At last, Farmer Bill gained admittance to his own home and darted inside. He was immediately confronted by the disembodied torso of Mama, which hovered in the window like a half-ghost.

"Help! I'm stuck fast, Farmer Bill!" she bleated.

Farmer Bill cursed and took hold of her arms, just as Dr. Dick took hold of her legs. Both tugged at the same time and Mama screeched in pain.

"Lemme go! Y'all're splitting me asunder!"

The gentlemen did as they were bade. Mama slid out of the window onto Dr. Dick, knocking him flat. Stunned, he lay motionless on the parched lawn.

"Dick! Wake up. Vakna!" she urged, fanning his face with one hand and jostling his limp carcass back to life with the other. In a moment he came to, just as Farmer Bill jogged around the corner of the house, hollering incoherently and dragging a python-green garden hose. The unlucky sharecropper tripped over the pair and went sprawling in the grass, the hose springing away from his grasp.

And that was when the trio heard an unnatural squawking sound. They froze and listened.

"It's got at the duck coop!" Farmer Bill exclaimed.

They hightailed it across the yard to the coop, dragging the hose between them, but it was too late. The whole thing went up in a surging inferno. Charred feathers flew heavenward to twirl with malevolent orange sparks among the cruel white stars in a tragic tango.

As the flames ebbed, Farmer Bill turned to Mama and Dr. Dick, snorting like an angry bull.

"I suppose we wouldn't be able to trouble you for a duck egg?" Dr. Dick ventured.

Farmer Bill did not react well to the request. As Dr. Dick once again fled over hill and dale from the enraged agriculturalist, Mama had a thought.

She crept onto the porch, opened the unlocked front door, and slipped into the dark farmhouse. She skulked to the kitchen. Next to the battered zinc washtub that served as a sink she spied an old-timey icebox.

She opened it. Inside, she discovered a treasure trove. Shoved behind a dented tin can brimming with goat's milk was a chipped blue china dish containing three smooth duck eggs.

She snatched one.

She dashed out the front door, her chilly prize cupped in both hands.

"Duck egg! C'mon, Dick!" she shouted.

Dr. Dick careened around the livestock barn, his arms

pinwheeling, and made tracks for the Oldsmobile. He threw himself behind the wheel and Mama dove through the passenger door as Farmer Bill wheezed his way across the dark yard.

"Go, go on, Dick!" Mama cried, tossing him the car keys.

Dr. Dick slammed the car door. He jammed the key in the ignition. He turned it. The engine sputtered. He turned the key again.

"Quit flooding the sucker and get going!"

Dr. Dick turned the key one more time. Just then, the barrel of the shotgun poked through the open driver's side window and kissed his left cheek.

At this very instant, 3-J and I were swerving onto Main Street, harried from the highway by a posse of trucks and motorcycles. Just as we sped past the Pubic Library, 3-J hit the brakes, sending me jolting against the windshield. Straddling the breadth of Main Street were a pair of bulky semis. They blocked our only path of escape.

"What do we do?" I said.

3-J considered. He opened his mouth to spout some wisdom, but before it could make its way from his brainpan to his talking hole, our pursuers swarmed around us on all sides. Brilliant headlights dazzled our eyes. Motorcycle tailpipes snarled and truck engines chortled as a loud voice boomed, "Come out, the two of you!"

I tried to look at 3-J, but he was invisible in the white-washing light.

"Don't make me tell you twice!" the voice insisted.

3-J and I inched our way out of his truck, our hands raised like criminals cornered by the sheriff-mayor. We squinted and blinked in the blinding glare.

Dr. Flo emerged from the bright beyond and stepped up to us.

"Now then," she said. "I'm quite upset with both of you."

"Back me up, Ruby," 3-J muttered out of the corner of his mouth.

"You are clearly operating under some ill intent. I've a good mind to uncover what it is before turning you over to the unsubtle but not ineffective machinations of the sheriff-mayor," she continued.

The horde began to press forward, gleeful grins gleaming. I knew we were done for. I squeezed my eyes shut.

At that moment, 3-J sprang forward and seized Dr. Flo in his arms.

Emitting a yawp like a Soviet weightlifter going for the bronze medal at the Olympics, he initiated an impressive overhead press and lifted her chubby little body horizontally above his head like a barbell.

"Stop—stop, everyone! He's got Dr. Flo!" cried one of the bikers.

"Put me down at once, Mr. J!" Dr. Flo ordered from on high, trying to squirm out of his grip while maintaining her regal dignity.

"Back!" shouted 3-J, brandishing Dr. Flo at the rabble.

The circle of attackers parted. 3-J bounded through a breach in the bodies, toting Dr. Flo over his head.

I considered the situation for all of two seconds, then ran after him down sultry, swarthy Main Street. Behind us, a general cry of alarm went up. The roadway began to vibrate under the pounding feet of our adversaries.

As he reached the Swedish Embassy & Beauty Parlor & Coffee Shop, 3-J paused for a split second, considering a flight to the refuge of foreign soil. Instead, he scrambled up the sidewalk to Dr. Flo's home turf.

"Sanitary!" 3-J bellowed from the threshold of the clinic. "Sanitary, sanitary!"

"Sanctuary!" I corrected.

The crowd menaced us from the sidewalk with profane threats and lighters jerry-rigged into flame-spouting torches. 3-J laughed, turned away from Dr. Flo's enraged devotees, and thrust himself face-first against the closed clinic door.

"It's locked, you oaf," Dr. Flo snapped from above his head.

"Gimme key!" 3-J said.

"No, absolutely not. I don't for a moment approve of this vigilante—"

"Gimme key!"

3-J flexed his biceps and pumped her up and down.

A key ring fell out of her pocket.

I scooped it up when it hit the concrete, shoved the shiniest key into the lock, and gained ingress.

We rushed inside and slammed the door. The crowd began to pound on it. I turned the deadbolt and shoved a couple waiting room stools against the thick wood for good measure.

3-J set Dr. Flo down, breathing hard and rubbing his arms. The waiting room was quite dark. I hunted for a light switch, discovered one, and flicked it. Surgically bright fluorescence bleached the space. A loud siren began to scream. I clapped my hands over my ears.

"What's that?" I shrieked.

"You've set off the security alarm. Now the sheriff-mayor is coming," Dr. Flo shouted with satisfaction.

"How d'you shut it off?" I cried.

"There is a keypad into which the password must be entered. You didn't do it when we entered, so..." she shrugged and seated herself upon a stool to await the arrival of the Five-0.

"Gimme password!" said 3-J.

"No."

"Gimme password now!"

"No," said Dr. Flo, crossing her arms over her grandmotherly bosom.

I decided to disengage myself from their bickering and make hay of this sorry situation. If anyone had a syringe, it would be Dr. Flo. She had jabbed me countless times over the years.

I moved through the dim space past a red door marked

"Emergency Exit" and made for the exam rooms. It only took a slim minute of hunting to locate several fine specimens. I returned to the waiting room armed with the biggest syringe of all, just as the sheriff-mayor's cop car pulled up out front, its lights shooting red and blue sparkles through the closed Venetian blinds.

Through the falcon-shriek siren and the shrill security alarm came an unintelligible jabbering from the sheriff-mayor's bullhorn. 3-J unlocked the front door, opened it a crack, and stuck his head out.

"What?" he shouted.

The sheriff-mayor fired his sidearm at 3-J in response. 3-J ducked back inside, grabbed Dr. Flo under the arms, and held her like a shield before his body.

"You'll never take us alive!"

Bullets flew again, heedless of Dr. Flo. 3-J pulled himself and the town physician back inside, and slammed the door.

"You're trapped," said Dr. Flo. "Give yourself up and accept your lawful punishment. There is no alternative."

"Let's go out the emergency exit," I said.

Dr. Flo was not in favor of my suggestion, but 3-J was. Hoisting Dr. Flo under his arm like a football, 3-J jogged past the twenty-yard line and through the end zone, winding up out of bounds in a narrow back alley.

It was deserted.

"Help! Attention! Help!" Dr. Flo called.

3-J mashed a hand over her mouth. She bit him. He yelped and withdrew his hand.

"The dangers of a human bite far exceed those of the common dog," she informed him.

Behind us, we could hear a loud *slam-slam-slam*! The truckers, urged on by the sheriff-mayor, were attempting to batter down the front door of the clinic. 3-J slung Dr. Flo over his shoulder and we insinuated ourselves into the darkness. Down the alley we crept.

We stole through the ranks of idling trucks, which stood abandoned along Main Street, searching for 3-J's rig.

There it was! My fellow abscondee and I looked at each other.

"On three," said 3-J.

"One," I said.

"Two," he said.

"Help!" Dr. Flo shouted.

3-J and I lit out for the truck just as the throng broke through the clinic door. Dr. Flo's voice, lost in the hubbub, floated away into the night.

3-J chucked Dr. Flo into the front seat. I clambered after her. He cranked the engine and swung his head this way and that, the steering wheel following suit. Across from the Tree of Contemplation, a chink had appeared in the wall of blocking vehicles. 3-J floored the gas and upshifted. We barreled down the road, straight for the parked trucks. I braced myself for impact.

With a tooth-aching *scriiiiiiitch*! of metal-on-metal, 3-J's semi slipped between the two trucks.

We shot down Main Street and out of town to the liberty of the open road.

"Think we made it," I panted. "Think we're okay."

"Yeeeeee-haaaaaaw! Hell yeah!" exclaimed 3-J, pumping his fist in exultation.

He glanced over at the scowling doctor beside him.

His grin faded.

"Your situation has just gone from serious to dire, sir," she said.

Meanwhile, Dr. Dick and Mama were stammering at gun-toting Farmer Bill from the insecurity of Mama's car.

"Get out," Farmer Bill ordered.

"Now, now, wait—" said Dr. Dick.

Farmer Bill racked the shotgun.

Dr. Dick and Mama got out of the car, their hands up.

"Give back m'egg," said Farmer Bill, leveling the shotgun at Mama.

Mama clutched it between her hooters.

"No! We need it!" she said.

Farmer Bill took a step toward her, the barrel of the shotgun pointed at the shadowy spot between her knockers.

"What she means what she's saying what the situation appeahs to be is there's an orthodontist or I suppose a drug deala of sorts and she lost her traila to a trucka today and she requiahs this egg for reasons that aren't entirely cleah and we came out here to purchase it but Crystal-Lynn dropped her lighta when I kissed her and it set the grass on fire and this is all a very unfortunate misundastanding!" babbled Dr. Dick.

Farmer Bill cocked his hoary head.

"You talking about the Tooth Witch?" he inquired.

Dr. Dick said, "Um?"

Farmer Bill lowered the shotgun.

"Well," said Farmer Bill. "Since it's for the Tooth Witch, I don't guess I can deny it to y'all. But tomorrow, the two of you best turn up at the Celestial Temple of Psychedelic Truth and City Administration to answer for your high crimes. Duck murderers!"

"Yes, sir, Farmer Bill," said Mama.

Dr. Dick frowned.

"What do you mean, the Celestial Temple of Psychedelic—"

"Get in the damned car, Dick!"

Dr. Dick hastily resumed his place behind the wheel and Mama slid in beside him, cradling the duck egg. He turned the key and put the car in motion. Away they sped.

They rode in silence.

"I'm thinking of giving up the smokes," said Mama at last, in a shaky voice.

"And five: The hedonist lifestyle is by its very nature a state of degeneration and degradation. Without forward progress, humankind finds its condition to be identical to the vegetative state of the lesser flora and fauna. Are we no better than the lowly amoeba? Shall we not aspire to more than the ignoble algae? Do we not wish to transcend our base instincts? I rest my case," concluded Dr. Flo, as we pulled into the Somwärin Trailer Park and RV Pleasure Garden.

3-J's truck shuddered to a stop out front of the Bejou family trailer just in time to see Mama and Dr. Dick getting out of the Oldsmobile.

"Only women can be trusted to handle delicate things when it counts," Mama was saying. "You'll smash it."

"I've held premature babies on the brink of death and a beating human heart in the ER, and you won't trust me to hold a duck egg?" Dr. Dick said.

"Fine!" Mama snapped. "Hold the damned thing," and she thrust the egg into Dr. Dick's hands.

"Careful!" Dr. Dick exclaimed. "You almost made me drop it."

"Oh, joy," said Dr. Flo, as I helped her down from 3-J's rig.

3-J jumped out of his truck and strolled over to his good buddy. He clapped a hand on Dr. Dick's shoulder and gave it a squeeze. Dr. Dick flinched in surprise and nearly released the egg.

"Hey, Dick! I see y'all found Farmer Bill's no problem," said 3-J. "Good on you!"

He slapped Dr. Dick heartily on the back. Dr. Dick was knocked off balance. He clutched the egg to keep from dropping it. The shell cracked.

"Dammit!"

"Didn't I tell you?" said Mama.

Dr. Flo stepped forward and eyed Dr. Dick up and down, her gaze lingering on the oozing yellow goo he cradled in his hands.

"I should have suspected you were behind this," she said. "You are in deep trouble, young man. Kidnapping is a felony. I intend to see to it you're sent to prison for a very long time, where there will be no women-parts available for your so-called examinations."

Dr. Dick stuttered, sputtered, then shouted "Gah!" He stomped into the trailer, cupping the viscous glop with both hands.

Dr. Flo tsk-tsked and shook her head. She turned to Mama.

"Take me back to town," she commanded. "I'll settle that charlatan's hash first thing in the morning."

There was no time to eavesdrop on Mama's reply. The moment had come for 3-J and me to harvest Bitch-Girl's blood.

Our trek through the wilds of the trailer park was masked by the dense black of the night. Here and there, little pools of warm yellow light spilled onto the ground from the trailers that towered on either side of our trail. We walked with hunched backs and ready hands, the better to spring and strike.

"Now, remember," said 3-J in a low voice. "That dog's a fearsome beast. There's no telling what mortal wounds she might inflict. This may be our last night on earth."

I nodded.

"If I die," 3-J said. "I want you to have my package. You're the only person who appreciates it like I do."

I was touched.

I parted my lips to reply, but lo! There she was.

We stopped dead.

As before, Bitch-Girl was tethered out front of her master's trailer, her leprous body suffused with sickly ochre light that leaked from a fly-specked bulb above the porch. But now, she was wide awake and gnawing on a beer bottle with her formidable yellow fangs. She hadn't caught wind of us.

Yet.

"The element of surprise!" 3-J whispered.

He hunched and tensed his muscles, the syringe at the ready. He leapt.

Bitch-Girl looked up.

She dropped the beer bottle and growled.

3-J pulled back in mid-vault and tripped over his own feet.

Bitch-Girl jumped to her four scabby paws and charged at him.

"Waaaaah!" cried 3-J.

The chain, secured around her neck with an old bicycle lock, caught and bent the rusty drainpipe. 3-J flung himself aside like an action figure tossed by an invisible child. Bitch-Girl's foam-covered tusks rent the void of space where 3-J's right hand should have been. I searched the ground for one of my trusty two-by-fours fend her off, but the field of combat was bereft of armaments.

3-J scuttled backwards through the dirt, crab-style, to me.

"Lemme re-think this a moment," he panted.

"Gimme that syringe. I can take her. I know her ways."

"No. I guess a man's gotta do his manly duty," 3-J said.

"I sure do think I can do it better," I said.

But he just hitched his belt up, cocked the plunger of the syringe back, and let out a rebel yell.

"Yeeeeeeee-haaaaaaw!"

He ran full tilt at Bitch-Girl.

The ensuing battle produced a ten-foot-tall tornado of grit that swirled in the dim circle of saffron porchlight. All I could make out within the dun cyclone was a mass of thrashing limbs as man and beast became one in their fatal combat. Barks and yelps emerged from the throats of both combatants. There was a bang of aluminum on aluminum, and Bitch-Girl's owner appeared in the doorway of the trailer. She rubbed her eyes and gazed about myopically.

"What-all's goin' on out here? Woke my babies with this ruckus."

"Just borrowing some of Bitch-Girl's blood, ma'am," I replied.

"Oh yeah? Well, dontcha come crying to me when y'all git bit," she said.

She leaned against the screen door and squinted at 3-J as he wrestled the snarling, snapping dog to the ground. He sat on her writhing, flea-colonized body. He raised his arm above his head.

"The moment of truth!" he cried.

He brought his arm down in a savage arc, stabbing the dog in the neck with the syringe. He depressed the plunger. He waited.

"Nothing's happening!" he cried.

"Didja pull the plunger out?" I demanded.

"Yeah! Did that before I jumped her."

"Ya gotta stick the needle in first, then pull the plunger out!" I said.

"You mean I gotta wrassle her a-ground all over again?"

"No, just pull the plunger out now!" I shouted.

Bitch-Girl's red eyes were a-gleam with blood lust. Her gnarled muscles worked as her muzzle slammed closed again and again, seeking man-flesh. It was only a matter of time before she overcame Daddy's bestest friend in the world. 3-J drew back the plunger of the syringe with his thick thumb. The syringe filled with wine-red gore. Bitch-Girl let out a howl like Beelzebub down in hell. 3-J yanked the needle free of her scruff.

"On three," he said. "One—"

But Bitch-Girl threw him off, her body snapping taut like the crack of a whip. She clamped her jaws onto 3-J's wrist. His thumb reflexively depressed the plunger and a thin thread of blood squirted skyward.

I scooped up a fistful of dirt and flung it into Bitch-Girl's face. She squeezed her eyes shut and shook her head, snorting. 3-J wrested his wrist from her maw and together we took off running.

"Git 'em, Bitch-Girl!" cawed the dog's owner, releasing the chain from the drainpipe.

Freed, Bitch-Girl galloped after us, dragging the industrial-grade chain behind her. The dog's barks sounded and resounded from one end of Texas to the other. 3-J and I sprinted for the safety of the Bejou double-wide. It seemed impossibly far away. I could feel Bitch-Girl's sulfurous breath burning my calves. We weren't going to make it!

We dove for the front door, our feet tangling in the broken

metal stairs. 3-J kicked the front door in since there was no time for keys or knobs. We toppled into the living room. 3-J frantically slammed the off-hinges door into the jam. A massive crash shook it and a volley of fierce barks thundered just outside the trailer. I crawled over to Dr. Dick, who was sitting on the couch staring wide-eyed at 3-J as he strained to hold the door closed.

"Get me a brace, Ruby!" 3-J shouted.

I regained my feet and dashed into the kitchen. Pearl and the Tooth Witch looked up from the steaming stove in surprise. My eyes roved the kitchen. The broom was too spindly and the kitchen chairs too flimsy for such a task. Then I saw Opal, still flat on her back. I grasped the end of the table and began to shove it across the linoleum and into the living room.

"Help me, Pearl!" I cried.

Pearl and the Tooth Witch rushed to my side and helped me push the table across the scrabbly living room carpet. It went skimming over the worn shag, carrying Opal along for the ride. 3-J dropped to his knees just in time as the table crashed against the door.

"Don't leave me here! Help!" said Opal.

The Tooth Witch and I grabbed her arms and pulled her out of danger as 3-J crawled out from under the sturdy piece of Nordic furniture. The five of us backed up to the couch and pressed close to Dr. Dick, staring at the door. The table rattled but held.

Some more barks. A howl of wrath.

Then silence.

3-J collapsed on the couch next to Dr. Dick, his hand dropping in manly companionship onto Dr. Dick's upper thigh, which perturbed Dr. Dick. I fell to the floor next to Pearl, who was clinging to Dr. Dick's lower leg. Opal slumped against his shoulder, her cheek pressing his. The Tooth Witch hopped onto his lap and put both arms around his neck.

"Well…" said Dr. Dick uncomfortably. He cleared his throat thrice.

"Here…kennel juice…how-how…" wheezed 3-J, holding out the syringe to the Tooth Witch.

"Preeshaydit," she responded, accepting the half-full syringe and snuggling up against Dr. Dick's chest, with no apparent intention of rising.

Suddenly the door began to thud again!

All of us—including Dr. Dick—screamed.

The table rattled and shifted.

The door opened a crack and a skinny white limb inserted itself.

"Goddamn it, what the hell happened to my door? The hell?"

Mama shoved her way through the narrow crevasse between the door and the jam.

We let out sighs of relief.

She stared at us, flummoxed, and planted her hands on her hips.

"Well, ain't y'all cozy? Meanwhile, my ears are getting a third-degree scalding from Dr. Flo, and I'm having to promise all kinds of uncomfortable things, and I don't know what-all any of us are gonna do tomorrow when we're called to account! Well?" she said.

We glanced at one another. We rose.

"Guess that's that, then," said 3-J.

He and the Tooth Witch toddled off to the kitchen.

"Don't stick yourselves with that syringe," Dr. Dick admonished, following them. "The risks of bloodborne pathogens are not negligible."

"Feels good to stand up finally," Opal commented, following the crowd, and Pearl trotted gamely behind her.

Mama threw up her hands, incredulous.

"Sheesh!" she exclaimed, then stomped off to the kitchen herself.

I took a moment to set my nerves in order. I eyed the broken door. I pressed my palm to my racing heart. Is this what Daddy felt when he committed his notorious acts of mischief?

Did I like it?

Rather than confront what I sensed would be an unsettling answer to this question, I headed into the kitchen, where I found everyone hovering around the stove.

"Hey, wha—" I said.

"Shhh!" Opal hissed.

She, 3-J, Mama, and Pearl glowered at me. Dr. Dick shrugged.

I joined them at the stove. The Tooth Witch was stirring a steaming pot and muttering.

"We can't talk." Dr. Dick said. "She already yelled at me, and—"

The Tooth Witch whirled and pointed a claw-shaped finger at Dr. Dick.

"Ratchet jaw!" she proclaimed in a wild tremolo.

Dr. Dick made an apologetic gesture and she returned to her stirring and muttering. Presently, her mutter became a chant.

"Mickey's friend junior, big sleep, roger beep," she intoned, pouring the broken duck egg, shell and all, into the pot. "Kennel juice, big word at your back door, that's a four."

She squirted the syringeful of dog's blood into the bubbling mess.

She turned to us.

"Prince Harry plumbing."

"What?" said Opal.

"Aw, fack! The facken ginja root!"

One would presume this came from obscene 3-J or profane Mama. But no—thus spake our rapidly white trashifying Dr. Dick.

"Who was supposed to get it?" I said.

"I dunno, but I ain't goin' back out there!" said Mama.

"She's gonna be mad," said 3-J.

"Oh, for Gawd's sake!" exclaimed Dr. Dick.

He marched over to the fridge and grabbed the carrot, then rummaged through the cupboards until he found the ginger.

"Ginja," he held up the tin. "Root," he held up the carrot.

He handed both to the Tooth Witch.

She gave him a baleful look, then tossed the carrot and the contents of the tin into the boiling brew.

"Base station, base station in the big blue, come on, come on," the Tooth Witch chanted, rolling her head around in ever-widening circles.

She swung her skull in 3-J's direction and crooked her finger.

"Buffalo bawlin'," she said.

"Huh?" said 3-J.

"That's all of it," said Mama. "Ain't it?"

"Buffalo bawlin'," the Tooth Witch repeated.

She gripped 3-J's ratty shirtfront and hauled him close to the pot.

"Bawl," she commanded.

She shoved his face over the pot and waited.

"Whoa, that stinks!" 3-J said.

"Bawl, bawl," she barked.

"I can't do it. I don't cry."

"Think about a sad movie," Pearl said.

"Think about a sad clown! Not the creepy kid-murdering kind," Opal said.

"Onion?" suggested Dr. Dick.

"Maybe Dr. Dick oughta punch ya one," I said.

Dr. Dick and 3-J eyed each other in masculine discomfort.

"That-there's a bad idea. Menfolk prefer to avoid physical contact with one another," said the man who had lately rested his hand for a long time on Dr. Dick's upper thigh.

"Billy Big Rigger ain't bundled out in the attic, gotta spend alla his green stamps feeding the bears like a gear jammer," the Tooth Witch scolded.

She held up the pot to catch his tears of shame, but none came.

She set the pot back down on the burner and began to bawl herself, peeking at him between her twig-like fingers to see if it was having the desired effect.

3-J shook his head.

"Sorry. I just ain't the crying type. Maybe ol' Dick here—"

"No! No way!" Dr. Dick took a step back. "I've done my fair share tonight—fah, fah, fah more than my fair share! I was attacked by a dawg, I was chased around a dirt fam by a lunatic, I had a shotgun pointed at me, and to top it all off, I had the pleasure of watching a coop filled with ducks go up in flames, just because I happened to kiss—uh, ratha, certain circumstances…um."

My sisters and I squealed.

"And for what?" Dr. Dick resumed, his face crimson. "One single egg, for gawd-knows what kinda unsanitary soup or stew—or worse yet, an illegal narcotic—"

He was cut off by a loud sob.

All eyes in the kitchen turned to 3-J.

He was weeping.

"Them poor ducks! Couldn't fly, couldn't waddle away. Just hadta sit waiting for hot death to come and take 'em!" he moaned.

"Four-four and a ten-four!" crowed the Tooth Witch, grasping the handles of the pot and hauling the steaming concoction over to 3-J. She held it under his face to catch his free-flowing tears. When she had enough, she carried the pot back to the stove and thunked it onto the burner.

"Waaaaah!" 3-J wailed, unable to stop.

The Tooth Witch gave the liquid a final counterclockwise swirl with her wooden spoon, then she upended the pot, pouring the hot fluid into an old orange juice carton. She folded the top closed and put it in the fridge.

"Having shutter trouble," she said, giving us a nod.

She walked out of the kitchen. We heard the TV begin to jabber.

"That's it?" Opal said.

"What the hell was the point?" Mama said.

"Wonder if anything good's on?" mused Pearl.

Mama, my sisters, and Dr. Dick followed the witch into the living room. I stayed behind, staring at 3-J.

He sobbed on.

I thought I ought to comfort him.

I awkwardly patted his shoulder, and he grabbed me in a tight embrace.

"Let me tell ya my tragic life's story, Ruby," he keened.

Thirty-two pages of single-spaced text later...

"And that's how I came to have a soft spot in my heart for defenseless animals. But not that she-beast Bitch-Girl," he concluded, swiping at his eyes.

And with that, he staggered out the side door to his truck, dropping a badly-aimed pat on my head on the way.

The clock above the refrigerator read 10:21. I shuffled off to the living room. It was dark and deserted, except for the Tooth Witch, who had made a nest on the couch and was sawing logs. It seemed everyone had gone to bed. I switched the TV on and settled onto the floor in the shadows just south of the sleeping dental enchantress.

My enjoyment of the tail-end of Sissy Spacek's so-so collaboration with Whoopi Goldberg in *The Long Walk Home* was interrupted by the appearance of Dr. Dick in the hallway. He was pursued by Mama, who looked mighty distressed.

"Crystal-Lynn, I'm exhausted," he said, striding into the living room. "I've got to get some sleep. And not in that imported ahmchair of yours. I'll come back early tomorrow, I promise."

"Just stay until midnight—"

"He's not going to come here that late," said Dr. Dick, yanking his tweed jacket out of our humble coat closet and slinging it over one arm.

"That's his prime crazy-making hour!" said Mama. "It's at the midnight hour he's most likely to show up, just to vex me. Stay a little longer."

"No," said Dr. Dick. "I'm going home. I'll be back tomorrow."

"Can't you just—"

But Dr. Dick lifted one side of the off-hinges front door, ducked under it like a tent flap, and departed.

Oblivious to my presence in the dim recesses of the floor-region, Mama slumped in defeat.

Dr. Dick returned.

She perked up.

"Forgot my wallet," he said.

"For goodness sake," Mama grumbled. "Well, where'd ya leave it?"

"If I knew, I wouldn't have forgotten it. That orthodontist witch or whateva she is took it out of my pocket earlier," he retorted, following Mama out of the living room.

I heard rustling and murmurs in the kitchen, then in the bathroom, then in the hall. Then in the sanctum sanctorum of Mama's bedroom.

I heard the bedroom door close.

The murmurs ceased.

I waited for them to emerge.

They didn't emerge.

The movie ended. Still they didn't emerge.

I watched three episodes of "The Dukes of Hazzard."

The clock in the kitchen struck midnight.

Still they didn't emerge.

I crept down the hall and glanced at the closed door.

I went into us-girl's room and crawled into bed.

I fell asleep, full of thoughts.

Chapter Eleven
Daddy

Saturday, June 21
Midsummer morning

We Bejous were not unfamiliar with the interior landscape of the Somwärin jail and courthouse, both housed within the Celestial Temple of Psychedelic Truth and City Administration.

Between Daddy's propensity for malicious mischief, Mama's periodic public outpourings of profanity, and my own budding career as a troublemaker, we had become accustomed to the atmosphere of the incarceration cells located in what was once the Sanctuary of Groovy Good Vibes. We were also intimately acquainted with the layout of the courtroom, situated in the former Far Out Cannabis Chapel and Make-Out Pad. Even 3-J, in town for but a brief spell once a year, was a cognoscenti of the drunk tank, where the legend, "Bonkers Acid Meditation and Pooping Room," still shone forth in glow-in-the-dark paint.

Poor Dr. Dick, however, was like a babe in the woods.

Ever since the sheriff-mayor burst into the trailer at first light, cuffing everyone in sight and stripping 3-J and Dr. Dick of their shirts in a fruitless search for weapons, the young gynecologist and obstetrician had been most agitated. While we—we being Mama, 3-J, Pearl, and my own self—slouched in our communal jail cell, the unhappy physician paced and vented his spleen.

"This isn't legal," he said for the fourteenth time. "I know my rights—sheriff, I know my rights! I demand access to a lawya and my legally mandated telephone call."

"We're in the jailhouse now," sang 3-J. "We're in the j—"

"Stop it," Dr. Dick said.

I sighed. I was so bored.

I stared through the bars at the sheriff-mayor. In the police station proper, which stood within a ring of thirteen freaky, hallucinogen-themed cells like ours, he was **meddling** with a margarita machine. Surrounded by a forest of day-glo magic mushrooms that bedecked the walls and ceiling and floor, he measured and poured and salted and sampled with increasing satisfaction.

Scattered throughout the room were sturdy, well-polished Fack Sex desks, which belonged to the deputies. But today— just like every day that I'd found myself in the police station on one side of the bars or the other—they were unoccupied.

It was suspected by cannier Somwärinites, such as Dr. Flo, that the sheriff-mayor had no deputies and was our town's sole law enforcement officer. But even the most cynical among us felt it was better not to verify this fact because it would lead to the revelation of one of two unsettling truths:

1. Our town had a cabal of secret policemen who walked among us disguised as regular citizens

Or…

2. Our town's only lawman was dangerously delusional.

"We weren't propahly Mirandized," Dr. Dick resumed. "You neva informed any of us of our rights. I know my rights—I have the right to remain silent!"

"Use it!" Mama snapped.

Dr. Dick glared at her and kept pacing.

"I should have gone home last night when I had the chance," he muttered.

"How come he didn't go home?" Pearl whispered to me.

"I believe," I whispered back. "That he and Mama did the dirty disco."

Pearl's mouth fell open. She covered it with both hands. She began to giggle and so did I.

"Quit that tittering," Mama said. "We ain't in a tittering place."

"We're in the jailhouse now," sang 3-J. "We're—"

"Stop singing that song!" Dr. Dick said.

The phone on the sheriff-mayor's desk rang.

"Yellow?" he said, not picking it up.

The sheriff-mayor was more than slightly drunk.

As the phone continued to ring, he scratched his head in bewilderment, took another slug of margarita, sat on the edge of his desk, stared into the distance, belched, then absently picked up the receiver.

He pressed it to his ear. He said nothing. He nodded and hung up.

"Looks like alla y'alls're on deck," he announced.

With veering steps and three wrong turns, the sheriff-mayor conducted my criminal colleagues and me out of the jail, past the erstwhile Shrine to Our Lady of the Outta Sight Electric Flower Power that now housed the utilities bureau, and down the hall festooned with Somwärin's current indictments. The solemn passport photo of the Swedish ambassador, a blurry photocopy of Daddy's CDL, and a bug-eyed crayon caricature of the as-yet-unphotographed Dr. Dick stared at us as we trudged by.

"Where are you taking us?" demanded Dr. Dick, still shirtless, now shifty-eyed. "Are you releasing us?"

"Nope," said the sheriff-mayor, steering himself and 3-J headlong into the wall and bouncing them off the wainscoting like a pair of bumper cars. "Y'all're fixing to stand trial."

"Today?" Mama said. "I ain't never been called to trial on Midsummer. This-here's a high holiday!"

"You wanna see the judge today when he's good 'n' jolly, or tomorrow when he's a hungover viper of vengeance?" the sheriff-mayor countered, walking backwards to give Mama the eye, stumbling over his own spit-shined boots, and locking both hands around 3-J's neck to right himself.

"Today," Mama said.

"What's he talking about? What are you talking about?" Dr. Dick said. "I can't enta a courtroom like this!"

"Might help your chances," said the sheriff-mayor, giving Dr. Dick's bare chest a good once-over. "Nah, it won't."

The sheriff-mayor came to an unsteady halt in front of a massive pair of double doors. The outer surface of each oaken portal was carved with thick-lipped ovoids meant to represent the mystic yoni, and spiky leaves meant to represent the wacky tobaccy.

"In we go," the sheriff-mayor announced, shoving the fearsome gates of Somwärin's hall of justice inward with his meaty mitts.

We squinted as the radiance of the courtroom burst over us. The ceiling scintillated in the fluorescent light, encrusted as it was with a mildly pornographic mandala made of broken Mello Yello bottles and scraps of Billy Beer cans.

On the floor of the courtroom, a wild mob of justice-mad drunks jeered at the sight of us.

Pearl recoiled. Mama stiffened her spine and ratcheted her head as high as it would go, but her lips trembled. Dr. Dick began to hyperventilate. Mama reached for Dr. Dick's hand and squeezed it.

3-J guffawed and waved at a band of his trucker brethren, who were gathered around the judge's bench essaying a wobbly keg stand. When they waved back, they dropped His Honor himself, who landed with a squawk. As the sheriff-mayor swerved us hither and yon through the packed courtroom in an inebriated quest for the defendants' table, the judge untangled himself from his voluminous black robe and bounded to his place upon the high bench.

"Order!" the judge called out, banging his gavel.

The crowd in the courtroom paid him no heed. Their rough voices brayed on. Bottles passed from hand to hand. A young gentleman attempted to scale the swirly purple and orange tromp l'oeil "Highway to High Daze!" painted on the back wall. Bright red Solo cups soared through the air like swallows returning to Capistrano. It was the sort of bedlam only seen in our fair town on Midsummer morning. It was positively restrained compared to what was to come by nightfall.

"Or…der! Or…der! Or…der!" the judge chanted in a merry sing-song, drumming along with his justice hammer like a cheerleader at half-time.

"SHUT Y'ALL'S GOL-DANGED TRAPS!" bellowed the sheriff-mayor.

Silence descended upon the citizenry and criminal element

in the courtroom.

Except for Dr. Dick.

"You!" he exclaimed when he got a load of the judge. Dr. Barney, hazy of eye and askew of hair, gave Dr. Dick a friendly nod in response.

"Well, hey there, Dick! Didn't fancy I'd be seeing you in my courtroom so early into your tenor in this town. Tender. Tenure—ten-yooooore. Let's see what brings you by on this fine Midsummer morning. Bailiff? Where's that pesky docket? Bring 'er on over, and—aw, what the heck. Let's all do a shot!"

"You can't—this is—you're not a judge!" Dr. Dick sputtered. But his words went down like a leaky boat under the tsunami of exultant shouts.

"You heard the judge: Everybody take a shot!"

"Shot time!"

"Don't mind if I do!"

"Shot, shot, shot!"

Our friends and neighbors withdrew their poisons of preference from purses and pockets, and tipped back. Dr. Barney pulled a half-full bottle of Jim Beam from the depths of his robe and took a healthy slug. Standing guard over us at the defendants' table, the sheriff-mayor obtained a flask from his gunless revolver holster and swigged. He declined to share with 3-J, which perceptibly saddened the accused kidnapper.

"Ahhhh!" said Dr. Barney, swiping his black sleeve over his lips and slamming the bottle down on the judicial bench. "Wheeew! What've we got on the menu today?"

"Your honor, we got two duck arsonists, two felonious kidnappers, a hit-and-run on a house, and Pearl Bejou," replied the none-too-steady bailiff.

Little Pearl, who was standing next to me, piped up.

"How come I'm on trial? I didn't do anything bad."

"Well, how about it, Sheriff-Mayor Dolan? What're you charging Pearl Bejou with?"

"She's a known party-wrecker with a violent temper."

"Eayaheyeh," rumbled Dr. Barney, with a flap of his hand. "That's not a chargeable offense. Case dismissed."

A rowdy cheer went up, then went right back down when the sheriff-mayor spun around to glower at the gallery.

"Next case, bailiff. Woo-ee! Rate we're going, we'll be outta here in time to do some serious swallowing before the clock strikes noon."

"Calling William Swiftland Harris versus Dr. Richard Grant and Crystal-Lynn Bejou," slurred the bailiff, wobbling from one foot to the other.

In the gallery, Farmer Bill removed his countrified hat and rose. At the defendants' table, Mama jumped to her feet and prodded Dr. Dick to do likewise. He glanced down at the place his shirt was supposed to be, then stood, then crossed his arms over his bare chest, then uncrossed them, then assumed a posture of affected indignance with one hand thrust into his pants pocket and the other balled in a fist on the tabletop. From the twitching of his eyelids, I could tell he wanted to fidget on, but restrained himself out of deference to the dignity of the courtroom.

"Alrighty, let's take a look…" Dr. Barney said, studying the thin file that the bailiff flung at him. "It appears that Mr. Harris has brought charges against Dr. Dick and Mrs. Bejou for trespassing, destruction of property, robbery, arson, and assault—"

"Assault? He threatened us with a shotgun!" Dr. Dick said.

"It's Ms. Bejou! Ms!" Mama said.

Dr. Barney banged his gavel and hissed, "Shhhhh!"

"I know my rights," Dr. Dick said. "None of us can be tried without legal representation. And you certainly aren't qualified to renda judgement—"

Dr. Barney banged his gavel. He frowned. He crooked his finger at Dr. Dick.

"C'mere," he said.

The spectators went, "Ooooooh," as Dr. Dick approached the bench.

Dr. Barney leaned down from the seat of judicial power and gave Dr. Dick a stern look.

"Fun fact," said Dr. Barney. "Here in Somwärin, we don't

have any lawyers. I'm just a mail-order certified justice of the peace myself. We try our criminals on the quick so they can get back to work without upsetting the higher-ups at the Fack Sex Corporation. Do you want to upset the higher-ups at Fack Sex? No, you don't. Now, get back to that table and keep your mouth shut, Dick, or I'll charge you with contempt of court."

With a sullen shrug, Dr. Dick stumped back to his co-conspirator.

Justice of the Peace Barney fluffed his black robe, gazed around him, and let out a little humming sound. Then, "I think this calls for another shot, bailiff."

As before:

"You heard the judge: Everybody take a shot!"

"Shot time!"

"Don't mind if I do!"

"Shot, shot, shot!"

"This is outrageous."

The last comment being from Dr. Dick.

"Okie-dokie," gasped the judge, as he banged the nearly empty bottle down instead of the gavel. "Lemme hear it, Mr. Farmer Bill."

"Your honor," began Farmer Bill. "Late last night them-two with malice aforethought encroached themselves onto m'farmland, set a mighty blaze, stole one duck egg—"

"Yeah, yeah, I already heard all about it from the Swedish ambassador this morning," interrupted the magistrate. "What I'm really interested in is why? Well, Dick? Now's your chance to shine!"

Dr. Dick cleared his throat.

"In lieu of making a formal statement in this specious court of law," he said. "Let me go on the recad asserting this entire process is illegal and will be reported to the attorney general of Texas the minute I'm released from custody. I know my rights—"

"I'm gonna make a rule," Justice of the Peace Barney cut in. "Every time Dr. Dick says, 'I know my rights,' everybody take a shot."

The hoots of approval put a scowl on Dr. Dick's face.

"Eh," said Dr. Barney. "I don't really care why you did it. I'm sure you had your reasons. The question is, are you gonna do it again?"

Dr. Dick opened his mouth to reply, but Mama cut him off with a loud, "No, your honor—we won't!"

"And are you sorry?"

"Yes, we are, your honor. Very, very sorry!" Mama hollered over Dr. Dick's huffy, "I have no intention of making a declaration that could be construed as an admission of guilt."

"Well, in that case," said Judge Barney. "I'm ordering the two of you to rebuild Farmer Duck's bill coop to his satisfaction, and repopulate it with poultry at your own expense. Case—"

"That's ridiculous! I'm not a carpenta!"

"Dismissed!"

And Dr. Barney banged the gavel aslant, causing it to rebound and hit him smack on the end of his nose.

"Where do you even buy ducks?"

"Dick, shut the hell up," Mama said. "He let us off easy."

"Next contestant!" said Dr. Barney.

"Calling Ruby Bejou and John Jesse James Whitehead," mumbled the bailiff from her slumping place on the floor. She held up the file and waved it around until Dr. Barney thrust himself over the benchtop, snagged it, and reeled it in to peruse.

"Two complainants for this case," he said. "Charge the first: kidnapping. Wow. That's a serious crime."

Dr. Barney studied 3-J, aghast. 3-J grinned, slung an arm around my shoulders, and gave the judge a thumbs-up.

"You kidnapped this young girl, sir?"

"Nope," said 3-J. "Me 'n' this young girl kidnapped Dr. Flo."

"Ruby Bejou took part in a felonious abduction? Wow," said Dr. Barney. "Kidnapping's a federal offense, even for a juvenile. Yikes. Not sure how to handle this one."

In the gallery, Dr. Flo rose.

"I decline to press charges against either party," she said.

"Huh," said Dr. Barney. "Well, that takes care of that. Charge the second: cruelty to animals."

His face clouded. His cheeks reddened. His eyes narrowed.

"That's an even more serious crime," he growled, scanning the police report. "Cruelty to animals is something I take very, very, *very* seriously—oh, it was Bitch-Girl. Case dismissed."

"Ha!" 3-J exulted, pumping his fist over his head. "Just as the all-powerful CB promised, I'm free as a bird! Freebird, freeeeee—" he began to sing.

"Stop singing that song!" Dr. Dick said.

"Suck-stained," agreed Dr. Barney. "By golly, I'm drunk. Sheriff-mayor, how about you trundle that breathalyzer over here and lemme take a pull offa her."

The sheriff-mayor staggered over with the sticky unit and Dr. Barney stumbled down from the bench to slobber over the mouthpiece. The congregation availed itself of the break in the action to partake, Dr. Dick shook his head in disgust, and 3-J made talking-into-a-CB gestures at his fellow truckers, who huzzahed in approbation. It appeared that 3-J wasn't the only convert to Daddy's way-out philosophy. I glanced over at Mama, who was watching 3-J and his pals with suspicion.

"Yep, yep, yep. I'm every which way but sober. I'm guessing I got one more trial left in me. Let's wrapper upper," enunciated Justice of the Peace Barney, yanking the final file from beneath his snoring bailiff. He squinted at the police report therein, opened his eyes very wide, then squinted again.

"Wuhhh…wheeeee…aw, heck, I can't pronounce this darned name. Somebody versus Billy Ray Edgar. Single charge: destruction of property. Says here he ran over her house with his truck. Well, this should be interesting!"

The sheriff-mayor dragged a fella out from underneath the defendants' table, where he'd been residing, passed out, unbeknownst to me or my accomplices. The sheriff-mayor propped the limp sot against 3-J and removed his unmistakable trucker's baseball cap as a sign of respect.

"I spy the defendant," said Dr. Barney, peering with his

little eye. "But where's the complainant?"

In the gallery, a tiny figure stood. Unable to see over the big boozers that surrounded her, she clambered onto one of the pew-like seats and waved her arms to attract the judge's gaze.

When Dr. Barney and the courtroom populace discerned that "Wuhhh…wheeeee" was the Tooth Witch, they collectively shrank back, gripping their pockets and coin purses spasmodically.

"What in heaven's name did you do to her, man?" whispered the judge. "God help you."

"That trailer jumped right out in fronta my truck," the trucker replied. "I oughta sue it for damaging my rig."

"I see," said Dr. Barney.

He gulped.

He took a bracing bolt of bourbon.

He crossed himself.

He met the Tooth Witch's eyes and shuddered.

"And what's your testimony, madam?"

The Tooth Witch hopped down from her seat, clutching a large black purse in both hands.

She scuttled out of the gallery and into the courtroom.

She approached the bench.

She opened her mouth wide, wide, wide.

"Get horizontal, this-here's the magic mile," the Tooth Witch proclaimed.

She spun around, reached into her purse, and pulled out an orange juice carton.

She flung it at the house-wrecker. Its contents splattered across his flannel button-down, coating him with sticky, foul-smelling brown fluid.

"Augh!" he cried.

"Ten six-six-six!" she shouted.

And, *bang*! A puff of white smoke burst forth swallowed the Tooth Witch. Screams rang out in the hall of justice. When the smoke cleared, the wicked enchantress was gone.

"Everybody here saw that, too?" said Justice of the Peace

Barney. "Not just me? Okay, then."

He turned to the juicy trucker as the smoke crept up to the ceiling.

"I guess I'll go ahead and pronounce sentence in the absence of your accuser. You, sir—"

But the trucker's lawful punishment was to remain forever unknown, for at that moment the pale smoke reached the smoke detectors embedded within the psychedelic Sistine Chapel ceiling. The sprinklers went off, spraying us lustily with cold water.

"Oh my! Everybody out!" Justice of the Peace Barney cried, and everyone scrambled for the doors.

Outside, I scampered through the bright sunlight. Hot on my heels followed the accessory to my wrongdoings, Dr. Dick and his criminal confederate, innocent Pearl, and Judge Barney, with his black robe flapping like the wings of a bat.

We regrouped under the dire limbs of the Tree of Contemplation and looked askance at our judicial representative.

Dr. Barney shrugged and pulled his administrative robe off over his head.

"My authority ends once I step outside the courtroom. Guess it's back to the Vet 'n' Pet Shop. Coming, Dick? I've got a bottle of twenty-year-old Scotch stashed in the bunny hutch that I wouldn't mind sharing."

Dr. Dick glanced down at his naked, wet chest.

"I think I need to get myself togetha first."

Dr. Barney shrugged and headed off, dragging his robes of office behind him in the dirt.

"I'm hungry," Pearl said.

"Me too," I said.

"Me too," 3-J said.

It was going to be a long walk back to the trailer park on empty stomachs.

"Let's get something to eat at the Swedish Embassy & Beauty Parlor & Coffee Shop!" I said.

"Yeah!" Pearl said.

"Yeah!" 3-J said.

"I dunno," Mama said. "You know how the ambassador gets on Midsummer."

"Please, Mama?" wheedled Pearl. "He bakes the best Midsummer cake of all."

"And because of our lengthy incarceration, you ain't got time to bake our traditional cake," I said.

"Unless you plan to forgo drinking to toil over a hot stove," 3-J said.

"Let's get a bite to eat at the Swedish Embassy & Beauty Parlor & Coffee Shop," Mama said.

"I can't go to a restaurant like this," Dr. Dick protested. "My shirts are in my apartment, and my apartment key is at your place. Let's get a ride back to the traila park and sort ourselves out first."

Mama gave Dr. Dick's glistening chest a lusty-eyed up and down. She seemed torn between opposing carnal cravings for food and whatever NC-17 "sorting out" he'd offered her last night.

She bit her lip.

Just then, Sheriff-Mayor Dolan tromped by, a forty-ounce bottle of malt liquor duct-taped to each hand.

"Sheriff-mayor," Mama called. "You're the one who dragged us here—you're gonna give us a ride home, right?"

The sheriff-mayor paused his game of Edward Fortyhands and came to a halt beneath the Tree of Contemplation to laugh. He laughed and laughed and laughed. He leaned up against the frightful instrument of civil obedience. And he laughed some more.

"Nope," he said, when he had recovered his composure. "Only criminals ride in my patrol car. Y'all're hoofing it home, unless one of ya feels like committing a new crime before the sun's yet high…not that I'd put it past you Bejous."

He began to laugh again. Then his eyes fell upon Dr. Dick.

"You," he growled, his mood shifting. "You're still under indictment. Had ya in my clutches and I letcha go. Get over here so's I can stuff you back in that jail cell!"

He clanked his bottle-hands together and took a stumbling step in our general direction.

"Come on," I urged, tugging at Dr. Dick's arm. "Let's take refuge in Sweden, which has no codified extradition process with Somwärin."

"Good idea," said Mama, taking his other arm and pulling him toward the Swedish Embassy & Beauty Parlor & Coffee Shop.

"But," Dr. Dick began.

"The Swedish ambassador forgoes the 'No shoes, no shirt, no service' edict on Midsummer," said 3-J, shoving Dr. Dick along from behind. "Crystal-Lynn, take your shirt off in solidarity with me 'n' my brother male here."

Mama opened her mouth to make an acidic retort when Dr. Flo came skimming out of nowhere and blocked our path. Our drenched posse jolted to a dripping halt in the middle of Main Street.

Dr. Dick emitted a nearly inaudible groan.

Dr. Flo strode up to him and pursed her lips in distaste.

"You will have noticed," she said. "That I did not file kidnapping charges against you, sir, though I know you were behind last night's outrageous violation of my personal liberty. However…I require informal retribution."

"Forget it," said Dr. Dick.

"We can do this off the books, or not only will I formally accuse you, I'll reinstate the charges against this innocent girl and this good friend of yours."

Dr. Dick crossed his arms over his damp chest.

"What precisely is it you want?"

"I don't want," she said. "I demand that you take over my Motel Rounds. Permanently. Starting tonight."

"I'm an ob-gyn, not a paramedic, dammit!"

"I'm not a paramedic either, mister!" Dr. Flo said. "Hell's bells, do you know what I am? Do you?"

The corners of Dr. Dick's lips twitched. He seemed to be pondering whether to prefix his reply of "itch" with a saucy W or an offensive B.

"You're a general practitiona," he said.

"Wrong. I am a forensic pathologist," she said. "I was Chief Regional Pathologist for the Federal Bureau of Investigation for fifteen years. Then, I came here…for reasons I will not speak of. Now I'm a general practitioner, a paramedic, a notary public, St. Lucia Day choir director, and anything the town requires me to be. Adapt, doctor. 'Adapt or die,' Charles Darwin."

She folded her arms across her dry, fully-clothed chest and raised her eyebrows.

"Do we have a deal?"

"Do I have a choice?" said Dr. Dick.

Dr. Flo just smirked in response, then pointed at Mama.

"You," she said.

"What'd I do? I wasn't involved! I drove you home, didn't I? Helped you out, like a neighborly neighbor," Mama bleated.

"You must confront that ex-husband of yours before the Midsummer sun sets," said Dr. Flo. "No more tricks, no more hiding behind dubious protectors like the new Motel Rounds physician here. Get rid of him yourself."

"But he's nuts!"

"He's a mere man," Dr. Flo said. "Call upon your womanly strength and oust him, as the sub-Saharan lioness does when the king of the jungle has outstayed his welcome."

"But," Mama whined. "But…"

Dr. Flo brushed her aside and turned her attention to 3-J.

"As for you, vile, freakish, beast of a man," she said. "Get yourself cleaned up. You're beyond redemption in every way besides personal hygiene."

I braced myself. It was my turn.

Dr. Flo turned to me.

She looked into my eyes.

She stepped close to me and took me by the shoulder.

"Find something," she whispered into my ear. "To stave off your boredom, Ruby. Something legal. Learn from my mistakes."

And with that, Dr. Flo executed a crisp half-circle turn and marched across Main Street toward her clinic's dented door. She dodged a trio of dizzy bat enthusiasts who were watching the Fack Sex warehouse supervisor orbit a baseball bat. As she spun, she sloshed a mug of frothy beer across Dr. Flo's sensible shoes. Dr. Flo just shook her head and disappeared into the clinic.

Alone again in the middle of Main Street.

We were silent. The golden sun set our wet clothes to steaming. The joyous cries of the beer pong players on the lawn out front of the Pubic Library tickled our eardrums.

"Well, that does it," Dr. Dick said at last. "I'm a paramedic and a construction worka now, apparently. Four years of college, four of med school, two of residency. I'm a licensed medical dacta, but what does that matta?"

He paused for breath and ramped way up.

"I'm a dacta," he cried. "And I'm in debt up to my eyeballs, and I'm stuck in this gawd-forsaken town, so why not make a facken career change and become a facken carpenta, and build a duck-facken-coop for fack's sake!"

He threw up his bare arms in frustration, showering us with drops of water.

He fell to brooding.

3-J turned to me.

"Hey, we got off scot-free, huh Ruby!" he said, giving me a high-five.

Dr. Dick glared at us.

"Then you rebuild that stupid bird house," he said.

"Nah. I gotta go get cleaned up or Dr. Flo'll get me. She's one tough lady," 3-J said. "Dang, I guess I gotta skip the cake and hit the shower. Well, them's the breaks."

And off he strode, a true philosopher. Dr. Dick scowled at his retreating back.

"Come on, Dick," said Mama. "You're just hot and hungry. Let's get some tasty Midsummer cake in ya and you'll see how much brighter things look."

"Hmf," he replied. But his features softened as Mama beamed one of her coaxing smiles at him and encircled his bare waist with her arm.

Into the Swedish Embassy & Beauty Parlor & Coffee Shop we traipsed, pausing on the threshold to wring out our garments so as not to import U.S. resources into an allied territory without a permit. The moment we crossed the border into Sweden, we were hit with an arctic air front and a dissonance of Norwegian death metal turned up to eleven.

The joint was crowded with glum drunks who crouched over plates of blue-and-yellow frosted cake and mugs of adulterated coffee. In between the tables wove the Swedish ambassador, stoic, sorrowful, and thoroughly sloshed.

"Ah," he called, upon catching sight of us. "Veldumden tell kindergarten…Sweden. Oh, my beloved Sweden!"

A lock of blond hair fell across his forehead. He emitted a sob. He composed himself.

"Shall you enjoy a slice of cake today?"

"Sure!" Pearl chirped, popping herself into a chair at our favorite table. "A big one."

"And a coffee?" said the Swedish ambassador, reaching behind the counter to obtain a bottle of deadly aquavit and four shot glasses.

"No, no," said Dr. Dick.

"Hell, yes!" said Mama.

"It is a joyous day," said the Swedish ambassador joylessly, as he plunked four cups brimming with hot coffee down on our table, followed by four empty shot glasses. "It is the longest day of the year. The longest journey into night, when blissful sleep obliterates our grief. Oh, God!"

He let out another sob.

"I have composed a poem for the occasion," he said, dribbling the above-legal proof alcohol into the shot glasses. "I will recite it for you."

"No, that's fine," Mama said. "Bring on over four slices of cake and that'll do us."

"Long is the light, the day shall never end," said the Swedish ambassador, leaning upon our table. "Forever we must trudge, without a hope, without a friend."

"Just the cake, thanks," said Mama.

"Endless is our weeping, eternal is our pain," the Swedish ambassador replied, wavering away to the kitchen. "Our laughter turns to sobbing, the sunshine turns to rain."

"See, Dick?" said Mama, corralling the brimming shot glasses for herself. "Your situation ain't nearly as bleak as it could be."

"I suppose so," Dr. Dick conceded, his dour expression easing a bit. "Even in a propa court of law with propa lawyas, our sentences could have been fah worse."

"Wonder what was up with that smoke? Wonder what happened to the Tooth Witch?" I said.

"Doomed to greater woe with every passing year, my heart cries on, on, but nobody shall hear," the Swedish ambassador concluded, clunking four plates of delectable Midsummer cake onto the tabletop.

"Mmm!" Pearl enthused, seizing the biggest chunk of cake before I could snatch it.

"Could we have forks?" Dr. Dick said.

"Who needs forks?" Mama grinned, swiping up a slice of sugary goodness in one hand and a shot of hard liquor in the other.

"For I have been exiled far from my native land," the Swedish ambassador resumed. "Never am I joyful, I am a wretched man…d."

"Happy Midsummer, everyone," Mama said, holding up her cake and smiling around the table at her daughters and her lover.

We each picked up a wedge of cake, even Dr. Dick. We held our holiday treats aloft.

"Happy Mids—" we began.

But at that very moment, the door swung open.

A vicious blast of heat burst through the calm, cool air of the Swedish Embassy & Beauty Parlor & Coffee Shop. On the threshold stood a sweaty, crazed-looking man. Breathing hard, he gripped the doorknob for a moment, then staggered into our midst. His hair was wild and his face was red and he wore a countrified straw hat.

"Thar y'are!" he exclaimed when he caught sight of Mama and Dr. Dick. "Been hunting high and low in the heat for the two of you. Let's getta move on, we're burnin' daylight!"

"Please, Farmer Bill," Mama said, for it was indeed he. "Me 'n' Dr. Dick'll be over bright and early tomorrow to fix up your duck coop, I promise. I aim to drink myself silly today. It's Midsummer, after all."

"I don't celebrate Midsummer," rumbled Farmer Bill. "Ain't no such thing as a holiday on a working farm."

"The solace of the grave awaits, I long for gentle death," droned the Swedish ambassador. "To wipe away my anguish and take away my…meth? Seth? Peth? Can you suggest an English word?"

"Breath," said Dr. Dick. "Let's just get it over with, Crystal-Lynn."

He set down his untasted cake and rose. He held out his hand to her.

Mama remained seated. She stubbornly retained her hold on her cake and her booze.

"And take away my breath," said the Swedish ambassador. "Go with Farmer Bill, fröken. There is nothing but misery to be had on Midsummer. Whatever torments he offers you, embrace them willingly and hasten your end upon this sad, sad earth."

"Fine," Mama grumped, flinging down her cake and shot glass. "This is the worst Midsummer ever."

She took Dr. Dick's hand and rose.

"You girls head straight home, you hear? There ain't nothing but trouble in town today."

And she left.

And of course Pearl and I did not go straight home.

But Mama was right: There was nothing but trouble in town on this Midsummer day, for the town was overrun with truckers. They were everywhere—disrupting the shotgunning competition in the alley behind the Vet 'n' Pet Shop, knocking over the cans in the towering beeramid that the teachers had labored to construct in the school parking lot, tying the Whisky a Go-Go dancers to the maypole with their own rainbow ribbons.

They were rowdy, they were obscene, and they were growing violent. And it was only early afternoon. There were hours upon hours of daylight drinking left to go. At last, fed up with their destructive shenanigans, Pearl and I fled to the one sanctuary no trucker ever dared violate: the Fack Sex Furniture Distribution Warehouse.

It was a dreary choice, for the only Midsummer entertainment offered on corporate property during Midsummer was the annual outdoor theatrical production, *The Passion of Fack Sex*, a six-hour cyclical play about the history of the international organization.

When we arrived, the tipsy thespians on the rickety stage just outside the employee entrance were midway through Act Two: Opening for Business.

Clad in goofy embroidered Swedish bunder and 1970s porn star mustaches, the Lady Principal and Miz Jackson were endeavoring to impersonate the founder and CEO of Fack Sex and his smarmy co-founder, who would be denounced as an embezzler at the climax of act four. Pearl and I were more than familiar with the dramatic denouements of *The Passion of Fack Sex*, having sat through it one or twenty times over the years.

"We are ready to open for business," announced the Lady Principal, DBA the founder and CEO of Fack Sex. "There is a crowd lined up around the block. Everyone in Stockholm is eager to browse our fine furniture innovations. Let's open the door and let them in."

He/she rattled the door ineffectually.

"But the door is locked! Where is the key?"

Miz Jackson, fighting off an inebriated giggling fit, replied, "I cannot find it anywhere! It was in one of my pockets. I have checked pocket one, pocket two, pocket three, pocket four, and pocket five!"

And she indicated each pocket on her person and each pouch in her briefcase.

"Have you checked…pocket six?" inquired the founder and CEO of Fack Sex, with a fourth-wall-smashing smirk at the audience. Pearl and I cheered, along with the handful of attendees who had not yet fallen into alcohol-induced blackout.

The soon-to-be-disgraced co-founder fumbled in his sixth pocket and discovered the key.

"Ah ha!" he cried, holding it aloft like a lightning rod. "Now let us open our store for business."

"But wait!" said the founder and CEO of Fack Sex. "We still don't have a name for our wonderful furniture company."

The duo pondered for a moment. Their musing was interrupted by some half-hearted pounding on the flimsy cardboard door constructed from Fack Sex shipping containers.

"There's no time—open the door!" said the founder and CEO of Fack Sex.

Miz Jackson hastened to perform her pantomime. Mama's lady friends staggered on stage, blinking in surprise.

They stood stock-still for a minute and a half.

"Oh yeah!" the blonde blurted at last. "We want to buy many pieces of furniture. We are Swedish."

"But what is…um…but what is…um…" the brunette fumbled.

"But what is the name of this fine store?" the other blonde declaimed in a Shakespearean accent.

"Welcome," boomed the Lady Principal, pitching her voice as low as it would go. "Welcome to…"

And she looked from the co-founder, to the key, to the pocket on his butt where the key had been discovered. Then she looked at the audience. We held our breaths.

"Welcome to…Pocket Six!" she cried. "Fack Sex!"

We spectators burst into applause.

But then the unthinkable happened. In the midst of the most glorious moment of the eighteen-act play, four score and seven truckers descended upon the theater. They mocked, they chortled, they flung empty beer cans, they flung full beer cans, and they chased the actors off the stage, all the while chanting,

"CB! CB! CB!"

Pearl and I ran for cover. Then, seeing the marauding truckers were raising hell everywhere—from Fack Sex at one end of town to the Pubic Library at the other—we sprinted for home.

"Mama was right, and so was the not-yet-newspaper," I grumped, as we jogged along the dirt road out of town. "This is the worst Midsummer ever."

"Don't say that," Pearl replied, panting to keep up with me. "There's still five hours of daylight left. Anything could happen."

Far from the madding crowd, the trailer park was peaceable and trucker-free. Our neighbors were scattered about upon the ground, empty bottles clutched in their hands. Even Bitch-Girl had succumbed. She was sprawled belly-up across Quentin Keeton's front porch, a warty tongue lolling from one side of her maw, a drained bottle of Pabst Blue Ribbon from the other.

Our pace slowed. We savored the serenity. Perhaps this Midsummer would turn itself around after all.

As we strolled past the grimmest corner of the trailer park, I stopped and stared in surprise. The Tooth Witch's up-ended caravan was gone. In its place knelt a wall-eyed trucker. His hands were wrapped around an antiquated wooden yardstick. He placed it on the ground, then lifted it, then placed it again. Down his flannel shirtfront ran a sticky, brownish stain. I couldn't be sure, but I could've sworn I heard him murmuring, "Ten six-six-six…ten six-six-six…"

"Hurry up, Ruby!" called Pearl.

I glanced at my little sister, who was trotting up our front steps, then glanced back at the Tooth Witch's property. The trucker had vanished.

The Bejou family trailer was a shambles. Fancy clothes were draped over every stick of furniture. Scribbled-upon sheets of notebook paper tiled every inch of floorspace. Makeup and hair curlers and nail polish bottles and bobby pins littered every flat surface. The walls were papered with stylish ladies clipped from fashion magazines. Opal had been busy in our absence.

I waded through the dreck and hallooed, but my big sister was nowhere to be seen. Nor was my little sister. Sisterless, I shoved aside a heap of nylons and settled onto the couch. What to do now?

A patter of footsteps caused my ears to perk up. Pearl came scooting through the wreckage with a shining quarter in one hand, a cream-colored rectangle of cardstock in the other, and an inscrutable expression on her face. She opened the front door.

"Where're you off to?"

"Gotta make a call," was all she would say.

"Why dontcha use our phone—"

But she just banged the off-hinges front door behind her and was gone.

I peered at the clock. 5:00 p.m.

At 5:01 p.m. on the dot, 3-J emerged from the bathroom wearing nothing but a threadbare pink towel, which he had carelessly wrapped around his waist like a sarong. He plopped down next to me on the couch, all shaven and combed and smelling of soap and cleanliness. I'd never seen him looking so peachy and pure, like a prize piglet all slicked up for the county fair.

"Ahhhh!" he groaned luxuriously. "Ain't it amazing how clean a five-hour shower can getcha?"

I had no reply to offer, but a shriek of dismay from deep within the trailer served as an adequate answer.

"I look obscene!" cried a voice. "Help!"

Opal trotted into the living room decked out in one of her bikinis. The bottom, a sparkly blue and pink contraption, had a tasteful sort of lewdness to it. But the top was indeed obscene, the huge starfish-shaped cups sliding indecently off her much-reduced jugs.

"This-here's the smallest bikini top I got! I can't take to the stage wearing this," she wailed. "What do I do?"

3-J sat up with a wolfish leer smeared across his mug. He

unhinged his jaw to say that which I dared not image. But he was interrupted by the return of Mama and Dr. Dick, who, forgetting the door was as-yet unrepaired, knocked it clean to the floor with a loud thud.

Dr. Dick strolled in, looking tired and pleased. Mama stomped in, looking ready to kill.

"Put some damned clothes on, 3-J!" she hollered, as Dr. Dick hoisted the door back into place behind them. "What kinda flesh pot has this place become while I'm away laboring in the hot, hellish sun?"

Opal surged at Mama, tugged her sagging bikini top over her titties.

"Help, Mama! I'm obscene."

"Are we livin' in a sinful bathhouse back in Roman times, like on that PBS show I watched that one night with my lady friends and we played the drinking game where you take a shot every time they say 'Pax Romana?' Clothes! Put some on, people—it ain't that hot! Hell, never mind: Let's all git naked and walk around like a buncha nudist Swedes."

Mama angrily made to unbutton her blouse, then was overcome with frustration and weariness. She flopped down in Dr. Dick's least favorite chair and glared at the ceiling.

"I'm so tired! Lookit these calluses on my hands. I hate Farmer Bill! And I hate that one over there."

"You mean Dr. Dick?" I said, pointing at her brand-new lover, who was placidly emerging from the kitchen with a cold beer in each hand. 3-J held out his hand eagerly, but Dr. Dick gave one to Mama and took a sip from the other.

"Yeah, that one there was having the time of his life, yucking it up with ol' Farmer Bill while I shoveled ashes like a slave woman."

Dr. Dick considered the open seating options (the floor, or next to nearly-naked 3-J) and perched himself on the arm of Mama's fåtölj.

"Not true," he said. "William and I were buying materials at the lumba yard in Big City. Then we had to draft the blueprints for the coop, measure it out, and prep the foundation."

Mama snorted.

"If you say so."

She took a slug of her beer. Dr. Dick's hand curved around the back of her neck and began to knead. She lost her scowl.

"I have to admit," he said. "Dacta Barney's unorthodox punishment was a stroke of luck for us. It's incredible how fast that coop came togetha! There's nothing left to do but fill it with ducks. Who'd have thought we could build a whole duck coop in just one day?"

We stared at him, dumbfounded.

"How long did you think it would take to build a duck coop?" said Opal.

I was the only one who heard his murmured admission, "Six months."

Everyone heard his suggestion, however: "Well, in any event, I'm starved. What does everyone say to pizza?"

Oh, the shouts of acclaim, the jubilant approval that met his suggestion! Dr. Dick ordered it delivery-style, which was very aristocratic. Mama located her pincushion in the back of her closet and set to pinning Opal's bikini top, Pearl returned from making her mysterious phone call, and the pizza man pulled up after narrowly avoiding a drunken collision with 3-J's parked semi.

We took the pizza outside to eat at the picnic table. The Midsummer sun was easing closer to the horizon, smudging the sky with shades of pink and lemon and violet. I watched Mama and Dr. Dick as we ate. They sat side-by-side, acting innocent. But their faces betrayed the truth. Mama's frown was completely gone. Dr. Dick wore a tiny smile. Mama leaned close and whispered something in Dr. Dick's ear. They both grinned, then quickly assumed unconvincing poker faces.

The sun began to go down. The sky turned orange, then ochre, then orchid. We all sat back, sated and smiling. Our plates were empty, as was Mama's beer bottle.

"Want anotha?" Dr. Dick inquired.

"Nah," she said.

"You?" he asked 3-J, who astonished him by vigorously

shaking his head.

"Sun's almost down," 3-J said. "On Midsummer, all drinkin' must stop once the throbbing celestial orb penetrates the moist, yielding horizon."

A gentle breeze began to blow, wafting away the day's heat.

Mama's hand drifted to Dr. Dick's knee.

"Maybe this ain't the worst Midsummer ever," she said. "I do wish I'd gotten a bite of that cake, though."

Dr. Dick's arm glided around her shoulders.

"I think I'm ready for the pageant," Opal announced. "I think I've got a real shot at the crown."

Mama and Dr. Dick snuggled up close to each other. I burst into giggles.

"Quit it!" Opal cried.

Pearl opened her mouth to admonish me. I jerked my head at Mama and Dr. Dick. She began to giggle as well.

"Don't ruin my confidence!" Opal said.

"Sorry," Pearl and I tittered in unison.

"Knock it off," commanded Mama, perfunctorily and preoccupied with passion.

"This is really inappropriate, girls—very unkind to your sista," Dr. Dick began, step-dadishly.

He hesitated. He looked from me to Pearl. He frowned.

"Wait," he said. "Why are you really laughing?"

Mama shushed him.

"Don't humor their humor," she said. "Never leads to aught but more strife. And if there's one thing I've learned to avoid with them girls, it's stri…"

Mama trailed off.

Her eyes were fixed upon the horizon.

"What's that?" she whispered.

"What?" said Opal.

"Shhh!" Mama hissed. "Listen…"

We grew still and strained our ears.

In the distance, there was a strange lowing sound. Gradually, it grew louder, coalescing first into an engine-like thrum, then a deep hum that seemed to be coming from the outskirts of the trailer park. The sun was fully down now. Fireflies darted about, trailing alien-green phosphorescence. Flickering yellow lights joined the fireflies, bobbing about just beyond the furthermost trailers.

Mama, my sisters, and I glanced at each other in dread. Then, one by one, our gazes strayed to 3-J.

The humming sound wasn't just coming from afar—it was coming from him as well.

Mama's eyes grew huge.

"Oh no," she whispered.

The flickering yellow lights merged into a straight line at the edge of the trailer park. They glimmered in the navy-blue darkness, coming closer and closer. When they were within a stone's throw of our trailer, they resolved into dozens upon dozens of lighters held aloft by a line of men that stretched a quarter mile in either direction. The men were humming, just like 3-J.

"Dear God, it's The Police," Mama gasped.

"What?" Dr. Dick said, staring at the men who had stopped marching and stood staring at us. Their eyes glittered in the lighter-light like flat stones embedded in taboo idols.

The truckers, for that is what they were, ceased their humming and lifted their voices in song.

"I won't share you with another boy, I know my mind is made up. So put away your makeup. Told you once, I won't tell you again…" they sang, standing in a semi-circle surrounding our property.

3-J rose and pulled a book of matches from beneath his towel. He lit one and turned to Mama.

"Cryyyyyyystal Lynn! You don't have to put on the red light! Cryyyyyyystal Lynn! You don't have to sell your body to the night!" he sang in a tender twang, waving the match soulfully at her until it burned his fingers.

"Ow!"

He lit another and recommenced.

"Cryyyyyyystal Lynn! You don't have to put on the red light!"

The truckers, some two-hundred strong, joined his chorus. "You don't have to put on the red light!"

"Oh lordy!" Mama cried, covering her face with her hands.

She backed up against Dr. Dick's bare chest. His hands grasped her upper arms protectively, but I was too alarmed by the flame-bearing truckers to giggle.

When the song quavered to its conclusion, 3-J approached the truckers and accepted an object wrapped in a bit of toilet paper. He moved down the line and received a slip of paper with writing on both sides. He turned to Mama. He cleared his throat and began to read from the paper in a speechifying voice.

"Crystal-Lynn: Your once and future husband has sent us to bestow upon you our rendition of your and his song, the 1978 hit 'Roxanne' by The Police, and also this…*thing*."

He stepped up to Mama and handed the toilet paper wrapped…*thing* to her. She unwrapped it with a trembling hand and uncovered a chunky, chipped motel ashtray.

"What…what the hell's this?" she said.

"A token of undying esteem. And, uh, please also accept and remit this-here unpaid bill for the Blue Water Travelodge in Doyotte, Alabama."

3-J awkwardly thrust the bill, with its penciled speech running along the tip line, at Mama. Faced with her slack-jawed silence, he waved at the truckers and they began to hum again, very softly.

"Your ex-husband wishes you to prepare yourself. His coming is imminent," 3-J said.

"Imminent? When? Tonight? Tomorrow? Just tell me!" Mama cried.

3-J merely smiled and began to hum himself. The truckers turned and walked away in a line. Clad in his ceremonial towel, 3-J followed them, lighting matches and tossing them over his shoulder at Mama and Dr. Dick as he and his unionized cohorts vanished into the night.

When we were alone, Mama let out a little moan and dashed inside. Dr. Dick followed her. My sisters and I stared at one another, our faces a triple mirror of shock and awe. Daddy had carried out plenty of astonishing acts in the past, but never before had he mustered a gang of men to serenade (and subtly menace) his ex-wife en plein air. We each opened our mouths, one after the other, to say something. But none of us could speak. Wordlessly, we repaired to the interior of the trailer.

Mama was pacing the living room in a panic.

"Crystal-Lynn, calm down," Dr. Dick was saying. "This is all going according to plan. When your ex-husband shows up, you'll tell him that you're in a new relationship. And the best part is, it won't be a lie."

"It won't work," Mama said. "I can't believe I thought this dumb scheme of Ruby's could—"

She stopped pacing.

"What do you mean, it won't be a lie?"

Dr. Dick encircled her waist with his arm.

"Afta what happened last night," he said. "Well, now it's the truth. Isn't it?"

"I—you—that was—what?" Mama dithered, pulling away from Dr. Dick. "This is all too much; my mind's a muddle!"

"Was it…was it just part of the act for you?" Dr. Dick said.

His face was a mixture of bewilderment and hurt.

"What? I just—I can't—" Mama vacillated.

"Crystal-Lynn, are we togetha now, or aren't we?"

"I—I don't…know," she said.

But what he heard was, "I—I don't…no."

His face fell. His shoulders sagged. He inhaled.

As he exhaled, his expression hardened and his spine stiffened.

"Very well," he said. "It's cleah I've behaved inappropriately. I was wrong to get romantically involved with the motha of two of my patients. Even if it was only an act."

"No, Dick," Mama began. "I just need to—"

But Dr. Dick didn't let her finish. He turned, grabbed his jacket from the back of the fåtölj, and slid the detached front door aside.

"I have Motel Rounds," he said. "Goodbye."

And he exited.

Mama slumped. Her face was stricken.

Dr. Dick returned.

Mama brightened.

"Forgot my keys," he said.

"Dick," she said. "Can we—"

He snatched the shining key ring from the grubby ändbordet.

"Wait," Mama said. "Don't go."

He ducked back out the door.

This time he did not return, though Mama waited for over an hour, her mien gradually growing more anguished. At last, she sighed, long and hard and deep.

"Well, it's over," she said. "Dick was a nice man. He treated me right. He was sensible and steady. And he had the best bedroom know-how I ever—never you mind! Oh, Jesus! I done lost my only chance for happiness with a good man on this bleak, barren earth."

"Oh, Mama," Opal said, rushing to embrace her.

"Maybe he'll come back," Pearl said, patting Mama's arm.

"Nah, he's gone for good," I said.

My sisters glared at me. But Mama nodded.

"Ruby's right," she said. "And the Swedish ambassador was right, too. There ain't nothing but misery to be had on Midsummer. I've been arrested, put on trial, and forced to labor in the hot sun. My crazy ex is on his way and my lover left me. I couldn't drink myself goofy and I didn't get so much as a crumb of Midsummer cake."

A wild look took possession of her eyes.

"Can't do nothing about none of it," she said. "Except the cake. I'll be danged if I let every danged thing go wrong with this danged holiday!"

"What're you gonna do, Mama?" asked Pearl.

"Get y'all's shoes on," Mama commanded. "We're going to the Swedish Embassy & Beauty Parlor & Coffee Shop and get us our Midsummer cake!"

"But Mama, it's nearly ten at night," Opal said. "You think

the Swedish Embassy & Beauty Parlor & Coffee Shop'll still be open?"

"It's always open until midnight on Midsummer," Mama replied, rustling her purse out from under the sofa.

"You think the Swedish ambassador'll still be conscious?" I said.

"He's Nordic," said Mama, jamming her feet into a pair of sky-blue high heels with bows on the toes. "He's got the drinkin' constitution of a Russian, an Irishman, and an elderly Greek woman rolled into one."

"You think he's still got any cake?" said Pearl.

"If he don't," Mama said, flinging the front door to the floor with a humorless, frenzied laugh. "I'll add eighty-eight lines to that poem of his, and I won't stop my gloomy rhyming until he whips us up a cake all our own. And I'll eat the whole thing myself!"

And with that, Mama marched out the front door.

"Don't eat it all—I want a slice, too," Pearl wailed, following Mama.

Looking worried, Opal dogged the two out the door.

"How's about you let me drive, Mama?" I heard her say.

"I'm as sober as a judge who ain't Dr. Barney," came the reply. "And you failed your driver's license exam three times before the only straight man at the Big City DMV came back from vacation and got a load of you."

I started to follow my family, then I faltered.

I had a bad feeling about this nocturnal excursion into town.

A very bad feeling.

The Oldsmobile engine sputtered to life.

Three car doors slammed.

"Wait!" I cried.

I dashed out the front door and threw myself upon the car.

"I got a bad feeling about this, Mama!" I said, splaying myself across the windshield like a dead bug.

"Git!" Mama ordered, turning on the windshield wipers.

I leapt off the hood of the car. I hesitated, then I jumped

into the backseat and slammed the door just as Mama put the car in high gear.

Away we sped toward town, the reflection of Mama's eyes in the rearview mirror alternating between grim and glum. Now and again, Opal or Pearl ventured an optimistic word or two regarding the probable return of Dr. Dick. But Mama merely snorted and replied, "You girls don't know nothing about the hearts of men."

I may have known nothing about the hearts of men, but I had a sixth sense when it came to the urges of truckers. The moment the Oldsmobile humped onto the outermost end of Main Street, we were assaulted by the bright orange glare of licking flames and flashing police lights and high beam truck headlights, conjoined with the hullabaloo of rebel yells and sirens and diesel engines and CB radios turned up full blast.

Mama slammed on the brakes.

Shielding our eyes and covering our ears, my sisters and I shrank into the depths of the backseat. Main Street was awash in chaos. Drunken truckers swarmed high and low, scuttling through the night in a dark mass that left aught but devastation in its wake. Sparkling glass from broken windows spangled every inch of sidewalk. Fires blazed where fires ought not to blaze. The stench from the river of Budweiser that flowed down the roadway was overpowering.

Mama wrenched the steering wheel hard to port and swung the car in a breakneck U-turn. She floored the accelerator, evacuating us from the demilitarized zone.

"The not-yet-newspaper predicted this," Opal exclaimed. "Remember? 'Midsummer shall bring MISFORTUNE and CHAOS on a scale never before seen in Somwärin.'"

"Hush that talk," Mama said, white-knuckling the steering wheel as the great outdoors flashed by the windows.

"No, not Midsummer," Pearl corrected. "The Trucker Jamboree."

"Y'all shush!" Mama said.

"My God," gasped Opal. "If it's this bad now, how much worse will it get?"

"For the last time," yelled Mama, turned her head to glower at Opal. "Be qu—"

"Look out!" Opal yelled back.

Mama swung her head back to the windshield, let out a scream, and slammed on the brakes.

Stopped dead in the middle of the road was a massive, blood-red semi. The Oldsmobile fishtailed, skidded, and came to a halt just inches from the naked lady silhouettes stamped on the truck's rear mud flaps.

"Sweet Jesus," panted Mama, pressing a hand to her bosom, then her forehead.

As soon as she had caught her breath, she honked at the semi.

Nothing happened.

She honked again.

We waited. The truck didn't move.

Mama honked a third time.

Opal cracked her door and stepped out into the night-shrouded road to carry out a reconnaissance mission on the motionless vehicle. The moment her feet touched asphalt, a brilliant orange semi with purple lightning bolts zigzagging across the hood and along both doors came barreling up behind us. Opal yelped and jumped back into the car just as the truck shuddered to a stop in the very place she'd been standing.

"What…what's happening?" Mama said, her hands trembling as they clenched the steering wheel.

As the words left her lips, two more semis rolled up, one careening to a halt next to the driver's side door, the other parking right up against our back bumper.

We were boxed in.

Mama began to hyperventilate in terror. My sisters and I followed suit.

All four trucks let loose an earsplitting cannonade of horn blasts and revved their engines. Trapped in the center of this prison on wheels, Mama had no choice but to depress the gas and roll along with the semis.

The trucks steered us out of town along a sinister, shadowy route that led straight to Motel Way. We passed a multitude of debauched traveler's inns, each more debased than the last. When we reached the penultimate motel—the very one at which I'd so recently sojourned with 3-J—the trucks eased to a stop. The two on either side of our car split off and parked some distance away. The other two didn't budge, their formidable frames pushed up snug against our front and back bumpers to prevent Mama from maneuvering her vehicle free.

I pressed my face to the window. The ring of trucks and the slumping gray motel were as they'd been last night, but the enormous circus tent was gone. In its place was an unlit pyre, or possibly a shrine, constructed of broken scraps of Fack Sex furniture. It towered two stories into the night sky. All around it stood leaping bonfires and hundreds upon hundreds of swaying truckers.

One of the truckers stopped swaying and made his way to our car. He tapped on the driver's side window with a grease-blackened knuckle and indicated through the jerking of his head that we were to get out.

Mama, my sisters, and I obeyed.

Without a word, the trucker led us through the huge parking lot. On all sides were men scrubbing their laundry in barrels of rainwater, burning hot dogs over fires lit in old coffee cans, throwing dirt clods at their flea-chewed dogs, swilling beer, and clutching disconnected CB mics into which they chanted, "Base station, base station in the big blue, come on, come on."

We were conducted to the foot of the immense furniture pile. Truckers surrounded us on all sides, making flight impossible. Their faces were turned expectantly toward the strange sculpture.

"What's happening, Mama?" whispered Pearl, her face white with fear.

Mama just shook her head and clutched my little sister close to her.

"CB!" chanted the truckers who surrounded the mighty

monument. "CB, CB, CB!"

"What do we do, Mama?" said Opal.

Mama shook her head.

"What do they want with us?" said Pearl.

Mama shook her head.

"Who will help us?" Opal cried.

"Dr. Flo!" Mama shouted.

Oh, the relief that flooded our veins as Dr. Flo's makeshift ambulance pulled into the midst of this scene of incomprehensible pagan liturgy! Opal let out a jubilant shriek, Pearl burst into happy tears, and Mama frantically waved both arms at the medical vehicle.

"Here! Over here!" she called. "Help us!"

The truckers stopped swaying, stopped chanting, and stopped staring at the looming woodpile. They turned to Dr. Flo's familiar vehicle and watched as it came to a halt a few paces from us.

The front door of the ambulance opened.

Out stepped 3-J.

Mama blanched in horror and her arms fell slack by her sides.

3-J, still kitted out in our pink towel, strode around to the rear of the ambulance, unlocked the back doors, and unloaded a gurney upon which Dr. Dick lay firmly strapped down.

"Not funny," Dr. Dick said. "I told you, I've taken over Dacta Flo's Motel Rounds! You're doing your fellow Teamstas a great disservice with this little prank, 3-J."

3-J unbuckled his civilian pal, helped him to stand, and clapped him on the shoulder.

"No hard feelings," 3-J said.

He turned to his compatriots and held up both arms in triumph.

"Now the family circle is complete!" he announced.

"What are you—" Dr. Dick said. Then he caught sight of Mama.

His expression darkened.

"Dick, I didn't have anything to do with this," Mama said.

"Are you alright—"

Her words stopped cold when a loud bang, as of heavy furniture falling, came from the wooden structure. The truckers turned away from us and stared with rapt eyes as a man emerged from the base of the great tower. His face was pale, his eyes were fiery, and he wore a long, gray beard, like a crazed biblical prophet.

I knew this man.

"Don!" shouted 3-J.

He ran to Daddy and embraced him. The two kissed each other, once, twice, on each bristly cheek, like degenerate Frenchmen.

"Ew," said Pearl.

"Cut it out!" 3-J snapped. "It's perfectly fine for two buddies to, y'know, share a friendly physical salutation—"

"Jesus Christ and his disciples were known to kiss each otha upon meeting," said Dr. Dick, cutting off 3-J's sputtering. "And today, the practice has been adopted by degenerate Frenchmen."

"See! Ha!" 3-J crowed.

"But," Dr. Dick continued, looking at 3-J. "The disciple Judas betrayed Jesus with a kiss. And," he turned to Daddy. "Frenchmen have a reputation for jealousy when it comes to their women."

Daddy scrutinized Dr. Dick. He narrowed his eyes. He snapped his fingers and four burly truckers sprang forward to help him mount a contraption constructed from a torn driver's seat and the glittering innards of a CB radio, which was bolted to the side of the monument ten feet off the ground.

When he was settled upon his lofty throne, he turned his hypnotic gaze on Dr. Dick with the force of a fire hose. Dr. Dick flinched but did not look away.

"This-here's the doctor of womanly parts?" he intoned.

His voice…his voice! It thrilled me from the tips of my toes to the tangles in my hair.

"Now, now, hold on a minute, Don—" Mama began.

Daddy raised his right hand in a magisterial gesture, not

unlike the pope or Lord Satan on the cover of a heavy metal album. To my surprise, Mama fell silent.

He beckoned to Dr. Dick.

Dr. Dick stepped toward him. Not a sound was heard in the parking lot but the crackling of the bonfires and the fearful gasping of my sisters.

Daddy beckoned again.

Dr. Dick stepped closer.

Daddy beckoned again. He kept beckoning and Dr. Dick kept stepping closer and closer, until they were nose-to-nose. With their schnozes touching, the two peered at each other, unblinking.

This went on for a solid five minutes. We girls and Mama began to fidget. 3-J shushed us.

"Don's lookin' into Dick's soul," he said.

"Hell, how long's he gotta look? Either it's there or it ain't," Mama said.

"All night, all day, and on into eternity if that's what it takes," 3-J replied.

"I ain't got that kinda time," Mama said. "Come on, girls, we're leaving!"

But the hulking truckers who surrounded us wouldn't budge. Mama cajoled, pleaded, sweet-talked, and threatened, but were as deaf and dumb as statues.

At last, 3-J let loose a sharp whistle to catch Mama's attention.

"Crystal-Lynn, Don will speak with you now," he said.

Mama went white.

"Girls…stick close to me."

We surrounded her, clinging to her with shaking hands as she crossed the empty space between the ring of truckers and the throne upon which Daddy sat. Dr. Dick had removed his nose from Daddy's and stood a handful of paces off, his arms crossed over his finally-shirted chest, his freedom impeded by the restraining hand of 3-J.

"After a long and thorough search," announced Daddy. "I located wisdom in the soul of this-here medicine man. Many things have been revealed to me. He has come to us from Afar. He is a Democrat. And he is not your boyfriend."

Mama's eyes went wide.

"For it was you," Daddy declaimed, pointing his finger at Mama like a condemning high priest. "You, with your infernal shilly-shallying, who put the kibosh on what was fixing to be a serious and satisfying relationship. Out of base cowardice."

Mama turned on Dr. Dick.

"How could you tell him that?"

"I didn't say a word," Dr. Dick replied. And though he appeared unamused by the general proceedings, he did not seem dissatisfied by Daddy's assessment of the situation.

Daddy held up his hand imperiously. Mama and Dr. Dick fell silent.

"I've learned from my good buddy—my bestest buddy—about the kinda life you're leading," Daddy said. "Though I trust 3-J as I trust my own eyes and ears, I want to see it for myself."

"Whaddya mean, the kinda life I'm leading? I run a tight ship, mister—not that you ever noticed when you were living with us. I pay the bills, I keep food in the fridge, I put—"

"Enough," Daddy thundered, making Mama, my sisters, and even Dr. Dick jump. "We will go to my once and future home now."

3-J released Dr. Dick and ran to assist Daddy to dismount his throne. Dr. Dick turned and strode toward the ambulance. The truckers parted to let him pass.

"Dick—wait!" Mama cried.

He turned to look at her. He let out a little sigh of regret, but his eyes were without pity.

"You made your choice, Crystal-Lynn. There's nothing I can do to help you now."

He climbed behind the wheel, turned the key in the ignition, and drove away.

Mama, my sisters, and I were ushered into the Oldsmobile. Daddy climbed into 3-J's rig. The ring of semis surrounding the parking lot roared to life. Our earlier captors returned to box in our car and away we motored, an honor guard of trucks filling the road behind us. As we drove, more and more trucks from the other motels joined the convoy. By the time we reached the Somwärin Trailer Park and RV Pleasure Garden, we were hemmed in by a mile-long escort of semis that smoked and growled demonically.

Only a handful of trucks could squeeze into the trailer park. Daddy's chauffeur parked in front of our trailer, jumped out, and clambered to open his pal's door. Then he scooted around to Mama's car, yanked her door open, and made urgent get-on-out gestures with both hands. Mama hesitated, then climbed out. My sisters and I did likewise.

A horde of truckers assembled in the vicinity of our trailer. They watched as Daddy strolled over to Mama. He reached out his hand to touch her, then did not. He turned to address his colleagues.

"Wait for me out here. I'm gonna spend time with my…*family*."

So menacing, the way he said that word. I shivered.

With trembling hands, Mama unlocked the side door. She stepped into the kitchen, followed by Opal and Pearl, followed by me. And finally, followed by Daddy.

As soon as we were all in the kitchen, Daddy closed the door.

He locked it.

He turned to Mama.

He crossed the room to her.

He grabbed her by the shoulders.

His face was awash in panic.

"You've gotta help me, Crystal-Lynn," he said. "I'm in way over my head this time!"

"Wha…" bleated Mama. "What? What, what?"

Daddy raked a hand through his hair, his eyes darting nervously to the unshaded window.

"I got myself in a terrible fix," he said, yanking the tattered old curtains to cover the all-revealing glass. "I made up that CB thing as a joke during a boring run through the Sonoran Desert but 3-J took it seriously and he told all my buddies about it and they believed every dang word and like an idiot I went along with it and now I'm the leader of a cult and I don't know how to call the whole thing off!"

Mama's face morphed from terrified to astonished to enraged to something beyond human emotion.

"You," she said. "You did this…as a joke?"

"At first," Daddy said. "But it spiraled outta control. If my fellow truckers find out the truth, who knows what kinda revenge they'll take? They're already on edge over the Incredible Collapsing Strip Circus from last night. I been playing this 'Chosen One' thing by ear for weeks and I think some of them are starting to get suspicious. This isn't even a real beard!"

He yanked the long, gray beard off, revealing a smooth-shaved chin.

"You gotta help me—what should I do?"

"What should you do?" Mama said. "I'll tell you what you should do."

I had heard plenty of profanity flow forth from Mama's mouth over the years. As a connoisseur of obscenity, I was a jaded, cynical sort. But the scatological storm of sacrilege and straight-up swearing that she unleased at him made my jaw drop.

"Fair enough," Daddy said, when she had finished. "But please, you gotta help me!"

Mama just spun around and marched out of the kitchen.

Daddy turned to my sisters, his face creased with supplication.

"Girls," he said.

But Opal and Pearl wore expressions of outrage just as baleful as Mama's. Without a word, they turned on their heels and huffed after their maternal ancestor.

Daddy let out a quavery breath. He lowered his head until his de-bearded chin touched his chest. He closed his eyes.

I turned to follow my sisters and my mama.

I paused.

I turned back.

"I'll help you, Daddy," I said.

Chapter Twelve
A Day Of Profound Regret

Sunday, June 22
Too early and too late

It was the day after Midsummer: a day to wallow in regret. I spent the first moments of the day after Midsummer pondering the living room rug with its pale, phantasmagoric stain shaped like Daddy. Then I went into the kitchen, looked out the window, and pondered the man shaped like Daddy seated atop the picnic table smoking a cigarette in the burning light of dawn. The rising sun limned his sooty silhouette with a blazing red aura that crackled and bristled like the spines of a fire dragon.

In fact, it was Daddy. The truckers were gone. He was all alone.

I hesitated.

I reached for the doorknob.

I released it.

I found that I was outside, sidling toward the picnic table.

Daddy turned to me. His face was obscured by sloe shadows cast by the brim of his baseball cap. He turned back to the ruddy sunrise and took a long, deep drag off his cigarette.

"This might be the worst trouble I ever caused, Ruby."

"How'd it all start, Daddy?"

He gave me a good, hard look in the eyes. I'd forgotten he had eyes just like mine: same color, same shape, same scheming squint. He shook his head.

"I don't dare tell you," he replied.

"Why not?"

"You got a gleam in your eyes. I know that gleam. I seen it in my own eyes in the rearview mirror when I get a notion to make trouble. I best not tell you, lest I give you ideas."

Daddy pulled a pack of Mexican cigarettes out of the

pocket of his red-checked flannel shirt and held it out to me.

"You smoke yet?"

I shook my head.

He shrugged.

"Well, give it time," he said.

He sighed.

"I wish I could skip town," he said. "Hop on the road and let my fellow truckers cool their jets here in Somwärin."

"Why dontcha?"

Daddy looked at me with alarm.

"I can't leave them alone," he said. "Not considering what they're planning."

"What're they gonna do?"

"I can't tell you," he said. "Word 'round the campfire is you already got one federal charge to your name, which you only dodged on account of the Machiavellian gamesmanship of Dr. Flo."

"Please tell me, Daddy."

Daddy rubbed his hand over the back of his neck.

"Well, alright," he said. "Tomorrow, at the Miss Somwärin pageant, my brother truckers are gonna lie in wait just outta sight. The moment Miss Somwärin is crowned, a mighty mob'll swarm the stage. And then…"

"What?

"No, I don't dare tell you."

"Please tell me! What're they gonna do?"

"It's too shocking to say," said Daddy. "They're gonna—"

"What're you doing here? You get offa Mama's property!"

"Yeah!"

Opal and Pearl, hands on hips, stood framed in the doorway leading to the kitchen.

Daddy obliged, sliding to the end of the picnic table, which lay across the property line shared with the Disgraced Modern Poetry Professor.

"Howdy, girls," he said. "I ain't on your mama's property. Come sit a spell with me 'n' your sister. We're having us an enlightening confab."

Opal and Pearl ignored him. They stepped outside, turned their backs to Daddy, and addressed me.

"We're going to town," said Opal. "The truckers trashed the school auditorium, so the Miss Somwärin pageant can't take place there as planned."

"They didn't cancel it?" Daddy said. "Did they?"

Opal ignored him.

"The warehouse supervisor over at Fack Sex said we can hold it there. She's opening the warehouse to the public—ain't that something, Ruby?"

Indeed it was something. My pulse quickened with excitement. Nobody was permitted to enter the Fack Sex Furniture Distribution Warehouse except Fack Sex employees. Since my tenderest years, the place had been a tantalizing enigma. My eyes were alight. I could tell because everything looked unaccountably bright. I turned to Daddy and saw the same glow in his eyes.

"Interesting," he said. "I didn't count on that happening."

Opal ignored him harder.

"It's the perfect place for the pageant. No mischief-making trucker'd dare set foot inside the Fack Sex Furniture Distribution Warehouse," she said.

"Don't be so sure," Daddy said.

Opal ignored him so hard her body began to shake.

"Me and the other contestants are going to the warehouse to help move pallets and set up a stage. You wanna come along?"

Oh, how I did!

But I was torn. I wanted to hear Daddy's story.

"And I'm going to the Swedish Embassy & Beauty Parlor & Coffee Shop," said Pearl. "I gotta meet with the ambassador about…the last step of a secret plan. You wanna come?"

A secret plan? I knew what that meant. The solution to the mystery of what Pearl was planning to do to Perdee Dora—and a luscious hot fudge sundae—would be mine if I went with her.

But I was itching to hear Daddy's story.

I bit my lower lip. Then I bit my upper lip.

I shook my head at my sisters.

Their faces went sour.

"Suit yourself," said Opal.

"Your loss," said Pearl.

And my sisters stomped away.

I watched them go with a peculiar blend of regret and resolve. I felt a firm hand fall upon my shoulder. I turned to Daddy.

"Ain't their fault," he said. "I haven't been much of a father to you girls over the years. I'd blame my nature, but I got free will, don't I? I've pondered this many a day and many a night when I'm rolling down the endless highway, all alone in my rig. We truckers are isolated in our trucks day after day and night after night. That's why we like talking on the CB. That isolation's what gave me the idea for my…prank."

Daddy stuck a fresh cigarette between his lips, lit it, and took a long drag.

"I ought never to have done it," he said. "It's brought nothing by trouble. And the worst is yet to come."

"What're the truckers gonna do, Daddy?"

"The moment Miss Somwärin's crown lands on her head, they're gonna snatch her up, carry her off to an undisclosed location out Motel Way, and lock her in a pay-by-the-day room. They're gonna hold her captive, and…"

Daddy closed his eyes. He shook his head in shame.

"They're gonna…"

"What?"

"They're gonna turn her into a trucker."

I gasped.

"Yes, it's incredible, but it's all too true," said Daddy. "They're gonna teach her to drive a big rig and school her for the commercial driver's licensing test and help her apply for membership in Texas Teamsters Union Local 666. By the time the Trucker Jamboree rolls around, she'll be a brother Teamster, ready to load up and hit the open road with us."

"No!" I cried, my hands flying to my mouth in horror.

Opal had a fair to middling chance of winning Miss Somwärin. What if Opal was transformed into a trucker?

I could see it now: Opal roaring home in her big rig, straight off weeks on the open road. Stinking of diesel fuel and chicken fried steak and the mangy mutt she kept up front in the passenger seat for companionship. Beer gut hanging over her greasy blue jeans. Eyes bloodshot from copious doses of NoDoz.

"Mama!" she'd bawl, while scudding her filthy, oil-grimed boots over our semi-clean shag rug. "Where the hell's muh grub? What's a working woman gotta do to get some vittles around this dump?"

She'd spy me huddled up on the couch. With a rough laugh, she'd toss a mildewed sleeping bag at me.

"Scoot that sweet ass of yours over to the laundry trailer and wash up muh bed for me. And then fetch me a six-pack of Lone Star and a tin of Skoal. Pearl! You better not've rustled through my Playgirls while I was out busting my butt to put food on y'all's table! Man, I best call my union rep 'bout that cow herd I clipped out in Oklahoma."

And then she'd let out a massive belch. And scratch her crotch.

"But that's not the worst of it," Daddy said.

"It's not?"

"Nope, that's just phase one of the master plan," he said. "The long con here is…no, I don't dare tell you."

"Tell me, please, Daddy!"

"I get the dread when I think about it, and I'm the one who came up with it," said Daddy. "I'd hate to get my own girl involved."

"I want to help you set things right."

"It ain't the kinda thing a kid should get mixed up in."

"I'm not a kid! I'm gonna be fifteen soon."

He eyed me. He nodded slowly.

"True that," said Daddy. "I guess I can tell you after all. While Miss Somwärin is learning the art of the long haul, the rest of my brethren are gonna show the town a good time, trucker style. One long Trucker Jamboree, day after day after day. When the time is ripe, Miss Somwärin will return, a convert to the Teamster life. And the rest of the town'll follow suit."

"You don't mean…"

My mouth hung open. I was appalled. All of Somwärin, transformed into truckers?

This was worse than the not-yet-newspaper predicted. This was worse than anything I could have imagined. The Gentleman Gym Teacher, Dr. Flo, the sheriff-mayor, the Swedish ambassador, Dr. Dick, even Mama—all careening about in semis, chowing down at grease-trap diners, raising Cain from one end of the continental U.S. to the other?

The hot sun beat down upon my pate, yet I felt cold all over.

"We gotta do something—we gotta stop them!" I cried.

Daddy opened his mouth to reply, but before he could, a familiar voice rang out.

"Don!" 3-J shouted.

He emerged from the cab of his semi, parked in its usual spot out front of the trailer. Daddy gave me a hush-up gesture and rose from the picnic table. As 3-J approached, Daddy remembered his fake beard, yanked it out of the back pocket of his jeans, and hastily affixed it to his chin.

3-J grabbed Daddy's bicep and leaned close to him.

"Muh! Muh!" went his mouth on both of Daddy's cheeks, then he gave Daddy a big hug for good measure.

"When'd you wake up? I been dozing in my bunk for hours," said 3-J. "Where'd all our buddies go?"

"I sent 'em away in the wee hours," replied Daddy. "I been powwowing in private with my middle girl."

"Betcha had a powerful lotta wisdom to impart," 3-J said. "C'mon, let's go to the strip club!"

"Not yet," said Daddy. "Step 'round the trailer with me. I gotta tell you what's on my mind."

Daddy steered 3-J out of sight, trampling a family of gnomes in the process.

Now was my chance. I crept across the dead lawn to 3-J's semi. I glanced over my shoulder, then unlatched the driver's side door and hoisted myself up into the cab.

The interior of the truck was stifling. Nevertheless, I pulled the door closed. I settled myself into the driver's seat and scanned the dials and dead lights and doodads that bejeweled the dashboard. At last my gaze fell upon the object of my search.

There it was.

The CB.

The cause of all this trouble.

Gulping nervously, I reached out and pressed the power button. Instantly a ruckus of static blasted forth. I began turning knobs and pushing buttons until a voice rang out, clear and confident.

"And in the central Texas area, the National Weather Service has issued a tornado warning for approximately ten a.m. tomorrow morning—"

I twisted a dial and the voice cut out. Just as I was reaching for the oblong microphone attached to a skinny spiral cord, I heard the side door from the kitchen bang open.

I ducked down. After a moment, I peeped out the driver's side window and espied Mama stepping from the kitchen into the yard. She pulled out her cigarettes and settled into the very spot Daddy had recently occupied at the picnic table. She stuck a cigarette between her lips, fumbled around her person for a lighter or a matchbook, then flicked the unlit smoke to the ground with a sigh.

"Aw, what's the use?" she muttered.

She made to stand.

She sat back down, dropped her chin into her hand, and began to mope.

Just as I was starting to have visions of a slow death by hyperthermia, 3-J and Daddy came strutting around the trailer and into her presence.

Mama leapt to her feet.

"What the hell're you still doing here?" she demanded.

"You get offa my property!"

"Howdy, Crystal-Lynn," said Daddy, reaching into his pocket and pulling out his cigarettes. "Smoke?"

"You know good and well I ain't got a taste for that Day of the Dead tobacco you favor," Mama said. "You take it and yourself back to Motel Way this very minute, and don't you come back. Go on, git!"

Daddy did not git. He offered Mama a winning grin. He opened his mouth to drawl something charming.

"Don't you deploy any of your fanciful sweet talk!" she interrupted. "You get off my property this instant."

"Now, Crystal-Lynn," said 3-J. "Don's here to reconcile, not squabble. Give him a chance."

"No," said Mama. "Leave. Right now. The both of you."

"It's been foretold," said 3-J. "You and Don will reunite. No longer must you settle for the inferior affection of Dr. Dick."

Mama's eyes flashed with rage and her body vibrated with wrath. She jabbed her index finger into Daddy's chest.

"Dick's twice the man you are!" she said. "I done wrong when I dithered. I shoulda said, 'Hell yes!' when he asked me to be with him. But I been burned by the likes of you for years, and it's made me gun-shy. I finally had me a good man, and I lost him on your account. Even when you ain't around, you bring me nothing but trouble!"

"Point taken," replied Daddy. "However—"

"However, y'all're meant to be together!" said 3-J. "You and Don. The CB said so. The CB is never wrong. Don's the Chosen One and you're the one he's chosen."

Mama pursed her lips. She removed her finger from Daddy's chest.

"You got until I count three to get off my property," she said. "One."

Daddy did not stir.

"Two."

Daddy smiled beatifically at Mama and crossed his arms over his chest.

I held my breath. None of Mama's daughters had ever dared to let her reach three. Surely Daddy was astute enough to flee while he had the chance.

Mama raised her eyebrows.

Daddy raised his.

"Don played you for a fool, 3-J. He made up that CB hooey as a joke, and you fell for it like the dummy you are. Three!"

Daddy's smirk melted into a stare of stupefaction.

"What?" said 3-J.

"Tell him, Don," said Mama.

"What's she mean, you made up the CB? Don? What's she mean?" said 3-J.

"Um," replied Daddy. He glanced at his bestest buddy, then at Mama. "Well played, baby doll."

"Don?" said 3-J, his voice no longer confused. "Did you lie to me?"

"Well," replied Daddy. "It can be said that every word a person utters ain't but the partial truth. See, a man's experience is colored by his personal perspective—"

"Sombitch! You did lie!" 3-J shouted. "How'd you do it? How'd you make the voice from The Great Beyond talk on our CBs all these months? Even when we was outta range? Even when our CBs was turned off? You meddled with the internal electronics of our radio transceivers, didn't you?"

"I might have done something like that," Daddy conceded. "However, I had a good reason—"

"I'm gonna sic the FCC on you!" 3-J shouted, jumping at Daddy, his hands reaching for the betrayer's throat.

Daddy, at long last, decided the moment had come to flee.

He took off running, with his irate pal in hot pursuit.

While Mama observed this, I took the opportunity to release myself from my scorching prison. I scooted to her side and watched as Daddy darted from one end of the trailer park to the other, followed by 3-J.

"You get over here and let me beat the living hell outta you, Don!" shouted 3-J, as the pair rounded the McMayberry brothers' school bus and pounded toward the laundry trailer.

Daddy sprang up onto the porch, dodged piles of empty detergent jugs, and jumped off the far side. He dashed back toward the Bejou family trailer.

"You're just making it worse for yourself!" bellowed 3-J, flinging himself over the end of the laundry trailer porch and charging through the dry dust after him.

Daddy halted in our yard, gave pitiless Mama a hasty once-over, then turned tail and sprang into the cab of 3-J's big rig. He fumbled with the sun visor, located the spare key, jammed it in the ignition, and roared off without a single backwards glance.

"Stop!"

3-J skidded into the yard just as his vehicle sped away.

"Bastardly bastard!" he panted. "Stole my truck! Grand theft auto! How could he?"

"He could," replied Mama. "Coz he's nothing but a troublemaker."

"Rotten ol' trick-playing lying Chosen-One-pretending-to-be scumbag!" 3-J cried. "I ain't gonna stand for it. He done played the wrong fella for a fool. I'm gonna—I'm gonna—"

He gasped for air, tipped his head back to the angry sun, and let out a howl.

Then he brooded for twelve solid hours. As the sun was beginning to creep toward the western horizon, he drew in a profound breath, raised his arms above his head, and shouted, "I'm gonna join forces with the one man who hates him as much as I do!"

As 3-J and I marched into town, the sublime, splendiferous sunset was unable to outshine the sublime, splendiferous rage burning in the eyes of Daddy's bestest buddy.

"Just you wait till I get my hands on him," 3-J muttered, flexing those very hands in anticipation as we plowed past the lawn chair graveyard. He said no more until we reached Main

Street, which lay in ruins despite the best efforts of the hungover natives to restore their primary thoroughfare to a functioning place of commerce and conveyance.

3-J stomped past the Lady Principal, who was scrubbing trucker expectorations and regurgitations from the front door of the Pubic Library.

He stomped past Dr. Flo's receptionist, who was sweeping sparkling drifts of broken glass into a soaring Matterhorn outside the clinic.

He stomped past the Handsomest Man in Somwärin, who was unwinding great furls of toilet paper from the fearsome arms of the Tree of Contemplation.

And he stomped past Dr. Barney, who was sopping up lakes of whiskey, vodka, beer, Scotch, Goldschläger, gin, absinthe, Stolichnaya, hard cider, brandy, cognac, Jägermeister, Old Crow, mezcal, Cointreau, mead, applejack, Maker's Mark, moonshine, Tanqueray, sangria, vermouth, champagne, schnapps, Bailey's Irish Cream, port, crème de menthe, sake, tequila, rum, Everclear, bourbon, and cooking sherry, which shimmered in the dying light of the sun outside the Vet 'n' Pet Shop.

3-J paused, then stomped up the steps that led to Dr. Dick's apartment.

I trailed him, apprehensive, anxious, and a-feared.

"3-J," I began.

3-J gave me nary a glance. With a primordial "Oof!" he shouldered the door open and barged right in.

We found Dr. Dick sitting in the little living room on a little sofa. He was drinking a beer and eating leftover Midsummer cake and listening to a Boston Redsox game on the radio. He looked up, surprised and annoyed, when we burst through his front door.

3-J stomped over to him and planted his hands on his blue-jeaned hips.

"Drunk! I might have known. Getting soused alone in his sad bachelor pad."

Dr. Dick, quite sober, glanced from 3-J to me.

"Is Somwärin a dry town all of a sudden? You should try a slice of cake. There's a whole box on the kitchen counta."

3-J lunged at him and grabbed his shirtfront. He shook Dr. Dick, who permitted this indignity with a shocked expression on his face.

"Sober up, man! There's an innocent girl present," 3-J said. "And I need your brainpower—not the half-witted ramblings of a drunken sot."

"3-J, what are you talking about? Quit that!" Dr. Dick said, dropping his beer and cake. "Dammit—Ruby, grab a papah towel."

3-J grunted in exasperation, released Dr. Dick's shirt, and shook his head.

"Guess we gots to do this the ol' fashioned way."

Before Dr. Dick could react, 3-J sprang forward like a jungle cat and snatched him up in a fireman's carry. As 3-J slung him over his shoulder, Dr. Dick began to squirm and kick.

"We are not—put me down! We are not repeating the nonsense of—I said, put me down! Of the otha night!" Dr. Dick said, bucking like a toddler in 3-J's arms.

3-J was unable to hold him. He dropped Dr. Dick with an apartment-shaking thud. Dr. Dick made to regain his feet, but 3-J was ready for that old tactic. He seized both of Dr. Dick's ankles and began to drag him across the slippery hardwood. Dr. Dick clawed at the frictionless floor, grabbing the doorjambs of the kitchen, then the hall, then the foyer, into which 3-J towed him in quick and confused succession. Ignoring his shouts of protest, 3-J hauled him hither and thither through the apartment until at last he discovered the bathroom.

3-J released Dr. Dick, slapped his protesting hands away, and hoisted him into his arms like a bride. He tossed him into the tub and turned on the water full bore.

"Sober up, you disgrace!" 3-J shouted.

Dr. Dick struggled to stand, slipped on the gleaming porcelain, and landed on his rump in the cold puddle gathering in the tub. He sprawled there, unresisting and glaring up at 3-J, as the water pattered down to soak him.

"Satisfied?" he inquired.

3-J let the water rain down upon the physician for another minute, then turned the shower off and stepped back with a pleased grunt. Dr. Dick rose, wrung himself out, and slopped back to the living room.

3-J followed him, and I followed 3-J.

"You may be wondering what brings me to your humble abode," said 3-J.

Dr. Dick ignored him. He retrieved the empty beer bottle from the floor and set it on the coffee table next to a half-full bottle of the same brand. He scraped the wad of mashed cake from the sofa cushion and made his soggy way into the little kitchen.

"Tonight's your lucky night," said 3-J. "For I bring news of our mutual nemesis."

Dr. Dick tossed his ruined snack into the garbage and dripped back into the living room.

"A great injustice has been done to me," said 3-J. "By the man you despise most of all."

"I don't despise anyone," said Dr. Dick. "Though I'm not terribly fond of you right now."

3-J let out a hoot of derision.

"You may be inclined to forgive and forget the crimes of that snake in the grass, but I ain't!" he replied. "Come, brother: Let's join forces and take him down together!"

3-J reached out his hand for a pact-sealing shake. Dr. Dick scorned it, crossing his arms over his chest.

"I don't want to get involved," he said.

3-J, his hand still extended, let out another hoot.

"Maybe you think you can take him down alone," he said. "Ha! You need me. My brawn plus your brainpower. Only if we join forces can we destroy your rival and my new enemy, Don Bejou!"

"No thanks," said Dr. Dick. "He's not my rival."

3-J dropped his hand. He gazed at Dr. Dick with disgust.

"You're right," said 3-J. "You're half the man he is."

"Some say I'm twice the man he is," replied Dr. Dick.

3-J's eyes narrowed at that familiar phrase. Those eyes of his drifted from Dr. Dick to the coffee table to the two beer bottles standing side-by-side in solidarity. One was half-drunk when we entered the apartment. The other…was also half-drunk when we entered.

"Say, Dick," he said in a slow, silken sort of voice. "Why don't you go change outta them wet duds?"

"I'll change afta you leave," replied Dr. Dick.

"Why not now? You must be powerful uncomfortable."

"I'm fine," said Dr. Dick, who did not appear to be anything other than uncomfortable as he shivered in his soaked garb.

"I'll fetch you a dry shirt," said 3-J, making to stride toward the one room into which he had not dragged Dr. Dick in his quest for the bathroom—the one room whose door was firmly closed.

Dr. Dick planted himself in 3-J's path.

"That's not necessary," he said.

"Why dontcha want me to help you out?" demanded 3-J, trying to shove past Dr. Dick and get at that closed door.

"I don't want you to trouble yourself," said Dr. Dick, grabbing 3-J by the forearms and struggling to strong-arm him back into the living room.

"Lemme get you some dry clothes, buddy!" shouted 3-J, swinging his fists at Dr. Dick.

"Don't botha, friend!" yelled Dr. Dick, shooting his own fists out in turn.

"Enough!" a deep voice intoned.

The door opened.

Out stepped Daddy.

3-J ceased his brawling and let out a bitter laugh.

"You're a helluva lot smarter than I gave ya credit for, 3-J," said Daddy. "First place you looked was the last place anyone'd expect to find me."

"The days of you pulling the wool over my eyes are over,"

3-J said. "And the days of me kicking your ass've just begun!"

He took a step toward Daddy.

"Whoa, whoa," said Dr. Dick, interposing himself between the pair. "If you two want to settle things in a primitive manna, I must insist you step outside."

"No need," said Daddy. "I've done you no wrong, pal."

His pal let out another bitter, triumphant laugh.

"Still playing the Chosen One, even when I know better?" said 3-J.

"Nobody's playing," said Daddy. "I don't play. I organize."

"Organize?" said 3-J. "Organize this!"

He turned to me.

"Ruby," he said in a low, terrible voice. "Go outside and raise the rabble."

"Why?" I said, a cold sensation sliding into my stomach.

"I think we both know it's high time for the Tree of Contemplation."

"No!" I cried.

"Yes!" 3-J cried.

"What?" Dr. Dick said.

"Can't we just try to talk sense into him?" I begged.

"His reign of trickery must end!" said 3-J. "The Tree of Contemplation is the only way."

"What the hell?" said Dr. Dick.

"Do it, Ruby!" 3-J shouted.

"No!" I shouted back.

"Ruby," Daddy said. "Do as 3-J says."

"No…" I moaned. But I knew I had no choice.

With dragging steps, I walked out of Dr. Dick's apartment, went down the stairs, and crossed Main Street. I slogged past the steps of the Celestial Temple of Psychedelic Truth and City Administration and approached the terrifying Tree of Contemplation, now cleansed of TP and looming in the gathering blue twilight.

I shuddered. I glanced up and down Main Street. All along the roadway, my fellow Somwärinites were still hard at work in the semi-dark, restoring their wrecked town to its former splendor.

With a heavy sigh, I located the old metal clapper and triangle affixed inconspicuously to a small concrete platform at the base of the Tree of Contemplation. I let out a little sob and struck the clapper against the triangle as hard as I could: once, twice, thrice, and then over and over and over as tears filled my eyes.

Presently, drawn by the distinctive *CLIII-ANG! CLIII-ANG! CLIII-ANG!* that no one from our fair town could ever mistake, a small crowd gathered on the lawn. They milled in the warm night air, conferring with each other. I decided a sufficient number had arrived to constitute a rabble. I dropped the clapper and turned to face the oblong plaque positioned on the platform.

"Hear ye, hear ye!" I read aloud, in the prescribed manner. "Know then that the Tree of Contemplation is a civic resource of peace and order. May the troubled mind of fill in the blank—I mean, may the troubled mind of Don Bejou receive enlightenment upon said Tree."

I stood up straight, faced the crowd, and sighed in regret.

The townsfolk, for their part, evinced the opposite of regret.

"Well, awright—Don Bejou, huh?"

"Never a better candidate for Treeing, in my opinion."

"And 'bout time, I say!"

"Where is the gentleman, sötnos?" the Swedish ambassador called from the doorway of the Swedish Embassy & Beauty Parlor & Coffee Shop across the street.

"3-J's got him cornered up in Dr. Dick's apartment over the Vet 'n' Pet Shop," I said.

"Better go give him a hand, I 'spect," said Dr. Barney. "No one ever climbs the Tree willingly."

Dr. Barney, the Gentleman Gym Teacher, and the Handsomest Man in Somwärin betook themselves in a gang down the crepuscular street. The Swedish ambassador glanced up at the sky.

"It is dark for such business," he said. "I shall fetch the

portable torches from last year's St. Lucia Festival. And the United Nations torture witness forms, which I must fill out and fax."

I shivered in the soft breeze. I dreaded what was about to happen.

The Swedish ambassador returned to the doorway bearing four man-high torches. He lit them and the flames licked upward, painting his face with dreadful shadows and frightful highlights. Dr. Flo's receptionist carried them across Main Street and sunk them into the ground around the Tree of Contemplation. The firelight lapped at the Tree, and the hulking contraption seemed to grow taller and more formidable.

The crowd murmured in approval, then fell into a solemn silence.

Presently a commotion was heard far up Main Street. In the gloom, we saw four men jogging along the deserted road. Hoisted high above their heads, flat on his back, lay Daddy. Behind them came Dr. Dick, who was objecting vociferously.

"It's an eight-legged horse for Don Bejou to ride on!" Dr. Barney panted, struggling to keep hold of Daddy's left leg.

"Hup! Hup! Hup!" the other men chanted, each grappling with a limb.

"What're you doing? Are you people insane?" Dr. Dick shouted.

3-J, Dr. Barney, the Gentleman Gym Teacher, and the Handsomest Man in Somwärin carried Daddy to the Tree of Contemplation, came to a halt, and set him on his feet. Their hands closed over his wrists and upper arms to keep him from fleeing, as so many attempted to do once they had been condemned to the Tree. The crowd closed in.

"What is this? Let him go!" said Dr. Dick, shoving his way through the mob.

3-J gripped Dr. Dick by the shoulder.

"Dick, we all know the time for this is long past. Make it easy on Don and let us get on with it."

"What's going on?" Dr. Dick stared wide-eyed at the

dozens of grim faces. His eyes jerked in alarm to the torches, then to the horrible, multi-armed behemoth that towered in the midst of the crowd.

"Wrong-thinking is Don's problem. Right-thinking will come to him on the Tree of Contemplation," said 3-J.

"The what?"

3-J jerked a thumb at the Tree of Contemplation. Dr. Dick turned to look at the Tree of Contemplation, then at the plaque that read, "The Tree of Contemplation."

"Let's get this over with. Who has the rope?" said Dr. Barney.

"This—this—I thought this was modern art!"

"No, Dick. This right here's a time-honored tool. She came over with the first Nordic corporate settlers way back in 1981. You've probably been wondering what keeps our town so peaceful and orderly. Well, you're looking at her," Dr. Barney said.

"This isn't legal, this is—Ruby! Go get the sheriff-mayah!"

I looked at Daddy, who stood passive and resigned. I shook my head.

"I can't, Dr. Dick. Better just let it happen," I said.

"Here is the rope," called the Swedish ambassador from the doorway of the Swedish Embassy & Beauty Parlor & Coffee Shop. He slung the thick coil high into the air. The Lady Principal trotted out into the road and caught it as it fell to earth.

"Now, boys!" cried 3-J.

He, Dr. Barney, and the Gentleman Gym Teacher fell upon Daddy, who put up a mighty struggle, as was traditional. He nearly wrested himself from their grasp, then the crowd surged around him and he was pressed back, back, back until he was mashed flat against the Tree of Contemplation. The Gentleman Gym Teacher and Dr. Barney hefted him up onto the Tree, pinning his arms and legs. 3-J seized the rope and advanced on Daddy.

"Stop it!" cried Dr. Dick.

Just then, the sheriff-mayor's patrol car rolled up Main

Street. It slowed, then stopped on the outskirts of our scene of unrest. Sheriff-Mayor Dolan got out and planted his fists on his leather gun belt.

"And just what's going on here?" he demanded.

"Thank Gawd!" Dr. Dick called out. "Sheriff—help him!"

"Well, well, well," said the sheriff-mayor, hitching at his belt and striding over to join the crowd on the lawn. "Been awhile since the ol' Tree of Contemplation's been occupied. Can't imagine how ya managed to avoid it for so long, Don. Need any help, fellas?"

"For Gawd's sake, stop them!" exclaimed Dr. Dick.

"Just relax and let us do our duty," said the sheriff-mayor.

"Ruby, go call someone! Call the deputies!" Dr. Dick ordered.

"We are the deputies," said the Gentleman Gym Teacher.

And he, Dr. Barney, and a considerable cohort of the crowd flashed their badges.

The cabal of secret policemen who walked among us disguised as regular citizens and the sheriff-mayor surged forward, shoving Dr. Dick aside. They lashed Daddy to the Tree of Contemplation, tying his wrists and ankles to four stout limbs positioned at irregular heights for that purpose. They settled him onto the shallowest branch, which served as an uncomfortable seat, then passed the rope around his waist several times for good measure, for Daddy was a known scrapper and escape artist.

"There we go, all snug an' secure!" proclaimed the sheriff-mayor.

Lashed to the Tree of Contemplation ten feet from the ground, Daddy ceased his struggles and turned his eyes heavenward.

"It is done," he said.

The men stepped back and shook hands with one another.

"Mighty fine knot-tying skills you got there, 3-J," said Dr. Barney.

"I've been known to practice when I'm on the road. But you tie a right powerful half-hitch," he replied.

"Pshaw," said Dr. Barney. "It's nowhere near as elegant as our Gentleman Gym Teacher's square knot."

"That is indeed most gracious of you, Dr. Barney," replied the Gentleman Gym Teacher. "Though I believe we can all agree Sheriff-Mayor Dolan's running bowline is far superior in both execution and effect."

"Darn tooting it is," said the sheriff-mayor.

"What the fack is happening?" Dr. Dick cried.

"The Tree of Contemplation," began the sheriff-mayor in a speech-making drawl. "Is a grand tradition dating back to the dawns of history. The Scandinavian god Odin showed us the way when he hung hisself from a big ol' tree to set his thinking aright. And what did he say when folks asked why? 'I sacrificed myself to myself!'"

In the flickering torchlight, the crowd murmured in approbation.

"And our own Lord and Savior, Mr. Jesus H. Christ—what about him? He let himself get hung off a cross—a wooden tree! And why?" said the sheriff-mayor. "For religious reasons."

"Amen!"

"And speaking of religion, lookit the Puritans. They liked to hang folks in wooden stocks. And what are stocks? Them's a tree-like thingy that holds ya still so's you can stop your wrong-thinking and start your right-thinking," the sheriff-mayor said.

"Hallelujah!"

"Det är rätt!"

"And there's probably plenty of similar examples," he concluded. "So, Don, we'll leave you to seek your right-thinking. Everybody outta here, show's over!"

The crowd began to disperse.

"Wait!" shouted Dr. Dick. "When are you going to take him down?"

"When the time's right," said Dr. Barney.

"When the hell's that?"

"He'll know. And so will we. The Tree never fails."

3-J, Dr. Dick, and I were left alone on the lawn.

"I'm getting him off that thing right now," said Dr. Dick, striding around the back of the Tree of Contemplation and fumbling at the knots that held Daddy in place. Daddy let out a sigh.

"I forgive alla y'all," he said.

This did not please 3-J.

"Still playing the Chosen One?" he taunted. "You ain't nothing but a fraud and a liar, Don Bejou! You ain't the Chosen One!"

"These *are* wicked good knots," Dr. Dick grunted, tugging impotently at the ropes.

"No, I ain't the Chosen One," said Daddy. "You are."

3-J's self-righteous scowl slid clean off his face and scampered away into the night, which had fully fallen on Main Street.

"What?" he said.

"I never proclaimed myself the Chosen One," said Daddy. "Search your memory. You know it's the truth."

"But…" said 3-J.

"Just our luck it was a lynch mob of forma Boy Scouts," said Dr. Dick, yanking at the knots that held Daddy's ankles. "3-J, give me your pocketknife."

"But…everybody said you was the Chosen One," 3-J said.

Daddy shook his head; at least, he vibrated it side to side as much as his bonds would allow.

"I'm just the organizer," he replied. "You were the Chosen One all along. Who told all our buddies about the mystical messages from The Great Beyond? Who encouraged them to listen to their CBs? Who kept right on believing, right up to the very end? You did."

"Ruby, do you have a pair of nail scissas? Anything?" Dr. Dick mumbled, taking his teeth to the implacable knot on Daddy's left wrist.

"Me?" said 3-J.

"I've been organizing for you every step of the way, Chosen One," said Daddy. "I even allowed myself to be Treed for you, my bestest buddy in all the world."

3-J's face fell into lines of ultimate sorrow.

"I didn't know!" he cried. "Crystal-Lynn was right, I am a dummy! I'm sorry, Don!"

"Good—help me cut him down," said Dr. Dick.

"I can't," said 3-J. "Once a body's Treed, nobody can unTree 'em. They gotta stay up till they got the right-thinking."

"Bullshit," said Dr. Dick.

"No, it's true," I said. "It's in the town charter."

Dr. Dick huffed in frustration, then his expression lit up with cunning. He lunged for one of the torches and seized it. He yanked it from the lawn and swung it at the Gordian knots that held Daddy. Sobbing, 3-J tackled him, knocking the torch away a split second before the fire could burn through the rope and liberate Daddy's Houdini-like hands.

Rolling to and fro over the crispy lawn, 3-J and Dr. Dick wrestled for supremacy. 3-J quickly gained the upper hand and sat upon Dr. Dick's chest, weeping.

"I done a terrible thing to my bestest buddy!" moaned 3-J, bedewing Dr. Dick with his tears.

"Get…off…" wheezed Dr. Dick.

"I'm the worst Chosen One ever!" 3-J wailed.

"Ruby," said Daddy.

I picked up the fallen torch and approached. The amber light cast by the flame gave his face a martyrly mein.

"Now that I'm outta action, it's all up to you," he said. "You gotta help me like you promised."

"But how?" I said.

Daddy glanced at 3-J, who still sat lamenting upon Dr. Dick, his back to us. He motioned with his head. I leaned closer.

Into my ear, he whispered six words…six innocent little words that would change Somwärin forever.

Chapter Thirteen
The Secret of Motel Way

Sunday, June 22
10:51 p.m.

On the day after Midsummer, an unprecedented evening edition of The Somwärin Soothsayer: A Not-Yet-Newspaper arrived on doorsteps all over town. It was printed on dire black paper with ghostly white ink. Everyone got a copy, including newcomer Dr. Dick, who was closing out his ninth day in Somwärin. He didn't hear the distinctive Plap! of the newspaper when it hit his front stoop, however, because he was slumped on his little couch between 3-J and me, who were likewise slumped. We three were in low spirits.

"I'll never forgive myself," said 3-J, his gaze aimed out Dr. Dick's window at the Tree of Contemplation, which stood illuminated by wavery torchlight across the street.

"I wonda if the Texas Ranjas could do something," said Dr. Dick. "The law and orda group, not the baseball team."

"There ain't nothing nobody can do," said 3-J miserably, dropping his head crotchward. "All hope is lost."

I started to nod in defeat when suddenly, out of the clear blue, I felt a surge of that which 3-J had just declared lost.

"Daddy knew a way to set everything right," I said.

"Don's on the Tree," said 3-J. "The only thing he can set right is his thinking."

"Then we'll do it," I said, jumping to my feet. "He told me his plan before the three of us abandoned him to his fate."

Dr. Dick looked uncomfortable with my choice of the verb "abandoned."

"What did he say, Ruby?" he inquired.

I cleared my throat, turned my eyes to 3-J, and declared, "He said, 'Tell 3-J to open his package.'"

The men were silent as they pondered these six astonishing word. Eventually 3-J began to sputter.

"Well—but—I can't do that!"

"You gotta!" I replied. "It's the only way to save Somwärin from the coming onslaught of miscreance and debauchery."

"I'm afraid I don't undastand," said Dr. Dick.

"But—but it's so special!" 3-J stammered. "It's my only memento of my bestest buddy, who's gonna descend from the Tree a changed man. Maybe he won't even be my buddy no more, between his new right-thinking and my cruel betrayal."

"It was Daddy's last wish," I said. "3-J, open your package."

3-J glanced out the window at his friend.

He turned to me.

He squared his shoulders.

He stood.

"I'll do it," he replied. "Where's my truck?"

"Crystal-Lynn's ex parked it in the alley," said Dr. Dick. "I told him he couldn't leave it there. It's sure to get towed, considering how it's blocking the dumpstas and—"

"To the alley!" proclaimed 3-J, seizing his new bestest buddy by the upper arm and giving a mighty jerk.

"3-J, I'm not getting involved in some kind of—"

But Dr. Dick's words wafted away as 3-J hauled him out the door and down the stairs.

As I followed the pair, I chanced to look down at the välkommen mat on the front stoop. A small, black packet of folded pages, like a half-burned deck of cards, lay upon it. I picked it up. Beneath the masthead, "The Somwärin Soothsayer: A Not-Yet-Newspaper," was a single, bold headline.

"Tornado Tomorrow," I read aloud.

"Ruby! C'mon!" called 3-J from the netherworld of the alley.

I shoved the not-yet-newspaper into my back pocket and hurried down the stairs.

The alley behind the Vet 'n' Pet Shop was lit with the dusky, coppery glare of a single streetlight, which revealed vast puddles of boozy ooze. My sneakers squelched through the muck, sending me skidding from one side of the narrow passageway to the other. I turned my head first to the left, then to the right. Sure enough, there stood 3-J's semi, its cherry-red paint gleaming in the tawny light, its rampant blue devils grinning with their customary insouciance, the impertinence of the invocation, "3-J outta the FIRES OF HELL YEEEEEAH!!!" undiminished by Daddy's thievery.

Dr. Dick stood before the toothy chrome grill with his arms crossed and a frown on his face. High above in the open driver's side door, 3-J's rear waggled from side to side.

"Found it!" he exclaimed, emerging with the eight-inch cube clutched in both hands. He jumped down from the cab and turned to Dr. Dick and me. His face was a mixture of curiosity and dismay.

"Do I really gotta open it?" he said.

I nodded. Dr. Dick shrugged.

3-J gave a little moan. He furrowed his brow. He bit his lip. He squeezed the beloved package to his chest. With a little sigh and a little cry, he tore into the bright yellow and red striped wrapping paper. The crisp covering fell away in shreds, revealing a white box with a lid. With trembling, grease-blackened fingers, 3-J grasped the lid and lifted it.

Dr. Dick, 3-J, and I peered into the box.

Inside, nestled on a bed of cheap motel toilet paper, lay a shiny silver key. It was attached to a clear rectangular keychain. It was identical to the keychains Daddy had deployed to torment the quondam Somwärin Sentinel editor and contemporary Somwärin Soothsayer oracle. No, not quite identical. Written on the slip of paper within the plastic rectangle was not a phone number, but an address.

"321 Motel Way, Somwärin, Texas," 3-J read aloud. "What can it mean?"

"It means that's where we gotta go," I said.

I grasped the latch on the passenger side door of 3-J's rig and tugged it open.

"You're right!" 3-J exclaimed, vaulting up into the captain's chair. "Hop aboard, Dick!"

Down in the befouled alley, Dr. Dick was diffident.

"I don't want to get involved in some kind of ill-advised," he paused, considering his descriptive options. "Misadvencha."

"Adventure," corrected 3-J, blasting his horn and making Dr. Dick jump. "We need ya, Dick. Who knows what mishaps me 'n' the troublemakingest girl in Somwärin will fall into without your steady sensibility?"

Dr. Dick compressed his lips.

He shook his head.

He hoisted himself up into the cab next to me.

3-J revved the motor, gave another blast of his horn, and away we drove.

The night sky was lit by a million gaudy stars as we rocketed down deserted Motel Way. The sketchy sector was lined with neon signs promising:

"Rooms rooms rooms!"

"Beer beer beer!"

"Girls girls girls (and a couple guys)!"

Dr. Dick gave evidence of increasing dismay as the strip clubs, gambling dens, and liquor lairs that bordered the road diminished in reputability. At last, on the outermost edge of Motel Way where tumbleweeds outnumbered truckers, Dr. Dick pointed out the window and said, "There it is—321 Motel Way!"

3-J slammed on his brakes and swiveled the wheel, sending Dr. Dick and me crashing against each other like bowling pins. His high beams revealed a lonesome sandwich board sign standing askew at the side of the road. Its chipped red and blue paint spelled out the words, "Somwärin Storage Locker."

Cautiously, 3-J pulled into the dark lot, which was unpaved and unlit. A single-story building loomed in the thick obscurity beyond the reach of the truck's headlights. 3-J killed the motor and took a deep breath to give himself courage. With a steadying glance at me, he opened his door and got out. I followed suit. Dr. Dick refused to budge.

"Do you have a flashlight?" he inquired.

"Good thinking, Dick!" called 3-J, from somewhere in the obsidian blackness. "Toolbox under the passenger seat. See—

this-here's why we brung you."

Dr. Dick rustled up the flashlight, got out of the truck, and herded 3-J and me to his side by swinging a crystal-clear beam of light around. When we were all together, he pointed the flashlight straight ahead. It cut through the gloom and revealed a gray steel door.

"Who can say what horrors lurk beyond that door?" said 3-J.

With much trepidation, our brave trio crept up to the portal. A little keyhole was situated above a grimy, industrial-grade brass knob. A lone coyote howled in the wilderness just beyond our circle of flashlight light. An owl hooted interrogatively. A chupacabra chattered.

Dr. Dick gulped. 3-J raised the silver key to the keyhole.

"Maybe we ought to—"

But Dr. Dick was forced to eat his suggestion as 3-J turned the key and the door swung slowly inward on shrieking hinges. A puff of sepulchral dust floated into our faces. The flashlight beam jittered as Dr. Dick sought to keep his hand steady.

"Don's storage locker," said 3-J. His words echoed in the darkness. "I ain't never been here."

"Nobody has," I replied.

3-J reached into his front pocket and pulled out his lighter. He positioned his thumb on the striker and fixed to flick it. Dr. Dick clapped a hand over it.

"Nah-uh—no way, I'm not going through that again," he said.

Dr. Dick aimed the flashlight to his left. Featureless gray cinderblocks were revealed. He aimed it to his right. Featureless gray cinderblocks and a single light switch were revealed. He reached out and flipped it.

"I've been struck blind!" wailed 3-J, as the space was flooded with searing white light. "Don laid a trap for intruders, and his loved ones've been caught in it. Cruel irony!"

After a moment, our eyes adjusted to the blazing fluorescents that marched along the high ceiling from one end of the space to the other. When we were able to peer about us, we did so in wonder.

I'd been hearing about Daddy's storage locker since my earliest days on this earth. I'd always pictured a cozy cubbyhole, like my locker at school. I was rendered breathless by the vast expanse that stretched before my eyes. It was as big as the football field out back of the school, and it was filled to bursting with boxes, crates, cartons, barrels, bundles, bales, trunks, parcels, packets, baskets, and a single enormous sailing ship.

"Wow!" said 3-J, turning slowly round and round and round, his eyes wide, his jaw ajar.

"Why do I have a feeling I'll be called to testify about this?" muttered Dr. Dick.

"Come on," I said. "There must be something in here that Daddy wanted us to find. Something that'll help us save Somwärin."

We set to combing through the mysterious artifacts, clambering over objects large and small, hunting among articles hidden and exposed. As I searched for I-knew-not-what, I uncovered several life-sized Scooby-Doo piñatas and a fat lady dress, knocked over a ceiling-high stack of books with "Somwärin Public Library" stamped on the spines, and stumbled over a battered cardboard box overflowing with beige sweatsuits.

"Will ya lookie here!" 3-J exclaimed, when he spied the sweatsuits. "I remember these—comfortablest clothes I ever wore in my life."

He reached into the box and grabbed a hooded sweatshirt and a pair of sweatpants. When he did so, a large manila envelope was revealed, nestled in amongst the ecru get-ups. As 3-J tugged the sweatshirt over his head, I read six words printed on the envelope in Daddy's all-capitals handwriting.

"OPEN IN THE EVENT OF TREEING."

I grasped the envelope and held it over my head.

"Dr. Dick!" I called. "I found it!"

From somewhere in the depths of the storage locker, there came the sound of crashing cymbals and a squawk. Presently,

Dr. Dick arrived at my side, his brown hair gone elderly gray with dust.

"What's inside, Ruby?" demanded 3-J, as he stepped into the sweatpants and pulled them up snug over his blue jeans.

I turned the envelope over and tore it open. I reached inside. Paper crinkled under my fingers. I grasped it and pulled out a folded newspaper. *Somwärin Sentinel*, read the masthead. Beneath it was a photo of a grinning gal wearing pasties and a Viking helmet. "Miss Somwärin crowned yesterday," ran the caption.

3-J, now clad all in beige from head to foot, let out a guffaw.

"That's one'a them papers me and Don and our brother truckers swiped one summer. We replaced 'em with old papers. What a prank!"

It was the last copy of the *Somwärin Sentinel* ever published, before madness overtook the editor and morphed him into the Soothsayer. But what did it mean? How could the last piece of legitimate journalism prevent the transformation of the entire population of Somwärin into truckers?

I sat down on a potato sack filled with doll's heads and puzzled about this. Dr. Dick settled himself in the lap of a papier-mâché Santa Claus to read the newspaper cover to cover. 3-J pranced and preened in his sweatsuit.

After a solid hour of hard thought, I gave up.

"We'll just have to ask him," I said.

"Ask who?" said Dr. Dick, who had reached the classified ads on the last page.

"The Soothsayer," I said.

In the pre-dawn gloom, 3-J humped his semi through the entrance of the Somwärin Trailer Park and RV Pleasure Garden. He killed the headlights and slowed to a crawl. We rolled past the Bejou family trailer, past the McMayberry brothers' school bus, past the laundry trailer, and past the empty spot where the Tooth Witch's caravan once stood. We edged our way to the trailer park limits, where the crackpots, cranks, and crazies congregated. At the backend of the dilapidated ice cream truck occupied by the Quiet Fella Who Was Undoubtedly A Serial Killer, 3-J braked and turned to me.

"You sure about this? I got a bad feeling in my bones."

No, I wasn't sure about this. The Soothsayer was Daddy's greatest enemy in the world.

"I'll go by myself," I said. "He's less likely to blow a kid to kingdom come."

"Good idea," said 3-J.

"Good idea? That's a terrible idea," said Dr. Dick. "We'll all go togetha."

"Nah-uh! I'm too spooked," said 3-J, pulling his off-white hood over his head and shuddering.

"Fine, stay here. I'm going with Ruby," Dr. Dick replied. "But stay put—got it? Don't wanda off somewhere."

3-J gave Dr. Dick a firm A-OK hand sign.

Dr. Dick and I got out of the semi cab and tiptoed through the remote ring of creepy vans and treehouses on wheels until we reached the very last domicile of all.

There it was: a sterling Airstream.

The Soothsayer's home was surrounded by a thicket of surveillance gear: cameras and listening bugs and motion detectors and recording devices. Some were cleverly concealed, some were mounted on metal poles, and some hovered on tiny helicopters a few feet off the ground. As we approached, they all turned toward us. A single floodlight welded to the roof of the Airstream ignited.

"Halt!" boomed a voice over static-riddled speakers buried somewhere in the soil near our feet. Shading our eyes against the glare, Dr. Dick and I froze in our tracks.

"State your purpose," the voice ordered.

"It's me, Ruby, from the trailer on the other side of the trailer park," I began.

"Selling Girl Scout cookies? At this hour of the morning?"

demanded the unseen Soothsayer. "Well, I'll take two boxes. Let me find my checkbook."

"No, actually I…uh…er…" I stammered. "Um…ah…so…"

"Her fatha's been tied to a sculpcha and she thinks you can help him," Dr. Dick declared, with East Coast indiscretion.

"Ruby…Bejou?" growled the disembodied voice. "Daughter of the patron saint of all evil? How dare you approach my home and hearth!"

Over the loudspeakers, there was a pause filled with the mechanical hum of electronic gear.

"You said something happened to Don Bejou?"

I nodded.

"He's on the Tree of Contemplation," I said.

The gleeful laughter of the Soothsayer lasted for seven solid minutes. When at last he regained his composure, he crowed, "This is the greatest day of my life! I'm going to buy every box of your cookies to celebrate!"

"Daddy left this in case he got Treed," I said, holding out the folded copy of the *Somwärin Sentinel*.

One of the front windows of the Airstream eased open a few inches. A little device shaped like a flying beetle shot out, seized the newspaper in its mechanical claws, and darted back through the window with it.

There was a long silence over the speakers. At last, the Soothsayer spoke.

"I thought I'd never see the last edition of the old girl again. Your father deserves to rot on the Tree of Contemplation for what he did to me."

"Daddy wants to set things right," I said. "He wants to save the town."

"Look at this: I mistakenly used a semicolon when I should have used a colon in the article about the Swedish ambassador's indictment trial…what were you saying?"

"The truckers are gonna destroy Somwärin!" I said.

"I know that," scoffed the Soothsayer. "I predicted that weeks ago."

"Don't you care?"

"Of course," he replied. "And I'd love to help you, but the fix is in and the future's been written."

"Has it?" I said. It was my worst fear confirmed. "Ain't there nothing we can do to change it?"

"Hmm," replied the Soothsayer. "Let me ask the fat Mesopotamian demigod to consult the tarot cards."

After a moment, the loudspeaker crackled to life.

"The demigod's sleeping. But the Virgin of Guadalupe says you, young lady, might be able to alter the course of events. But I won't tell you how."

My heart, which had soared, sank.

"Why not?"

"Because I despise your father above all entities that exist on this astral plane! Sure, I was a member of the Newspaper Guild and he's a Teamster, but besides that fraternal union bond, there's only rancor and ill-will between us. There's nothing that can compel me to assist the daughter of my mortal enemy. Nothing!"

At this moment, 3-J, still clad in his beige sweatsuit, came dashing up to Dr. Dick and took him by the arm.

"Dick! I wandered away from the semi and something grabbed me by the ankle. Something made of slime!"

The floodlight and the whirring spy copters and the shining lenses of the video cameras swung toward 3-J. A shriek of terror peeled forth from the speakers.

"It's back! The dummy is back!" screamed the Soothsayer. "Dear God, go away—haven't you tormented me enough?"

"I told you to wait in the truck," said Dr. Dick.

"Begone! Begone, foul specter!" cried the Soothsayer.

"I got lonely," said 3-J.

"All right, all right, I'll help you! Just don't let the dummy get me!" shouted the Soothsayer.

Out of the window flew the insectile device. It dropped a walkie-talkie at my feet.

"Go to the place I once called 'work.' When you arrive, summon me. I'll guide you to the one thing that can help you save the town. Just take the dummy away!"

A faint glimmer of sunlight was beginning to sparkle on the horizon as 3-J, Dr. Dick, and I prepared to take our leave of the Somwärin Trailer Park and RV Pleasure Garden.

"Hold on," said Dr. Dick, as 3-J drove us past the Bejou family trailer. "Let's stop in and see if your motha's awake, Ruby."

"Why?" I said.

"Well," said Dr. Dick, pinking up in the cheeks. "I'm sure she's worried about you. And…ratha…um…"

He wanted to go make things up with her. I rolled my eyes. 3-J brought the truck to a stop and threw open his door.

"Good idea, let's stop in," he said. "I'm starved."

Mama's car wasn't parked in its usual place outside. Inside, the trailer was deserted. Unperturbed, 3-J yanked open the refrigerator and began to shove Mama's hard-won grub into his gob. Dr. Dick returned from a discreet search of her bedroom with a disappointed look on his face. As 3-J closed the fridge, I discovered one of Mama's creatively spelled notes tacked up to the exterior with a bit of false nail glue.

"Ruby," it read. "Me & your sisters left for Fack Sex to get reddy for the pajant. Your in **BIG** trouble for staying out all nite! Sherrif-Mayer, if your the one reading this, go find Ruby coz she's gone missing."

Dr. Dick, reading the note over my shoulder, gave me a frown.

"We'd betta go to the warehouse and let her know you're safe and sound," he said.

"First we gotta find the one thing that will save the town," I replied.

"I'm sure she's frantic about you by now," Dr. Dick said.

"Ruby's right," mumbled 3-J through a mouthful of cold saffransbullar. "Besides, Crystal-Lynn can't be all that worried.

She's got two extra daughters to replace this one."

"I really think—" Dr. Dick persisted.

"Say," interrupted 3-J. "Notice who else's missing?"

"The Tooth Witch!" I said.

"I wonder where she could be?" he said.

"I wonder when she's coming back?" I said.

"I'm worried," he said.

"Me too," I said.

He looked at me and I looked at him. Then both of us looked at Dr. Dick.

"Oh, Dick," said 3-J in an oily, casual tone. "You wouldn't happen to have a bit of pocket change on ya?"

Dr. Dick reached into the front pocket of his slacks and pulled out a quarter, three dimes, and a penny. He held the coins out to 3-J. 3-J backed away in alarm.

"How's about you toss 'em on the kitchen table here," I suggested, making a scattering gesture with my hand.

"Why?" said Dr. Dick.

"Go on," said 3-J.

"Do it, Dr. Dick," I urged, my voice trembling in apprehension.

Dr. Dick looked at us quizzically, then deposited the coins in a tidy pile upon the kitchen table.

3-J and I gasped. We recoiled. We stared at the loose change, which gleamed with the menace of transmogrification.

Nothing happened.

The coins remained coins.

The Tooth Witch did not appear.

We watched the legal tender for ten minutes, then 3-J and I let out a pair of sighs.

"Guess she's gone for good," 3-J said sadly.

It was a bad omen. A very bad omen.

Like rats fleeing a sinking ship, if the Tooth Witch skipped town you could bet something truly wicked was just around the bend.

And it was heading your way.

Chapter Fourteen
The Deus Ex Sverige

Monday, June 23
8:03 a.m.

Fresh morning light poured through the plate glass windows of the Swedish Embassy & Beauty Parlor & Coffee Shop. The Swedish ambassador unlocked the front door, opened it, and flipped the cardboard sign that hung on a hook above the polished knob from the rejecting "stängd" side to the welcoming "öppen." He paused to admire Main Street, which looked most tempting and öppen, suffused as it was with golden sunbeams and topped by a dome of purest blue.

He hesitated, his hand on the shiny doorknob.

Main Street was empty. There was no one in sight.

He stuck his head out—just an inch. The gentle breeze—so long unfelt!—ruffled his blond hair and caressed his sun-deprived cheeks. He closed his eyes and inhaled deeply. Such a refreshing draught of outdoor scents! He lifted his right foot. He let it drift across the threshold. Freedom was a single step away…

"Go on, I double-dog-dare ya!" came a rough taunt, followed by a braying laugh.

The Swedish ambassador hastily withdrew both his head and his foot to the safety of his nation's consulate.

"Välkommen till Konungariket Sverige: För Sverige i tiden," he said, as the sheriff-mayor strutted up the sidewalk and shoved his way into the country of Sweden without presenting either his passport or diplomatic papers. "I am gratified that you can join this momentous political occasion."

"S'long as I ain't late for the pageant," said the lawman, clumping across the hardwood floor of the café and seating himself unbidden at the choicest table. "I don't aim to go without my yearly dose of lovelies to hobnob with some horn-head from across the pond."

"Indeed," replied the Swedish ambassador, joining him at the table. "But where is Mrs. Dolan?'

"Extracting herself from the car," said the sheriff-mayor, and a canny glint flashed in his eyes. "Why don't you be chivalrous and go give her your arm?"

"Ah," said the Swedish ambassador. "It would be too much of an honor. I shall defer such distinction to her husband."

"Muh," grumped the sheriff-mayor, temporarily thwarted. As another canny glint appeared in his eyes, the drowsy lady drifted through the door and gave the Swedish ambassador a hazy smile.

"So, where's this Harry Handjob fella?" said the sheriff-mayor, as his wife wandered to the beauty parlor section of the Swedish Embassy & Beauty Parlor & Coffee Shop.

"Häri Härison," said the Swedish ambassador. "You may refer to the honorable mayor of Härisverige as Borgmästare Härison. It is a great courtesy to do so."

"Nah, I ain't gonna do that," said the sheriff-mayor. "And I'll tell you a true fact: If'n he don't turn up within the next five minutes, I'm taking off."

"The flight of Borgmästare and Herr Härison landed at the Dallas/Fort Worth Airport at dawn," said the Swedish ambassador. "The couple rented a vehicle and should arrive at any moment."

"Hey, there we go—fella's bringing his wife. That should keep ya occupied," said the sheriff-mayor to Mrs. Dolan, who was running her fingers over the shampoo bottles like a pianist tickling the ivories. "Meanwhile, me 'n' the Borg'll take advantage of my mayoral privileges and slide into the Miss Somwärin contestants' dressing rooms for some good ol' pre-pageant adjudicatin'."

"Ah," said the Swedish ambassador, rising. "Here they are now."

The sheriff-mayor and the Swedish ambassador watched as a dingy 1990s-era Taurus with the legend "Rent-A-Ryde" slathered across the side in gold glitter paint rolled up outside the Swedish Embassy & Beauty Parlor & Coffee Shop. The sheriff-mayor grudgingly rose to stand with the Swedish ambassador. Mrs. Dolan seated herself upon one of the salon chairs and began to spin with infinitesimal slowness.

A tall, dour, blond gentleman exited the driver's side. He circled the "Ryde," opened the passenger door, and out stepped a tall, dour, blond lady. The pair looked with loathing at the building before them, exchanged an uneasy glance, then stepped up to the front door to do their diplomatic duty. The instant the couple made landfall in Sweden, the Swedish ambassador sprang forward and seized them in a duet of hearty handshakes.

"Välkommen till Konungariket Sverige: För Sverige i tiden!" he exclaimed. "Trevligt att träffas, Borgmästare Härison. God morgon, Herr Härison. Hur är det?"

"Bra," replied the lady.

The sheriff-mayor snickered like a seventh-grader.

Sensitive protocol expert that he was, the Swedish ambassador hastily put in, "But we must speak English for civility to the illustrious sheriff-mayor of Somwärin. Sheriff-Mayor Dolan, it is my honor and privilege to present—"

But the sheriff-mayor had no time for superficial statecraft. He rose, took two thundering steps that brought him toe-to-toe with the gentleman from Afar, and hijacked his hand in a bone-crushing howdy-do shake.

"Good to meet ya, Borg," said the sheriff-mayor. "How's the mayoring over in the hinterland? I got me two jobs—sheriff *and* mayor. I don't guess you could handle that, eh? Gloria! C'mon over and make nice with the mayor's missus."

The Swede grimaced and slid his eyes to the Swedish ambassador. The Swedish ambassador said, "Ah...um..." and the lady stuck her dour, blond head between that of the sheriff-mayor and her spouse.

"I am Borgmästare Härison," she said.

The sheriff-mayor did not release Herr Härison's hand.

"Harry's the Borg," he said.

"He is Sven. I am Häri," she said. "It is short for Härriet."

The sheriff-mayor dropped the false mayor's hand with a

grunt.

The Swedish ambassador forced his mouth to curve up in a frolicsome smile.

"Indeed, this is a humorous moment," he said. "Let us sit and laugh about it together."

"Hmf," replied Mayor Härison, seating herself in the sheriff-mayor's chair. Her husband, nursing his crushed hand, seated himself next to her. The sheriff-mayor, now chairless, was obliged to drag a lesser seat from one of the lesser tables. It caterwauled as the legs scraped across the hardwood floor. In the beauty parlor, Mrs. Dolan spun on.

"Well," grumbled the sheriff-mayor, with a dark look at the Swedish ambassador. "I guess we oughta make with the small talk."

"No small talk," said the Borg. "We will talk turkey. I have come these many thousands of kilometers for a reason."

"Oh yeah?" said the sheriff-mayor, his mighty oak-branch arms folded across his chest. "And what might that be?"

A chilly smile crept across Häri Härison's lips

"To proposition you."

Concealed behind a reeking dumpster in the alley behind the Pubic Library, Dr. Dick and I regarded the electronically monitored exterior of the formidable brick building with trepidation. Even from the back end, it appeared unbreachable. 3-J, for his part, was riddled with excitement.

"Miss November 1998, here I come," he said. "I can't wait to get my hands on my ol' *Playboy* at long last."

"Now then," said the voice of the Soothsayer, concentrated into a tinny jabber by the walkie-talkie. "What you have to do is disarm the heat, motion, and audio sensors, then deactivate the external alarm system."

"Right," 3-J said. "How?"

"Yeah, how?" I said.

"I'll talk you through it."

"But I'm banned for life from the Pubic Library," I said. "I can't get anywhere near the building."

The Soothsayer pondered this dilemma for a moment.

"Send the hootchie doctor," he suggested.

On my right, Dr. Dick shook his head at the walkie-talkie.

"Breaking and entering is illegal. Especially when it's a gov'ment building," he said.

"Come on, Dick," said 3-J. "Who's gonna know?"

"It's for a good cause," I said.

"Don would want you to do it," said 3-J.

"Mama would definitely want you to do it," I said.

Dr. Dick shook his head again, then sighed and stood.

"If I wind up back in that hippie jail," he said. "I'm counting on you to find a lawya to represent me—an out-of-towna."

Dr. Dick rolled up his shirt sleeves, which had dried into the crinkly texture of crepe paper. He took the walkie-talkie from me, stepped out from behind the dumpster, and approached the heavily fortified building.

"The control panel is to the left of the back door," we heard the walkie-talkie say. "Find it and open it."

Dr. Dick vanished from sight.

A moment later: "Did you open the control panel?"

"I'm trying," replied Dr. Dick, his voice tight with frustration.

"You have to remove the top screws first, then—"

"I don't have a screwdriva."

"Okay, no problem. There should be a red wire and a green wire leading to the power source above the door."

"I see them."

"Locate the splice between the wires and disengage it."

"Between which whyas?"

"The powered pair."

"Disengage the red whya from the green whya?"

"No, don't do that! The powered pair! The wires leading to the—"

"What? I don't undastand!"

"Just get the dummy over here!" the Soothsayer shouted. "It never had any problem bypassing the security system."

"Yes!" 3-J exulted, jumping to his feet. He drew out his pocketknife and extended the screwdriver tool.

"Hide your face from the cameras," I said.

"Right!" he said.

He tugged the strings of his sweatshirt hood tight to conceal his face and bounded out of sight.

Twenty seconds elapsed, then: "We're in! Hurry, Ruby."

I poked my head out from behind the dumpster.

"Are you sure it's safe?" I called.

"I installed this security system," replied the walkie-talkie. "I could disable it in my sleep. Unless the town sprang for a major upgrade, of course," and the Soothsayer snorted to demonstrate the unlikelihood of this wacky notion.

I darted to the back door. The video cameras gazed blankly into space, like me in math class. No alarm sounded. Dr. Dick turned the knob and pushed the door inward. In we went.

We stepped into a little anteroom lit only by eerie green light leaking from the sans-serif letters of the exit sign. I was filled with anticipation. 3-J was beside himself.

"Oh boy," he enthused, rubbing his hands together. "I'm a-gonna grab my *Playboy* and a whole poke of porn for all them lonely nights on the road."

"Don't touch the porn!" said the walkie-talkie. "The external security system is disabled, but everything in this place is alarmed."

Dr. Dick flicked on the flashlight and slid the beam of light to a closed wooden door labeled "Enter me, please, baby."

We obeyed. Velvet duskiness met our eyes. Dr. Dick thrust the flashlight into the library, seeking to penetrate the void. The darkness sucked at the flaccid shaft of light, draining its potency.

3-J's eager twitching slowed, then ceased.

"This is right spooky," he said.

"There's got to be a light switch someplace," Dr. Dick

replied.

He played the light over the walls, tickling the surfaces until he found a little white nodule.

"Ah, here we go," he said, reaching for it.

"Don't touch the light switch!" shouted the walkie-talkie. "I told you, everything is alarmed. Don't touch the light switches, don't touch the window shades, and for God's sake, don't touch the porn."

"I don't think I wanna touch the porn," whimpered 3-J. In the negligible illumination afforded by the flashlight, I saw him swiveling his head this way and that. His eyes were huge and terrified.

"Now, listen close," said the Soothsayer. "Go find the men's bathroom. In the third stall, behind the toilet bowl, you'll discover a very important article of mine that I was forced to leave behind when I resigned my post. This one thing you may remove from the Pubic Library with impunity. But nothing else."

"Where's the men's room?" I said.

"It's this way," said Dr. Dick, aiming the flashlight westward and striding through the darkness.

"How do you know?" said 3-J.

Dr. Dick cleared his throat.

"I have," he cleared his throat again. "Been here before. A few times."

"I don't wanna go in," 3-J blubbered. "It's scary."

"We gotta," I said. "Daddy's counting on us."

"Hold my hand, Ruby?" he said.

"Okay," I said, and immediately I regretted it as his sweaty paw enveloped mine in a slippery embrace that kept inadvertently jerking toward the porn fan in his jeans whenever he flinched in fear. And he flinched in fear many times.

He flinched when Dr. Dick ran the flashlight over towering shelves loaded with nudie magazines whose covers were alive with hostile nipples that stared at us like bestial eyes.

He flinched when we descried racks of DVDs decorated with genitalia that gaped like vicious jaws intent on swallowing us whole.

He did more than flinch when we came upon the blow-up sex doll seated at the librarian's desk.

"It's her! It's her!" he cried. "The librarian! Protect me, Dick!"

And he abandoned the dubious comfort of my adolescent hand for the greater satisfaction of an adult embrace. He threw himself through the dark at Dr. Dick and nearly knocked him to the worn wooden floor, which creaked creepily under their struggling footfalls.

"Quit it, 3-J!"

"Lemme hold your hand!"

"No!"

"Gimme your hand, buddy!"

"Okay, okay—just stop grabbing me there!"

Quiet descended again upon the Pubic Library, broken only by 3-J's fearful gasping and Dr. Dick's irritable grousing.

"Stop clowning around and get to the bathroom," said the Soothsayer. "The library will open for business in exactly eight minutes. I hate to think what the townspeople will do to the three of you if they catch you here."

We hustled past the wide-eyed and wider-mouthed latex librarian, ducked down a corridor, and slipped into a narrow hallway decorated with posters from which the legends, "Deep Throat," "Caligula," and "Flesh Gordon," shouted in 1970s tones. At last we came to a white door. Stenciled upon it in fleshy pink paint were the words, "Men: No masturbation in the second stall."

"Don't go in there, Dick," said 3-J. "It looks haunted!"

"It's fine," said Dr. Dick. "Just stay away from the urinals."

3-J let out a little moan and in the two went.

I stayed in the hall. I squinted into the shadowy abyss of the library. All at once, a thin shaft of light appeared in the center of the vast room.

I frowned. What was it?

I cautiously crept to the end of the hall and stuck my head into the dark room. The beam of light beckoned to me.

I knew I ought to stay put. I knew I ought to ignore the inviting illumination.

Into the library I advanced, placing my feet carefully on the rough wooden slats to avoid stumbling over an unseen chair, table, or sex swing.

When I reached the center of the library, I realized that the light was a sunbeam coming through a tiny tear in one of the thick canvas blinds that shaded the tall windows. Like a celestial arrow, it pointed directly at a low bookshelf, the top of which was covered with neat stacks of old periodicals. The sunbeam was dancing in a coaxing manner over the cover of one magazine in particular. I tiptoed up to it. A cheerleader with refulgent cleavage and generous pompoms smiled a welcoming smile up at me. All around her were encouraging phrases.

"Hot, Hot College Issue…"

"Love and Lust 101"

"Students Tell ALL in our Sizzling Campus Sex Survey"

"Interview with Mike Tyson"

Then I saw the masthead: *Playboy*.

I gasped.

I gasped again when I saw the date: November 1998.

It was 3-J's beloved dirty magazine, the object of his fondest desire.

From the bathroom came a crash and a curse.

The walkie-talkie jabbered.

I bit my lip.

My gaze became fixed upon the magazine.

An alarm suddenly began to bleat.

I looked up in shock to see the blinds rolling up, unaided by human hands, as the light fixtures set in the ceiling dawned to full wattage.

I looked down in even greater shock to see that I was clutching the *Playboy* in my hot little hands.

From the bathroom came shouts of distress.

"You fool!" shrieked the walkie-talkie.

"Wicked hell!" cried Dr. Dick.

"Run!" screamed 3-J.

Out into the now-bright library dashed 3-J, encumbered by the walkie-talkie and an oblong object. He was followed by Dr. Dick, who clutched a large rectangular item and a shiny lump of glass. 3-J threw himself upon the heavy wooden front door and began to shove it with all his might. It didn't budge.

"Out the back door!" the walkie-talkie ordered.

We stampeded past glossy images of schlongs and snatches and dongs and dugs. The alarm howled on. We pounded through the anteroom, the green light of the exit sign drawing us like a beacon. As before, 3-J threw himself upon the egress and began to shove.

Like its brother up front, it didn't budge.

"We're trapped!" said 3-J.

"Don't panic," said the Soothsayer in a panicked voice. "The town must have sprung for a major upgrade of the security system. The alarm triggered automatic door locks. You might be able to disable them, but you don't have much time. In the basement, behind the boiler, there's a locked electrical cage. It's high voltage, so you might get fatally shocked when you break it open. Now, inside the cage there's another cage—"

"*NAWAWHELLNOFUCKTHIS!*" shrieked 3-J, and he ran full-tilt at the back door, slamming his body into it like Wile E. Coyote.

The door didn't budge.

"Hurry!" shouted the Soothsayer.

With a feral cry, 3-J wound up to launch another assault on the door. Dr. Dick seized him by the back of his T-shirt, slung him aside, grasped the door knob, turned it, and pulled the door inward.

Out we went.

Around the building we hustled, striving to convey the casual innocence of regular folks enjoying a morning stroll as pugilistic townspeople advanced on the library to surprise the invaders trapped within. We scurried across the street to hide our guilt in the all-concealing shade of the Tree of

Contemplation.

"Idiots!" railed the Soothsayer, the instant we were safe. "I told you to take nothing but my personal article!"

I glanced at 3-J and Dr. Dick, whose eyes were glued to the walkie-talkie, and quickly stuffed the *Playboy* under my shirt.

"You said take whateva we found behind the toilet bowl," said Dr. Dick. "But the little nook contained three—"

"My instructions were perfectly clear!" cried the Soothsayer. "Don't ever call me again. We're through!"

And the walkie-talkie went silent.

Squatting together beneath Daddy's place of confinement, we members of the international thieves' guild examined our booty: a small glass object with words etched upon its smooth, clear surface; a framed clipping from the *Somwärin Sentinel*; and an empty bottle of Scotch.

Dr. Dick, 3-J, and I looked at each other.

Which of these peculiar things was the one that would save Somwärin?

Meanwhile, across town in the bowels of the Fack Sex Furniture Distribution Warehouse, the hopeful contestants for the title of Miss Somwärin were primping for the competition, which would start at ten o'clock.

The employee breakroom, with its bevy of cast-off bordssällskaps and lärostols deemed too uncomfortable for sale to the general public, was a-buzz with activity. Would-be beauty queens paced in their high heels, practicing their regal waves. Hair was teased tall and sprayed solid. Faces were brushed, slathered, smeared, dusted, and painted with the best makeup the Fack Sex employee grocery store had to offer. Winning smiles were smiled and speeches were speeched.

At the far end of the room, next to vending machines crammed with bottles of anemic Fruktsoda, venom-yellow Svenson's Sockerdricka, and Smurf-blue Vira Blåtira, sat Opal.

Behind her, Pearl was plying her comb and hairspray. In front of her, Mama was dipping in and out of her special occasion makeup stash, contained within a humongous picnic basket.

"I'm so nervous! But it's so exciting, Mama!" said Opal.

Mama smiled and gave Opal's hand a little squeeze.

"So anyway," continued Opal. "Yesterday, after we finished building the pageant stage, I swung by the Burger Bower to find out what my schedule for the week's gonna be. And when the owner got a load of my new chest, guess what he said?"

"What?" said Mama, flicking a mascara wand over Opal's eyelashes.

"'You're fired!'"

"No!" said Pearl, teasing the topmost hairs on Opal's head into a turret.

"Yeah-huh," said Opal. "So I said, 'Fine then. Gimme my final paycheck.' And he said, 'Fine then.' And I pulled out my contract, which, you'll recall, I drafted myself. I said, 'Lookie here: My contract says regardless of reason for, or date of, termination of employment, you owe me a commission equal to the total increase in sales from the start of my tenure as roof ornament to my final day of work.' And he was grumpy, coz sales increased three-thousand and twenty-eight percent after I got up on that roof. But he was fixing to take cash outta the till to pay me, and I said, 'You ain't got enough liquid capital on hand to cover what you owe me. Lookie here again: My contract says the commission continues for the rest of the year.' And he was right upset. 'You mean I gotta pay you for another six months that you ain't gonna work!?'"

"Six months?" said Mama in awe, tracing Opal's upper eyelid with a gold eyeliner pencil. "You got yourself a powerful contract negotiating skill, Opal."

Opal's lipstick-slicked lips curved up in a cunning smile.

"Not six months," she said. "Twelve."

"Twelve?" said Mama. "But the end of the year's in December—that's six months off."

"That's the end of the calendar year," replied Opal. "My contract was for the fiscal year. That ain't over until next

June."

Mama shook her head in admiration.

"Well, you had a better day than me," she said, loading a broom-sized brush with cotton candy colored blush.

"Didja get to talk things out with Dr. Dick?" asked Pearl, pinching her nose and blasting Opal's head with hairspray like an arachnophobe macing a spider.

Mama shook her head.

"I waited a bit, but he never came back. So I figured I might as well go to work. I tell you what, girls, I ain't never in my life gone to work stone sober on the day after Midsummer. It was quite an experience. Every-danged-body here was either a corpse, a zombie, or still drunker than an Icelander on the first day of kindergarten. Even the folks across the Atlantic. When I showed up, the supervisor's phone was ringing off the hook. I picked it up, and them Swedes on the other end was just as ruined as the warehouse folks stateside."

Pearl perked up.

"You took a call from the Fack Sex corporate office in Stockholm?"

Mama nodded, gluing three layers of sparkly false lashes into a Möbius-like configuration around Opal's eyes.

"Yes, indeedy I did. And it was most peculiar, what they had to say."

"What did they say?" Pearl demanded. "What were their exact words?"

"Den stora mannen är på flygplatsen," said Mama. "I dunno what them jibber-jabbery words mean—probably just some after-Midsummer good wishes."

Opal frowned in thought, cracking the thick layer of foundation on her forehead.

"It means, 'The big man is at the airport,'" she replied. "I wonder why they said that?"

If Mama or Opal had looked at my little sister, they would have seen that she wore a crafty smile. But neither of them was looking at Pearl because a terrible hush had fallen over the contestants and their armies of amateur beauticians.

Grinning like a minor demon, into the employee breakroom walked Perdee Dora.

"It all started a year ago," Daddy croaked from the Tree of Contemplation. "It was the day after the Trucker Jamboree."

On the leeward side of the terrible tool of public order, Dr. Dick, 3-J, and I unsquatted. Together, we stepped around to the front of the Tree.

"Me 'n' my fellow truckers were in a mile-long lineup outside the Fack Sex loading docks, each waiting for our turn to pull up and get our trailer filled with freight," continued Daddy, his voice ragged.

Pinioned askew on the splayed limbs of the Tree, his arms and legs looked thin and feeble. His face was white, with hectic stains running over his cheeks and down his throat. Dr. Dick studied Daddy. A worried frown darkened his face. He reached up and pressed two fingers to Daddy's neck.

"I'd enjoyed me plenty of rotten—hey, no funny stuff," Daddy said.

"I'm taking your pulse," replied Dr. Dick.

"Man likes to be an active participant in any amorous adventures that happen to befall him…what was I saying? Ah," he drew in a dry breath, let out a hacking cough, and resumed. "I'd enjoyed me plenty of rotten rum the night previous. I was tired. I was hungover. And I was bored."

Dr. Dick stood on tiptoe and gently grasped Daddy's left eyelid. He lifted it and peered into Daddy's eye.

"Have you been given any liquids today?" he said.

"Nah," replied Daddy. "3-J was on the CB jawing about—but here he is now. Remember that fateful day, buddy? The day I was hailed by The Great Beyond?"

"He's dehydrated," said Dr. Dick. "I'm going to get a bottle of watah."

He set the framed newspaper article and glass lump down

on the dead lawn, and jogged across Main Street to seek refreshment. 3-J and I gazed up at Daddy with supplicating eyes.

"Daddy," I said. "We did what you said. 3-J opened his package. We went to your storage locker. We found the newspaper and brought it to the Soothsayer. And we broke into the Pubic Library to get something that can save the town. But there were three somethings. How do we know which something is the right something?"

I held up the framed article in one hand and the glass blob in the other. 3-J tipped the bottle of Scotch back, his pink tongue fishing for any stray drops that might be lingering at the bottom.

"Over the CB, 3-J was saying, 'Y'all ever thought about how we say we gots a skull inside our head and a ribcage inside our chest and such, but our brains're *inside* our skulls and our hearts are *inside* our ribcages? We ain't got a skeleton inside us—we're inside a skeleton!' And Big Bobby Watson was saying, 'I gotta lay hands on two hundred three pesos and eighteen centavos by Friday—anyone wanna set me up with a charitable contribution?'"

At this moment, Dr. Dick trotted up with an open water bottle in his hand. Without preamble, he stuck it in Daddy's mouth.

Daddy sputtered.

"Drink," Dr. Dick said.

Daddy took a mouthful of water. He seemed to forget about it. He let it dribble from between his lips onto his shirt front, which was already soaked with sweat.

"And Rockin' Ron was saying—'"

"Your eyes are sunken and your skin is dry. You're going to start hallucinating soon and pass out," said Dr. Dick, pressing the bottle against Daddy's lips again. Daddy shook his head and refused to drink.

"'Rockin' Ron was saying, 'I'm retiring after this run, boys. That mean y'all're gonna have to get yourselves a new union organizer from the pool of yokels in Local 666. I'm countin' on one of y'all to step up to the plate, lest we gotta draw straws and one unlucky bastard gets his ass appointed, like happened to me. Whichever one of y'all gets the short straw, I'd advise you start your organizing with them warehouse drones up yonder inside Fack Sex.' And El Señor Poco Loco was saying, 'No pagaré por tus prostitutas sucias, Bobby Grande.' And gradually, alla them voices on the CB faded away…"

Dr. Dick set the bottle down in the grass. Daddy hadn't taken a single sip.

"We'll try again in a couple minutes," said Dr. Dick.

He sat down on the ground, his back pressed against the Tree of Contemplation. 3-J sat down beside him. He held out the empty Scotch bottle to his pal.

"What good d'ya suppose this would do the town?" he said.

Dr. Dick shrugged, picked up the framed article and scanned it.

"About as much good as an article on," he squinted at the text. "A failed attempt at unionizing within the Swedish-Texan corporate commonwealth of Somwärin."

I knelt down next to the men and picked up the glass doodad. It was shaped like a teardrop or maybe a flame. Along the fattest section, etched into the glass, were the words, "First Place, "Labor Loses Fight," Enrique Hernandez, Editor, *Somwärin Sentinel.*"

"But then all of a sudden, I heard a voice from The Great Beyond!" cried Daddy from his hanging place above us. "It knew me, hailed me by name. 'Don Bejou!' it boomed in a ringing voice that shimmied my windshield and my very soul."

"Maybe we're supposed to get the town good and drunk," said 3-J.

"The town got good and drunk yestaday," Dr. Dick replied, whipping his gaze back and forth across the yellowing newspaper.

"Maybe these-here letters are a code!" I said. "Maybe if we rearrange them, they'll spell out a message telling us what to do."

"I ain't never been called by The Great Beyond before. It

was a most powerful experience," rasped Daddy. "I didn't know what to do. Again the voice hailed me, urging in tones most powerful, 'Don Bejou! Advance!'"

Mentally I rearranged the letters. "Calligraphers' boots fit elf hindquarters. Modernize wieners on net lines," I said. "Is that a clue?"

"And a third time, the voice hailed me. 'Bejou, Don: Hotel Echo Bravo One Thirty-Three license number! Move your danged truck up!'" said Daddy. "That's when I came outta my doze and realized it weren't nothing but the Fack Sex warehouse supervisor hollering at me over the public address speakers outside the loading dock. I felt mighty foolish as I knocked my rig outta neutral and pulled forward. But it got me to thinking."

"Maybe there's a secret compartment," I said, pressing and prodding the smooth surface of the glass object. "Should we smash it open and see?"

"I got to thinking all along the highway outta town, and all along the route eastward to the first drop off," wheezed Daddy, his breathing becoming labored. "I jumped on the CB and radioed 3-J. '3-J,' I said. 'I been contacted by the supernatural.' And he said, 'Really? That's awesome, Don!' and he inquired after the nature and timbre of the voice, and what it said, and what I oughta do about it. I told him everything, 'cept the part where I figured out it was just the Fack Sex whip-cracker on the PA system. We spoke no more about it as I pulled into Dallas and 3-J pulled into Austin to begin our deliveries. But my buddy's credulous acceptance of my tale got stuck in my mind."

Dr. Dick, having come to the end of the article, tipped his head back to look up at Daddy. The physician's eyes were narrowed in thought.

"A couple weeks later, to fight the boredom during the long haul through the desert skipland, I introduced my buddies to the voice from The Great Beyond as a joke. But I also inadvertently introduced the notions of mystical messages and Chosen Ones and such. And that's how all the trouble started," concluded Daddy.

Dr. Dick rose, picked up the water bottle, and put it to Daddy's mouth. Daddy clamped his lips shut.

"If you don't drink, I'll have to start an IV," said Dr. Dick. "You need fluids."

"Gotta keep things going," said Daddy. "Man's gotta organize."

Dr. Dick gave Daddy the eye. Again he pressed his fingers to Daddy's neck. He leaned in close to Daddy.

"I think I undastand what you've really been up to all along," he said in a low voice.

"Don't jump to conclusions 'bout my motives," said Daddy. "Things ain't always what they appear."

"And sometimes they are," Dr. Dick replied. "I've seen *Norma Rae*."

Daddy replied with a string of rough coughs. Dr. Dick turned to 3-J and me.

"We need to get him off this thing immediately," he said. "His heart rate's too fast and his blood presha's dropping."

"But we can't," said 3-J.

"It's forbidden to remove a Treed person before their time," I said.

Dr. Dick opened his mouth to respond. But his words were co-opted by a shout from the other end of Main Street.

"Hey! They've Treed Don!"

"Get him offa there!"

A gang of irate truckers, with menace in their eyes and knot-untying fingers on their hands, was advancing on us.

"Ha-ha-ha-ha," said the Swedish ambassador, as the sheriff-mayor concluded a tirade on the subject of why he would ever and always reject the sexual favors of the leader of his sister city; a tirade that started with "municipal incest" and concluded with "I like my gals rotund in the rack."

"Är han en idiot?" inquired Häri Härison in a sour voice.

"Ja," replied the Swedish ambassador. Then, turning to the sheriff-mayor, he explained, "Borgmästare Härison intends nothing of innuendo."

"I am propositioning you a swap," she said.

"A swap, eh?"

The sheriff-mayor eyed her unrotund rack, then gave her husband a scrutinizing once-over.

"Gloria!" he called. "Get on over here and appraise this fella. The wife ain't to my liking, but you might have a better opinion of the gent."

"Not a spouse swap," the Borg snapped. "A town swap."

"It is a tradition in the province where Härisverige makes its home. The mayors of nearby town often trade posts for a month or two," said the Swedish ambassador.

"Why the hell'd they wanna do that?" demanded the sheriff-mayor, as his wife drifted over and began to inspect Herr Härison with her hands.

"For civic betterment," said Mayor Härison. "In Somwärin, I will learn about your town's infrastructure regulations and taxation structure. In Härisverige, you will learn how to be a mayor."

"Hm," replied the sheriff-mayor. "I dunno what I thinka that."

"He's fine and firm," opined Mrs. Dolan, squeezing Herr Härison's chin in one hand and his thigh in the other. "Let's swap."

The sheriff-mayor shrugged.

"Lady's choice."

"My husband will remain in Härisverige," said the Borg. "It is I who will swap households with you."

The sheriff-mayor reached out and squeezed the discomfited gentleman's chin and thigh in his turn. He shrugged again.

"I can make it work," he said. He stuck his massive right duke across the table at the mayor of Härisverige. "Let's shake on it."

She accepted his thick hand and shook it with a barely disguised moue of distaste.

"We shall swap in six months' time," she said. "At midwinter."

The Swedish ambassador flinched.

"Midvinter?" he said in horror.

"Ja," said the mayor of Härisverige.

"Han kommer bli galen!" cried the Swedish ambassador.

The Borg smiled her chilly smile.

"Jag hoppas det," she replied in an ominous voice. And then she laughed a malevolent laugh while the Swedish ambassador murmured a prayer under his breath.

The sheriff-mayor was oblivious to these unlucky portents. He slapped his hands together, interlaced his sausage fingers, and cracked his knuckles.

"I'd say this calls for a tour of the town we'll be Yankee swappin' come Christmas," he said, rising.

"Certainly," his Swedish counterpart replied, also rising.

"Bra idé!" said Herr Härison, also-also rising. Fleeing the questing hands of Mrs. Dolan, he made a break for the door of the Swedish Embassy & Beauty Parlor & Coffee Shop. He tugged it open and leapt outside.

"Don't you run off, now," said Mrs. Dolan, pursuing him in slow motion. "I want to check those pearly chompers of yours."

"After you," said the sheriff-mayor, holding the door open, his thick arm crooked and his hand a-waving to guide the Borg onto American soil.

She stepped outside. He turned to the Swedish ambassador. There was a wicked glint in his beady eyes.

"And now you," purred the sheriff-mayor.

The Swedish ambassador glanced from his waiting countrymen to the Mephistophelean sheriff-mayor.

He turned pale.

He swallowed hard.

He began to sweat.

While the sheriff-mayor was flubbing cross-cultural negotiations between the independent Scandinavian nation of Sweden and the Swedish-Texan corporate commonwealth of Somwärin, his daughter was doing a cook's tour of the contestants in the Fack Sex employee breakroom, spreading ill-will and stealing confidence with each stop on her circuit.

"What on earth is that nasty child doing here?" Mama murmured.

"She's singing the opening song at the pageant," replied Opal.

My nuclear family couldn't hear what Perdee Dora was saying to each of the contestants, but the devastation she wrought was clear. Optimistic smiles faded. Foreheads creased in consternation. Tears were shed.

At last, the thirteen-year-old approached the vending machines and my family. She ignored Pearl, Mama, and Opal. She inserted three quarters into the soda machine's coin slot and treated herself to a frosty enbärsdricka. She popped it open, took a big slug, and gave Mama a good, long look. She turned to Opal.

"I didn't know you had a brother," she said.

Mama winced. Her hand flew to her short hair, then she gritted her teeth and forced an indulgent smile to form on her face.

"That's cute, Perdee Dora," she said.

Perdee Dora did a stagy double-take.

"Oh, Ms. Bejou!" she cried. "I didn't recognize you. That new hairdo makes you look fifteen, twenty years younger!"

Mama gritted her teeth and fabricated a laugh.

Perdee Dora turned back to Opal.

"Are you just fit to *bust* with excitement?"

Perfectly pleased with her new bust, Opal was not to be cowed by Perdee Dora's subtle taunts. She nodded and beamed a happy smile.

"I just hope you don't fall," said Perdee Dora.

Opal's smile vanished like the sun going behind a cloud. No longer overcompensating for all that extra poundage up front, my sister was unsteady on flat feet and precarious in high heels. Falling on stage in front of the whole town was her greatest fear. Her lower lip began to tremble.

"Good luck!" chirped Perdee Dora.

Now it was Pearl's turn.

Icy soda in hand, Perdee Dora turned to face Pearl. Pearl braced herself for another dousing. But it was not to be.

"Listen, Pearl," said Perdee Dora in a soft, conciliatory tone. "We oughtn't carry on feuding all summer. We oughta bury the hatchet right here and now."

Pearl eyed her skeptically.

"I mean," said Perdee Dora. "I didn't say sorry for tramping your toes at my party."

Nor was she saying sorry now. Everyone in the employee breakroom drifted closer, the better to eavesdrop.

"And I didn't say sorry after I dumped that nasty, sticky, smelly ol' milkshake on ya."

Mama and Opal glanced at each other, then at Perdee Dora, then at Pearl.

"But," said Perdee Dora, with a big, fat smile on her little, slim face. "I just gotta say sorry for the disgraceful, shameful situation you're in right now, what with your daddy being up the Tree of Contemplation."

Each and every person in the employee breakroom gasped, sucking in so much air the place briefly became a vacuum.

Perdee Dora had violated Somwärin's greatest taboo.

It was unthinkable: No one spoke of a Treeing with the loved ones of the Treed. But Perdee Dora had done far, far worse. She had called attention to the embarrassment Daddy's Treeing lent Pearl in front of a crowd.

No one had ever done such a thing in the history of Somwärin. The humiliation was beyond comprehension. Pearl could never show her face in town again. There was nothing she could do to right this wrong Perdee Dora had done her. Nothing at all.

To everyone's surprise, Pearl just smiled.

She advanced on Perdee Dora.

She darted her head out like a cobra striking.

"A word in your ear," said Pearl.

She whispered something into Perdee Dora's earring-heavy ear. Something nobody overheard, strain their own earring-heavy ears as they might. Something that made Perdee Dora's cheeks drain of color.

"You wouldn't dare," Perdee Dora said.

Pearl didn't answer. The smirk, formerly a long-term lodger on Perdee Dora's mug, packed its bags and moved to my little sister's lips.

The sky was growing overcast. The sun slipped behind black clouds. A low rumbling could be heard just beyond the horizon.

"Y'all best back away and let us cut Don down!"

"Then y'all best run for y'all's lives, lest we Tree ya ourselves!"

The truckers stormed toward the Tree of Contemplation, and Dr. Dick raised his palms in a "have at it" gesture. But 3-J and I stood our ground.

"Ya can't unTree him," I said.

"Brothers," said 3-J. "Us-all know good and well there's nobody that can unTree a man once he's been condemned."

The Truckers stopped. They conferred.

"We disagree!"

They began to advance once again. Just then, the doors of the Celestial Temple of Psychedelic Truth and City Administration flew open. Out marched the deputies.

"Fantastic," muttered Dr. Dick.

"Disband!" shouted Dr. Barney, flashing his badge. "With the sheriff-mayor temporarily out of the country, we're empowered to make any and all arrests we see fit."

"Kindly depart at once and we'll forget all about this uncouth melee," said the Gentleman Gym Teacher, crossing his arms over his milk-white broadcloth blazer.

The truckers conferred.

"Not without Don!"

"There'll be no unTreeing today or any day," replied Dr. Flo's receptionist. "When Don Bejou's thinking turns right, down he'll come."

"Don, is your thinking right?" inquired El Señor Poco Loco.

"Not even a little," replied Daddy.

"Doesn't matter—cut him down!" shouted Big Bobby Watson.

The truckers surged forward. The deputies lunged at the truckers. Dr. Dick jumped between the disparate mobs, his arms upraised.

"Let's discuss this in a civilized manna!" he cried. "First things first: Mr. Bejou is severely dehydrated. While you people are resolving your dispute, let me start an IV to give him fluids."

The truckers conferred.

"Okay, Motel Rounds Doc, we'll allow you to treat Don. Then we'll cut him down!"

The deputies conferred.

"No—no IV," said the Disgraced Modern Poetry Professor. "You're the hootchie doctor. Mr. Bejou doesn't have a hootchie. He has a dingle-dong. And nobody's cutting this man down!"

With that, the two factions surrounded the Tree of Contemplation and commenced a turf war.

"Ruby," called Daddy, his body hidden by the flailing limbs of the truckers and deputies. "3-J. Crystal-Lynn's lover. Don't linger here. Y'all gotta finish what I started."

"I don't wanna leave you!" I said.

"We can't do it without you," said 3-J.

"Yes, you can," said Daddy. "I'm just the organizer. I've organized all I can. Now it's up to y'all."

3-J and I squared our shoulders. The wind began to whip our hair. We nodded first at Daddy, then at each other, then at

Dr. Dick.

Dr. Dick shook his head in response.

"You two are on your own," he said. "This man needs medical attention. I intend to make sure he gets it."

We watched as Dr. Dick walked up Main Street, his body black against the ominous, greenish-gray clouds.

3-J turned to me.

"I guess it's like Don said—it's all up to us now," he said.

"What should we do?" I said.

3-J pondered this for a moment. He stared at the framed newspaper article abandoned on the grass. A light dawned in his eyes.

"We gotta go to where it all began," he said. "We gotta find the voice from The Great Beyond!"

"Let me get this straight," said Dr. Flo. "You want me to cart a peripheral intravenous kit out to the Tree of Contemplation, infuse a solution of saline into Don Bejou, and then convince the masses to remove the gentleman from his place of lawful punishment—all because they won't listen to you? Have I got it right?"

Dr. Dick, alone in the waiting room of Dr. Flo's clinic with the lady herself, forced himself to nod.

"Yes," he said.

"Is this man your patient?"

"No," said Dr. Dick.

"Then what possible business of yours is this?"

Dr. Dick turned his head to the large windows and stared out at the darkening sky, striving for composure.

"I disagree with the method of punishment," he said. "It's putting his health in danja. His circulation has been compromised for more than twelve hours, and his—"

Dr. Flo stepped out from behind the reception desk and approached Dr. Dick.

"What business is it," she repeated. "Of *yours*?"

Dr. Dick scowled and opened his mouth to reply, but she cut him off.

"We do things in a certain way here in Somwärin. This is exactly why I objected to bringing in another doctor. I told you once, now I'll tell you again: adapt or die. You must adapt to us, not the other way around."

In the ten-second silence that followed, Dr. Dick wound up for a cleansing, obscenity-infused discourse on the myriad ways he had adapted in the week and a half he'd spent in town. But the words became meaningless when he glanced out the window at Daddy strapped to the Tree of Contemplation. Instead, he gave a helpless flap of his arms.

"I just don't want him to suffa."

Dr. Flo considered this.

"And that's all there is to it?"

"Yes," he said.

She considered this further.

"Well," she said at last. "I don't want him to suffer, either. And I have nothing to do until the pageant starts. But I'm not interested in playing field medic. We will remove him, bring him back here for rehydration therapy, then either return him to the Tree or retain him until the sheriff-mayor returns from Swedish terrain. The man is under *EXTREME!* indictment, after all—we must tread carefully and see which way the wind is blowing."

"Thank you," said Dr. Dick.

He held out his hand to her. She eyed it.

"I still won't shake your hand," she said. "God knows where it's been."

"Now we are all outside," said Mayor Härison, her blond hair whipped into a mohawk by the wind. "All except you, Ambassador."

"Join us, won't you?" murmured Mrs. Dolan. "The hail is lovely this time of year."

And indeed, as the words left her lips, jagged bits of ice began to fall from the turbulent sky.

"Vad är detta?" cried the Borg, tipping her head up at the frigid bombardment.

"Gode Gud!" exclaimed Mr. The Borg, tugging his jacket over his fair head.

"Let us go back into the embassy," said Mayor Härison.

"Aw, this ain't nothing but a picturesque summer shower," said the sheriff-mayor. "Don't be a pansy, Harry. If ya wanna run this town in my stead, ya best get a liking for the feeling of nature on your face!"

"Very well, very well," she replied with a scowl. "Come, Ambassador. Let us make a brisk circuit of the town, then we shall come to terms with our town swap over nourishing cups of coffee."

"Yes, come, Ambassador," said the sheriff-mayor, beckoning with both hands. "I promise, I ain't gonna scoop ya up on that silly ol' indictment of years gone by."

The Swedish ambassador grimaced.

The view of the great, wild world just through the doorway was captivating.

Ice shards fell from the stygian sky.

The wind shrieked, launching debris through the air with the swiftness and determination of fallen angels come to reap the souls of the damned.

Behind the diplomatic party, as yet unnoticed by the town's lawman, a brawl was in progress at the dead center of Main Street. The Gentleman Gym Teacher swatted at truckers with his broad-brimmed white hat. The Disgraced Modern Poetry Professor bashed the heads of friend and foe alike with his weighty worst-seller of free verse. Dr. Barney chucked dog biscuits like grenades.

Looming over it all, like a grotesque simulacrum of the Lord of Hell, the Tree of Contemplation seemed to rejoice in the chaos both natural and man-made.

The entire scene was as inviting as heaven to the Swedish ambassador. He so longed to step outside! He so longed to trust the sheriff-mayor.

The sheriff-mayor sensed his indecision. He gave the governmental representative a smile of affirmation.

"Honest Injun," he said. "You really think I'd detain you, in front of our honored guests from Afar? That'd be plumb loco!"

The Swedish ambassador darted his eyes from his mortal foe to the public anarchy to the apocalyptic meteorology.

He lifted his left foot. He stuck it out the door. The toe of his leather brogue was instantly assailed by hail.

"This is nonsense!" said the mayor of Härisverige impatiently. "Allt är bra—kom hit!"

"Ja, kom hit!" urged the soaked first gentleman of Härisverige.

"Come," said Mrs. Dolan, her arms outstretched, her palms cupped to catch the hail. "It's raining diamonds!"

"Come, yes, come, come," crooned the sheriff-mayor.

The Swedish ambassador bit the inside of his cheek. He placed his left foot on the sidewalk outside the sanctity of Mother Sweden. He hesitated. He drew in a deep breath. Hope surged within him.

With a reckless cry, he brought his right foot out to join its twin on American soil.

"There, you see? All is well," said Häri Härison.

"Bra jobb, Ambassadör," said Herr Härison.

"Ha-HA!" said the sheriff-mayor, and he fell upon the Swedish ambassador, seizing him in a half nelson. "Caught ya at last!"

"What can you be doing, Mr. Mayor—" said Mayor Härison. But her words were cut off by a mighty roar coming from the north.

While the truckers and deputies surged this way and that along Main Street, Dr. Dick and Dr. Flo sought to spring Daddy from his Nordic Golgotha. As Dr. Flo sawed at Daddy's bonds with a scalpel, Dr. Dick clambered from limb to limb trying to loosen the ropes. Their hair became seeded with sparkling ice cubes, their clothes stuck to their bodies like soaked tissue, and their hands grew raw from the biting gusts of air that increased in velocity by the second.

All of a sudden the hail, which had started abruptly, ceased just as abruptly.

There was a moment of eerie calm that caused Dr. Dick to stop his scrambling and Dr. Flo to take a sabbatical from her sawing. Dr. Dick looked at Dr. Flo and Dr. Flo looked at Dr. Dick. Before either could say a word, the wind hit with a ferocity that took the medical colleagues' breath away.

Over the roar of the gale, Daddy shouted something to Dr. Dick.

"What?" he shouted back.

To the north, a column of sooty clouds appeared on the horizon.

Daddy shouted again.

Dr. Dick tugged at the cords holding Daddy's chest to the Tree of Contemplation, paying him no heed.

Daddy shouted a third time, and this time everyone on Main Street heard it.

"TORNADO!"

The truckers and deputies suspended their skirmish, the sheriff-mayor detained his detention of the Swedish ambassador, and the town's medical personnel desisted in their efforts to free Somwärin's Most Wanted.

At the northern edge of town, a thin funnel touched down.

It was heading up Main Street, straight for the crowd.

"Take cover!" shouted the deputies, and they bolted for the safety of the Celestial Temple of Psychedelic Truth and City Administration.

"Save the porn," cried the truckers, sprinting for the Pubic Library.

"Herregud!" cried Häri.

"Springa!" cried her husband.

And they darted back into the Swedish Embassy & Beauty Parlor & Coffee Shop.

"Arg!" cried the sheriff-mayor. He made to follow the Swedes back to Sweden, then caught himself. "You ain't slipping through my fingers via the intricacies of international law again!"

As Mrs. Dolan wandered into the Vet 'n' Pet Shop, shoved along by Dr. Barney, her husband galumphed down Main Street directly into the path of the oncoming twister, dragging the hapless Swedish ambassador in his wake. He threw both himself and his quarry through the open door of Dr. Flo's clinic, just as the tornado slithered past the junior and senior high school.

"Run, man!" ordered Dr. Flo, already halfway across Main Street. "Leave him!"

Desperately yanking at Daddy's bonds, Dr. Dick did not obey.

"You can't save him," she shouted. "You've done all you can."

"I can't leave him here to die!" he shouted back, pulling on the ropes with all his might.

Dr. Flo jogged back to Dr. Dick and grabbed his arm.

"Don't be a fool! Run!"

"No!" said Dr. Dick, straining at the knots.

Daddy raised his head and gave Dr. Dick a hard look.

"You do as Dr. Flo says," he said. "You run for it now— you hear? Go! Git!"

Dr. Dick glanced from Daddy to Dr. Flo to Daddy again with a stricken expression on his face.

"I won't leave you," he said to Daddy.

The tornado was nearly upon them. There was no time left.

"Like hell you won't!" said Daddy. "Run, dammit!"

A metal garbage can came flying through the air, nearly clipping Dr. Dick in the skull. He reluctantly backed away from the Tree of Contemplation, gave Daddy a regret-filled look, and broke into a dash. He and Dr. Flo made it to the staircase leading to his apartment, scrambled up and up and up, and forced the front door open. Dr. Dick slammed it shut against the howling wind. Panting, they hurried to the window and watched in horror as the tornado struck Main Street.

The lithe little funnel twirled lazily up the roadway, its slender girth no wider than Scarlett O'Hara's corseted waist. It idled by the Vet 'n' Pet Shop, meandered over to the Pubic Library, pirouetted indolently in indecision, then drifted to the Tree of Contemplation. It gave the Tree a languid spin on its base, like a nouveau riche madame nonchalantly rotating a jewelry rack in a fine department store.

It lifted the Tree of Contemplation a foot or so off the ground. It held the Tree suspended for a heartbeat, rotating the structure and my daddy as if testing their weight. Then, almost as an afterthought, the wee whirlwind carried the Tree of Contemplation and Daddy gently out of town and out of sight.

The dark clouds cleared. The sun came out. And so did the townsfolk.

They congregated on Main Street, dazed and astonished. There was nothing but a six-foot deep oval hole in the earth where the Tree of Contemplation once stood. Apart from the loss of the Dark Ages torture device and its latest victim, Somwärin was unharmed.

The truckers looked at the deputies and the deputies looked at the sheriff-mayor and the sheriff-mayor looked at his prisoner. Should they start brawling once again?

Their conundrum was cut short by an acerbic, complaining trill that pierced the air and sent a shudder down every spine.

"It's the näverlur!" exclaimed Dr. Flo's assistant.

"The pageant is about to begin!" said Big Bobby Watson.

"Guess I'd better hustle to the judging stand," said Dr. Barney, taking off for Fack Sex in a double-time trot. He was followed by the general assembly—all except Dr. Flo, Dr. Dick, the Swedish ambassador, and—

"Ha-HA!" bellowed the sheriff-mayor, seizing Dr. Dick in a headlock. "Ain't this my lucky day? Two indictments with one stone."

The birchbark horn bleated again, and the officer of the law gave a hearty yank on his arrestees.

"Don't wanna miss the pageant on account of the likes of y'all. We'll take 'er in, then it's off to jail with the both of you."

"Å nej!" moaned the Swedish ambassador.

"This is illegal!" Dr. Dick gasped, his windpipe darned near flattened by the meaty forearm of the sheriff-mayor. "Dacta Flo—do something!"

Dr. Flo folded her hands neatly and shook her head.

"I'm afraid not," she replied. "An indictment's an indictment. You must do your time and learn your lesson. But if and when you're released, come and see me. I may have a small space available for you in my clinic…Dr. Grant."

"Gah…" he gasped as the sheriff-mayor lugged him up Main Street by the throat.

"A very small space, as that's all your kind requires," Dr. Flo called.

Standing in one of the wide loading bay doors, which had been thrown open to reveal a landscape lightly dusted with detritus and melting hail, the Fack Sex warehouse supervisor inhaled deeply and gave a final tootle on the näverlur. Inside the warehouse, early-comers seated in the sinuous rows of lärostol chairs clapped their hands over their ears.

"Now's our chance!" mouthed 3-J.

We skulked along the far wall of the warehouse, past a slapdash stage constructed of castoff loading pallets. Tucked between shelves that soared to the ceiling was a metal staircase, vetted and approved by the Occupational Safety and Health Administration of the United States and the Arbetsmiljöverket of Sweden. We cast a last glance at the supervisor, whose back was still turned, and the audience, whose eyes were squeezed shut in auditory agony. We scurried up the slip-proof rubber treads, our hands gliding along the regulation five-inch circumference handrail.

At the top of the staircase was a steel door inset with frosted shatter-proof safety glass. The mysterious word "Förman" was spelled out thereupon in black letters.

"What's in here?" I whispered.

"Shhh!" hissed 3-J.

He whipped off his beige sweatshirt.

He wrapped it around his fist.

He eyed the glass and took a deep breath.

He wound up and braced himself for impact.

He reconsidered.

With Dr. Dickish sensibility, he reached out his unwrapped hand and tried the knob.

The door swung inward on silent hinges approved by a nationally recognized testing laboratory.

A snug, fluorescent-lit room with a window overlooking the warehouse below greeted our eyes. We darted inside, closed the door behind us, and took a look around.

"Ah ha!" crowed 3-J.

Tossing the sweatshirt aside, he dropped into a lumbar-supporting office chair not of Fack Sex manufacture, which was positioned at a small desk. Upon the desktop were piles of payroll forms, scads of ballpoint pens with no caps, three empty Styrofoam coffee cups, and a queer microphone on a slim stalk that sprouted from a panel covered with buttons and dials.

3-J grasped the panel and drew it closer.

At this point, it finally occurred to me what 3-J's plan was.

"You're gonna use the PA system and pretend to be the voice from The Great Beyond!" I accused.

3-J froze.

He looked at me with wide eyes.

His mouth fell open.

"That's a great idea!" he exclaimed. "I'm gonna do that instead."

He studied the microphone and its planter box of twiddly

controls.

"This-here ain't like any CB I've encountered," he mused.

I crept to the window and peeped down into the warehouse. Drawn like rats to the Pied Piper's pied piping, the townsfolk were streaming through the loading bay doors. Down on the concrete floor, they jostled for seats, throwing elbows and baring their teeth to guard their territory. At the foot of the stage stood the judges' table, draped with a sequin-augmented Swedish flag. Dr. Barney and Mrs. Dolan were settling themselves on either side of the blow-up sex doll from the Pubic Library.

It looked like any old Miss Somwärin pageant. But then I spied a trucker.

He was cleverly camouflaged by a bokskåp box shoved against a wall a few feet from the stage.

Then I sussed out another upon a high shelf above the crowd, his body concealed by piles of furniture assembly instruction booklets.

And another, lurking beneath the stage like a slug under Farmer Bill's outhouse.

And another and another and another...

I turned to 3-J in horror.

"There's truckers hiding all over this place!"

"Mm-hm," he replied, twisting a knob and pressing first one button, then another.

"How'd they get in?"

"Who can say? All's I know's they'll pop out the second Miss Somwärin is crowned and grab her. Then it's out them bay doors and off to Motel Way. There's dozens more fellas out yonder in the scrubland, and still more on the edge of town, all waiting to defend their brothers from the enraged townsfolk. But," said 3-J, waggling the microphone experimentally on its stiff stem. "I'm gonna put a stop to alla that with a message from The Great Beyond, just like Don heard one year ago."

"What're you gonna say?" I inquired.

3-J stopped twiddling and fiddling. He cocked his head.

"I don't rightly know," he said.

"It oughta be something mystical," I said.

"Yeah," he said. "Like what?"

"Hmm…" I mused.

"Umm…" he agreed.

We cogitated in dumb silence. Then, as not a single idea was coming to mind, the amplified voice of the Fack Sex warehouse supervisor filled my empty head.

"Välkommen, y'all!" she blared into a hand-held microphone from the stage below. A former Miss Somwärin herself, she wore her Viking crown and pageant pasties. Happily, the latter objects were affixed to the exterior of her "Förman" T-shirt, transforming the *ö* and the *a* into winking vowels of obscenity.

"It's my pleasure to introduce the emcee—y'all know who he is!"

And without introducing him, she turned the microphone over to the Gentleman Gym Teacher. The crowd, several hundred strong, applauded.

"Thank—"

The warehouse supervisor snatched the microphone out of the Gentleman Gym Teacher's hand.

"But first, we gotta honor the Employee of the Year! Dr. Barney, ya got the battle-axe?"

At the judges' table, Dr. Barney stood, hefted the double-headed weapon, and held it up for all to see. Without a word of warning, he flung it at the warehouse supervisor. The crowd gasped. It sailed through the air, turning end-over-end, and embedded itself in the stage floor between her feet. The crowd burst into cheers. Dr. Barney bowed and resumed his seat.

"Righty-dighty," said the warehouse supervisor, yanking the death-dealer out of the rough wood and leaning it against her shoulder. "Will the Employee of the Year please c'mon up here and swing the battle-axe during the singing of the Miss Somwärin theme song?"

The crowd murmured in confusion. Who was the Employee of the Year?

"C'mon now," said the supervisor. "Don't be bashful."

The Gentleman Gym Teacher dipped his head with genial gentility and murmured something into the supervisor's ear.

"I know that!" snapped the supervisor. "Y'all, it's my privilege to announce the Employee of the Year…are ya ready? The Employee of the Year is—are ya listening? The Employee of the Year is none other than…the one and only person in the history of Fack Sex to show up the day after Midsummer sober and fit to work…Ms. Crystal-Lynn Bejou!"

Down on the warehouse floor, there were squeals and cheers and a wild banging together of hands. Mama shoved her way through the standing-room-only crowd, her palms pressed to her cheeks in astonishment. She mounted the stage with the courtly assistance of the Gentleman Gym Teacher and stepped to center stage. She waved her arm like a windshield wiper in a thunderstorm at her lady friends, who stood on their chairs shrieking with delight. Then she composed herself for the solemn duty that awaited her. She took a deep breath and held out her hands to accept the battle-axe. At a nod from the Gentleman Gym Teacher, she began to swing the axe in elaborate curlicues above her head, kicking her legs high like a Rockette and tossing her hair for emphasis.

A hush fell over the crowd as Perdee Dora swooped onstage from behind the chintzy patchwork curtains. The child beamed at the crowd and yanked the microphone out of the Gentleman Gym Teacher's hand with nary a "by your leave, sire." For an instant, Mama appeared to be considering whether she ought to use the sharp skull-slicer to separate the lassie's head from her shoulders. Then she shook herself and resumed her swinging and kicking and tossing.

"In nineteen-hundred and eighty-one," shrilled Perdee Dora, about an octave too high and a half-tone too sharp. "They put their horny helmets on. They put their horny helmets on, to conquer Boscoe Counteee! With quality home furnishings at affordable prices…"

Mama dipped and shimmied, the axe shining in the industrial shop lights that had been duct taped together to form a spotlight.

"Now we are Somwärin town, Somwärin town, Somwärin town," shrieked Perdee Dora. "Now we are Somwärin town, instead of Boscoe County! Thanks to...IKEAAAAAAAA!"

The silence that followed was thick and hard and full of bile. Perdee Dora let out a mean little giggle, made an "Oops!" gesture of false contrition, and dropped the microphone on the splintery stage floor. Mama, frozen in horror with the battle-axe poised above her head like a medieval executioner in mid-execution, again appeared to consider the feasibility of ridding our dear town of its worst citizen. But she allowed Perdee Dora to sashay by unbeheaded.

And that was the moment it happened.

Pearl's ghastly revenge.

It fell upon Perdee Dora in the form of a bucket of vile pig's blood, as seen every year in the Sissy Spacek Movie Marathon crowd-favorite, *Carrie*.

Drenched in red gore, Perdee Dora let out an unhuman howl and set the entire warehouse on fire with her mind.

But no. That didn't happen. Nothing happened. Perdee Dora slid behind the curtains, the Gentleman Gym Teacher retrieved the microphone from the uncouth ground and made a little bow to Mama, and Mama marched off the stage with the battle-axe slung over one shoulder.

"Good ladies and fine gentlemen," the Gentleman Gym Teacher said in his smoothest parliamentarian voice, which was identical to the one he used to hector the high school football team when they were down in the fourth quarter. "Please give your very warmest welcome to this year's contestants in the Miss Somwärin beauty pageant!"

Behind him, the patchwork curtains slid open and there they were! Three dozen of Somwärin's most eligible bachelorettes, decked out in their shiniest frocks and their biggest hair and their heaviest makeup. Four girls from the left stood Opal, smiling the most radiant smile I'd ever seen on her face.

"There she is!" came a shout.

"Grab her, boys!"

And before anyone could blink, the hidden truckers I'd been playing "Where's Waldo?" with popped out of their places of concealment and surged toward the stage.

Screams rang out. One of them came from me.

"What's happening?" I cried.

"Dang, they weren't supposed to emerge until after Miss Somwārin's crowned," said 3-J, jabbing at the buttons of the PA microphone. "They jumped the gun."

"Say something to call them off!"

"I can't figure this thing out!"

"Push the 'Talk' button!"

3-J pressed the red button and a whine of feedback from the horn-shaped speakers situated throughout the warehouse notified us that the mic was live.

"I don't know what to say," he whispered in distress, as the truckers and the townsfolk braced themselves for battle.

"But you're the Chosen One," I replied.

"I don't know what to say!" he insisted.

"The Chosen One oughta know what to say!"

3-J rubbed his palms over his face like a gambler who'd tossed in his last chip on a losing hand.

"I ain't the Chosen One," he moaned. "I ain't—I can feel it. Don was wrong."

And then he let out a mighty yell.

"Don!"

Everyone in the warehouse froze and stared up at the speakers, which had hollered the evocative name. Then their eyes drifted to the central loading bay door.

Standing there within the towering opening was Daddy.

He was windblown and wild-eyed. His hair stood up like the quills of a porcupine. His shirt was torn from collar to cuffs. He had no shoes. And he was covered in dust.

He regarded the shocked faces, staggered a few steps into the warehouse, and gave his disheveled frame a little shudder like a hound dog roused from sleep.

El Señor Poco Loco spoke first.

"Don defeated the Tree of Contemplation!"

"The Tree itself unTreed him," breathed Dr. Flo's receptionist in awe.

"This is unprecedented," said Dr. Barney.

"It's a sign!" shouted Big Bobby Watson.

"Let's steal ALL the Miss Somwärins!"

"We'll turn 'em all into truckers!"

"Steal the Employee of the Year, too!"

The truckers, their faces enflamed with cultish fervor, flung themselves at the stage from all sides. The warehouse was overtaken with chaos. Daddy stood alone by the loading bay doors, backgrounded by cloudless blue sky, dazed and mute. I watched in horror as Mama swung the battle-axe in great arcs to fend off the handsy truckers. On the stage, baseball-hatted men were plucking the would-be Miss Somwärins like daisies from a flower garden. They gathered them into shrieking bouquets and slung them over their shoulders. The Gentleman Gym Teacher bellowed indistinctly into the microphone and the sheriff-mayor swung Dr. Dick and the Swedish ambassador at the assailants like maces made of flesh. The townspeople threw fists and the truckers threw steel-toed boots.

3-J sat motionless as the anarchy unfolded below.

"Stop them!" I cried. "Save Opal and Mama!"

"I can't," he moaned. "I dunno what to say."

"Then I'll save 'em myself!"

I bolted out of the Förman's office and took to the stairs that led down into the warehouse. But I stopped dead when I saw the full extent of the free-for-all.

It was out of control.

3-J couldn't stop such a riot.

I couldn't stop such a riot.

Even Daddy couldn't stop such a riot.

Nobody could stop such a riot.

Suddenly, the riot stopped.

Every soul in the warehouse turned to stone as a Great and Terrible Presence made itself felt.

The Deus ex Sverige had arrived.

The founder and CEO of Fack Sex stood in the central loading bay door. He was flanked by hulking, gray-suited Swedes with unamused countenances. The founder and CEO of Fack Sex swept the scene with his steely blue glare. Without a word, everybody disentangled themselves from their co-combatants, righted their chairs, and seated themselves facing the stage.

The founder and CEO of Fack Sex marched through the thick silence to the stage. He mounted it. His sensible Skoaktiebolaget dress shoes resounded on the wooden floor like claps of thunder as he stepped into the spotlight. He withdrew the microphone from the stunned hand of the Gentleman Gym Teacher, scowled at the crowd, and opened his mouth to speak.

Just then, 3-J finally channeled the voice from The Great Beyond.

"Unionization," boomed the PA system.

But before he could conjure a second mystical word, the founder and CEO of Fack Sex threw a glower at three of his hulkingest, unamusedest flunkies and they shoved past me up the stairs. A squawk was heard over the PA system, then the Swedes emerged lugging a beige-clad figure that kicked and struggled to no avail. Out the nearest loading door they dragged him, and silence returned to the warehouse.

The founder and CEO of Fack Sex, looking more disapproving than ever, frowned at the crowd. He raised the microphone and began to speak. A wrathful string of words in the Skånska dialect shot out at us. His timid American employees glanced at one another in confusion. The cowed truckers scratched their heads. With annoyance, the founder and CEO of Fack Sex repeated the last six words, which clearly constituted a question.

Opal hesitantly stepped forward and cleared her throat.

"Y'all," she called out. "He says he's come here coz a brave young whistleblower contacted the head office in Stockholm. Do y'all know what it was about?"

The crowd murmured in the negatory.

The founder and CEO of Fack Sex raised a fist and began to harangue the listening folks. His eyes shot lightning bolts of censure that caused heads to bow in shame, though nobody knew what for.

"He says, y'all've been harboring a viper in y'all's titties. A viper like the devil snake in the Holy Bible, trying to lead alla y'all astray by ruining the morale of his future employees."

A speculative buzz spread through the congregation.

"Där är HONNNNNN!" he shouted, pointing into the midst of the crowd.

"I think he means," said Opal with a nervous gulp. "Perdee Dora."

And indeed, it was Perdee Dora at which his Jehovian finger pointed. She was standing next to her father, her arms crossed over her chest and a surly scowl on her face. A chain of vicious vowels and cruel consonants flew from the founder and CEO of Fack Sex's mouth.

"Um," said Opal, when at last he fell silent. "I don't guess I better say mosta them words. He ain't happy that Perdee Dora's tormenting his soon-to-be staff—and that y'all're letting her do it. He says she'll be the ruin of the entire blamed town before she's done—mark his words."

The crowd turned to glare at Perdee Dora, who stuck out her lower lip and glared right back.

"And," continued Opal. "He ain't happy about how it takes y'all warehouse workers so long to load the trucks every summer. It's costing him thousands and thousands of Euros to keep the truckers on standby for days, waiting for their loads."

"That's—" shouted Mama. "That's—that's also Perdee Dora's fault!"

Her coworkers jumped to their feet and joined their voices with hers in agreement. Perdee Dora placed her hands on her hips and began bickering with them, but her words were lost in the clamor.

The sight of his daughter being denounced by the entire town caused the sheriff-mayor to swivel his head from side to side in consternation. With his hands employed as restraints, he was unable to shield her from the excoriation of the businessman from abroad or the civilians from the homeland. So he opened his jaws wide and hollered across the warehouse at the one and only distraction that might capture the attention of the crowd.

"Indictment! Don Bejou, you get over here and join these two degenerates in jail for the duration! *EXTREME!* indictment!"

The founder and CEO of Fack Sex stepped to the edge of the stage, pointed at the sheriff-mayor, and shouted back, "No! End indictments now!"

That was that.

Daddy, unmindful of his surroundings and temporarily deaf from the whirling winds, did not register the wondrous news. But the Swedish ambassador did. When the sheriff-mayor's dumbfounded hand fell away from his upper arm, the Swede lit out across the warehouse in a jubilant prance, laughing madly.

"At last!" he shouted. "At last, after such a span of years! Free, free, free!"

Half-strangled, Dr. Dick contented himself with sinking to the concrete floor at the sheriff-mayor's feet, where he rubbed his windpipe and inhaled raggedly.

The founder and CEO of Fack Sex snapped a single sentence at the Swedish ambassador, who ceased his frolicking and hurried to join Somwärin's corporate visitor on the stage.

"But of course," said the Swedish ambassador. "I must do my duty."

He looked at the founder and CEO of Fack Sex expectantly. The old gentleman turned to Opal.

"Tack, Fröken Somwärin," said the founder and CEO of Fack Sex with a gruff nod.

"He wishes to express his thanks to Miss Somwärin," translated the Swedish ambassador.

That also was that.

Dr. Barney shrugged and held out a silken sash that in no way resembled pasties, and a sparkly tiara that in no way resembled Viking horns. The Gentleman Gym Teacher crossed the stage, accepted them, and decked my sister out in the winner's trimmings. Opal blushed and beamed. Her co-competitors glowered and growled.

"No fair!" the bravest dared to mutter. Her mutter was met with mutters of agreement.

Luckily, at this very moment, a new distraction roared up.

Just outside the loading bay doors, a loud horn sounded. Within three seconds, a hefty semi truck pulled into view. Behind the wheel was a wall-eyed trucker who stared in a fixed manner at the view before him. His rig was pulling a spanking new trailer lashed to a flatbed with dozens of colorful bungee cords. Straddling the roof of the trailer was a wee figure, who rode the mobile home like Ahab astride Moby Dick. The truck slowed to a stop and let loose another blast of its horn. The personage atop the trailer waved at the crowd within the warehouse.

"The Tooth Witch!" someone shouted.

The entire population of the pageant sprang up and clustered at the loading bay doors to take in the sight of the long-lost fang fairy.

"Ten-forty-four, good neighbors!" the Tooth Witch called out. "Swapping the greasy side up. Gonna fingerprint with the bedbugger. Y'all wanna convoy it? Ten-eighty-five's the Somwärin Trailer Park and RV Pleasure Garden. C'mon back!"

The truckers let out a series of rebel yells at this news…whatever it was. The driver behind the wheel gave another honk of his horn and pulled away at a snail's clip. His brother Teamsters flowed forth from the loading bay doors to follow him, and the rest of the pageant-goers swiftly followed suit. Even I began to march along with the parade that was heading up Main Street in the direction of my trailer park home.

When I reached the place where the Tree of Contemplation once stood, I stopped. Daddy was seated just south of the hole, which was all the tornado had left behind. Next to him knelt Dr. Dick.

"You're sure you're alright?" Dr. Dick was saying.

"Well," replied Daddy. "My thinking ain't. In fact, I'd say it's wronger than it's ever been. But the frame's sound."

"There you are!" cried Mama, jogging up the sidewalk and seizing me in a smothering embrace. "Thought you were lost for good! Where you been all night and all day? Not with this one here, I hope—"

Then she saw "this one" was accompanied by her erstwhile lover, and her words came to an abrupt halt.

Dr. Dick stood awkwardly.

Mama released me and took a step toward him.

"Dick, I—"

"Crystal-Lynn, I—"

But before they could say more, a rattle-trap pickup truck assembled around the dawn of the automotive age humpity-humped up to the sidewalk. The engine hocked up wads of congealed oil as the tailpipe pleaded for a mercy killing.

"Top of the mornin'!" bellowed Farmer Bill, leaning out the glassless driver's window. "Hop in, missy—we're runnin' late."

"We finished that blasted coop!" Mama said. "Put a roof on it and a sturdy door and everything."

"True that," replied Farmer Bill. "Now's the final step: Fill 'er with ducks. We gotta hightail it if we aim to reach the Mexican border by sundown. Bring your cash bag; them replenishment ducks are on your tab by order of the court."

"Not today," Mama said. "I'm beat from the brouhaha."

"I'd like to volunteer to go on your behalf, Crystal-Lynn," said Daddy, his eyes avidly taking in the open-air accommodations of the truck bed, the rusty egg incubators roosting in the back, and invisible Mexico far to the south.

Dr. Dick shouldered past him and hopped into the bed of the pickup.

"Come on, Crystal-Lynn. It might be fun," he said, holding his hand out to her. "Besides, we'll have plenty of time to talk on the way."

A smile formed on Mama's lips. She held her own hand out, joined it with Dr. Dick's, and let him hoist her up.

The two settled in to sit on a pair of burlap sacks. They

leaned back against the incubators and Farmer Bill gunned the engine. As he and his cargo receded into the distance, I could see that they were still holding hands.

Epilogue

Monday, June 23
Sunset

At sundown just a handful of days into summer, a gang of truckers descended upon the Somwärin Trailer Park and RV Pleasure Garden. Big-rig toolboxes in hand, they set about battening down the Tooth Witch's new digs against future hit-and-runs.

My sisters were at the Swedish Embassy & Beauty Parlor & Coffee Shop attending an impromptu reception for the visiting Swedish nationals hosted by the Swedish ambassador, who kept darting out into Main Street to caper in the gathering twilight. Mama and Dr. Dick were also on foreign soil, bartering for duck eggs in Los Estados Unidos Mexicanos, and 3-J was standing in the Bejou family kitchen gaping at a pile of slick, sharp wolf fangs scattered across the table where a stack of coins once stood.

Just another summer evening in Somwärin, Texas.

I went outside and climbed atop the picnic table. The dying sun's rays were fractured by thin clouds that carved garnet gullies across a sky as golden as honey.

"Lookie who we have here," called Daddy, strolling just as casual as you please around the corner of the Bejou family double-wide. He was still wearing his tornado-torn clothes, but he'd smoothed down his hair and looked a good deal less shell-shocked.

"Now that the EXTREME! indictment's been lifted, I can walk free in Somwärin," he said. "Your mama ain't gonna be happy about that."

He climbed up to sit beside me on the weathered old tabletop.

"Daddy," I said. "I ain't exactly sure what happened today, but I don't guess I helped you much."

401

"Aw, Ruby-gal," he said. "Ya helped me plenty."

I shook my head.

"I don't guess I did," I said. "But I got something here that'll help you more 'n' you know."

"Oh yeah? What's that?"

I pulled a flat object from under my shirt. I'd wrapped the old Playboy in copies of the not-yet-newspaper and scrawled "For 3-J" across the top. I held it out to Daddy.

"Now, what might this-here thingy be?" said Daddy, turning the object over and over, shaking it, and giving it a sniff.

"It's 3-J's new package. If you give it to him, I'll bet dollars to donuts the two of you'll be best buddies again in no time flat."

A slow grin spread itself over Daddy's face.

"What's inside?"

"I ain't telling," I said. "That way, both of you can try and guess over the CB when y'all're lonely on the road. And if y'all ever decide to open it, 3-J'll find the thing he wants most of all inside."

Daddy said nothing. He just clapped a hand on my shoulder, gave it a squeeze, and smiled at me.

Daddy and I gazed at the setting sun in silence.

"Summer's barely started," I said.

"Yep," he said.

"I hope I don't get bored," I said.

"Same here," Daddy said.

THE END

www.ingramcontent.com/pod-product-compliance
Lightning Source LLC
Chambersburg PA
CBHW071642260626
47170CB00001B/204